GODLESS CREATURES

by
Gabriel Blake

Godless Creatures

First published in 2020 by DRF Publishing.
Copyright © 2020 by Gabriel Blake

Print ISBN: 978-1-9996636-3-6
eBook ISBN: 978-1-9996636-2-9

Cover art by Farrukh Bala
Edited by DRF Publishing
Written by Gabriel Blake

www.gabrielblake.com

'The price of vengeance is to sacrifice a part of yourself.'

1

Wednesday 13 February

'I think even you can deduce the cause of death here, DCI Baxendale. If it wasn't the rope around his neck, you can be sure the castration and disembowelment would have done the trick,' said Arthur Potts, forensic pathologist.

The two men, wearing white protective suits, gloves, and plastic overshoes, stared up at the naked body suspended over the stairway of the large, impressive entrance hall – his innards scattered over the wooden steps and parquet flooring. Looking a little worse for wear, a second, younger detective appeared behind them. He had already removed himself from the crime scene once, and after a second glimpse of the grisly spectacle, his cheeks swelled like a blowfish, and he was out of the front door like a whippet.

'The youth of today,' said the detective.

'I quite agree.'

'He was the same a couple of months back when you were away,' said Baxendale.

'Ah, yes. The body on the bed, force-fed hydrochloric acid. I recall the pictures – a particularly nasty business. My esteemed colleague said it made *her* feel queasy, and believe me, Olivia has a much stronger stomach than I do.'

'I didn't fare too well on that one either,' admitted Baxendale.

They turned their attention back to the dangling corpse.

'What's with all the little black holes in his body?'

Arthur said, 'It's not easy to tell from down here, but those are nails. Six-inch nails, to be precise – hammered into his body. If you follow me, I'll show you some more grisly findings.'

The pathologist led the detective down the hall and through the kitchen to another, smaller staircase. They climbed the stairs and walked along the landing.

Arthur pointed to the parquet floor. 'As you can see from the trail of blood, the body was dragged from the study, just along here.'

Baxendale glanced over the bannister to view the body directly below, sickened by the sight of the man's entrails. He contemplated the aforementioned crime a couple of months earlier and whether the two could be connected. Gruesome murders so close together, gentlemen of a similar age; it could not be disregarded.

As they entered the bright and airy study, Harry Baxendale was blinded by an abundance of light permitted by the wall-to-wall window. Long teal curtains dangled on either side, matching the paintwork surrounding the huge, intricately carved antique wooden fireplace. Overstuffed bookshelves lined the walls from floor to ceiling. His eyes adjusted, and he focused on the large wooden desk in the centre of the room. A luxurious leather chair was positioned in front of the desk. Blood covered the dark oak floorboards beneath.

Arthur Potts explained the scene. 'The man was stripped and forced to sit in the chair. His arms were splayed out behind him across the desk and secured with six-inch nails driven through his hands. With his feet *pinned* to the floor, nails were hammered into various parts of his body. From the amount of blood pooled here under the chair at the edge of the seat, I'd say this is where he was castrated. As you can see, the nails are still in place on the desk and floor, so when his hands and feet were removed, they were viciously ripped away. He was then dragged along the landing and down the stairs. This was an extreme level of torture, and nobody goes to this much trouble just for the hell of it.'

'No, they don't,' replied the detective. 'So, where are his nuts?' he asked, scanning the floor.

'Good question. As yet, the man's testicles remain unaccounted for.'

DCI Baxendale stepped out of the room onto the landing. 'So why not hang and drop the body from up here?'

'Another good question, and I can only think of one reason – an agonisingly slow death.'

'So they dragged the man downstairs, put a rope around his neck, disembowelled him, and pulled him up gently so as not to strangle and kill him too quickly?'

'Seems that way. I think the killer wanted to watch him suffer until the end. It's highly likely the victim would have lost consciousness from the strangulation rather than from the loss of blood.'

'How long?'

'Somewhere between eight and twenty seconds.'

'And how long before death?'

'Ten to twenty minutes.'

'Jesus Christ! What kind of person does this?'

'Well, that's your job, Detective, but I'll state the obvious and say revenge. This attack was premeditated, brutal, and heartless – carried out by someone who held one hell of a grudge.

And in my experience, anyone who kills in such a methodical way will rarely leave trace evidence.'

Harry Baxendale nodded in agreement and said, 'I'll keep my officers out of your way and let you finish.'

'Detective, I'm sure you've already alluded to the thought, but do you think there is a connection between this and the acid murder?'

'Could be. Two different but very extreme deaths. I doubt it's a coincidence.' The detective took another look over the bannister, grimaced, and walked along the landing towards the back staircase.

Outside the mansion, the officers chatted, smoked cigarettes, and drank steaming takeaway tea to help ward off the cold February morning. Harry made a quick call to update his superior and approached the men, noticing the young detective constable with the temperamental stomach had removed his protective clothing.

'Who told you to take off your coveralls?'

'Nobody, guv,' he answered, clearly intimidated.

Harry didn't follow up; instead, he scrounged a cigarette. He was about to take a puff when a police constable approached; the pathologist wanted to see him.

'I'll be right there,' said Harry, drawing in a long puff before stomping it out on the ground. Turning to the young DC, he said, 'Put your crime scene suit back on and be ready to get your arse inside the house.'

'Yes, guv.'

Stepping through the open doorway, Harry viewed the body on the floor of the hallway, taken down by the forensic team. Potts leaned over the victim as Harry wandered closer.

'What is it, Arthur?'

'Balls, DCI Baxendale!' said Potts, glancing up at Harry.

'I beg your pardon?'

'Balls. You wanted to know the location of the gentleman's testicles – well, I've found them.'

'Where were they?'

'If you look here,' he said, widening the man's jaw, 'at some stage during his torture, they were stuffed into his mouth. Judging by the bite marks on the one testicle I *can* see, I'd say he was forced to eat them. The meaty remnants in his mouth are quite likely from the other.'

Harry winced at the thought and instinctively guarded his own testicles as Arthur Potts continued.

'I'll retrieve this one when I get the body to the morgue. I'm fairly confident I'll find pieces of the other either in his oesophagus or in the contents of his stomach over there on the steps.'

2

Saturday 27 July
Elaine & Harper

Elaine's nerves had taken control of her life many times over the years, but this was different – the kind of nerves you welcomed, coming with a flurry of emotions: excitement, anticipation, and eagerness, to name a few. It was exhilarating to be doing something she hadn't imagined doing again. Doubt had called plenty of times, and she questioned whether this was the right path to take.

In the past, the burden of anxiety had prohibited her from moving forward, preventing her from making the correct choices and leaving her with regrets about the things she'd missed, especially when it came to significant events in her children's lives. Now, here she was, finally in control; her decisions, her children, her mind – her life. Freedom! A simple yet powerful word, too frequently taken for granted. An overwhelming feeling of free will, something that had withheld itself from her until the sixteenth of August, nearly three years ago.

Elaine Davis's life changed forever on that godforsaken day, as did many lives. Unlike most, hers changed for the better. Yes, she gained horrendous memories, which she soon considered necessary, but she also gained her children. Elaine learned the hard way that sometimes you have to rectify the past in order to repair the present.

The aftermath for others was catastrophic. Even her children had to endure the loss of their father and soon-to-be stepmother on the day of the massacre. The ramifications stretched far and wide. For some people living in and around the town of Helmsley, North Yorkshire, the recovery from the shock of what had happened was ongoing. Healing was a process, and it would take time.

Standing behind two low-level gates under a wooden shelter with a slated roof, Elaine turned to the man beside her.

She smiled. 'Thank you, Harper. I wasn't sure you would come.'

His bold blue eyes gazed into hers. 'How could I not?' He checked the footpath above the steps to make sure nobody else was around and gestured with his head. 'Come on. I'll walk you to the door.'

They climbed the four concrete steps and strolled purposefully along a straight path enclosed on either side by a line of low trees and grass verges. With the trees in full leaf, you could barely see between them to the clear blue sky above. The sunshine blinked through small gaps, creating a dappled effect on the shaded path. A pleasant silence lingered in the air as they walked. Sunlight enveloped them as they cleared the cover of the trees. They passed through the wrought-iron gates and came to a stop under a shaded archway. Ahead of them were two enormous brown doors.

'I wish you could come inside with me,' she said.

Used to having Harper by her side, facing this without him would prove difficult. Together, they had planned and carried out several brutal murders in pursuit of revenge against those who had torn their lives apart. The bond between them grew ever stronger, reinforced by their childhood suffering.

He placed a hand on her shoulder. 'We both know that's not possible. I'll hang around for a while and watch from a distance.'

Elaine knew he was right. This was something she had to do on her own. It was risky for him to have come *this* far.

Harper removed his hand and altered his stance to appear serious. 'I think it's time. You need to go inside before we are seen,' he said. 'Are you nervous?'

'A little.'

'You'll be fine.' He smiled. 'You can do this. Now get in there and knock 'em dead.'

He kissed her cheek and stepped back into the bright, beautiful morning, his shadow cast upon the corner of the sandstone wall.

Elaine composed herself, opened the large door, and stepped inside. He watched the door close behind her and strolled back along the path to the top of the concrete steps, a doleful look on his face; yet there was something else: pride.

In his younger days at Rampton Secure Hospital, before he had accepted Liam's fate and taken on the role of Harper Darmody, he frequently contemplated from the bed in his small room all the special life events that would elude him. He never dreamed he would be free and, in truth, he wasn't, not in the eyes of the law. Nevertheless, he was here, and it felt good; it felt – just.

Harper took the first step down and paused, deep in thought. He turned, stepped back up, and marched towards the double doors. He hesitated, wondering if he should go beyond this point. Why should he miss out yet again?

Under no circumstances was Harper to enter the building; *that* was the agreed plan. Elaine had asked him to escort her as far as the external door. The consequences of him being recognised would be disastrous for both of them. When he watched her go through the door, it never crossed his mind. Until he thought back to those long solitary days in Rampton, everything had gone accordingly: he had waited for everyone to go inside, and when the coast was clear, he stepped out of hiding and met her at the bottom of the steps under the lychgate. Yes, it was risky to go against the plan, but he deemed it a risk worth taking. Cautiously, he opened the door and entered.

In casual attire, he hoped to be inconspicuous and that everyone's attention would remain focused where it should be. Head down, he soft-shoed to the back of the church, happy not to have missed Elaine's last few steps down the aisle towards Tom Burgess, who stood patiently waiting for his beautiful bride-to-be.

As Harper peeked out from behind the marble pillar, he thought about all the special occasions that had happened without him: Elaine's first marriage, the birth of his nephews and niece, birthdays and Christmases. For so long he'd wanted to play a role in his sister's life, and, if only for a short time, he was. He just wanted a taste of what it was like to be normal.

Harper Darmody, though, was anything *but* normal. It may well have been his name, but somewhere inside his tangled mind lived the remnants of Liam Bennett, the man he should have grown up to be. The little boy who was physically and mentally abused, a battered and broken child locked away forever to hide the shameful immorality of others. It aggrieved him and always would. As much as he'd laid claim to Liam being a long time dead, he sensed him more and more, growing inside – becoming stronger. He could even pinpoint when these feelings first developed: the moment Elaine chose to help him instead of handing him over to the police.

*

On the day of the massacre, nine bodies were discovered on Elaine's property. It was assumed Harper's body would be recovered soon after, unlikely to survive the three gunshot wounds without urgent medical attention. In the days that followed, there wasn't a trace of him from the moment Elaine and Lenny Grey watched him walk out of the front door.

Harper managed to get far enough away from Sablefall Farm to avoid detection, taking respite in derelict outbuildings he stumbled across. Some nights, he slept under the stars. For food, he rummaged through bins, feeding on scraps. He discarded his bloody police uniform and stole various garments from washing lines, some of which he tore apart to use as makeshift bandages.

Eventually, he happened across a dilapidated, empty cottage with running water and an intact roof to shelter him from the elements. Dirty old clothes and towels were strewn about the place. In the only bedroom, up a narrow staircase, was an unsound double bed with a tattered mattress. At least he wouldn't have to sleep on the bare wooden floor with the mice he'd seen scurrying for cover.

A shabby chest of drawers provided some folded bed sheets, which he tore up to dress his wounds as best he could. He holed up in the tiny house for a while to regain his strength; however, he became feverish and lost track of the days. Time had become irrelevant. He'd all but accepted his inevitable death when he heard a vehicle in the distance. From the small broken window, he saw the setting sun and the headlights of a police car approaching. Determined not to be sent back to Rampton or any other prison, Harper mustered enough energy to make his escape out of the back door and across the wheat fields. With the bloodstained sheets and torn clothing, it wouldn't take the police long to discover who had been hiding in the cottage. The area would soon be crawling with them.

It occurred to him the only safe place was back at Elaine's house in their father's secret hiding place. He was hopeful Elaine hadn't found it yet and equally optimistic that the police wouldn't expect him to retrace his steps and return to the scene of the crime, especially while a police presence remained in the area. Over the next few days, travelling only by night, he staggered back to Sablefall Farm, all the while succumbing further to infection.

Cautiously approaching the house, he didn't know for sure if it was late at night or the early hours of the morning. Lights were absent from the windows, and there were no signs of activity. He passed two large skips at the rear of the property; it appeared the house was undergoing a complete refurbishment. It came as no surprise when he found a spare key (no doubt left for the workmen) underneath a sturdy granite pot a few feet from the kitchen door. Even in his current state, he couldn't help but smile to himself. Didn't Elaine realise there were some very unsavoury characters about? He let himself in and returned the key, locking the door from the inside.

The house was empty and peaceful. The smell of fresh paint and silicone sealant lingered in the air of the nearly completed state-of-the-art kitchen. He raided the brand-new fridge for food and drink, knowing Elaine would assume the workmen had taken advantage of her generosity.

In the bathroom, he found some dressings and a bottle of antiseptic. He cleaned the wounds on his neck and shoulder, which seemed to be healing okay; he'd been fortunate with those injuries. The bullet to his neck had ricocheted and exited the skin without causing major damage. As for the shoulder wound, the bullet had passed clean through. His stomach, however, was a different matter. Slow and steady, sucking in air through gritted teeth, he peeled the discoloured and sticky makeshift bandage from his skin. The entire area around the bullet entry had swollen and reddened; yellow pus seeped from the partially scabbed wound. He'd changed the dressing before slipping into his father's hiding place: a medium-sized room beneath the kitchen, accessible by a ladder.

Harper was thankful that the alcove in the kitchen had remained untouched by the refurbishments. It housed a unique revolving cupboard of two halves, built into the recess before the family moved in all those years ago. The light still worked from when he had changed it before; not the brightest bulb, but much better than complete darkness. He settled on the futon and, after a few minutes, closed his eyes. He hadn't expected sleep to find him and was surprised to wake a few hours later to the sound of workmen stomping above and chattering loudly. Within an hour or so, the workmen left, and all was quiet.

Later in the day, voices returned, Elaine's among them. As the hours wore on, he realised she must have moved back into the house with the children. Drenched in sweat and growing weaker from the infection, Elaine had become his only option. If he didn't get help soon, he would die. Somehow, he needed to let her know where he was without letting the children or anyone else see him. He waited patiently until late at night before making his move.

The bottom half of the kitchen cupboard rotated slowly until it opened to reveal the canned food on the bottom shelf. The shelf lifted by an inch and rolled forward, exposing the dark cavity. Void of colour, Harper emerged from the black hole beneath the storage unit, placed the shelf to the side, and climbed out.

Feverish and in pain, he crept upstairs, looked in on Elaine to see her sound asleep, then continued to Michael's room and on to Emily's. He removed Matthew the teddy bear (which once belonged to her brother Charlie) from her grasp and headed back downstairs and out onto the freshly painted porch. Seated on the swing bench under the bright moon, Harper chose to place his fate in Elaine's hands.

Wincing, he peeled back the bandage, forced his index finger into the hole in his stomach to make it bleed, and smeared blood on the back of the teddy bear. He placed the bear on the bench next to him. Sweat oozed from the pores of his skin as he lumbered back inside the house and locked up. He left a second speck of blood on the front door behind the handle and another on the architrave above the kitchen door. Further smears were made on the floor in front of the cupboard and on the shelf, which he rolled back into place as he descended into the darkness beneath the kitchen. Now, all he could do was wait and see whether Elaine would find the clues and help him or simply call the police.

Harper's eyes swept around the ornate interior of the church. The artwork on the walls and ceiling was exquisite, and the stained-glass windows were exceptional. Vague memories of Liam attending church as a child sprang to mind. What a joke his so-called parents were – *hypocrites*.

He glanced over the congregation. When a church wedding had first been suggested by Tom, Elaine had told Harper she wasn't sure, concerned nobody would show up. After what had happened, people reacted in different ways, some holding her to account. There had been a few extremely unpleasant comments, and some had snubbed her completely, but in time, her association with Tom saw tensions decrease. Everybody loved Tom.

Harper's slight smile faded. It occurred to him that some of the people in this very church had probably held funerals for loved ones here; loved ones whose lives he had shown no mercy in taking away. He caught the gaze of a small boy wearing a cute smile. He couldn't bring himself to smile back and knew it was time to leave. It felt wrong to be in the same room as these people. What was this? Compassion! Why did he no longer feel empty and numb? His unexpected time spent with Elaine had started to change things. The re-emergence of Liam was stirring up emotions relinquished long ago.

Taking one more glance at Elaine, he lowered his head and left the church. He stopped to take a deep breath and continued along the path, taking in the weathered, heartfelt messages on time-worn tombstones. What was happening? Being sympathetic, attending weddings, admiring craftsmanship – this wasn't something he would do. This was Liam, and this was Elaine's doing. Was she responsible for bringing Liam Bennett slowly back to life? Whatever it was, he wasn't sure he liked it. As far as he was concerned, Liam had gone away and left him to carry out the retribution. Did Liam think he could just waltz back into his head and take over now that their task was almost complete? He couldn't just let that happen and do nothing. At present, both personalities needed each other, but could they both occupy the same space once the last person on the kill list had been crossed off? Probably not.

He'd accepted that Elaine was right to control and restrain Harper. He wouldn't have got far in pursuit of vengeance if he'd continued down his carefree, violent path. Their best chance of accomplishing their objective was to work together.

Under the lychgate, Harper noticed a man staring at him from across the road. His fear that he had been recognised was soon allayed when the stranger smiled, waved, and shouted, 'Beautiful day for a wedding!' The man puffed on his vape and entered a bookshop.

Harper's confidence increased, and against his better judgement, he strolled into Market Place to look around. He hadn't ventured into town since the night he'd first caught the attention of Elaine at The Royal Oak, and as he passed the library, he found himself right outside the pub. Moving on, Harper gazed through shop windows and even entered some to browse.

He wandered towards the monument of William Duncombe, sat on the steps beneath it, and observed the people of Helmsley going about their daily business. This was the first time he'd been out on his own in three years. Elaine had taken him to a few places that he'd enjoyed, but to be out alone in public without a purpose was new and welcome. Never in his life had he walked into a delicatessen or gift shop; simple pleasures that had previously been non-existent for him. People didn't know how lucky they were.

The church bells burst to life in jubilation for the happy couple. Harper viewed the church steeple standing tall above the rooftops. It was time to get back, especially if he wanted to catch sight of Elaine before she was whisked away on her honeymoon – a honeymoon with a hidden agenda.

Harper watched from the entrance to a courtyard between a charity shop and the bookshop he had seen earlier. Locals gathered, all wanting to share in the glorious moment of the bride and groom. The town needed happiness, and Elaine and Tom were delighted to share theirs with everyone.

Some of the children attending the wedding rushed down the steps, through the lychgate, and out onto the pavement, closing the small wooden gates behind them. Among the children was Elaine's nine-year-old daughter, Emily. Tom and Elaine walked down the steps and handed the children coins to open the gates and let them pass. It was a nice touch to bring back an old tradition that had all but faded over time.

Elaine hugged and kissed a woman. Harper guessed she was Lila. Elaine had talked about her often; how the two had become best friends when she returned to the care of her mother while Liam was detained indefinitely. Next up were the children. First was Michael, who, at fifteen, looked so grown up and, despite being embarrassed, let his mother give him an affectionate and prolonged hug. Then it was Emily's turn, whom she lifted, pulled to her chest, and squeezed.

As the happy couple said their goodbyes and waved to the gathered crowd, Elaine glanced around; it didn't take her long to catch sight of Harper. True to his word, he'd stuck around to watch from afar. Not so long ago, she had accepted that Liam was lost to circumstance and history, but over time, she sensed him beneath Harper's outer shell. The name he went by now no longer mattered to her because, deep down, she knew it was her brother smiling back. Their sad but happy eyes held each other. Elaine felt awash with a sense of resounding fulfilment at having him there. It wasn't in the way she would have wished, but it was better than not having him there at all. What the future held when their revenge was complete was irrelevant at that moment in time. She would never forget the day she discovered him, weak and on the edge of death.

*

Upon finding Matthew on the bench, Elaine was stumped as to how he got there. She knew Emily couldn't have left him because she couldn't have unlocked the front door to get out. When the children appeared on the porch seconds later, she put it out of her mind.

Later that night, after she'd put the children to bed, she took a book and a glass of wine out onto the porch. She was about to sit down when she observed a faint red stain on the bench, exactly where she'd found the bear that morning. Elaine ran her finger over the dried stain. Blood. She didn't hesitate and rushed upstairs to Emily's room. She gently removed the bear from under her daughter's arm, trying not to wake her – and there it was, a visible bloodstain on the back of the bear's leg.

Her heart raced. A sign from Harper? It had to be. He was close. She scampered down the stairs and out onto the porch, wondering where he could be. The house! He had to be inside the house. Elaine entered and closed the front door, instantly observing a small spot of blood behind the handle. For the next clue, she scanned the hallway to no avail. She searched the lounge and dining room, increasingly frustrated and unable to find anything.

She explored the cupboard under the stairs, fell backwards onto the hall floor, and just lay there, wondering if her cruel mind was up to its old tricks, toying with her as it used to. She gazed up and, by chance, caught sight of a bloodstain smeared above the kitchen door. Jumping up in excitement, she raced into the kitchen. How could he possibly be in this room? Everything was new, everything except for . . .

She turned towards the old rotating cupboard and saw it, a faint red stain on the floor in front of the unit. Elaine rotated the bottom half of the cupboard and gazed inside to see nothing obvious. Convinced there had to be an opening, she pressed her hands against the sides and back, trying to force something to give way. Increasingly frustrated, Elaine pressed down on the shelf and then tried to slide it, but nothing happened. It didn't make any sense.

She placed her hands under the lip of the shelf above the wooden plinth and lifted it to hear a click. It rose a little and rolled slightly towards her. She climbed to her feet and pulled the shelf forward until she was staring down into a dark abyss. Elaine's eyes adjusted to see a faint light. She recalled Harper telling her he'd found their father's hiding place, but she'd expected it to be a small space, not a room. After retrieving a torch and removing the shelf, she shone the light into the hole and saw the ladder. She climbed down.

Not wanting to draw attention to Harper, Elaine turned to Tom and kissed him, greeted by loud cheers and applause from the crowd, who threw more confetti. The couple climbed into the white limousine and disappeared behind the tinted windows.

A tear fell. For the most part, happiness flowed through Harper, but it was tinged with sadness and a sense of loss. Sister or not, having Elaine back in his life after so many years still felt new to him. Now it was as though he was losing her all over again. She'd assured him that everything would be okay and nothing would change. But how could it not? They could never have a typical relationship. He knew she was kidding herself.

For several months, while she nursed him back to health, the basement under the kitchen had become his temporary home, but they both knew it was never a permanent solution. He couldn't go on hiding whenever the children were about or when company came calling. He now lived in a fairly new caravan on a small site a couple of miles away in the village of Beadlam. Harper didn't mind being alone; he'd grown accustomed to it, and though he was, in a manner of speaking, *free*, it hardly ever felt that way.

Unbeknownst to Harper, Elaine had started to make alternative arrangements. After the honeymoon, she would inform him about his impending move to a detached cottage she'd recently purchased on the edge of a town called Kirbymoorside, approximately six miles from Helmsley. Owning a property development business had its advantages; she had already sent tradespeople to get the cottage up to scratch and would have it fully furnished soon after. She was very excited about it and hoped Harper would be too. A minor change was also in store at her house. Even though Tom had been spending most of his time there, he hadn't yet moved in on a permanent basis. That would happen within a day or two of their return.

She wound down the window as the limo's engine started, all smiles as the car slowly pulled away. She looked for Harper; her smile faded slightly when she saw he was gone. While she was away, the children would stay with their grandparents, and Harper would stay at the house. At first, he was reluctant to return, but Elaine convinced him it might be nice to have a bit more room. He was, however, under strict instructions not to leave the property and to remain out of sight until she arrived home. If she had known he'd already strayed into town, she would have been furious with him, mostly out of concern.

3

Harper

Contemplation. Harper had done so much of it over the years, from the young boy separated from his sister right up to his escape three years ago. The week ahead would be no different, with plenty more time on his hands to think about what would happen when he and Elaine reached their endgame. His original plan was to kill every person involved in their childhood abuse and then take his own life. He was no longer sure about the latter. He'd found a new desire to live but failed to understand why or where it had come from.

The complexities of his mind ran deep. His experiences of so much cruelty had shattered any illusions that life could be good, happy, or worth living. Society had shown him nothing but hatred, and in turn, he'd reciprocated. So why the sudden change? What could possibly come from deciding life was all of a sudden worthwhile? With Liam lingering beneath the surface, change was coming, and there wasn't much Harper could do about it.

As Liam Bennett, he was diagnosed with schizophrenia at the tender age of thirteen. A little later, doctors concluded he also had what is now called dissociative identity disorder. Traumatised by the brutal assaults inflicted upon him, Liam created an alter ego as a coping mechanism. For him, it was a lifeline, a new beginning. A metamorphosis from the debilitated boy fast fading into oblivion to the birth of the man, Harper Darmody – the name given to him by the authorities to hide him in the system and to protect those who had committed the atrocities against him and Elaine. Through Harper, he would find strength, determination, and hunger.

Hunger for revenge.

Hunger for blood.

Outside on the front porch, staring blindly into the night, he manipulated the swing bench back and forth with his feet. One of Elaine's stipulations was that he remained inside the house during daylight hours. "Like a vampire," he'd joked. Although he'd been presumed dead, he still remained the most wanted man in the United Kingdom. When the evenings drew in, he couldn't wait to step outside. He found solace in the night, like a cloak concealing him from prying eyes. Sablefall Farm may have been secluded, but it had become a destination for dark tourists: tourism associated with extreme tragedy or the macabre.

Barely an hour passed when Harper didn't turn his mind back to the day he'd ended so many lives. He hated and regretted what he'd done, but knowing it was wrong and feeling sorry for his victims were two very different things. It confused the hell out of him as to why he felt no remorse. He knew the meaning of guilt – he just couldn't feel it. He wished he could, wanted to, but empathy was not part of his make-up, not until today anyway, when he looked around the church. Only then did it occur to him that some of the people were likely relatives or friends of those he'd killed.

The weight of guilt fell upon him like a shadow, a darkening; his spirit tainted with a deathly gloom. When Harper looked into the boy's eyes, he saw himself before the abuse; the impact was sheer devastation. His heart took a battering as the heavy burden of remorse breached his stone-cold exterior. He'd never have thought the innocent eyes of a young boy would possess the power to find his conscience.

He heard the sound of a car engine chugging along. Through the trees, he saw headlights out on the main road; the vehicle displayed a stop-start motion. The driver's obvious problems became worse as the car spluttered to a halt. Harper stayed put and observed from the porch as the driver opened the bonnet in an attempt to discover what was wrong. Numerous attempts were made to restart the engine without success. As well as growing tired of watching, he felt a chill in the air from the sharp drop in temperature. He went inside the house and made a cup of tea, pouring in a splash of whisky instead of milk.

The living room was cosy with a subtle warm glow, aided by the crackle of burning logs in the fire. Harper settled into the armchair. He was comfortable; not a term he'd been accustomed to during his life. He sipped his tea and relaxed in the chair. His thoughts drifted back to when Elaine had found him in the secret basement.

A short distance from the futon where he lay, topless and feverish, the bulb on the bare brick wall flickered like an old Victorian street lamp. It offered little light in the cold, dark room that could become his tomb if Elaine failed to find the clues he had left for her. With his strength fading fast, he'd come to accept that, in all likelihood, he would die. As his eyes grew heavy, light flooded down the wall and the ladder in the corner of the room. A long pause followed as he awaited his fate, and then, like an angel, Elaine descended into the basement. Ignited energy surged through him – reinvigorated – relieved.

She gingerly approached the futon, shining the bright torch over his shuddering body.

'You came. I hoped you would,' he said.

His words calmed her. 'I owe you,' she answered. 'And I failed you.' Her voice was sombre as she observed the wounds on his body – wounds she'd helped inflict.

'You owe me nothing,' he coughed before continuing, 'and you can't fail someone you never knew existed.'

Elaine placed her hand on his forehead. 'You're burning up.'

'One minute I'm hot, the next I'm so cold. I have an infection. I think it's pretty bad,' he said, reaching out to direct the torch in her hand to highlight his stomach.

Delicately, she lifted the bandage. 'Okay! I need to get you upstairs. Can you walk? Do you think you can climb the ladder?'

'I can make it. I could really do with some water, though.'

'Right, sit yourself up and I'll fetch some.'

When Elaine returned minutes later with a bottle of water, a towel, and a blanket, Harper was sitting upright on the edge of the futon.

'Here,' she said, passing him the bottle.

As he unscrewed the lid and gulped down the water, Elaine wiped the sweat from his body with the towel and then draped the blanket over his shoulders.

'So, this was Father's hiding place!' she said, shooting a quick glance around the soulless room.

'Yeah, this is it. Do you remember when I said I left something for you to see?'

From Elaine's knowing expression, it was clear she did.

'On the table against the wall,' he said, pointing to the dark side of the room. 'But I must warn you, you won't like what you find.'

Torch in hand, she shone a light in search of the table. Upon it sat a small, red wooden box.

Elaine moved towards the box with no idea what she was about to discover. She rested her hand on top of the dusty box and paused to take a deep breath. The hinge at the back of the box squeaked as she slowly raised the lid.

A loud knock on the front door forced Harper from his cogitation. He placed his tea on the table but stayed in his seat, hoping whoever it was would soon go away. The person knocked again. He got to his feet and stood still, thinking. Elaine had told him it was doubtful anyone would call, especially as all her friends knew she was on her honeymoon; nevertheless, she'd warned him that if anyone did come to the house, he was not to answer the door.

Harper stepped out onto the porch as the person headed down the steps. The hooded stranger clearly failed to hear him open the door, and for a second, he debated whether to let them walk away.

'Can I help you?' he called out.

The stranger turned to face him and pulled down the hood of her thick coat.

'Oh, hi. I'm so glad you're home,' she said, relieved as she came back up the steps. As she approached, he was immediately taken with her kind eyes and soft, warm, dimpled smile.

'I'm sorry to trouble you. My car has broken down on the road there.' She pointed. 'I've called the recovery service, but I saw your house and wondered if you'd be kind enough to let me use your bathroom?' she begged, the palms of her hands coming together.

Out of his comfort zone and a little rattled, Harper walked into the house without saying a word. The lady looked bemused when he returned seconds later.

'Sorry, I forgot to say yes. You can. Use the bathroom, I mean.' He finally got there. 'It's this way,' he continued.

She followed and closed the front door behind her. 'Thank you so much for this.'

Rather than give directions or point along the hall, Harper walked her right to the bathroom door and opened it.

'Here you go,' he said.

The woman passed by him and stood in the doorway. An awkwardness arose as she waited for him to leave, but he found it difficult to let his gaze drop from hers.

She reached for the door handle. 'Do you mind if I?'

He realised he was preventing her from closing the door. 'Of course,' he answered and stepped back. 'Sorry.'

Harper was out of his depth. Completely unprepared. A man who relied on being in control of situations. When he re-entered Elaine's life, it was easy; he'd calculated and manipulated every step of the way. This was entirely different. A first.

'Idiot!' he whispered and slapped the side of his head with the palm of his hand as he walked into the kitchen.

He fetched a glass from the cupboard and filled it with water at the sink. He sipped slowly while staring at his reflection in the window. Before he knew it, she was standing a few feet behind him.

'Thank you so much,' she said.

Caught by surprise once again, he turned. 'You're welcome.' He smiled. 'The kettle has not long boiled. Would you like some tea?'

'Only if it's no trouble.'

'No trouble,' he replied, seemingly over his earlier nerves and attempting to take charge. 'Did they say how long they would be?' he asked, fetching a cup from the cupboard.

'Within the hour. So hopefully, I'll be out of your way very soon.'

Harper turned to face her. 'Don't be silly, you're not in my way.' He gestured to a chair at the table. 'Take a seat.'

'Thank you.'

'Do you take milk or sugar?'

'One sugar, please, and just a dash of milk,' she said as she sat down. 'Do you live out here alone?'

'No, it's not my house. I'm, er—' He thought about his answer. 'I'm looking after the place for the week. For a friend.'

'Wow, it must be nice to have a friend like you,' she said as he brought the tea over to the table.

'Oh, I don't know about that,' he said, smiling as he sat opposite her. 'I can't say there isn't something in it for me. I'm fond of the countryside. I enjoy solitude and natural silence. In the city, it's more – contrived.'

'So true. I never thought about it that way before,' she said, sipping her tea. 'Which city?'

'Pardon?'

'From what you said, I assume you're here escaping from a city.'

'Oh, I'm originally from London but moved up this way a very long time ago.' He needed to shift the line of questioning onto her. 'What about you? Do you live around here?'

'No, I live in York, though I'm moving to London soon to start a new job. I'm on my way to Pickering for a family wedding – a cousin I haven't seen for years. You know how it is.'

'Actually, I do,' he said, sipping his tea. 'What is it you do, for work, I mean?'

'I work for a small literary agency, but when I move to London, I'll be working for what we in the literary world call "one of the big five." I'm very excited.'

'I bet. That sounds great.'

'So what about you? What do you do?'

Obviously, a lie was forthcoming, but fortunately, the phone in the living room started to ring.

'Please excuse me for a minute,' he said and left the kitchen, marching down the hall.

The woman checked her phone and glanced around the room. She spotted a book on the worktop. Intrigued to see what the man might be reading, she went to take a peek: *The Dancing Bear* by Leonard Grey. The title rang a bell. She picked it up and read the synopsis on the back. She'd heard of the novel but hadn't read it. Flipping through the first few pages, she saw it was signed by the author with a short handwritten dedication to someone called Elaine. Her phone pinged. She looked at the message, put the book back where she'd found it, and returned to her seat to finish her tea.

Harper reappeared. 'I'm sorry about that. It was my friend checking up on me.'

She laughed. 'Probably making sure you're not up to any mischief. Anyway, I just received a text, and the recovery van is going to be here in about five minutes, so I guess I should go and wait by the car.'

For the second time today, a sad emptiness engulfed him. The first time was earlier when he saw Elaine about to leave with Tom. Now it was because of this beautiful woman who had appeared out of nowhere. He wasn't used to meeting strangers, but it was certainly nice to have company, if only for a short time. Harper was instantly taken with her, and for some unknown reason, he didn't want it to end.

'I'll walk down and wait with you if you like,' he offered.

'No, I couldn't possibly take up any more of your time. You've already been more than generous.'

'I honestly don't mind,' he said sincerely.

Her eyes lit up. 'I can tell you don't.' She smiled. 'Okay then.'

They headed along the hallway and out onto the porch. As he was about to pull the front door closed, the flashing amber lights of the breakdown van illuminated the dark road below. Her phone pinged again to let her know the van had arrived.

'I don't suppose you need me to come down with you now,' he said, dispirited.

'No, I guess not.' She looked just as disappointed.

'Thank you again for the tea, oh, and for the use of the bathroom,' she said, raising her eyebrows with slight embarrassment.

'My pleasure. Thank you.'

'For what?' she asked, puzzled.

'For breaking down and knocking on my door,' he casually answered.

She blushed and gave him an affectionate smile. 'I'd better get down there. Goodbye then,' she said reluctantly, turning and walking towards the porch steps.

Harper wasn't used to days full of difficult, unexpected, and undesirable emotions. Was this feeling of not wanting her to leave really so unwelcome? No, it wasn't. When the woman stopped, turned, and headed back towards him, a delightful warmth countered the burgeoning cold.

She reached into her handbag. 'I have never done this before in my life, but I hate regrets, and believe me, I have a few,' she said. 'This is not one I want to have hanging over me.' She handed him a card. 'My number is on there. I'm up here for a couple of weeks, and it would be nice to perhaps go for a coffee or a bite to eat.'

'I'd like that,' he said, taking the card from her.

'Good. I'm glad.' She smiled and carried on her way. At the bottom of the steps, she looked back. 'I forgot to ask your name.'

Caught off guard, he said, 'Simon.' The first name that came into his head.

He watched her walk away with a bounce in her step and soon realised he didn't know her name. He stared at the card. Alice. Her name was Alice Shaw. When she was out of sight, he turned to go inside the house.

'Simon,' he said. 'Where the hell did I get Simon from?'

4

Elaine

So many beautiful Greek islands to choose from, but for a reason unknown to Tom, Elaine chose the island of Symi.

"Perfect," Tom had said. "Symi it is."

It wasn't difficult to manipulate Tom into a honeymoon destination. Why wouldn't he want to please his new bride?

Elaine helped Tom through some difficult times concerning his rehabilitation from the injuries sustained to his chest three years earlier. There were some tough decisions to be made about his future in the Yorkshire Police. The ruptured diaphragm, fractured breastbone, severe bruising to his lungs, *and* the pellets that penetrated the stab vest were not the only things that left him reeling from the aftereffects of that day. For him, it was the emotional toll of so many deaths, including the loss of close colleagues. Retirement was a viable option, and after lengthy consideration, he took on the role of Police Family Liaison Officer.

The friendship between them developed fairly quickly when Elaine first moved back to the area. There was immediate chemistry between them, which continued over time and grew into something a little more special. It was probably helped by Tom knowing so much about her past and the secret he'd helped her keep about Harper Darmody being her brother. Of course, it wasn't a secret any longer, not since the release of Leonard Grey's book, which sparked immense controversy and a very short investigation into the historical crimes committed against Liam and Elaine Bennett.

There wasn't much to find, not after thirty years and a cover-up. Files and such information had almost certainly been destroyed, and after the early flurry of interest, the case remained open but was no longer a priority. Other than their father, Elaine had omitted the names of the other people involved. However, there was one link out there that could bring her world crumbling down and put a stop to their revenge: Elaine's former psychiatrist, Dr Graham Walker. Hence, that was why Symi was her favoured destination.

Dr Walker had retired to the Greek island with his wife. He had been Elaine's therapist since she was a child, until she moved back to Yorkshire, that is. Under strict instructions, it was his responsibility to monitor her behaviour throughout her life. If he had more information, perhaps he could be compelled to share it before his death.

In the build-up to the holiday, Elaine deliberated on how she would slip away from Tom's side just long enough to take care of her personal business. She had even considered drugging him, a measure she hoped would not be necessary. Fortunately, Tom and hot weather were not a good combination, something she remembered from when he'd visited her property on numerous occasions while investigating the disappearance of Police Constable Andrew James. Since their arrival, the height of the afternoon sun had been too much for Tom. For the last three days, he'd found going back to the room unavoidable, the heat sapping his energy. Today would undoubtedly be no different.

At a table outside a taverna overlooking the beautiful, bustling harbour of Gialos, Tom and Elaine were less than a couple of feet from the tranquil turquoise sea, where many boats were moored and others came and went. Colourful buildings and restaurants lined the main strip, and houses painted yellow, orange, and blue speckled the mountainside, ascending to the heavenly blue sky.

Elaine could read Tom very well, and as soon as he started shifting in his chair and fiddling with his straw trilby hat, she knew it was only a matter of time before he made his apologies and left for the apartment. In the meantime, she had been keeping a watchful eye on a restaurant a couple of doors along, where Dr Walker and his wife were inside having lunch. People, in general, were creatures of habit, and this was the fourth time she had seen them frequent this particular place. Tom would usually leave before the couple left the premises. Shortly after, they would make the six-minute walk along Akti Pavlou and part ways at the steep steps between two buildings, with Dr Walker ascending the steps to their indigo-coloured two-storey stone house, while Mrs Walker continued on to a friend's house.

On schedule, Tom reached for Elaine's hand across the table. 'You don't mind if I head back for a little while, do you?'

She smiled. 'No, of course not, sweetheart, it's fine.'

'You going to be okay?' he said, rising from his chair.

'Yeah! I'll probably sit here and watch people for a little longer, then maybe have a wander.'

Tom took his sunglasses from the table. 'All right, I'll see you in a bit,' he said.

As he turned and strolled away, Elaine noticed the familiar sweat patch across the top of his light blue shirt. She knew he would have preferred to spend their honeymoon somewhere cooler, possibly the Arctic, but she had personal business to take care of and would make it up to him at some stage in the future. She hated to deceive Tom in this way, but it *was* necessary.

Elaine waited patiently in her flimsy deep red dress and sandals, sunning her already tanned legs and watching the world go by. The Walkers were still inside the restaurant. A waiter approached. He removed the plates and empty glasses and asked in broken English if she wanted another drink.

'Tequila sunrise, please.'

By the time Dr Walker and his wife stepped out from the shadows of the overhead awning, Elaine had finished her cocktail. They were in the restaurant slightly longer than she had witnessed in the previous three days, but she didn't mind; there was plenty of time to spare. Though her face was partly obscured behind sunglasses and a wide-brimmed beige sun hat, Elaine still turned her eyes to the sea as they passed by. She reached inside her clutch bag and placed cash on the table for the bill and tip. Rising from the chair, she signalled to the waiter, gestured towards the money, and followed the couple.

Elaine paused by a narrow passage below a sharp climb of concrete steps and watched as the couple came to a standstill further along, below another set of steps. This was a repeat of the other times she had followed the couple. Dr Walker planted a kiss on his wife's cheek, and she walked on as if heading elsewhere. Elaine recognised the pained look on his face as he glanced up at what must have appeared to be an almost vertical climb. He was probably asking himself why, at his age, he had chosen to live on the side of a mountain.

Elaine scaled the steps next to her, knowing she would easily beat Dr Walker to the summit. Once at the top, she paced quickly along the path and stared down at the doctor. She removed her hat, nestled her sunglasses into her short brown hair, and sat on the top step. Taking the odd breather during his ascent, he eventually made it to the top, where Elaine patiently waited, her arms resting on her knees, the hat dangling from her hand.

'Hello, Dr Walker,' she said.

Graham Walker stopped a few steps from her, startled to see Elaine towering over him. The expression on his face revealed he had imagined this day might come. He took a moment to regain his breath.

'Mrs Davis. I assume this is no chance encounter?' he questioned, already knowing the answer.

'You're right, Dr Walker. This is not mere happenstance.'

'I always wondered if our paths would once again cross,' he said, his accent as posh now as it had been on the day she met him all those years ago. 'And here you are.'

'Here I am,' she said, spreading her arms wide.

'I guess you have questions?'

'Not really,' came her blunt reply. 'I did, but they're no longer necessary.' There was no need for explanations. Dr Walker knew he was, in part, responsible for the cover-up of a terrible crime.

'I see.' A flustered and frightened man, he hopelessly attempted to find words that could save his life. 'You don't have to do this, you know.'

Elaine grabbed her clutch bag and got to her feet. Her eyes burned into his. 'Yes, I'm afraid I do.' She moved down a step.

'But why? It's not as if I had a choice. This is bigger than you could possibly imagine. I'm not one of those who hurt you. I was never party to the awful things they did to you. I helped you!'

Dr Walker's fear amplified as she stalked down another step, edging closer.

'There is always a choice, and you helped keep it quiet instead of reporting it to the authorities. You. Did. Nothing.'

Graham's countenance changed from fear to acceptance. 'You're right. Of course, you're right. I don't deserve your forgiveness or your mercy. I played my part, and I deserve what's coming.'

He turned his back to her and stood on the edge of the step. He'd had a long and distinguished career with one almighty stain he could never escape. It must have haunted him, disgusted him. It would continue to do so as long as he lived. It was justice, and she was justified.

Only an arm's length away, she raised her hand towards his back. Reluctance crept over her. This was not as easy as she thought it would be. She stared down between the two overshadowing buildings on either side of about one hundred and twenty steps. A dreadfully long way to the bottom. Daunting. She leaned forward and saw Dr Walker's left eye, closed in expectation. A tear ran down his cheek and dripped from his chin. He no doubt felt her presence over his shoulder. Could he also feel her hesitation?

Elaine wrestled with her emotions and her conscience. Did she need to do this? Was killing this man completely necessary? What would it achieve? Her doleful eyes gazed along the length of her arm to her fingertips, an inch from his back. Her mind was clouded, full of doubt. Slowly, she withdrew her arm.

'I'm so sorry, Elaine. This should not be your burden,' said a melancholic Dr Walker. With his feet planted firmly on the ground, he let his body fall forward.

Elaine watched as Dr Walker tumbled, struck, and fell down the steps. Over and over she heard the thunderous thud of his head, limbs, and torso on the concrete. Blood splattered against the walls and steps. His despairing yells turned to silence as the dead weight of his body crashed down every single step until he rolled out onto the pavement below.

One sluggish step at a time, she descended, following the fresh red trail in his wake. A passer-by hurried to him, then someone else closed in. Other people appeared from nowhere. An elderly woman shouted up to her in Greek, probably asking what had happened. She peered over the shoulders of the small gathering. All heads were bowed as they stared in shock and horror at the old man's crumpled and battered body, a heap of broken bones and torn flesh.

For over an hour, Elaine walked the streets and eventually stopped at a bar for a few strong drinks. It was out of character for her, but under the circumstances, they were very much needed. She had mixed feelings. The whole point of going to the island was to kill Dr Walker, and she'd succeeded. Although not by her own hand, she'd played her part by showing up to confront him. She should have been happy – mission accomplished. But as the guilt churned in her stomach, her feelings were a long way from satisfaction. He was an old man who had wanted to live out his golden years with his wife. He would never have said a word to anyone.

Later, when Elaine returned to the apartment, she presented a side of her that Tom had not yet seen or known existed: a fierce desire and intense passion. Elaine was insatiable, and the sex was rough and hard. Her overall state of mind was a cocktail of confusion, frustration, alcohol, and guilt.

5

The Boy

The room was long and narrow. Curled up in a tiny metal bed, the boy whimpered. A faulty white fluorescent strip light stuttered off, then sparked instantly back to life. He buried his head in the pillow, his tousled dark brown hair almost pasted to the cotton pillowcase with blood, sweat, and plenty of tears. He pulled the dark blue quilt up to his pale, frightened, and bruised little face. To the left of the bed was a small, grimy washbasin with a long hairline crack on the outside. Beside the basin was an exposed, grotty toilet with no seat, and in the corner was a cramped shower cubicle that looked as though it had been built by an incompetent DIY enthusiast.

He guessed he'd been in this room for about a month, although it felt longer – much longer. In truth, he did not know. When he woke in the room that first day, he screamed and shouted to no avail and soon noticed the walls and doors were covered in a dark, padded material – possibly some kind of soundproofing. There were no windows, perhaps boarded up. As hopeless as it might have been, he cried aloud until the man entered the room and glared at him. After a prolonged silence, he spoke. That was the day he learned the rules, of which there were three:

1. *Don't talk.*

2. *Don't scream.*

3. *Don't try to escape.*

The rules were simple enough, but to ensure he would never forget them, the man slapped him hard across the face after informing him of each one, knocking him to the floor every time and forcing him to rise to his feet. The fading bruise on his left cheek and the healing cut on his lip were indications of how hard he'd been hit. Words were rarely exchanged thereafter, only commands.

Every single day, he wondered if it would be his last. Sometimes he wished for it. For the first few days, he hoped and prayed his parents would find him; after a few more, it didn't matter who saved him. Someone. Anyone. When unanswered, hopes and prayers fade until all that remains is the all-consuming reality of dashed, empty wishes, cast aside for the sickening ache within to cease and the physical pain to stop. Death.

Music boomed from two speakers high up in the corners of the room. Parts 3 and 4 of Gustav Mahler's Symphony No. 5, the man had told him. The boy didn't care what it was, but he knew what it meant. The sound forced his young body to tremble. An awful, uncomfortable sickness formed in his stomach. He resisted the urge to shove his fingers down the back of his throat to force out the horrific darkness building inside. The music played for so long, and when it ended, it started again.

The door opened and, for a second, before it was closed, natural light flooded the room. Heavy feet clomped slowly down the three creaky steps. Tears amassed and crept from the boy's eyes. He did his best to remain still, but his trembling muscles made it impossible. His attempts to hide under the covers always failed, and yet he continued to try. Deep down, he knew there was no escape from the ordeal to come. Hefty footsteps stomped across the floor and paused somewhere in between, possibly by the side of the bed; he couldn't be sure. He was certain the monster's eyes were upon him.

Scanning.

Burrowing.

The leaden footsteps proceeded across the room, away from him. He peeked over the covers as another door opened. There was an unassuming glare from an unseen energy source, likely a weary bulb, aged and ready to burn out. The sound of drawers sliding open and gliding to a clacking close in the other room unnerved him. The shuffling continued for a few minutes, all while the never-ending music rumbled on. His heart thumped emphatically, the terror within intensifying.

Footsteps.

A door closing.

Silence.

The boy waited for the fluorescent white light to flick off. *A click!* Pitch black. Now he awaited the red light. *Click!* There it was.

The boy always had an inkling of what was to come, and yet it did not prevent him from becoming more anxious and distressed following the intense delay that came before the switching on of the red light. With the cover pulled ever tighter to his face, he waited . . . and waited. The pretence inside his head of not really being there never helped or made a difference. The quilt was ripped from him, exposing his almost naked and bruised twelve-year-old frame. Skinny and weak, his underpants drooped around his bony waist. He couldn't recall what had happened to his clothes or what he had been wearing when he was first brought there.

A shackle linked to a chain bolted to the floor restrained his left ankle. The chain was long enough for him to reach the facilities and the small table across from him, but not the doors. The boy turned to face the burly half-naked man at the edge of the bed. The red glow of the bulb made his appearance all the more terrifying, transforming a human into a demon. His jet-black hair was swept back with gel. Scars, old and recent, covered his torso.

On this occasion, the boy perceived unfamiliarity. Usually, by now, the man would force the boy to punch, whip, cut, and make him bleed by any means possible. If the boy caused him enough pain, the man would leave him be. If not, the monster would be brutal. The man and the monster. The boy detested both, but at least with the man, he knew he would survive for another day.

What was the monster waiting for? It seemed impossible to believe, but it made things worse. Anything different could not be good. The boy's dark eyes widened in alarm when the monster opened its mouth to reveal bright white, serrated teeth – hideous, frightful, and designed for a specific purpose. Helpless, the poor boy, consumed with terror, *screamed*. Was the man finished with him? Was this the end? He knew he'd grown weaker since he'd been there, but perhaps he was too broken, surplus to the monster's requirements. Tears streamed down the petrified boy's face. His deafening cries bounced off the padded walls.

The beast lunged across the bed towards the boy, a demon flying through the air to catch its ill-fated prey. The sharp teeth penetrated the young boy's thigh, extreme agony shooting through his body as he glared down at the monster feasting on his leg.

The red beast raised its head, blood trickling from the side of its mouth. The terrified boy needed to show anger and strength; it was the only way to survive, the only way to stave off the attack. He wasn't ready to die, not yet, not like this.

Against all odds, instead of believing this was the end, he salvaged the will to fight for his life – a desire to show he was not as weak as he appeared. He had learned that the monster did not like weakness. The boy *yelled* at the top of his lungs, hurled his chained ankle towards the monster's face, and struck him with the metal shackle, knocking him from the bed. The beast hit the floor with a thump. The boy rose from the bed and kicked him repeatedly – his face, his body – it didn't matter where. He lashed out until he had no more energy to continue. The boy collapsed onto the bloodied bed. The man pressed a button on a tiny remote control to turn off the music. Silence fell over the room for what seemed like an eternity.

The man rolled onto his back and laughed aloud. He removed the ghastly teeth from his mouth and glanced up at the boy. 'From the moment I took you, I had a feeling you'd be the toughest one yet. The other boys were so weak and unworthy. Not a challenge at all, but *you* . . . you're different. I started to doubt myself, thinking you'd become as useless as the others.'

The boy watched from the edge of the bed as the man climbed to his feet. He hoped he might have kept death at bay for a little longer, renewed hope that he might yet be rescued.

'You saved your life today, boy. I thought you were finished, but you have proved me wrong. I like that,' the man said as he left the room.

Once again, the boy heard drawers opening and closing. He gazed down at his leg and removed his hand to look at the excruciating wound. He blanched at the sight. Minutes later, the man reappeared, holding a metal bucket in one hand and a plain white carrier bag in the other. He switched the light from red back to dim white and walked over to the bed. The bucket clattered to the floor, and he tossed the bag onto the bed.

'For water,' he said, pointing to the bucket. 'In the bag are bandages and other items to treat and dress the wound.' He carried on across the room, up the three creaky steps and through the door, quietly closing it behind him.

The boy let out an almighty sigh of relief. It was the first time he wasn't sad to be alive.

6

Lenny

Lenny Grey always favoured a full English breakfast over anything else, and today was no exception. Inside a greasy spoon in Chingford, he tucked into his fry-up. He'd given up cigarettes, but that was as far as his steps towards healthy living had taken him. He wasn't far from Tumbling Bay, a place he'd visited earlier in the day and on two previous occasions. The first time was eight years ago when the body of Elaine Davis's ten-year-old son, Charlie, was discovered, and yet it still burned fresh in his memory.

Elaine had kept her word and acquired Lenny's services. A lengthy conversation revealed she respected his determined nature and how his commitment showed no bounds – a quality she'd come to admire. She had witnessed it first-hand when he'd wrongly suspected her and her then-husband, Robert, of involvement in their son's murder. Lenny was relentless in his pursuit until a restraining order kept him away. He'd always had a sixth sense about certain things and was adamant at the time that there was more to the case of Charlie – more to Elaine. It took an awful lot for him to admit he'd been wrong.

Lenny and Elaine had an unorthodox relationship. What started as pure anger and hostility had developed into something else entirely. Not quite a friendship, but no longer hatred. They had found common ground and needed each other. Elaine hired Lenny to write her and Liam's story from their preadolescence right up to the consequences of their traumatic childhood three years ago. She also wanted him to look into the death of her son and find his killer. She'd said, "If anyone can find the person responsible, it's you."

The last couple of years had seen Lenny's life change significantly. Not long ago, he was a broke, money-grabbing opportunist who had attempted to blackmail Elaine. When she offered to change his life substantially, he jumped at the chance. She had been more than generous. Even before the book's release, Elaine had cleared his debts, paid him a considerable sum, and purchased an apartment in London where he now lived rent-free.

The truth is, money wasn't an obsession for him; it never had been. As long as he had a set of wheels, a roof over his head, and no financial worries, he was somewhat happier. What he truly wanted was to earn back his self-respect. It was important to him. Writing the book was one thing; finding Charlie's killer was everything. Seeing that poor boy's body in the long, wet grass on that dark, windy night haunted him; it taunted him.

Many times over the past two years, he'd staked out circus tents and questioned clowns. Lenny had never had a problem with clowns, but by God, he detested them now. He'd travelled the length of the country in his quest for answers; unfortunately, he'd reached a dead end every time. How wrong he'd been to think Elaine or her husband had anything at all to do with their son's murder – something he deeply regretted and needed to make right.

It was time to step up the hunt and find the person responsible. He'd already visited the park in North London from which Charlie had been taken, and today he'd stood on the spot where his body was found. All he had to go on was one witness statement: a boy getting into a car with a man dressed as a clown in the car park. It wasn't much, but it was a start.

He'd arranged to meet the witness in a few days. Until then, he'd been going over his old notes and the details supplied to him during the course of the investigation by his old friend, DCI Colin Hargreaves. Many of his old contacts in the force had moved on or retired, so there wasn't much information available. The case wasn't closed, but with a lack of both evidence and resources, it didn't take precedence over new investigations.

As Lenny chewed on a mouthful of black pudding, his mobile phone hummed and danced on the table next to his cup of strong tea. He glanced down at the screen before answering and saw Elaine's name, which, considering she was on her honeymoon, came as a surprise. She'd called for an update, and he informed her he'd arranged to meet the witness in the next few days. He hadn't expected her to be thinking about his inquiries at this time, although it should have been obvious; she probably thought about her son every single day.

Within seconds of her call, his phone buzzed again. This time it was DCI Hargreaves. The pair had fallen out over something trivial a while back, so seeing his name was quite unexpected.

'Colin! I hope you're calling to apologise,' he said, tongue in cheek.

'Shut up and listen, Lenny. Are you still looking into the Charlie Davis murder?'

'Not much escapes your attention, does it?'

'I'll take that as a yes. I don't suppose you're anywhere near Waltham Abbey?'

'It just so happens I'm not too far away. Why, what's going on?' asked Lenny, recognising the urgency in Colin's tone.

'There is something you need to see.'

'What? Just tell me!'

After a prolonged pause, DCI Hargreaves continued, 'I'm looking at the remains of two young boys. The thing is, I have a nasty suspicion that whoever killed these boys murdered Charlie Davis.'

Lenny's mind went blank. A dark cloud shrouded his thoughts. Wind and rain slammed against him. Blinded by the black night, his fingertips caressed the long, wet grass as he trudged forward. Beset by a flood of light, he was forced to shield his eyes. Lenny continued towards the brightness. The light illuminated the ground ahead like a runway. His eyes slowly adjusted, and he saw Charlie lying in the saturated grass. Lenny was back at Tumbling Bay, and it wasn't the first time he'd relived that night. He closed in on the young boy's body, focusing on Charlie's closed eyes.

'Lenny!' a distorted childlike voice called out.

He spun around to investigate and returned his gaze to Charlie, who was now standing directly in front of him, his prominent eyes wide and aglow, the purest white he'd ever seen. They glared at him with intent. Startled, Lenny stumbled backwards and plunged into the long grass. He glanced up at Charlie, his deathly pale face exactly as he'd remembered, with a speck of mud across his cheek and his hair matted and darkened by the rain. The boy turned his head and pointed towards the line of trees along the canal.

'What, Charlie? What are you trying to tell me?'

'Lenny!' A sharp, deeper voice attempted to get his attention.

He resisted the interruption as Charlie's head tilted, his proud eyes once more bearing down on him. Lenny watched in astonishment as the heavy rain constructed a wall of water around the outline of Charlie's body. The boy's mouth opened wide, and a bright light burst from within, momentarily impairing Lenny's vision. The wall of water whirled at speed around the boy and fashioned itself into three lines. Charlie spread his arms, and the lines of water streamed into his white eyes and mouth. His body liquefied until only water in the shape of a small boy remained.

Lenny climbed to his feet and reached a hand forward to touch the watery apparition. His hand passed through the body of water, and Charlie froze solid, like a flawless ice sculpture, Lenny's hand trapped inside. He tried to pull it free, but it wouldn't budge. Cracks formed and spread all over Charlie's body before breaking into millions of tiny ice crystals. Mesmerised, Lenny watched the beautiful crystals sprinkle upwards and vanish into the night sky. A clunking sound of metal distracted him. Lenny stared down at the fork he'd dropped onto the tiled floor of the café.

'Lenny! Are you still there?' Hargreaves waited for a response.

Lenny raised his clenched hand and let his fingers steadily uncurl to reveal water seeping between them. He observed the droplets hit the floor, bounce, scatter, and dissipate.

'Text me the postcode. I'm on my way,' said Lenny, ending the call. In one swift movement, he got to his feet and swiped his leather jacket from the back of the chair. There was no time to fathom what had occurred in his mind. He needed to return to the reality of the harrowing news he'd just received. More young lives had been taken.

*

According to the satnav, which Lenny hated, he was approximately eight miles from the crime scene. He didn't trust all these computer gadgets. Before he condemned his old Renault Laguna to the scrapyard and upgraded to an Audi, he had found his way around with an A-Z road atlas he'd had in his possession since the '80s.

"Like a caveman frozen in time." That's what Elaine said when she put a brand-new laptop in front of him and watched in amusement as he tried to work out how to turn it on. It wasn't as though he hadn't used a computer before. Elaine was unaware that he'd been growing increasingly forgetful of late. Little things. Simple things. He hoped it was nothing more than tiredness or a sign of ageing.

The satnav displayed a journey of twenty-seven minutes. It didn't take as long as that to find his way to Nazeing. He parked next to a few other police vehicles outside Broxbourne Sailing Club. Through the side window, he saw Colin walking his way and climbed out to meet him.

'Hiya, Len. Enough potholes for you?' quipped Hargreaves, referring to the unkempt dirt track known as Meadgate Road.

'Potholes! More like bloody sinkholes,' Lenny retorted.

'New car?' asked Colin.

'Yeah, well, it was until you decided to bring me down here, off-roading. I do miss the old girl, though.'

'You would,' said Colin. 'Still, you must be doing okay for yourself. You look well.'

'Cheers. Things ain't too bad. I'm trying a bit of a health kick.'

Colin pointed. 'Is that egg yolk on your shirt?'

Lenny glanced down at the stain: egg yolk mixed with brown sauce. 'You know how it is. One step at a time.' He smiled.

'Anyway, time to get serious. Are you still chasing clowns?'

Lenny narrowed his eyes. 'You're a funny fucker, ain't ya?'

'All right, no more clown jokes, I promise,' said Colin. 'Come on, I'll take you to the scene. I must warn you though, Len, it's not a pretty sight.'

'A dead child never is,' he answered as they walked.

They walked over to an unnamed gated road, now used as a footpath. It was an old shortcut from Meadgate Road to Nursery Road, to save going around the warehouses, industrial units, and commercial units. They ducked under the police tape and headed along the wide gravel path. Bushes and trees lined the path on either side of them, with glimpses now and then of the River Lea, which formed many small lakes and bodies of water in that part of London.

Further along the track, Colin stopped. 'It's just through here,' he said, pointing to a narrow beaten path in the bushes.

'If this weren't so serious, I'd have to think twice before disappearing into the bushes with you,' said Lenny, in an attempt to lighten the mood.

Colin remained silent as he led the way until they came to a small clearing close to the water's edge. Lenny glanced out across the lake. The sun bounced off the ripples in the water as a small boat with police divers on board made its way to a larger clearing on the far side.

'Looks like the divers have finished their search of the lake,' said Colin.

As Lenny turned, he observed a woman dressed in a white protective suit standing next to the two covered bodies. She looked to be in her mid to late forties.

Colin made the introduction, 'Lenny Grey, this is Olivia Reid, the forensic pathologist. Miss Reid kindly agreed to hold off the removal of the bodies until you arrived.'

'Pleased to meet you,' said Lenny, offering his hand. 'Thank you for waiting for me,' he continued, moving his other hand to conceal the food stain on his shirt.

'Likewise, and no problem.' She smiled. 'I've actually heard of you, Mr Grey.'

Lenny glared at Colin. 'Good things, I hope?'

'Don't look at me. I didn't know,' said Colin.

'Not from DCI Hargreaves,' she said. 'I read your book on the Helmsley siblings. Interesting, tragic, and very sad.'

'Yes, certainly emotional. Not pleasant to write about or to be a part of.'

'I couldn't begin to imagine. Anyway – shall we?' Olivia gestured to the bodies.

As she uncovered the almost skeletal remains of the boys, Lenny took a step back, aghast.

'The boys are Caucasian, of similar age, approximately ten or eleven. It's hard to say exactly how long they've been in the water. If I had to hazard a guess from what I've examined so far, I'd say four years minimum. I'll know more when I get them back to the lab. As you can see, these boys did not die by drowning. They were decapitated using some kind of saw, as were the legs, hands, and feet. This was probably done to make it easier to dispose of them in those woven sacks there.' She pointed to one side. 'Possibly postal sacks. Again, we'll examine the material and see if we can find any information regarding their use and where they may have come from.'

'What makes a person capable of doing something like this?' Lenny posed the question to nobody in particular.

'I'd say someone with an extremely disturbed mind,' Olivia answered. 'I'd also say these poor boys would have undoubtedly suffered severe injuries and abuse before death.'

'What makes you say that?' asked Colin.

'There are various indentations on the bones, but besides those, if someone could do this after death, it doesn't take a genius to work out what they were capable of before. Anyway, I'd better get these boys moved,' Olivia replied, covering them up.

'Thank you, Olivia,' said Colin.

'Yes, thank you,' said Lenny. 'It was nice to meet you. Although, I wish it could have been under better circumstances.'

'Oh well, you can't pick and choose the moments to meet the people you'd like to. Perhaps we'll meet under different circumstances next time,' she said.

'I hope so,' said Lenny with a half-smile.

Colin watched Lenny wander to the edge of the water and followed. Side by side, the two men looked despondent.

'Why did you want me to come here, Col?'

'I needed you to see everything. The bodies, how mutilated they are, the location. If we're going to find this sick bastard, I need you to see what he sees. Take in how he thinks and why he chose to dump those boys in this place. You've invested yourself in finding out who took and murdered Charlie Davis. If I miss something, I know that you won't,' said Colin.

'Who found them?'

'A teenager was flying a drone from a nearby house. Both sacks had been weighed down by rocks. At some point, one bag split, releasing the rocks, and up it came. It snagged on a fallen branch by the low-hanging trees over there. No doubt the kid wanted to see what it was and flew his drone closer. When he watched the footage back, he saw what looked like a skull on the bank.'

'What makes you think it's the same killer?' asked Lenny.

'Two boys of similar age, and Charlie's body was found no more than eight miles from here. Also, there are only two years, give or take, between the murders. I know the Davis boy wasn't mutilated like these poor souls, but it can't be a coincidence, Lenny.'

Lenny was silent. Thinking. Taking everything in. 'What if Charlie was the first?' he said.

The men looked at each other. Colin pressed him to elaborate, 'Go on . . .'

'Every serial killer has to start somewhere, and the first one is always the most difficult. That's when the line is crossed, and there is no going back. Charlie was kept alive for over a week before he was found. Something didn't go to plan. The kid barely had a scratch on him. When you find out the identities of these boys, I think you'll find they were killed at different times. If that is the case, which I believe it to be, it's unlikely they are the only victims over a period of eight years. I think your gut instinct was right – we have a serial killer targeting children – seemingly young boys, and he could be local to the area. He knew where to dispose of those boys long before he took their lives. I think there could be more sacks out there in the waterways, Col.'

'I agree,' said Colin, having already had comparable thoughts. 'Help me catch this monster, Lenny,' DCI Hargreaves pleaded.

Lenny looked over at the two small covered bodies, then turned to face his friend. For a few seconds, the two men stared at each other. Lenny eventually nodded and shook Colin's hand.

'I've been bound to Charlie Davis from the beginning. I've never stopped wanting to find his killer, but of course, you already knew that.' He trudged through the bushes and headed back to his car.

7

Harper

Liam, Harper, and now Simon. It was becoming difficult to keep up with whom he was supposed to be as he prepared to meet Alice in Pickering for a wander around the town, followed by dinner. They'd talked on the phone a couple of times since he first called her. On one occasion, the call lasted for over an hour, a massive achievement for him. He'd never spoken so many words in such a short space of time. To be fair, Alice did most of the talking. Everything happening to him now was new and unexpected. It seemed a different path was being laid out ahead of him, and with no idea where it would lead and limited options available, he was eager to follow.

Outside the house, in the driver's seat of Elaine's car, Harper debated whether to go ahead with his plan. He had been practising around the property and had taken to it quite well, barring plenty of stalls and nearly crashing into the stone shed. Now, having never had a proper lesson due to being incarcerated since childhood, he was about to take the car out onto the main road for the first time in his life. One straight road, Alice had told him. A short trip along the A170. How hard could it be? He took a deep breath, started the engine, and set off down the driveway.

The journey to Pickering went much better than expected. Alice had made it sound like a straightforward journey, and she was right. He used the car park she'd suggested on Vivis Lane. After feeding money into the machine and displaying the ticket on the dashboard, he walked to Elizabeth Botham's Tea Rooms as per their arrangement. As he passed a bookshop, he failed to spot Alice through the shop window, frantically waving to get his attention.

Hovering by the door outside the tearoom, Harper pondered whether meeting her was such a good idea. He knew what Elaine would think. A tap on his shoulder caught him off guard. He turned sharply to find Alice with a puzzled expression on her face, which quickly changed into the brightest of smiles.

'Didn't you hear me calling?' she asked.

'No, sorry.'

'I've been chasing you up the road, shouting your name. People must have thought I was as mad as a March hare,' she said, looking around, embarrassed.

Harper needed to get used to being called Simon, and fast. He smiled. 'You were chasing me?'

Alice blushed. 'Well, walking fast.'

'Sorry, I was miles away. Nerves, I guess,' he said.

'I make you nervous? Cute! Anyway, I'm glad you found your way.'

'Piece of cake!' said Harper, not realising his unintentional pun on the cakes in the shop window in front of them.

'Mmm, sharp wit as well as cute. I like it. Speaking of cake, you have to try the teacake in here,' she said, opening the door and leading the way. 'Watch your step.'

While at the table drinking a cup of strong Yorkshire tea, it occurred to Harper how easy and natural it was to talk to Alice.

Aside from the many conversations with Elaine, which certainly helped prepare him for an occasion such as this, he hadn't had much interaction with people outside Rampton Hospital, and even then, it was mostly with the staff.

'What do you think?' she asked, excitedly referring to the teacake.

'It's good!' he replied with a mouthful.

'Only good! Hard to please, eh?'

'No! It's pretty amazing.'

'I just knew you'd love it.'

Harper swallowed what was left of his cake and sipped more tea.

'If you live in York, how come you know about this place?' he asked.

'I grew up here. As I mentioned before, I'm here for my cousin's wedding, so I'm staying with my parents. If I'm in town, I always make a point of coming here.'

When they finished their tea, they walked around the corner to Beck Isle Museum, another place she'd visited more times than she could remember. It was full of fascinating artefacts, with so many rooms, all recreated to depict the Victorian era, including a sweet shop, a chemist, barbers, and a pub. Harper was fascinated. Alice seemed to be in her element explaining things to him. He observed her with complete adoration, loving how she spoke with such knowledge and passion. He'd never experienced this kind of joy from being in the company of anyone.

They wandered from the museum to another of her favourite places: Birdgate Chocolatiers. She enjoyed showing him the flavoured chocolates on display and pointing out her preferences. She purchased Mint Crunch, Rose Cream, and a bar of Yorkshire

Pudding and Golden Syrup. Alice couldn't wait for him to try the Rose Cream chocolates that she loved so much.

'Open up,' she said.

They hadn't yet moved away from the counter, and although a little embarrassed, Harper happily obliged. A few seconds passed as he sampled her offering.

'Mmm, oh wow, that is special,' he said, much to the delight of Alice and the young man behind the counter.

After browsing in various shops, they ambled along to Willowgate Bistro, where she had booked a table for dinner. It all seemed strange to Harper, as if he had slipped into a parallel universe and this was how his life should have been. Alice's company had a calming effect on him. Silences were rare, and when they did occur, neither of them appeared to feel awkward.

'So, tell me, Simon. What do you do for a living?'

He'd prepared a cover story. 'I'm between jobs right now, working out my next step in life.'

'Okay, so what did you do before?'

'I was a nurse at a high-security hospital.' It hurt to lie, but there was no alternative.

'Wow! Aren't those places full of, like, extremely dangerous people?'

'Yes, they are.' The truth felt better. 'The hospitals themselves are probably not as bad as the stories you've heard.'

'So why leave? Did you not enjoy it there?'

'I hated it.' Another truth.

'Have you any idea about what you want to do next?'

'To be honest, I don't have a clue!'

'Have you ever been married? Any children? God, I'm so nosy, aren't I?'

He smiled. 'I don't mind. But the answer is no to both questions.'

'How come? I mean, you're not exactly a young man any more,' she said, sticking a fork into her steak. 'You must have had some kind of long-term relationship in your life?'

'Well, it's nice of you to point out that you think I'm old,' he joked. Though, in truth, he hadn't taken into account that he was in his early forties and she was possibly ten to fifteen years younger.

'Oh no! That did sound bad, didn't it? I just meant—'

Harper laughed. 'It's okay. I know what you meant. There hasn't been anyone.'

'What, nobody ever? Not a single girlfriend?'

He saw she was getting more and more curious. 'I've had girlfriends, yes,' he lied. 'Just nothing serious.'

'Why is that, Simon? Is there something wrong with you?' she teased.

'Plenty.' He smiled. On a more serious note, he said, 'Not everybody gets to find that special someone or a place where they belong. For some people, life has other plans.'

'I don't believe that! I like to think there is someone out there for everyone.'

'That's sweet!'

She rested her knife and fork on the table and reached for her glass of wine. 'Is that sarcasm I detect, mister?' she asked with a wry smile.

'Not on a first date,' he jested.

'Is that what this is, a date?'

'Isn't it?'

Alice found it difficult not to blush and changed the subject. 'I meant to ask before, how come you don't have a mobile phone?'

'Never found the need.'

'Everybody has a mobile these days.'

'Not everybody.' He grinned.

'Evidently! You certainly are a strange one.'

'How so?'

'I'm still working on that. I hope I'm not being intrusive,' she said. 'But I noticed a scar on your neck earlier.'

It wasn't exactly a question, but Harper knew it probably demanded an answer. 'Oh,' he said, subconsciously reaching up to touch it, or perhaps to conceal it. 'It happened at work a long time ago. One of a few scars, I'm afraid. It's what comes from working with dangerous people.' He hadn't thought to prepare excuses for his scars but had always been quick to offer answers, whether the truth or a lie.

'Probably not as bad as the stories I've heard, eh?' she said with a sly glance. 'It actually looks fairly recent.'

'It's never healed properly and occasionally flares up. I must be a slow healer.'

She seemed to accept his answer, and why wouldn't she? Alice had no reason to doubt anything he told her. The evening drifted along smoothly, and they chatted about all sorts of things. He enjoyed listening to tales of her growing up in Pickering and sharing various events from her life, such as being run over by a car when she was little and almost dying, failing her driving test eleven times, bad dates, and how much she loved her job. When they'd finished their dessert and drinks, he insisted on driving her home, which was less than five minutes from town.

As they reached the car, she said, 'I have completely hogged the conversation today, haven't I? I'm so embarrassed. All I've done is interrogate you and go on about myself.'

'It's fine. I've loved listening to you,' he said, happy not to have contributed much more than he already had. It also meant he didn't have to tell her too many lies.

'Yes, but I still hardly know anything about you,' she said.

Harper slammed on the brakes to avoid colliding with another car as they left the car park. 'Sorry about that,' he said, continuing onwards. 'There isn't much else to know other than what I've already told you. I haven't had the opportunity to do much of anything.'

'You must have travelled abroad?'

'Nope! I've never left the country.'

Harper stalled the car further along the road and looked at Alice apologetically.

'Been driving long?' she joked.

'Not very, Miss "twelve times to pass,"' he replied, to which she gave an open-mouthed smile. 'Anyway,' he said, restarting the car and continuing the short journey, 'as I told you, all I've done since I left school is go to work.'

'Take the next turning on the right, and then the first left, please,' she said and returned to the main conversation. 'All work and no play is not good for you, you know? Hey! Maybe that's what you should do now – travel. There's a big, beautiful world out there. Perhaps you should go and see it.'

'Who knows what the future holds?' he said.

'Okay, just here is fine. Thank you for bringing me home.'

'My pleasure! And thank you.'

'What for?' she asked with a broad smile.

'For giving me a truly wonderful day,' he said sincerely.

'It has been lovely, hasn't it?' she said, removing her seatbelt.

The silence grew as they stared at each other. It was the first time he'd felt awkward all day. He recalled kissing Elaine on the porch when he had come back into her life, posing as someone else, but that was different. On that occasion, he had a motive. This time, he had no idea *what* to do. Did she want him to kiss her or not? Should he make the first move or wait? The choice was soon taken away from him when Alice opened the car door and stepped out. Still beaming, she turned and leaned down, one hand resting on the door.

'You're a mystery, Simon.'

'Is that good or bad?'

'Oh, I love a mystery,' she answered. 'Call me later,' she said and closed the car door.

She walked up the path to a pleasant-looking house and turned to wave before going inside and closing the door. He didn't know if he'd passed or failed some kind of kiss or not-to-kiss test. The way she waited, the alluring look in her eyes – she wanted him to kiss her – of course, she did. *Idiot*! He knew he'd turned down her invitation and felt foolish. Shitty. Like he'd ruined the entire day. He wanted to freeze time, turn it back, and relive the moment. However, she didn't leave as though she were upset or disappointed, and she did say to call her later. For a second, he closed his eyes, hoping he hadn't offended her and messed everything up between them. With a sigh, Harper pulled away and headed home.

8

Elaine

With the honeymoon over, it was back to reality for Tom and Elaine. While she returned home, Tom went straight to London. He'd been asked by an old colleague in the force to attend a meeting about becoming a volunteer Force Ambassador for police officers injured or traumatised as a result of their policing role. He was certainly giving it due consideration. Unlike currently serving military personnel and veterans, there was no specialist care programme for the police. It was a charitable organisation called Police Care UK. Being injured on duty himself, the idea of helping others in a similar position felt very personal. With Tom already working as a Family Liaison Officer, it was just a case of whether he could manage both roles.

When the taxi pulled away, Harper came out of the house to help Elaine with the suitcases and bags.

'Well, how did it go?' Harper asked as he picked up two cases.

'It's done,' she answered bluntly, angry at how forthright he was.

'I meant the honeymoon,' he said.

His comeback surprised her. She hadn't expected him to ask about the honeymoon. Up to that point, he'd shown no real interest in her relationship other than to show up at the church before the wedding, as she'd asked.

'Can we talk about this later? I just want to get in, take a bath, and then have a nice cup of tea,' she said.

Harper understood and told her to leave the bags for him and get herself settled. She took him up on his offer and trudged up the steps to the house. Though tired from the journey and thoughts of Dr Walker, Elaine couldn't help but sense something different about her brother. She glanced around the front of the house, not really knowing what she was looking for, and then disappeared inside.

With her bath nearly ready, an impatient Elaine stepped in, letting the bath fill to the brim before turning off the taps. She sank below the bubbles and lay her head back, eyes closed. Elaine's body may have felt relaxed; her mind, though, was anything but. Dr Walker's last words about not letting his death be her burden stayed with her. Constant visions of him falling violently down the steps in Symi troubled her. His wasn't the only death that sent her mind spiralling. Since the murder of Denley Parker, she and Harper had exacted revenge on two others from their list. First came Alan Whitehall . . .

As Mr Whitehall entered his swanky London apartment, a gloved Harper crept up and grabbed him from behind, holding him tightly while Elaine injected propofol into a vein in his neck. While he was out for the count, they stripped him naked, tied him to his bed, and propped his mouth open. For an older man, Whitehall's body was in decent condition. They grew impatient waiting for him to wake up and debated the size of the dose they had given him, worried they had killed him too soon. When he finally woke, they explained who they were and placed safety masks over their faces. The terror in his eyes and relentless muffled screams told them he remembered exactly who they were.

To drown out any yells of pain, Elaine turned on the radio and tuned it to the first song she could find, Led Zeppelin's 'Your Time Is Gonna Come.' Though not by design, the song seemed appropriate. Wearing chemical-resistant gloves, Harper proceeded to pour a few drops of concentrated sulphuric acid over the man's genital area. Mr Whitehall struggled and shifted frantically on the bed. Harper continued with the torture until the man passed out. They waited less than sixty seconds to see if he would come around on his own. He didn't. Elaine slapped his face to wake him and then inserted a plastic funnel into his open mouth. Tears trickled down the old man's face.

Harper stared into Mr Whitehall's eyes. Sympathy was not on the agenda. He poured a ready-made mix of sulphuric acid and hydrogen peroxide through the funnel, a slow, constant flow of burning liquid filling his insides. In unbearable agony, the man's body shook uncontrollably. His muscles grew tense, and the veins in his body strained under the surface of his skin. Froth spewed from the corners of his mouth, his teeth dissolving. All the while, Harper kept pouring until there was nothing left in the plastic bottle. It didn't take long for Alan Whitehall to die, most likely from heart failure, his body cooking from the inside out – a terrible and excruciating death.

While they observed, Elaine wondered if they were taking their retribution too far. Was there an unwritten rule on how far revenge should go? She felt happy and justified when they murdered Denley Parker. Why was this any different? Was it because, unlike Mr Whitehall, Denley Parker had been directly involved in her abuse? Harper didn't take much convincing when she said it was time to leave; another occasion when his reaction had taken her by surprise. At the time, she didn't know whether to interpret his thinking as job done or whether he too was having his own unanticipated crisis of conscience. She doubted it would be the latter; after all, this was Harper Darmody.

Next up, Malcolm Hayes. After some gruesome physical torture with a hammer and six-inch nails punched into various parts of his body, they castrated him and force-fed him his testicles. He passed out halfway through. Harper then dragged Malcolm down the stairs while Elaine dropped one end of the rope from the landing, which was tied into a noose and placed around his neck. She joined Harper downstairs, took a scalpel from a black satchel, and made an incision across his abdomen. Harper went back upstairs and heaved him up, eventually tying the rope to the bannister. The pair stood below and watched Mr Hayes, who at one point regained consciousness. Malcolm's face started to turn from a strained red to a pale shade of blue, his insides sliding from his belly onto the steps below.

The last name on the list was former Home Secretary Sir Edward Horner, the son of Judge Lawrence Horner. Judge Horner was the man responsible for the cover-up and separation of the siblings in order to protect his son. The evil old bastard was fortunate to have passed away years ago. Edward's father wasn't the only one to have escaped the wrath of Harper and Elaine. Timothy Hazlewood, a professor of psychiatry, personal friend of Judge Horner, and co-signatory of the court order to detain Liam Bennett indefinitely and have Elaine monitored throughout her life, had also died of natural causes. As much as Elaine would have liked to have seen the two men pay for their part in the crime, she felt relieved that it was almost over. She couldn't take much more of all this death. At least an end was in sight. Life could then return to some kind of normality.

Her head resting against the bath, Elaine opened her eyes and gazed at the white ceiling. Raising her hands to soak her face, she noticed red water dripping through her fingers. Confused, she lowered her eyes to see a bath full of blood and the head of a young boy above the water level. The boy stared at her, his dark wet hair almost covering his equally dark eyes.

'Help me!' he pleaded.

Elaine panicked and pushed herself backwards, away from the boy, her legs slipping and sliding until she managed to heave herself over the side of the bath and slump to the floor with a heavy thump. She calmed herself and gathered enough courage to glance over the edge of the tub. The boy had vanished, and the water was as it should be, with bubbles diminishing and a slight blue tinge from the bubble bath. Elaine hadn't experienced nightmares or hallucinations in quite some time, and she wasn't prepared for any kind of setback. Decisively, she picked herself up and grabbed the towel.

Later on in the living room, Elaine explained to Harper what had happened in Symi: how Dr Walker had voluntarily taken a dive and how it had made her feel uneasy, that perhaps his death had been unnecessary.

Harper listened with a blank expression on his face and asked, 'Don't you believe in what we're doing – what we've done so far? Do you think nobody deserves to be punished for what they did to us?'

'No! I'm just saying I'm not sure Dr Walker deserved to die.'

'But you didn't kill him.'

'As good as,' she answered.

'From what you say, it was his guilt that pushed him down those steps.'

'But if I hadn't shown up, brought it all flooding back . . . he'd still be alive.'

'You can't know that for certain. He may not have died at that particular moment, but you can be sure that what happened never left his thoughts, just as it never left ours. Sooner or later, whether anybody likes it or not, the past catches up.'

'I'm just tired, Harper. Tired of killing,' she said.

'And you think I'm not?'

'No, I don't. I think you love it. I think you live for it.'

'Rubbish! I told you what I wanted to do.'

'Yes! You did. Right before you lost the plot, went on some crazy murder spree, and killed all those innocent people.'

Harper shot to his feet. 'You think I don't know that!' he shouted. 'You think I don't regret what happened that day!' He walked over to the window.

'Do you regret what happened?'

'Yes – I do,' he replied softly. 'I hate the monster I became. When I arrived back here, I was hell-bent on revenge. Nothing would stop me or get in my way. After I opened up to you about what happened in that barn, I relived the whole nightmare. Every person I encountered immediately afterwards wore the faces of those evil bastards.'

'What about me?'

'What do you mean?' he asked, turning to face her.

'In the hallway with the shotgun. Would you have killed me?'

He paused, downcast. 'Yes. Until the second bullet hit me, you were just another face. Unrecognisable to me. You should have stayed in the barn.'

'Is that why you left me tied up? Did you know what would unfold?'

'Partly. What I said at the time stands, but yes, I had an idea of what *could* happen. I wanted you to be safe.' Despondent, Harper walked back to the sofa and flopped down. 'I want the same as you,' he said. 'For all this to end. Something is happening to me. I think I'm losing who I am.'

'I have no idea what you're talking about.'

'I don't feel like the man who tricked his way back into your life. The man who committed such an atrocious act. The thing is, I am, and I did, and I'm not sure it's something I can live with. I'm no good, Elaine.'

'Then neither am I,' she replied.

'That's not true. You are nothing like me. You're so much better than you know. I was wrong to come looking for you, and I ruined everything that was good in your life by coming back. I am a godless creature.'

'No! You are not! Those men – they were godless creatures, and they have paid for it with their lives.'

'What about the others, Elaine? The police officers, Robert, Chloe, the doctor? What did they do? They didn't deserve to die, and there is nothing you can say to justify my actions.'

'You're right. There isn't. But the men who destroyed our lives and many others share equal responsibility for what you did that day. Think about it. Suppose none of this ever happened to you. Would you have taken the lives of those people?'

He shrugged. 'Probably not, no.'

His head dropped. Elaine went over and sat beside him. 'We're close now,' she whispered, placing an arm around him. 'Just one more to go, and it's over.'

Harper rested his head on her shoulder. 'I don't want to die, Elaine. I want to live. I want the life I deserve. The life I should have had.'

Tears formed in her eyes as she consoled her brother. 'I know.' She tenderly kissed his head. 'I know.'

9

The Boy

A few days had passed, and the wound on the boy's leg healed slowly. He had rinsed the gash with water and used the saline solution from the bag to clean the area. So far, he couldn't see any signs of infection but wondered if it was too early to tell. His childlike attempts to keep the wound clean had been mostly guesswork.

He hadn't seen the monster since their last encounter. The man, though, continued to enter the room twice a day with food and water. Not a word was exchanged. The food remained basic and rarely changed – always a sandwich with variations of ham, cheese, or tomato. If he was really lucky, he'd get all three. Now and then, he'd receive a piece of fruit, usually an apple or a banana. The boy made sure to chew every mouthful many times to aid digestion and gain as many nutrients as possible, something he'd learned as an army cadet. He exercised first thing in the morning and last thing at night – mostly push-ups and sit-ups. He'd attempted jogging on the spot, but the heavy sound of the chain rattling against the wooden floor put a stop to that. Keeping fit, healthy, and strong had become a priority.

The monster's return was inevitable. It would be foolish to believe otherwise. He had to make sure he was ready to take him on again, having worked out that this was what the man wanted: for him to do what the man himself could not and hold back the monster. It crossed his mind that if he hadn't fought back the last time, some other boy would likely be in this room with a chain around his ankle. Another victim. The longer he held out, the greater the chance of rescue. If not, at least he might have saved another boy's life.

Over time, he'd determined the difference between night and day. He couldn't be certain about the days of the week; he'd lost track of those. However, when the very first meal was brought in, he saw a flash of daylight as the door opened. When the second meal came, it was much later, so he knew it must be evening.

As soon as his food was delivered in the morning, he would listen for noise. Occasionally, he would catch the sound of a loud thud, and for a while afterwards – complete silence. Sometimes he'd hear footsteps above, and every so often, the sound of a television in another room. Aromas frequently crept under the door when the man cooked. The smell of bacon or burnt toast was another recognisable sign of morning. After a while, he'd started to sense time like his pet cat, Flint, who always knew when it was time to eat.

Days would drift by without a sound. Occasionally, he'd observe the man strolling across the floor and entering the room at the other end, then reappearing moments later, carrying a toolbox and various other tools. Much later, he would return the tools to the room. Perhaps the man had a job? On some days, a heavy rumbling and vibration would continue for hours on end. The boy was unable to identify what could be causing it.

The door to the room opened, and daylight oozed through the narrow opening. The man carried a paper plate containing the boy's sandwich and a thin plastic cup of water towards the table. Without a word, he put them down and left, closing the door behind him. The boy climbed off the bed and pressed his ear to the floor, listening over the usual background noise of what must be a water pipe running beneath the floorboards. Then came what he was waiting for: the vibration of heavy footsteps followed by a dull thud.

It always pleased him to hear what he considered to be an outer door closing. A prolonged silence would follow. He assumed the man had gone out. The boy went straight over to the table for his sandwich: ham and tomato. He ate only half of the sandwich, savouring every bite. The other half he wrapped up tightly in the plastic bag that had previously contained bandages, plasters, and saline solution. He'd save the rest for the afternoon. After a shower, he lay on the bed for a while. Eventually, he took his daily walk back and forth across the room as far as his chain would allow, followed by another lie-down. Being held captive with nothing to occupy his mind, time was a cruel adversary.

He napped until the afternoon, ate the rest of his sandwich, and carried out his regular daily exercises. During his push-ups, he collapsed to the floor, out of breath, doing fewer than on any previous day. Although he'd given his all to keep his strength up, it wasn't good enough. He was growing weaker.

Rolling onto his back, he stared up at the ceiling. Trickles of sweat coursed down the sides of his face. Turning his head, he perceived markings under the table. He crawled over for a closer look. Names had been scratched into the wood. *Charlie, Harry, Kevin, Jason, Ian* and *Tom* were at the front of fourteen other names, all of them male. Beside each name was a series of numbers. The last name on the list – *Will*. He noticed that a screw securing the leg to the table wasn't all the way in. He twisted it until it came free in his hand. Staring back at the names, he realised what he'd discovered: boys who had been imprisoned here before him, and there could even be some who hadn't added theirs. They'd used the screw to mark their names. It then hit him what the numbers were – dates.

His body shuddered, his skin crawled, and his heart drummed. Each boy who had discovered these names must have felt as terrified as he did right now. The boys all remembered the date they were taken and, like him, probably not much thereafter. He looked again at the names and dates of the first and last children. *Charlie* was the first, and *Will* must have been the last, not long before *he* had woken to find himself in this godforsaken place. Eight years and fourteen boys, all of them murdered. His chest tightened. A horrid burning sensation – a constant ache in his stomach followed by a dreadful sinking feeling. Any possibility of rescue was gone. It was only a matter of time. He would become number fifteen – and it terrified him.

10

Lenny

Asleep in the car, his face distorted against the driver's side window, drool trickled from the side of Lenny's mouth and coated the misted glass. He'd had a rough night. Since he'd seen the skeletal remains of the two boys, he'd hardly slept at all. Instead of festering in his bed, he decided to set off early for his meeting with the only reliable witness to come forward in the Charlie Davis case. In all likelihood, she'd repeat the statement she'd given to the police at the time, but he had to start somewhere.

The glare from the August sun heated the glass and caused Lenny to open his eyes. As he moved, he grimaced, groaned, and reached up to soothe his stiff neck. He wiped the drool from his face and searched around for something to wipe his hands on. The dirty paper towel that was wrapped around his bacon sandwich would have to do. A loud, moaning yawn escaped him. He rubbed his hands upwards against the grain of stubble on his face.

'Blimey,' he muttered with another yawn and wiped away tired tears.

Checking his watch, he saw it was 9.17 a.m. 'Bollocks!' He was nearly twenty minutes late.

Lenny checked his face in the rear-view mirror. 'Beautiful.'

Upon closing the car door, he glanced at his reflection in the glass and tidied himself. He marched across the road, through the open gate, and up the path. The front door opened before he had a chance to ring the bell.

'Mr Grey?' said a well-dressed middle-aged woman. She appeared none too pleased with his tardiness.

'Sorry I'm late, Mrs Wells.'

'Hmm! I informed you over the phone that I had to leave for work at ten, Mr Grey. Lucky for you, the meeting I'm attending has been put back an hour,' she said.

'Lucky me,' he mumbled sarcastically, hoping his words were out of earshot.

'Pardon?' she queried.

'Erm! Lucky for me,' he answered in a heightened, cheery, and overly sincere tone.

'Yes, well, I suppose you'd better come inside, hadn't you?' she said, shooting an ambivalent glance his way.

Mrs Wells led Lenny into the sitting room.

'Please, take a seat, Mr Grey.' She gestured towards a fancy sofa.

'Lovely,' he said. 'You can call me Lenny.'

'Do you mind if I don't?' she replied, one eyebrow raised. This was a woman who knew how to make someone feel uncomfortable. 'Tea?'

'I'd love some.' He smiled. As she left the room, Lenny sighed. An arduous twenty minutes lay ahead.

Taking in the pristine room, he immediately noticed the absence of a television. Just the sofa, a book display unit, and a small table sat between him and a matching single armchair. At least there was a window. On the shiny, dust-free sill stood a framed photograph of a young man dressed in graduation robes, a diploma scroll in his hand. Her son, perhaps? He took out a pad and pen from his inside jacket pocket and looked through some notes he had prepared.

Moments later, she reappeared carrying a silver tray, placed it on the table, and sat in the armchair. A plate on the tray was loaded with a mouth-watering selection of biscuits, all beautifully laid out. Though eager to reach for one, he managed to restrain himself until she offered. Best not to add to her preconceived notion of him. She delicately poured tea into the china cups and then reached for the tiniest tongs he had ever seen.

'Sugar?' she asked.

'Er, no thank you, Mrs Wells.'

She dropped two lumps into her cup with the tongs and then poured a pitiful amount of milk from a small jug into her cup only.

'Help yourself to milk,' she said.

Oh, how he'd wanted her to say biscuits instead of milk.

Lenny poured some milk into his cup, attempting to act as refined as he could. Mrs Wells reached for a biscuit. *Bitch!* She was doing this on purpose. She'd probably seen the hunger in his eyes. She held it gently between her fingers for a moment, as though teasing him, and finally took a modest bite.

'Biscuit, Mr Grey?'

About bloody time. 'Oh,' he said, pretending he'd only just noticed them sitting there, looking delicious, calling to him. 'Thank you very much.'

'So, you want to ask me about the statement I gave all those years ago?'

'Yes, Mrs Wells, if you don't mind?' he answered with a mouthful of chocolate digestive.

'I don't mind – it's just, well . . . you're not a detective, and you don't work for the police. I find that rather strange.'

'It's not strange, Mrs Wells. I'm looking into the case on behalf of the boy's mother. She wants justice for her son.'

'I can't say I blame her. I would too. It's ghastly that nobody has been punished for such a dreadful crime. I'll gladly help if I can, Mr Grey.'

Her words pleased him. Perhaps this wouldn't be as difficult as he'd first thought. He took another biscuit, this time a custard cream, which he dipped in his tea, much to the dismay of his host.

'Right, I have the notes from your statement here, but I think it would be better if you told me in your own words what you saw on the night in question. As much detail as you can, if you will, Mrs Wells.' Lenny lifted the cup from the saucer, taking several sips while Mrs Wells relaxed in her chair.

'I'd taken my son to the circus. I wasn't too impressed, but my son seemed to enjoy himself. When we left the tent, I remember this bumptious gentleman – well, I say gentleman, but I think I'm being far too polite. Anyway, he almost knocked me over. I think he must have worked for the circus.' Sitting forward, she took the saucer in her hand and sipped tea from the cup. 'There were all these ghastly clowns outside. A couple were handing out balloons to the children, and we had to force our way through the crowd.'

Lenny listened with intent, jotting down the odd note while she spoke. However, this did not prevent him from taking another custard cream.

'I was accompanied by a gentleman friend. All above board, Mr Grey, nothing sordid! We strolled around the fair, and my son went on some of the rides. As we were walking back towards the car, there was some kind of commotion. At the time, I had no idea what it was about, but later, when I heard about the missing boy, I put two and two together.

'We had a little trouble finding the car as there were a lot more cars parked than when we arrived. During our search, I noticed a seemingly scruffy clown walking between the cars a few rows across. He appeared to be in a hurry. What drew my attention in the first place was a yellow balloon. At first, I thought he was alone, you see – but then I caught sight of a young boy being pulled along by the hand and assumed they were together.

'My son located our car and made himself comfortable in the back seat. My friend climbed into the driver's side, and as I was about to enter the car myself . . . I don't know why, but I glanced across the car park and saw the yellow balloon floating up into the sky. That was when I first saw the boy with the man. He was almost shoving the young boy into the back of the car. I thought to myself, now there's an angry parent, thinking the boy must have got lost or something along those lines. At the time, it didn't enter my mind that the man could be taking the boy by force. I mean, you never imagine you're going to witness something so horrid yourself, do you?'

'No, I suppose not,' Lenny answered as he bit into a Hobnob, crumbs falling onto his lap, hoping she didn't notice.

'After I saw the boy bundled into the car, the man drove off rather quickly. It crosses my mind sometimes, you know,' Mrs Wells cast her eyes to the window, possibly gazing at the photograph of her own son, 'whether I should have realised something was wrong or done something more.'

Lenny finally saw through her robotic facade. He finished his tea and placed the cup on the saucer. 'You couldn't have known, Mrs Wells. Most people would have assumed the same as you,' he said.

'It doesn't stop you wondering, though.'

As she took a final sip from her cup, Lenny clocked her raising an eyebrow at the biscuit situation. Out of the ten biscuits on the plate, there were only two left.

He quickly asked, 'Was there anything about the man or the car that stood out, for example, the colour or type of car?'

'Not particularly. As I said previously, it was quite dark in the car park, away from the lights of the fair. However, he was a well-built man, white, with dark hair. He was too far away to make out his face. I couldn't see the whole car through the gap. It was likely black or blue, but I really can't be certain.'

'Did you take any pictures of your son that evening? There could be a chance you caught something on camera.'

Mrs Wells looked surprised. 'Now there's a question I wasn't asked before, but as a matter of fact, I did. I took them with a mobile phone, which, as you can probably guess, I don't have now. I didn't even think to offer that information to the police. It just didn't occur to me.'

'I can't say I'm shocked. It's probably not a question I'd have thought to ask a few years ago, but these days, taking pictures with phones is all the rage. I don't suppose you downloaded the pictures to a computer or anything?'

Mrs Wells shook her head. 'No, I'm afraid not.' She glanced at the dainty silver watch on her wrist. 'I have to get ready to leave for my meeting now. I'm on the school board, you see.'

Lenny wasn't surprised to learn Mrs Wells was a member of the school board. 'Of course. I think that's all I need. You've pretty much confirmed what was in your original statement. I'd hoped perhaps something else might come to mind,' said Lenny.

Mrs Wells stood up and bent down to collect the tray. She moved the tray towards Lenny, her eyes suggesting he might as well take the last two biscuits on the plate.

'Oh, go on then,' he said.

'I'll just take this to the kitchen,' said Mrs Wells, the corners of her mouth slightly curled upwards, almost into a smile.

Lenny returned the pen and pad to his jacket pocket and stepped into the hallway.

'Sorry I couldn't be more helpful, Mr Grey,' she said, pacing along the hall towards him.

'Not to worry. It was worth a shot,' he said. 'Would you mind if I left my card – just in case?'

'You can leave it, of course, but if my mind hasn't remembered anything different in eight years, I very much doubt it will now,' she said, taking the card.

She showed Lenny out of the front door.

'Thank you for your time, Mrs Wells. I really appreciate it,' he said, walking away.

She called out, 'I hope you find the man responsible for what happened to that poor little boy.'

Turning to face her, he said, 'So do I, Mrs Wells.' He continued on his way. 'So do I,' he muttered again under his breath.

'Oh, and try not to sleep in your car too often. It must be very uncomfortable.'

He smiled. The lady had a sense of humour after all. When he arrived at his car, he reached into his jacket pocket, pulled out four biscuits, and bit into a Hobnob.

11

Harper

With Tom Burgess moving in with Elaine, it was time for Harper to go back to Beadlam, back to the caravan he'd called home since recovering from his injuries. As yet, he knew nothing about the big move to the cottage in Kirbymoorside. It would be one hell of a surprise and certainly unexpected. Until recently, he'd intentionally kept any thoughts of the future at bay. Over the past couple of years, Elaine had taught and shown him so much. She'd tried to convince him that it might be possible to have a normal life once they'd finished what they had to do, and now he'd met Alice; it wasn't so unimaginable. Of course, he wasn't stupid. He didn't imagine he'd ride off happily into the sunset with her in particular, but it was a comfort knowing people like her existed – people who could find pleasure in his company and wouldn't see through him – see the blood on his hands.

On the sofa, Harper waited. He'd been ready for over an hour. With Alice's car now repaired, she was on her way to pick him up and take *him* to dinner – her treat. They'd spoken a few times since their first date, and he was thrilled when she'd asked to see him again, which meant he had to come clean about where he was living. It worried him that she'd be put off by the caravan. She wasn't. If anything, she seemed more intrigued. This would be their third meeting, and Harper had no idea if this was leading anywhere in a romantic sense, but he enjoyed her company, and she obviously felt the same way.

When she arrived, he opted to go straight outside to meet her. With his social skills being somewhat rudimentary, he didn't know whether he should invite her inside. Did he even want to? He wasn't sure how much of himself he wanted to reveal. He'd barely pushed the door closed when—

'Whoa there, fella!' she said. 'What's your rush?'

Alice had already decided she was going in. She no doubt wanted to get a glimpse of how he lived and learn as much as she could about him. Harper pulled the door open and let her enter, amused by her assertiveness.

'Wow!' she said with a look of surprise. 'Spotless. Not what I expected at all.'

'What did you expect?'

'Guy stuff. Mess.'

'Sorry to disappoint you.'

'Oh, believe me, it's not a disappointment. It's nice to see a man who keeps a clean abode.' She ran her finger over a shelf, checking for dust. Not a speck. 'Sorry, I've been watching too much *Four in a Bed*. How long have you lived here?'

'A little over two years. It's just temporary until I figure out my next move.'

'That's so cool. It must be wonderful to have the freedom and time to decide what to do with the rest of your life.'

'Yeah, I guess it is,' he said, appearing more relaxed. 'Did you want a drink or something?'

'No, I'm fine, thank you,' she said, still taking in how pristine everything was. 'We should probably get going – the table is booked for half seven. I just wanted to have a look around. You already know how nosy I am.'

'Where are we off to?'

'A little Italian place in Helmsley. La Trattoria. Have you heard of it?'

'No, I can't say it rings a bell,' said Harper, taken aback at the mention of Helmsley, though he tried not to let it show. Helmsley wasn't the ideal place for a night out; not only was there a chance of him being recognised, but he also ran the risk of bumping into Elaine. He hadn't told her about Alice because he wasn't sure how she'd react, and considering Alice would be leaving in a few days, it didn't seem necessary.

Although busy, Alice managed to find a space in Market Place car park, a few feet from the door of the restaurant. Harper remembered passing it on the day of Elaine's wedding when he'd decided to go for a wander. A beautiful sunny evening meant there were quite a few people milling about in the town. Helmsley was always busy in the summer. Once through the door, he looked around, relieved to see no sign of Elaine. They were seated at a table by a young waitress who immediately took their drink order.

'It looks nice here, doesn't it?' said Alice.

'It does. I thought you'd been here before.'

'No. My parents recommended the place. Apparently, the food is delicious.'

Alice glanced up from the menu. 'Not long now before I have to go home,' she said. 'Are you going to miss me?'

'Not at all,' Harper said with a straight face. When Alice fell for his blunt reply, he broke into a smile. 'Of course, I'll miss you. It's been an unexpected pleasure. To meet you, I mean.'

Harper failed to notice the heartwarming impact of his words on her.

Having decided what they wanted from the menu, the waitress returned with their drinks and took their food order.

Alice stared at him while she sipped her lemonade and said, 'How would you like to come to my cousin's wedding reception on Saturday?'

Dumbstruck, Harper met her question with silence.

'You don't have to. It was just a thought,' she said to fill the gap.

'With you?' he asked.

'No, silly. With my mother. Of course, with me.'

He smiled. 'I'd like that very much.'

At the end of their wonderful meal, Alice drove him home. He invited her inside for coffee, which she readily accepted. Totally at ease with each other, they talked for a while on the sofa, albeit a couple of feet apart. Harper didn't want to overstep any boundaries. He listened attentively to every word she spoke; she seemed to love that about him.

Alice excused herself to use the bathroom. Out of his depth, Harper felt a tad uncomfortable. It had nothing to do with the company. Being with Alice was the closest to normal he'd ever imagined possible, even if he did feel like an awkward, nervous teenager on a first date with no idea what to do. With his mind in turmoil, he thought about who he really was – a killer. There was no escaping it. Gentle thoughts and emotions had no place in a man like him. But they *were* there, and he liked how good they made him feel. Did the true nature of a good person exist within the depths of his complexity? If so, Alice had unearthed something buried and lost long ago.

When she reappeared and sat down next to him, closer than before, his heart fluttered. *What the hell was that?* A tingling sensation at the top of his shoulders crawled slowly up the back of his neck. It was the most wonderful itch you didn't want to scratch, a buzz you never wanted to end. Powerful and prolonged. He'd never felt anything like it. The side of her leg pressed against his. Harper had never been prone to nerves, but on this occasion, there was no holding them back, no matter how hard he tried.

He glanced at a small clock on the side unit; it was getting late. Should he tell her so? Wasn't that what people said in the movies when they wanted someone to leave? But he didn't want her to leave. However, he did want to save himself from what he believed to be an involuntary weakness. He turned to face Alice and saw her staring right back at him with her beguiling, dimpled smile. Gazing into her eyes, the heavy weight of his world lifted. Whenever he was in her company, she freed him from the affliction that was his life.

Alice inched her face closer and stopped a fraction from his. The sides of their noses nuzzled, and he felt her warm breath caress his lips like a prelude to a kiss. Her bottom lip nestled between his. Electricity bolted through his veins, adding more light to his dark heart. The touch of her tongue, a sensual prod, enticed his lips to part. Harper didn't resist. Couldn't! Her soft hands embraced the sides of his face as she moved her body to straddle him. Mesmerised and lost within her kiss, he became overwhelmed by new sensations and an emotion he could not remember – happiness.

The first true kiss of his life, full of care and affection. Seconds passed, and he realised her lips were no longer on his. He opened his eyes, relieved to see her irresistible smile. For one tiny instant, he believed he'd imagined the whole thing. How could something so magnificent happen to him? Alice slowly climbed to her feet and stood in front of him. She held out her hand, pulled him up, and led him to the bedroom.

12

Tom held the door open for Elaine as they left The Black Swan Hotel, where they'd been for dinner and a drink to celebrate officially moving in together. Hand in hand, they wandered across the road to Market Place, where they'd parked.

'I'm so full. I wish I hadn't eaten so much,' Elaine said, her hand comforting her stomach.

'What did you expect? You ordered nearly every item on the menu,' Tom joked.

Elaine returned a dagger-like stare. 'I did not!'

As they reached the car, Elaine glanced across the square and hesitated, astonished to see Harper leaving La Trattoria with a woman. *What on earth did he think he was doing?* With Tom standing a few feet away, she couldn't say or do anything, but inside she was raging. She'd warned him over and over for his own sake not to show his face in town. The one exception was the day of her wedding. What excuse could he possibly have this time? By the looks of it, a date. If recognised and captured, it would be a disaster for both of them.

Tom opened the passenger door and no doubt noticed Elaine's pale face. 'You okay, sweetheart? You're looking a bit peaky there.'

Elaine faked a smile. 'Yeah, just a little queasy. I'll be fine by the time we get home.' She wouldn't be fine, not until she'd had strong words with Harper.

'I'd offer to drive, but I've had too much to drink,' said Tom.

In the morning, she'd leave Michael in charge of Emily and head straight over to confront him. It would drive her crazy to let this simmer any longer than necessary. The sooner the cottage in Kirbymoorside was ready, the better. At least he'd be further away from Helmsley.

As soon as Tom left for work, Elaine was out the door like a whippet. Michael wasn't thrilled about keeping an eye on his annoying little sister. Approximately four miles from Beadlam, she was outside his caravan in less than ten minutes. Another car parked out front caught her eye. She guessed whoever he'd left the restaurant with yesterday evening had spent the night. This could make things a little tricky. Elaine put on her happy face and knocked loudly.

Harper opened the door, and the aroma of frying bacon hit Elaine. From his carefree expression, she guessed he'd seen her pull up. He invited her in and told her to take a seat.

'Tea or coffee?' he asked.

Last night's bedroom antics were written all over his face. 'Coffee, please,' she replied.

The mystery woman was nowhere to be seen, which meant she could be hiding in the bedroom or perhaps taking a shower.

With the kettle on the boil, Harper sat at the table beside her and leaned in close. 'Listen, I have a friend here,' he whispered. 'Oh yeah, and my name is Simon.'

Elaine turned to face him. 'What?' she mouthed, barely making a sound.

'I'll explain in a bit.' He went to finish making the coffee.

Though not yet revealing her anger, it pleased her that he'd had the good sense to use a different name. As he placed a steaming mug in front of her, his guest appeared.

'Alice, this is Elaine, whose house I was looking after.'

'Hi there,' said Alice, a tinge of embarrassment shining through.

Elaine returned the smile. 'Hello.'

'Did you want another cup of tea?' Harper asked Alice.

'No, I need to make a move. I have a few things to do today, including buying a dress for the wedding.'

Elaine directed her shocked eyes at Harper. He immediately shook his head to indicate that it wasn't what she was thinking.

Alice opened the door and stared at Elaine. 'It was nice to meet you. Maybe we'll meet again sometime. Bye.'

Elaine forced another smile and waved as they stepped outside. She jumped out of her seat and spied on the pair through the window as they shared a kiss and a cuddle. Elaine rushed back to her seat before he returned. When he did, she waited for the door to close, dropped the friendly persona, and glared at him.

Smirking, he said, 'I know what you thought. You thought I was getting married.'

'Only for a second,' she said, and after a brief pause, alluded to his earlier statement. '*Simon*?'

'I know. For some reason, it was the first name that popped into my head.'

'So, what's going on? Oh, please tell me you did not just bed the bride-to-be?'

He laughed. 'Don't be silly. I did not just bed the bride-to-be.'

'I'm glad you think this is funny,' Elaine snapped.

'Well, she isn't getting married. It's her cousin's wedding.'

'I'm not talking about that.'

'What then? Am I not allowed to have friends or see anyone?'

'Not in Helmsley, no.'

'What are you talking about?'

'La Trattoria! Ring any bells?' she said, getting to her feet.

'Oh! I see. You know about that?' he said, like a boy who'd been caught with his hand in the cookie jar.

'Yes! I do. I also know you used my car.'

'Ah!'

'Harper, you can't even drive.'

'I just wanted to have a go,' he said. 'Anyway, how did you know I was in Helmsley?'

'Well, it just so happens I was in town having dinner with Tom last night, and on our way back to the car, guess who came ambling out of the Italian restaurant?'

'I was careful. And I was hardly ambling.'

'Are you kidding? You were as blasé as a cat strolling out of a fishmonger's with a large salmon between its teeth.'

Harper sat down, elbows on the table, face in hands. 'Look, I know I shouldn't have gone into town, but she booked the restaurant. What could I say? Oh, I'm so sorry, Alice, I can't go to Helmsley because I killed a few of the residents there a short while back.'

'Do you think I don't realise how difficult things are for you? Because I do!'

'No, you don't!' He slammed his hands on the table in frustration. 'You haven't got a clue. Do you understand how much

I struggle to live with what's in my head? I can barely sleep at night, and when I do, I wake up thinking I should kill myself – that none of this revenge shit matters any more.'

Harper stood and went to the fridge. He grabbed a carton of milk and poured some into a glass on the draining board. 'At first, it felt right, but now – now it just seems pointless.' He gulped down the milk and said, 'It's not going to take away the past. And the crimes I've committed since breaking out of Rampton have only served to ruin any future I might have. Well, at least that's what I thought until . . .'

'Until what?'

'Until I met Alice.'

Elaine frowned and flopped down on the sofa. 'Oh my God. You bloody well like her.'

'Yes, I bloody well do!' Harper fired back.

'So you're going to be Simon forever now, are you? Because I'll be honest, Liam, I'm starting to lose track.' Elaine let out a frustrated sigh. 'At this rate, you'll end up with more aliases than Butch Cassidy.'

Harper sat down with a smile on his face.

'What are you grinning for?' she asked.

'You called me Liam.'

'There, you see how confused I am.' Burying her face in her hands, Elaine chuckled to herself. 'I have no idea why I'm laughing. This is serious.'

'I know it is. Look, I'll keep out of Helmsley, I promise.'

She'd said her piece, and he was probably expecting her to leave, but Elaine decided this would be as good a time as any to tell him about his new lodgings. 'There is one other thing I've been meaning to talk to you about.'

'And that is?' he asked, curious.

'I've bought a cottage for you.'

He appeared shocked. 'You've bought me a cottage? Why?'

'You can't live in a caravan forever.' His dubious expression was plain to see. 'You'd have a lot more space,' she added, hoping to sell the idea to him.

'Where is this cottage?'

With excitement, she said, 'It's in Kirbymoorside. It should be ready for you to move into in a couple of weeks.'

'I drove past there on the way to—'

Elaine's eyes widened, prompting him not to complete the sentence.

'I'm not being funny, Elaine, but I might not want to move to Kirbymoorside.'

'You're kidding, right? Got other plans, have you?' she queried with a hint of sarcasm.

'Not right now – but that's not to say I won't want to move on to a different place at some point.'

'Oh – I see.'

He sighed. 'What do you think you see, Elaine?'

'That you believe your new girlfriend is going to whisk you away to some "happily ever after." Well, I'm sorry, Harper, but I have news for you – there is no happily ever after. You of all people should know there is no fairy-tale ending to all this.'

'That's not what I think is going to happen at all, but she has opened my eyes to something new.'

'Like what?'

'The possibility that others could see me for who I want to be, not for who I was. When I'm with her, I get these brief moments when my head feels so light, clear, and free. Like I don't have to carry this lorry load of shit around with me forever, and it feels fucking great, Elaine.'

A striking silence lingered before Elaine took a deep breath and said, '*You selfish bastard*! What about me? Yes, I was struggling three years ago, but that was nothing new. Then, out of nowhere, you manipulated your way back into my life, piled all the sick shit I had no memory of on me, killed people, turned *me* into a murderer, and now you want to be the one to run off with a clear head and forget all about it. Well, thank you, Harper. Thank you very much.'

'Don't forget, you were already a murderer. It was *you* who killed our father.' He smirked.

'Oh yeah, great! Another thing I didn't remember, and until we went to pay Denley Parker a visit, you thought you'd killed him. Also, the way you just said "*our* father" – means you've changed your identity yet again. Jesus, I honestly can't keep up.'

Harper sat up. 'All right, when you put it like that, it doesn't sound good. I clearly didn't phrase or do things as well as I should have, but I'm not saying I'm going to forget what happened to us as children. All I was trying to say is I've rarely felt I could live with myself, and now, for the first time in my life – I can see a future out there for me, and by me – I think I mean Liam.'

'Liam? I don't understand. Is this about what you said before, about losing who you are and not being the person you were three years ago?'

'Yes, for a while now I've felt confused, frustrated, and changeable. I don't know if it's the medication or something else, but I feel . . . I don't know how to explain it. It's as though Harper is fading away and Liam is coming back. At times it's so hard. It's like there is this war in my head, a battle of wills, so to speak – and I'm not sure who I am any more. I don't really know if I want to be either of them.'

'Perhaps you're neither.'

Harper looked perplexed. 'What does that even mean?'

'Okay. Just hear me out,' she said. 'By the time you arrived at Rampton, you were already a scared, traumatised, and broken young boy. In your mind, you eventually killed Liam off and created a new, tougher, vengeful personality as a way to cope. It helped you gain a new focus to move forward. As Harper, you had no plans to live any longer than was necessary. Now you say that has changed. So what if Harper has played his part? You created him to get you through a terrible trauma. You were once the victim, and then you were something else altogether. Now, it could be you're neither of those people. Maybe it's time to let both Liam and Harper go.'

She rose to her feet, walked over, and placed her hand on his shoulder. 'I was being selfish. The world is a big place, and you've seen none of it. You are in a unique position where you can go anywhere you want to go, be anyone you want to be . . . except Simon.' She smiled. 'I just don't see you as a Simon.'

Elaine realised she couldn't keep him all to herself. Her brother was best left in the past. If he was set on leaving, she knew he'd only make it with her help. To most people, everything she'd said would sound incomprehensible, but she could tell he understood. Liam was the past he didn't want to go back to, and Harper was the violent present he needed to walk away from. She should have read the signs; seen it coming. If he wanted to leave, she had to let him go. Perhaps it would be better for both of them.

'How could I go anywhere in the world?' he asked.

'There are ways around such things. Besides, I know someone who can help. Just leave it to me,' she said. 'Oh, I almost forgot.' Elaine placed a mobile phone and a piece of paper on the table.

'Your number is on the paper. I've put my number in the phone already. You'll have to add your girlfriend's.' She smirked and walked over to the door. 'Two days. Are you still okay to go through with it?' she asked, referring to the final name on their list.

'Yes. We have to finish what we started.'

'Good. I'll call you tomorrow then. If I do get you a new identity, is there a particular name you'd prefer?'

Harper smiled. 'You choose.'

13

The Boy

The boy wrapped the chain around the metal post at the end of the bed and looped it around his neck. With his feet stretched out in front of him, he let his body drop, his bottom hovering just above the floor. His eyes reddened and bulged, the veins protruding through the delicate skin of his small neck. It was no good; he couldn't do it. He pulled his feet back towards his body and raised himself, easing the tension in the chain. He'd failed for the third time in an effort to end his life this way. If he could just make it to the point of passing out, he knew it would work, but his survival instincts always kicked in before he got that far. He unwound the chain from his red and badly bruised neck. The colour of his face slowly returned to normal.

Since his discovery of the other boys' names, he had fallen into despair. If things weren't bad enough already, knowing he would die any day now was too much to bear. There would be no saviour. Taking matters into his own hands seemed the best option, but even suicide proved too difficult. He had considered *not* putting up a fight the next time the monster made an appearance – but that did not necessarily mean the end. It just meant more pain.

He frequently reminisced about his parents and little sister, all the fun and eventful days out to various amazing places, and how he would never get to do any of those things again. So many dreams unfulfilled and memories unmade. He missed them right now. His friends, too. Everything seemed like a young lifetime ago, out of reach and fading further into the distance. Imagining the relentless hurt and unbearable suffering his mum and dad must be going through was unavoidable.

The boy glanced down and ran his tiny, bony fingers over the rusted bolt that secured the chain to the floor, willing it to come undone and release him. He wrapped the chain around his hand and yanked it in a half-hearted attempt to pull the bolt loose, something he'd tried a hundred times or more already. It didn't budge. It never budged. He dropped the chain in frustration and flung himself onto the bed. Tears streamed down his gaunt face. He let out a weak, gut-wrenching scream that diminished into a tortured, tired, and torpid cry, his voice as broken as his soul.

Raising his head, he stared at the table. He dragged his skin and bones across the floor and examined the names etched into the wood. Twisting the screw loose, he lay on his back and added his name and the date he was taken – something he hadn't wanted to do. It felt too final, accepting his fate and giving up. But the end was near. The monster *would* eventually kill him; of that, he was certain. It was just a question of whether he would beat the monster to it.

When he'd finished adding his name to the list of other poor souls, he struggled to his feet and idled over to the toilet. He sat down on the grotty, cold porcelain pan. With his elbows on his knees and his head down, he stared at his pale, skeletal feet and the dark wooden floor around them. His feet were as white and grubby as the porcelain. He recalled the time his dad stood on the toilet at home to put up a new plasterboard ceiling. While banging in clout nails, he dropped the hammer, which cracked and broke the back of the pan.

The boy's eyes grew wide as a burst of energy surged through him. He pulled up his underpants and flushed the toilet. Raising his foot, he whacked the shackle against the back of the pan. Although it hurt his ankle, tearing through the skin and causing it to bleed, he had to continue until he broke off a piece of porcelain. Unsatisfied with the first fragment that came free, he carried on. Finally, a second piece broke off, and he stopped. He reached down behind the pan to pick it up. It was a thick piece, about three inches long and angled to a sharp point – exactly what he needed.

With his eyes transfixed on the broken shard of porcelain, he traipsed over to the bed. He sat down, turned his wrist over, and glared at the protruding vein. He rested the sharp end against his skin, attempting to build up the courage to slice through it.

Heavy footsteps above indicated the man had returned. The boy had lost track of time and would have to be patient. The last thing he needed was for the man to intervene and take away his makeshift weapon. He'd wait until later that night. Not long now, and he would be free. He hid the broken porcelain behind the toilet pan. It would be safe there.

Within the hour, the man entered the room with the boy's sandwich, fruit, and a small cup of water. He placed the paper plate and cup on the table, took his customary glance around the room to check everything was as it should be, and left, shutting the door behind him. The boy doubted the man would return until breakfast.

*

On the bed, the boy gazed up at the ceiling. It seemed like hours since he'd consumed his sandwich and fruit. He lay thinking about the harrowing task of cutting his wrists, and even though he wanted to give up, the faint hope of rescue still lingered. Slowly and unintentionally, his eyes closed, and he drifted off to sleep.

His eyes flashed open to the sound of deafening music. 'No! No, please, not now.' The monster was ready to play. The boy shuddered as the door opened. Footsteps stomped across the room to the other door. The opening and closing of drawers was followed by the switching off of the fluorescent white light, replaced by the daunting red. He sat up and eyed the shirtless demon at the end of the bed. *Please, not the teeth.*

A wish granted as the monster spoke over the music. 'Stand up.'

The boy wasted no time. Trembling throughout, he climbed from the bed as fast as he could, doing his utmost to conceal his ever-weakening state.

The monster tossed something onto the mattress. 'You know what you have to do,' he said, dropping to his knees with his back to the boy, his arms splayed across the length of the bed.

The boy picked up what the monster had told him was a cat-o'-nine-tails. The scars on the man's back still looked raw from the last time he had used the whip on him. On that occasion, he had felt stronger, much stronger. He silently prayed to raise enough stamina and strength to reopen those old wounds and create new ones.

'Come on!' the monster shouted. 'Fucking hit me!'

The boy did not hesitate. He pulled back the whip and launched the first strike.

A restrained yell bellowed from the monster's lungs. 'You're going to have to do a lot better than that, boy!'

With the second hit, he drew blood. The boy took a deep breath before each lash and continued for just under seven minutes, growing weaker with every strike. Blood coursed down the monster's back from the lacerations as he yelled and groaned aloud. Even so, the boy couldn't help but wonder if he was causing as much pain now as he had on previous occasions. Over the next few minutes, the pauses between lashes increased until finally, the boy slumped to the floor.

Sluggish, the monster perched on the edge of the bed, the soles of his feet bathed in a small pool of his own blood. He stood and wandered towards his exhausted little prisoner, scowling down at him. He reached for the whip, snatched it from his limp grasp, and threw it onto the bed. The boy let out a sigh of relief. He had managed to keep the monster at bay once more, but he knew he wouldn't have the strength to do so again. Come tomorrow, he wouldn't have to.

The man walked over to use the toilet, as he always did when the session was over. The boy lay crumpled on the floor, weary but pleased that his immediate ordeal was over. His eyes sprang to life in realisation of his earlier misconception. He should never have taken it for granted that nothing would happen tonight. Something was wrong. There was no flush of the toilet, no changing of the lights. Footsteps approached. Shivering in fear, he wanted to run – to hide – to disappear. The broken piece of porcelain landed on the floor next to him. He scrabbled and writhed along the floor, as far as the chain would allow. Within seconds, the monster was bearing down on him.

'Please, please don't hurt me!' he pleaded. He lifted his gaze to see the whip come down and strike his fragile body. He curled into a ball to make himself as small a target as possible, but it did not help. The monster did not hold anything back as he whipped him repeatedly, tearing the sheath-like skin from his bones. Finally, he stopped and pulled him by his hair across the room. He tried to resist, digging his fingernails into the floorboards. He couldn't conceal his horror as two of his nails snapped from their tiny nail beds.

The monster dropped the boy, sat on the thin mattress, and glared at him. He held out the whip. 'You know what to do.'

The boy's tears ran dry, and his hollow sobs came to a halt. A whimper escaped his lips as he shifted his battered and bleeding body onto his knees. Certain he couldn't summon enough strength to thrash the monster, he knew this could be the end, but he refused to go down without a fight. Slowly, he crawled forward. He hesitated for a second, then launched himself upwards with force, ramming the top of his head into the face of the monster, hurtling him backwards onto the mattress and opening up the skin above his right eye. The boy straddled him and placed his small hands around his thick neck, squeezing as tightly as he could.

The monster laughed, and it dawned on the boy that his effort to strangle him was futile. He let himself fall onto the bed. When the monster's laughter stopped, the pair lay there, bleeding out in silence.

The man retrieved the small remote control from his back pocket and lowered the volume of the music. 'I love how you keep surprising me, boy.'

Rising from the bed, the man fetched the whip and flicked the lights from red to white, highlighting the vast amount of blood scattered about the place. He entered the other room and reappeared with some towels, clean bedding, and clean underwear for the boy. He placed the pile on the table and held a small towel against the cut above his eye. 'Clean yourself, the room, and change the bed.' He picked up the sharp piece of porcelain. 'Your life is not for you to take. You would do well to cast any such thoughts from your mind. Make this mistake again and my next guest will be your little sister.' He turned away and left.

Little sister! How did the man know about her? He must have been watching the whole family. There was no way he could allow that to happen. Any plans to end his life were instantly vanquished. He would have to see it through to the end, whenever the end might be. The boy touched a small cut on the top of his head and winced. He stared at the blood on his fingers. The man was always pleased when he fought back. When he launched himself headfirst at the monster, he did so believing he had nothing to lose except his life, which, in some strange way, was what he'd hoped to achieve. The music fell silent.

After a short rest, he sat up and examined the lash marks on his body. If he didn't feel so numb, the pain would be insufferable. He climbed off the bed, staggered over to the shower cubicle and, after filling the bucket with water, lumbered over to the table. Catching sight of the underwear, he couldn't help but wonder if it belonged to one of the boys who had preceded him. He grabbed a large towel and set to work, washing the blood from the floor and cleaning the spots off the walls. Once he'd completed that task, he stripped the bed and left the sheets in a pile in the corner of the room, along with his old underpants.

Taking a shower, the water ran red, blood rinsing from his body. His emotions stirred, and tears flowed. He dropped to his knees and sobbed, the water raining down upon his wounds. Over the next few minutes, the pain set in, increasing by the second. He struggled to dry himself before putting on a fresh pair of underpants. Using items from his first-aid stash, he treated the wounds. He then turned the mattress over and put on the new bedspread. The fresh smell of the clean white sheets and quilt was enough to make him want to flop down on the bed and pass out, and that was exactly what he did.

A few hours later, he woke to the sound of the room door closing. For a moment, he just lay there, waiting to hear the man's footsteps, but there were none. He sat up to find the room empty. The pile of bloodstained sheets and towels had been removed. Spying something on the table, he went over to investigate.

Stepping closer, he identified the McDonald's logo on the large brown paper bag. Inside were three hamburgers, chicken nuggets, fries, and an apple pie. There was also a large Coke and a strawberry milkshake. Was this some kind of trick – or perhaps a treat? He didn't understand and, several seconds later, didn't care. Excitement and hunger consumed him. The boy tore the bag apart, ripped open the boxes, and got stuck in. He bit into a burger, shoved a handful of fries into his mouth, and, while chomping away, took a sip of his milkshake.

14

Lenny

Fine dining didn't sit well with Lenny, which explained why he was eating a full rack of ribs in an American restaurant at Westfield Stratford City, a place he'd visited many times. He was a sucker for their barbecue ribs and loaded fries, but since he'd started his health kick, he had limited his visits to once a month instead of once a week. However, this evening was a special occasion: a date, and the last time Lenny took a woman out, Tony Blair was Prime Minister.

As he sucked the tender meat from the bone, Olivia Reid, the forensic pathologist he'd met a few days earlier, showed her burger no mercy. Neither seemed to show any signs of discomfort as they tucked into their messy hand food.

'I'm glad you called me,' she said. 'Did you get my number from Colin?'

'Not a chance. I thought about it, but he would have taken the piss and ribbed me about it for ages. Excuse the pun,' he said, his mouth full and a smile on his face as he waved a half-eaten rib in her direction.

'Ah, I see. You were embarrassed to let your friend know that you wanted to take me out.'

Lenny tossed the bare bone onto the plate. 'Not at all. I didn't mean it like that. It's just, well, you know how mates are.'

Olivia smiled. 'Oh, Lenny, I'm just teasing.' She sipped her lemonade. 'So how did you find me?'

'I searched for your place of work on Google.'

The waiter returned, took their dessert order, and cleared the table. The familiarity between Lenny and the waiter was clearly visible to Olivia.

'I assume you are a frequent visitor here,' she said.

'Not as frequent as I used to be. I'm trying to trim a few off the old waistline.' He laughed.

'Do you bring all your dates here?'

'Only the pretty ones.' He smiled.

'Ooh, very smooth.'

'No, actually, you're the first.'

'I'm honoured,' she said.

'You shouldn't be – I don't go on many dates.'

'What's your idea of many?'

'Put it this way, the last time I took a bird out, *Captain Corelli's Mandolin* was at the pictures.'

'But that came out years ago!'

'Exactly.' Lenny sucked the tender meat from his final rib.

When the pair finished their dessert, they walked and talked about all manner of things. They ended up in a bar and found a table in the corner where they sat down for a drink. Lenny revealed he'd never married or had children and discovered Olivia was four years divorced, also with no children. Not long after getting comfortable, Lenny's phone rang. It was Colin. He stared at Olivia and for a second thought about ignoring the call so as not to be rude, but he couldn't help himself, thinking it might be important to the case – and it was. Colin informed him about the discovery of a young boy's body in Harlow a couple of months earlier. Lenny agreed to meet the DCI the following day, and together they would drive to Parndon Lock Meadows.

'That didn't sound good,' said Olivia.

Lenny took a large sip of ale. 'No, it wasn't. They found another boy's body in Harlow a few weeks back.'

'Does Colin think it's the same killer?'

'He didn't say as much, but I'm sure he believes it is.'

'May I ask how you ended up involved in this case?'

'Charlie Davis.'

'The boy from your book?'

Lenny nodded.

'What makes you believe you're chasing the same person who killed Charlie?'

Lenny gulped the rest of his pint. 'Sometimes, you just know.'

Olivia could tell this news had lowered the mood of their otherwise enjoyable evening and asked if Lenny wanted to call it a night. He did, and she completely understood why. They took the Tube, and Lenny walked her home from the station.

'Well, here we are.' She pointed to an apartment building and turned to him.

'Look, I'm sorry our date took a downturn,' he said.

'Hey, it's fine. What kind of person would I be if I failed to understand why? Besides, I had a lovely time. And thank you for walking me home. Quite the gentleman.'

'Oh, I don't know about—'

Olivia placed her lips against his to prevent him from finishing the sentence.

'Call me again,' she said.

'You asking or telling?'

'Telling!' She smiled.

'In that case, I have no choice.'

Plagued by another terrible night's sleep, Lenny wasted no time driving up to Harlow at the break of dawn. At least he'd missed the morning rush hour, although that seemed to be getting earlier and earlier these days. He met DCI Hargreaves at a café for breakfast. Colin explained the discovery and how he'd been researching missing children and the deaths of young boys in the area over the past eight years. Without including the two boys whose remains had already been recovered, this was the most recent case. On the whole, the results were staggering. During his research, he'd discovered that every year in the United Kingdom, one child in every two hundred went missing. More shockingly, as many as seven in ten missing children were not reported at all. How could anyone fail to report a missing child?

Lenny left his car near the café, and they drove to Parndon Mill Lane in Colin's silver Mercedes. They parked at the side of the road just after a small bridge that crossed over the railway tracks. Lenny climbed out of the car and surveyed the surrounding area. There were numerous trees, a narrow road, train tracks, and a dirt path he presumed they would be heading down any minute.

Lenny said, 'I'd imagine there isn't much traffic coming through here at night. It must be very quiet.'

'There's only an old mill at the end of that road. It's a gallery and workplace for artists, designers, and architects,' Colin explained.

'So, quite a few people coming and going then?'

'Yeah, but it closes at five most days and doesn't open on Saturdays or Mondays.'

'Nice. Who wouldn't want a Monday off? Right, where are we off to then?'

'Follow me,' said Colin, leading the way down the dirt path, holding a manila folder.

Enclosed by trees and thick bushes, the path led them through a wooded area where they came to a stop overlooking a large pond.

'This is where a couple walking their dog found the body. The killer didn't bother to weigh the bag down on this occasion, and after a while, it floated to the surface. Unlike the others, he wasn't dismembered, but he was shoved into a hessian mailbag, which was then tied shut and thrown into the water. He was alive when he went in.'

Lenny was horrified. 'You what?'

'Alive. The boy drowned,' said Colin.

'Fucking animal.'

'You're not wrong there. The boy had bite marks all over his body.'

'I take it there were no DNA traces or matching dental records?'

Colin shook his head. 'Nothing. Forensics suspect he used some sort of mouth device with sharpened false teeth – possibly homemade. Here,' he said, holding out the case file.

Lenny opened it and skimmed through the paperwork. 'William Harvey, eleven years old. Reported missing on the second of March this year.' Lenny glanced up at Colin, exasperated by how recent this was. He carried on reading aloud, 'Body discovered on the twenty-seventh of May. Severe physical scarring.' Lenny shook his head in disgust.

'According to forensics, he was probably kept alive for up to a month or more,' said Colin.

Lenny moved on to the grim photographs. 'For Christ's sake, these look like lash wounds from a whip. What the hell are we dealing with here, Col?'

'An evil, sadistic, savage bastard. No doubt about it. And we need to stop him, Lenny. It's not going to be long before the press gets hold of this. I'm already under a lot of pressure from above. The mailbags link the boys' deaths, and so far we have three confirmed victims. They're putting me in charge of a task force to find this animal, so any information you dig up, please pass it on to me.'

'Same goes.'

'Obviously,' Colin agreed.

'Three?' enquired Lenny. 'You said three confirmed victims. What about Charlie Davis?'

'I'm sorry, Len. Even though *we* know it's probably the same guy, my superiors won't accept Charlie as one of this particular killer's victims. Different M.O. Between you and me, I don't think they want to admit this goes back as far as eight years.'

On their return to the car, Lenny asked Colin to drive down to Parndon Mill. He just wanted to see what was down there, and other than the mill, fields, the continuing railway tracks, and narrowboats on the canal, there wasn't much of note. There were no through roads – just another dead end. During the journey to drop Lenny back at his car, Colin had one more piece of information to divulge.

'While looking through the list of children who had disappeared from the north to the east of London and the surrounding areas, I came across a twelve-year-old boy called Danny Logan. He was reported missing on June thirtieth. Going by how long the Harvey boy was kept alive, there is every chance this kid is still breathing.'

'Where did he go missing from?'

Colin glanced across at Lenny. 'From the Community Festival at Finsbury Park. The same place where Charlie Davis was taken.'

15

Harper

Redemption for Edward Horner was out of the question. Even though Harper and Elaine were tired of death, they remained focused on their goal. As the last name on their list, it would be ridiculous to let him go unpunished after everything they'd been through. They had come too far to stop now. As guilty as the others, he would soon meet his own violent end.

As per usual, Elaine had done the groundwork and been meticulous in her planning of the where, when, and how. Graham Walker's decision to take matters into his own hands was something she could never have predicted.

Harper had his instructions, and because of Sir Edward's high profile as a former Home Secretary, both knew this would be a lot more complex than with previous victims. They drove down to London and arrived late in the afternoon. Elaine had booked a room at Riverside Tower Hotel, situated on the north bank of the River Thames. Sir Edward Horner would be attending a private fundraiser at the hotel for some friends and former colleagues.

Due to a number of high-profile guests, a small security detail and police presence were required. Elaine and Harper were not going to let a *minor* detail like that deter them. If everything went without a hitch, they would be safely on their way home early the next morning. Things would be different this time. They'd agreed to end Edward Horner's life quickly, without prolonged, rigorous torture and without fuss.

Elaine sneaked Harper into her room so he could change. At her request, he wore a pristine white shirt, black trousers, and black shoes – so he wouldn't look out of place. After hanging around the room for a while, going over their plan, she handed him her room key, and he left. Though his memories of growing up in a London suburb were long gone, this was Harper's first visit to the City of London.

Drenched in the evening sunshine outside the hotel, he leaned against the railing, overlooking the river and Tower Bridge. He had seen the world-famous bridge on television, but that didn't compare to seeing it up close. Across the water beyond the bridge was The Shard, and to his right was the Tower of London.

Tired of watching boats cruise up and down the river, he turned to face the tall hotel. A few feet away was the Girl with a Dolphin fountain. He didn't quite know what to make of the statue. He understood the dolphin jumping out of the water but couldn't grasp the naked woman flying through the air to attack it. Outside the entrance to the hotel were two uniformed police officers wearing fluorescent yellow high-visibility jackets. They weren't guarding the door as such; it was more a case of watching for suspicious activity. He wanted to go inside, find the bastard, kill him, and be done with it. Elaine explained it wasn't as straightforward as that, not with plain-clothes security officers hanging around. She certainly didn't want today to turn into another bloodbath.

Harper checked his new phone for the time – just gone seven. He guessed Elaine was still getting ready. She said she'd update him by text. Her aim was to befriend Sir Edward in the function room and, at some stage, lure him out of the hotel. Harper would then take care of the rest. She'd warned him it could take some time. Harper suggested that, going by the former Home Secretary's past inclinations, he might not even fancy her. Elaine laughed off his comment, telling him Edward had a weakness for both sexes and she just needed to put herself in his path.

So many people ambled along the riverbank, mostly tourists with a desire to see everything from every angle. Though not used to crowds, being surrounded by people helped his attempt to remain inconspicuous. Growing somewhat impatient, he didn't know whether to go up to the room and wait or to go for a walk.

Choosing the second option, he crossed to the centre of Tower Bridge to look over the edge and then made his way back, wandering along the north bank towards the Tower of London. As he sat on a bench overlooking the castle, his phone pinged with a message from Elaine. She'd found out through small talk with other guests which room Edward Horner was staying in. How people loved to gossip! Annoyingly for Harper, she failed to reveal the room number in the message. *Holding back intentionally? Very likely.* He texted back, asking her to tell him. 'Not yet,' she replied. He hoped to hear from her again before she made her move.

From the bench, he watched the world go by: so many tourists, speaking languages he couldn't understand. Their words were foreign to him, but their body language was universal – whether it was a young couple in love, another couple arguing, or a child crying for an ice cream from a nearby van.

Bored and hungry, he walked back towards the hotel, keeping an eye out for a place to get a bite to eat. After strolling around St Katharine Docks Marina, awestruck by the luxurious boats, he happened across a fairly busy restaurant. Perched on a high stool, watching nothing in particular on the television behind the bar, he got stuck into his burger and fries, regularly checking his phone for any messages. There were none. It had been over an hour since he'd last heard from Elaine, and it bothered him. He sipped slowly at his pint of Coke to kill time until he finally decided to head back to the hotel.

The sun was setting, and the tall buildings concealed and sapped the colour from the day as darkness loomed over the city. Walking down St Katharine's Way, his phone rang but stopped abruptly, barely breaking into the second ring. He tried to call Elaine back – she didn't answer. Worried, he sent a text message in case she was unable to talk. By the time he reached the hotel, she still hadn't replied.

The two police officers outside the doors earlier had gone. The same couldn't be said for the two officers patrolling the reception. Head down, Harper advanced to the stairs and up to the first floor. Several people were leaving the function room, the event visibly winding down. Though stern in their refusal to grant him access, the security staff at the door relented when he explained he was Mrs Grosvenor's driver (as if they were going to check) and only wanted to let her know the car was ready. They patted him down and let him enter.

Inside, he saw neither Elaine nor Edward Horner, although it wasn't difficult for him to spot a couple of plainclothes protection officers in the room. Harper thanked the men at the door and went straight upstairs. All was quiet as he approached Elaine's room. An unsettling feeling grew in the pit of his stomach. He used the key card and eased the door open.

Uncertain of what he expected to find, he discovered the room was empty. Although relieved, it didn't ease his concern. He wished he'd pressed her for the number of Sir Edward's suite earlier; however, he understood why she had refused. Elaine still didn't fully trust him, and to be fair, he didn't blame her. He had it within him to go off on a tangent and be reckless. She'd helped him immensely since his return; taught him self-control, kept him from self-destruction, and, most importantly, kept him free. He loved her for all that she'd done, but not being able to contact her right now frustrated the hell out of him.

Harper tried Elaine's phone again; still, there was no answer. He exited the room and checked the bar areas to no avail. Heading towards one of the lifts, he saw a young man, smartly dressed in his hotel uniform, carefully pushing a trolley covered with a crisp, white linen tablecloth. Balancing on top were two wine glasses, an ice bucket, a corkscrew, and two expensive bottles of wine. Instinct told Harper to follow, and the man kindly held the lift door open as he approached.

'Looks as though someone is planning to party into the early hours,' said Harper, hoping to build rapport as he slipped into the lift.

The young man turned. 'Yes, sir, it looks that way. Between us, whenever Sir Edward stays, he does tend to go over the top. He always empties the complimentary minibar too.'

Harper's instinct had paid off. 'He's obviously got company tonight.'

'He has a roving eye for anything that moves. There have been quite a few complaints about his behaviour, even from the staff. He gets a warning about his conduct, but nothing ever comes of it. Nobody wants to wait on him when he's here. On this occasion, I lost the toss.' He frowned.

Harper couldn't believe his luck. 'Chatty fellow, aren't you?' said Harper, slightly upscaling his accent. 'Seeing as I'm on my way to his room, we can let him know what you and the other members of staff at the hotel think of him. I'm sure he'll be delighted.'

The colour drained from the poor young man's face as he realised his mistake. 'I'm so sorry, sir. I didn't realise—'

'Save it!' interrupted Harper, a faint smirk on his face. He let the room service attendant leave the lift with the trolley and followed a few steps behind.

The young man stopped outside the room and turned to face Harper. 'Please, sir. I truly am sorry,' he begged. 'I could lose my job for this and get other members of staff into trouble.'

Harper let the poor sod fret a little longer. 'Sir Edward is a very dear friend of mine, but even I know how *damn* right salacious he can be at times. I'll tell you what – get out of here and we'll say no more about it,' he ordered in a firm but friendly tone.

The man thanked him and didn't waste any time doing as he was told, disappearing down the hall and out of sight.

Harper put his ear to the door and heard men's voices inside. He waited a little longer, hoping to hear Elaine's voice; instead, he heard a loud thud, possibly a door closing. He knocked, and a deep voice asked who it was.

'I've brought the wine, sir,' he said.

'Leave it there,' the man demanded.

'I'm afraid I can't do that, sir . . . we've had a complaint.'

The man muttered something before opening the door. 'Sir Edward will be outraged when I tell him about this,' said the older man, fuming. 'Bring it in,' he continued in the same angry tone.

'Yes, sir,' said Harper, pushing the trolley in with his hands resting on a tea towel he'd placed over the handle so as not to leave fingerprints. Within seconds, he noticed a mark on the man's face and a few spots of blood on his unbuttoned white shirt. 'Is Sir Edward not here?' asked Harper, removing the small tea towel from the trolley and wrapping it around the top of a bottle of wine, which he gripped firmly.

'Sir Edward is otherwise engaged,' the man responded, looking towards a closed door across the room. 'Now, who complained?' he asked, readying some folded banknotes.

Harper glared at the door, too preoccupied with what might be going on in the next room to answer.

'I asked, who complained?'

'The room below, sir.'

'Well, I'll be sure to pass on your message,' he said, offering the money. 'Now, get out!'

The man watched Harper lift the bottle from the ice bucket and turn to face him. 'I said, get ou—'

Harper forced the bottom of the bottle hard into the man's nose, instantly drawing blood. The man staggered backwards, dazed and confused, and dropped to his backside, his bloodied hands covering his nose.

'Bastard! You broke my nose,' the man said, glancing up, teary-eyed, from the floor.

'Here, let me see,' said Harper.

Shock and stupidity made the man remove his hands to allow Harper to strike the bottom of the bottle against his nose for a second time. The man was flat out on his back. Harper fell to his knees and thumped the bottle against the man's face until it smashed, the white wine rinsing the blood from his features.

With the man out cold, Harper got to his feet, his shirt peppered with red spots. The broken bottle wrapped in the bloody towel now formed a long, lethal shard. Harper glared across the room and paced towards the bedroom door, opening it quietly. Confronting him was the sight of a slightly overweight naked man having sex with a woman on the bed. It had to be Edward Horner, and he hoped to God it wasn't Elaine beneath him – but deep down, he knew it was likely.

Edward violently slapped the woman's face. Harper stormed over and rammed the broken bottle into Edward Horner's neck. He shoved the man from the bed and stared, horrified, at the bloody and battered face of a half-naked, unconscious Elaine. What had gone so wrong for this to happen? Edward Horner's gargling caught his attention. Harper strode around the bed and dropped to the floor beside the dumbfounded naked man.

'Remember me?' Harper asked, watching the horror flicker in Edward's eyes – a split second of recognition before he drove the shard into his face and neck. The gouging, slicing and splashing filled the silence of the room, but none of it disturbed the horrific echoes of Harper and Elaine's past suffering. Instead, he felt only the cold release of gratification; he'd ended the life of the last man on the list. By the time he was done, Edward's head was barely attached to his shoulders. The carpet was sodden and stained red.

Harper released the shard and marched purposefully back into the other room, where he grabbed the corkscrew from the trolley. He knelt over the somewhat conscious man on the floor and plunged the corkscrew first into his jugular and then through the side of his head. With no time to waste, he returned to the bedroom for Elaine, picking up her underwear and shoes from the floor and placing them in her handbag, along with the corkscrew and bloodied towel. He lowered Elaine's dress, lifted her gently from the bed, and carried her from the room, using his foot to pull the door closed behind them. There were a couple of narrow escapes along the way, but Harper managed to make it back to their room unnoticed.

16

Elaine

Wrapped in a towel after her shower, Elaine stood at the hotel room window watching Harper below, gazing out across the river. She doubted he would remember living in London. Every time she thought about all the things he'd missed, it moved her and reminded her of just how awful his life had been. Though it was not her fault, guilt consumed her for erasing him from her memory for so many years. He'd suffered in Helmsley, and three years ago, he had brought that suffering back in the worst possible way. The more she thought about it, the more she realised why it was best for him to leave, to go and find himself in the world. It didn't matter where, as long as he found what little happiness he could, maybe even a little peace.

Elaine continued to prepare herself for the invite-only fundraiser. An expensive new black-and-white polka dot dress lay on the bed behind her as she sat at the dressing table doing her make-up. Staring at her face in the mirror, she worried whether what Harper had said could be true about Edward not finding her attractive. Elaine cast her doubts aside; she couldn't afford them at this stage. She'd pulled a few strings to get on the list and managed to do so using the same fake name she'd used to book a room at the hotel: Dr Rowan Heder.

Dressed and ready to go, Elaine picked up the invitation and looked in the mirror. 'You can do this,' she said, taking a deep breath before leaving the room.

The Tower Suites were on the first floor. A long foyer with a fantastic view of Tower Bridge led to the large function room. A server standing behind a table handed her a glass of wine. Walking around, she estimated there were about three hundred guests. People sat and chatted at the numerous tables around the room, while others stood or roamed about, greeting friends and colleagues as soft music played in the background.

The event organiser made a speech from the stage, but other than that, there didn't appear to be any order to things. People sat wherever they wanted and, as expected, the event seemed to be more about drinking and socialising than raising funds for the children's charity. No doubt most of the people here would be putting this excuse for a knees-up on their expense accounts.

Elaine kept a close eye on her prey, observing from her chair and stalking him around the room, absorbing his behaviour. Sometimes the gentleman, sometimes the sleaze. An awful man who deemed it acceptable to place his hands on the backsides of women. Elaine could see some of them doing their best not to cringe at his touch, desperate to divert his attention elsewhere.

It wasn't just the women; he was very hands-on with some of the younger men in the room. Even the waiting staff didn't escape his repugnant behaviour – one particular young lady looked increasingly uncomfortable. This man believed himself to be very special, appearing to do as he pleased without bounds, oblivious to people's reactions and what they really thought of him. Some made excuses and walked away. Edward stood in front of the huge window in the foyer. She imagined striding over and shoving him through the glass, delighting in watching the shock on his face as he fell and broke on the concrete ground below. *Nice!* She'd better hold back on the wine and not get ahead of herself.

Throughout the evening, she managed to catch Edward Horner's eye by being in the right place and standing next to the right people, baiting him with subtle glances and flirtatious smiles. At a table in the corner, Elaine sat conversing with a middle-aged couple: Harvey and Nina Lawson, the only people in the room she found interesting and down-to-earth enough to spend time with.

It wasn't entirely unexpected when Sir Edward sat beside Elaine and asked the couple to introduce him to her. As they talked and laughed, he couldn't resist placing his hand on her bare knee. At one point, acid rose from her stomach and set her chest on fire. She remained calm and focused and allowed this dreadful man to believe he was in charge.

Harvey and Nina soon made their own excuse to get away, claiming Nina had an important meeting first thing in the morning. As they said their goodbyes, Nina leaned into Elaine. 'Watch yourself with him,' she whispered, referring to Sir Edward.

'I can assure you, I'll be fine,' Elaine replied.

When the couple walked away, Sir Edward turned to Elaine. 'Well, my dear, Dr Heder – why don't I get us another bottle of wine sent over, and you can tell me more about yourself?'

'Please, call me Rowan.' She smiled through clenched teeth.

'Like the comedian in *Mr Bean*.' He laughed deep and purposeful, wanting those nearby to hear. 'Now, how about that wine?' He signalled to a waiter.

One of Edward's cronies joined them, introducing himself as Peter Stafford. The two men left the wine to Elaine while they each had a glass of Scotch. As his so-called friends departed, he stood to bid farewell to some and flippantly raised his hand to wave at others.

Despite Elaine's protests, Peter insisted on keeping her glass topped up. Never much of a drinker, Elaine needed to keep her wits about her. She had been extra careful throughout the course of the evening, not drinking much at all, but for some reason, over the past fifteen minutes, she'd become intoxicated. She slurred her words and struggled with her coordination, becoming more than a little drowsy . . .

Elaine opened her eyes, her vision slightly impaired as she stared up at a plain white ceiling. With difficulty, she raised her head to find herself slumped on a hotel room sofa with a small table in front of her. Through bleary eyes, she saw her handbag on the table and could make out a figure sitting in a chair in the opposite corner of the room. She fought against her stupor to focus for a few seconds, long enough to see Edward Horner staring back at her. His hotel room.

Confused, angry, and with only fleeting moments of lucidity, she fought to stay awake, to remain aware of her situation. God help her if she closed her eyes again.

'You did this,' she slurred, lifting her fatigued arm to point at Edward before it flopped down beside her. 'You drugged me.'

'Peter slipped Rohypnol into the bottle of wine you were drinking. Just lie back and relax. We're going to have some fun together. Come morning, you won't remember a thing.'

Her head lolled and fell back onto the sofa. 'Bastard,' she mumbled. Although she'd tried not to drink much, she had no idea how much of the drug was in her system.

Rolling her head to the side, she made out her reflection in a gigantic mirror. Seconds later, it became clear that the top of her dress had been pulled down to expose her breasts. A man sucked her right nipple and ran his hand along her leg, underneath her dress. It was Sir Edward's friend – Peter. Horrified, she could do nothing to stop him. Her eyes closed. Out of nowhere, she summoned a burst of energy and lashed out, striking Peter in the face with her forearm.

'Bitch!' he shouted. Peter grabbed hold of her hair, lifted her head, and launched his fist into her face.

Edward said, 'I told you we should have made her drink the whole bottle.'

'I thought that would be enough to wipe her out,' said Peter.

Elaine started to mumble.

'What on earth is she saying?' asked Edward.

Peter leaned in to listen. 'She keeps repeating the same thing.'

'What?'

'A name – Liam Bennett,' said Peter, bemused, as though it meant very little. Edward's whisky glass hit the carpet. Peter now knew it meant something. Something huge.

Sir Edward got to his feet. 'My God,' he said, confounded.

'What? What is it? Who is Liam Bennett?' asked Peter, unsure of what was going on.

Without answering the question, Edward rushed over and closely studied her face. She glared at him and laughed.

'Who are you?' he asked, worried about her answer.

Attempting to smile, she said, 'Elaine Bennett,' and spat in his face.

Peter struck her again.

*

Edward Horner stepped back in shock with a blank expression. He rushed into the kitchen area, wiped the saliva from his face with a tea towel, and emptied the last of the whisky into a clean glass.

Peter followed closely behind. 'Edward, you need to tell me what's going on. Do you know this lady?'

Sir Edward sank the whisky, feeling the burn in the back of his throat. For a moment, he seemed lost for words, paralysed by fear. Finally, he found his voice. 'Do you recall I once told you about an incident many years ago on a Yorkshire farm?'

'The boy tied to a post?'

Edward nodded. 'Well, sitting on that sofa' – he pointed – 'is his fucking sister.' In a panic, Edward opened and slammed cupboards. 'Why is there no bloody alcohol in my room?' he shouted. 'You know, I always thought I was safe, especially from the boy. As for her, well, I could never be certain, but it always felt unlikely. I warned my father this could happen. This problem should have been dealt with years ago, but oh no, the pompous old bastard wouldn't be party to the murder of two little brats.'

'It's okay, Edward. Don't you see?' Peter smiled. 'We can do what your father couldn't and fix this. We can make this go away forever. By coming here, the silly bitch has made it easy for us.'

'What do you mean?'

'She wasn't using her real name. I bet she checked in under Dr Rowan Heder.' He smirked. 'We could get rid of her, and nobody would ever know she was here . . . but not before you've had your fun,' he said with a wide, mischievous grin.

*

Once again, Elaine was lucid. These brief spells did not last long and rallied her into action. She eased to the floor, propping her back upright against the edge of the sofa. With great effort, she willed her arm to reach for her handbag on the table and managed to pull at the strap until it dropped beside her. She slid her hand inside and fumbled to retrieve her phone from the bag. Using her finger, she typed in her code and scrolled to her last call. Out of the corner of her eye, she saw Peter returning. Elaine pressed Harper's name.

Standing over her, Peter said, 'Oh no, you don't, you silly girl.' He reached down for her phone as it started to call Harper. Not recognising the name, he turned it off, placed it inside her bag, and tossed it onto the sofa.

Peter held her head back and poured more wine from the bottle containing Rohypnol down her throat. He dragged Elaine along the floor into the bedroom, where he lifted and threw her onto the bed.

Edward was soon at his side. 'What are you doing, Peter?'

'Me, nothing. You, whatever you damn well want. She is all yours, my friend. And when you're finished, perhaps I will indulge myself, right before I strangle the life out of her, unless, of course, that's something you'd like to take care of personally.'

'What about the body? How will we dispose of her?'

'We'll squeeze her into a large suitcase and walk out of here,' said Peter.

'Won't she be too heavy to carry?'

'Oh, my dear boy . . . that is why they put wheels on suitcases.'

Edward smirked. 'I've always liked your style, Peter.'

'Right, while you busy yourself with your old acquaintance here, I'll call room service and get a couple of decent bottles of wine sent up. How does that sound?'

'Like a splendid idea,' said Edward, wasting no time stripping down to his matching white cotton underpants and vest.

Elaine's legs were moved. Able to glance down from the pillow, she observed Edward sliding her knickers over her ankles, having already removed her shoes. Elaine mustered the strength to kick Edward in the face with her heel, knocking him from the bed. Hearing the loud thud, Peter entered the room and helped Edward up from the floor.

Peter glared at her. 'You just don't learn, do you?'

He approached and punched her in the face. A bright flash exploded in her head, and a burning sensation rampaged across her cheek, quickly becoming a numbing vibration.

'Don't spoil that pretty face too much,' said Edward, soothing his bloodied lip.

'Fair enough. I have called room service, and they will bring the wine up shortly.'

'Good. I'll come out and wait with you until she comes round. I want this whore awake when I fuck her. I want to look her in the eyes. I want her to know what's happening.'

Elaine fought against a powerful urge to pass out and heard the men talking before they vacated the room. Lethargic and barely capable, she shifted her body to the edge of the bed and let her legs drop to the floor. She couldn't let this happen. Using her elbows, she lifted herself upright. Elaine climbed wearily to her feet; the room whirled around her. She drifted backwards and fell onto the bed. Impossible. There was no way to prevent any of this. She'd been so stupid to make herself an easy target for these horrific predators. It sank in that she wasn't going to leave the room alive. The door opened and slammed shut. Edward had returned.

'I'm going to do what I should have had the chance to do all those years ago,' he said as he swivelled her legs and body around on the bed.

A bell rang in the next room. Edward removed his underwear and climbed between her legs. He raised her skirt and tried to force himself inside her. Elaine attempted to prevent him from doing so, raising her weakened arms to hold him off. He slapped her across the face and stretched her arms above her head, bringing her wrists together to restrain them with one hand, while his other hand helped him enter her.

Tears seeped from the corners of her eyes. What had she done? This wasn't supposed to happen. The muscles in her arms relaxed as she gave up the fight. He released her wrists and instead used both hands to grip her legs tightly and hold them apart. With one final attempt, she struck out at Edward, scratching his cheek. His large, strong hand smacked her face. Then nothing. She opened her eyes – Edward was gone. Had she passed out? Was she dreaming? Hearing Harper's voice in the room, she realised that this was not the case. He'd come to save her, just as he had attempted to do all those years ago. Elaine smiled with relief and let her eyes close, knowing she was safe.

17

The Boy

After the man delivered his breakfast and vanished for the day, the light flickered off as normal; only this time, it failed to stutter back to life. As if things weren't bad enough, the poor boy would be in soul-destroying darkness for hours. Switching to the red light wasn't an option; the chain only allowed him to get so close, and even at full stretch, it was out of reach. That being said, the red light wouldn't have made him feel any more comfortable than sitting alone in the dark.

The man had been kind to him of late, which seemed unnervingly out of character, serving him hot meals instead of the cold sandwiches he'd become used to. Nothing fancy, but so much better than the monotony of before. Perhaps he was being rewarded for fighting back. He'd asked himself so many questions, none of which he could answer. He would never understand the man or why he'd been chosen to suffer in this way. Only two things were certain: the man respected his fighting spirit, and while he remained alive, another boy was safe.

Later that day, the man returned and entered the room carrying his old metal toolbox. The natural daylight streaking across the floor was heaven-sent. He would never have imagined how the spectacular simplicity of the sun could enrich the heart in the darkest of times. With his days numbered, he dreamed of spending just one more hour outside, though the chances of that happening were non-existent. He had accepted his fate, knowing he would never leave this dungeon alive.

The man glanced suspiciously up at the fluorescent light and then towards the bed. With it being so dark on his side of the room, he couldn't be sure whether the man could see him or not.

The man called into the shadows, 'Step out into the light, boy.'

He did as he was told, and as soon as their eyes connected, it became obvious what the man suspected.

'Is this your doing?'

'No,' the boy replied.

The man's expression grew less intense, acknowledging his truth. 'How long has it been out?'

'Almost as soon as you left.'

'Hopefully, it's just the tube and not the starter. I don't have a spare one of those.'

Leaving the door open to provide some light, the man walked across to the other room. The main door had never been left ajar for this long, and the boy made the most of the fresh air breezing in. Golden streaks of sunlight sprinkled across the floor and gleamed like an angel's pathway. The gentle rush of nature's breath caressed his face. He sucked air into his lungs as though it were a gift sent just for him – a wondrous respite from a nonsensical end.

The man reappeared carrying a flimsy wooden stepladder and a long, thin cardboard box, which he placed on the bed. First, he removed the old bulb, and then he pulled the new one from the box and placed the old one inside. As he climbed the ladder to install the new tube, footsteps stomped above. Partially obstructing the light streaming through the doorway, a mysterious shadow stretched across the length of the floor.

'Hello! Is anybody home?' a voice called out.

Stunned, the boy didn't know whether to stay silent or scream at the top of his lungs. From the bed, he looked up at the man on the ladder, who in turn glared down at him; his evil eyes expressing the words he did not say aloud. *Keep. Your. Mouth. Shut.*

'Hello, don't be alarmed, I'm a police officer!'

The boy's eyes lit up just as the fluorescent light flickered on. As the man stepped down, the boy quickly scrambled across the bed and slammed his feet into the rickety stepladder. The ladder collapsed beneath the man, and he dropped fast and hard, whacking his head against the bedpost. He hit the floor and didn't move.

'I'm coming down!' the officer shouted, no doubt hearing the commotion.

The boy wanted to scream, but nothing came out – tongue-tied, drunk with hope, elation, and the thought of escape. The police officer's shadow grew larger.

'I'm here,' the boy croaked. 'I'm here,' he repeated, eager to see his saviour.

A suited man stepped down into the room and immediately lowered his gaze to the prostrate body on the floor. Seconds later, he noticed the dishevelled boy on the bed.

'Danny?' he asked.

'Yes,' replied the boy, exhilarated to hear his name. Tears of joy and relief rolled down his cheeks. He'd heard his name called thousands of times, but to hear someone say it right now was exhilarating.

'Everything is going to be okay, Danny. My name is Colin. I'm with the police, and I'm going to get you out of here.'

Colin Hargreaves moved towards the bed, observing the shackle around the boy's ankle and the chain bolted to the floor. He examined the shackle. 'Danny, do you know where he keeps the key?'

'He keeps things in that room over there,' Danny answered, pointing to where the man had fetched the ladder. 'But I don't know where it is.'

'Okay, don't worry. I'll find it and come right back,' said Colin, rushing past the man on the floor.

Colin paused at the doorway to the room and looked back at the body. With his focus solely on Danny, he hadn't checked to see if the man lay dead or unconscious. He approached, crouched to feel for a pulse, and found the man still breathing. Drawing handcuffs from his side pocket, Colin attempted to secure Danny's abductor. The man rolled into him, knocking him off balance.

On the floor, with barely a couple of feet between them, the men glared at each other, hatred in their eyes. The man sprang forward, sinking his teeth into the detective's nose. Colin cried out and pushed him away. Hot blood gushed into his mouth. He put his hands to his face and discovered a piece of his nose was missing. Colin scowled at the man on his knees across from him and watched in horror as he pulled the piece of flesh from his bloodied mouth and smiled.

Screaming with rage, Colin shot to his feet and pounced on the man. They rolled about on the floor, throwing scattered punches at one another. Danny looked on, hoping and praying the police officer would get the better of the monster. Colin pinned him down and grabbed his head, continually bashing it against the floor. The man clenched his hands together and thumped them into the detective's face, forcing him to reel back in agony.

Gasping for breath, the two men clambered to their feet. Colin was in a bad way, doubled over, his face battered and bloodied. Other than a few marks, the man appeared to be in much better shape. They clashed again; the man forced Colin against the wall, throwing punch after punch into his stomach.

The detective launched an uppercut to the man's chin, knocking him to the ground. With no time to stop and catch his breath, Colin reached down for the stepladder and repeatedly whacked it against the man's body. The ladder broke into pieces, rungs flying around the room. Colin tossed what remained of the ladder aside, dropped to the floor at the end of the bed, and grabbed the metal chain that held the boy. He wrapped it around the man's neck and pulled tight.

Choking, the man placed his fingers between his neck and the chain, trying to pull it free, but it was hopeless. His other hand scrambled around the floor in a desperate bid to save himself. With luck on his side, his fingers touched the roughened wood of a ladder rung. He gripped it tightly and struck Colin in the centre of his face. The detective fell backwards, and the man quickly unwrapped the chain from around his neck. Climbing on top of Colin, he plunged the end of the rung several times into his face before collapsing with exhaustion on top of the detective.

Colin lay still, his face an utter mess, blood hiding much of the damage. One of his eyes had swollen shut, and blood gushed from the deep cut above it. Grabbing a handful of his adversary's hair, Colin lifted the man's head and stared into the black, soulless eyes of the monster.

The man brought his hands up to Colin's face and sank his thumbs deep into the hollows of his eyes until they gave way. Struggling to his feet, he picked up a thick, splintered piece of wood and drove it through Colin's heart.

For several minutes, the man lay on the floor next to the detective's body. On the bed, a distraught Danny cried in silence, shaking with terror at the violent confrontation he had witnessed. His chance of freedom – gone. A phone rang. The man reached into the detective's pocket, took out the phone, and switched it off. He rose from the floor and, without saying a word, staggered into the other room. He eventually reappeared carrying a long plastic sheet, a large hacksaw, and two large hessian bags, dropping the items beside Colin's body.

'Once again, this is *your* fault and *you* will clean it up,' he snarled. 'Lay the sheet out and roll the body onto it. It'll save on the mess. Strip him – then lop off his arms, legs, and head. Cut his legs into two parts. Put the pieces in one bag and the torso in the other. I'll pick up some more cleaning products and, just like before, I want it spotless in here,' he said, leaving the room and closing the door behind him.

For what seemed like an eternity, Danny sat, gazing at the detective's body. It was traumatising to process what had occurred just under an hour ago. So close to being set free, only to be left devastated by the outcome. If the policeman had handcuffed the man when he'd first entered the room, everything could have turned out so differently. Danny's mindset was back to dashed hopes and shattered dreams, and it was only a matter of time before he endured a similar fate to the police officer.

Danny laid out the plastic sheet and wrapped his hands around the piece of wood in Colin's chest. He gagged at the dreadful squelching sound as he prised it free. Using every ounce of strength, he rolled the body onto the sheet. Next, he carried out the painstaking process of stripping the officer of his clothes. While removing the detective's trousers, he heard a jingling noise coming from the man's trouser pocket. He reached inside and fished out a set of keys, one of which was obviously a car key.

The detective had come to save his life – his reward – to be cut into pieces. It sickened Danny, and he couldn't shake it off. An excess of guilt and sadness surged through him. The man had said it was *his* fault. Whether he was responsible or not, it didn't matter now, nor would it ever. No one could take the pain of blame away from him. If, by some miracle, he *did* manage to come through this harrowing ordeal alive, it would leave an impenetrable scar on his soul.

With the hacksaw gripped tightly in his trembling hand, about to carry out a grotesque task beyond his imagination, he had an unthinkable decision to make: where to begin?

The neck. No!

The legs. No!

A wicked and atrocious choice. Danny hovered the hacksaw over the top of the unfortunate detective's arm and let the blade rest on the skin.

'I'm so sorry,' cried Danny as he manoeuvred the saw back and forth through the officer's flesh.

*

Back from the shop, the man entered the room with two carrier bags full of cleaning products. Danny had been sitting in wait on the floor, concealed by a blanket of blood, his knees tucked under his arms with his back against the side of the bed. The whites of his tired eyes contrasted beneath the red veil covering his sorrowful face. His dark pupils were like tiny black dots on a whiteboard. It hadn't escaped the man that Danny had been busy in his absence. The head and limbs had been removed and placed into one hessian bag, just as he'd requested. The man's eyes fell upon him. His gaze lingered.

'Why haven't you put the torso in a bag?' he asked, unperturbed by the gruesome sight in front of him.

'It was too heavy,' Danny declared.

The man put down the carrier bags and said, 'Come on. Hold open the hessian bag.'

Together, the two of them bagged the torso, and the man didn't stop there. For some reason, he helped Danny clean the entire room. They cleaned in silence for hours. When they'd finished, the man removed the hessian bags and left the boy alone to clean himself up. Before doing so, Danny took a well-deserved rest. About an hour later, he heard a door slam and a heavy dragging sound across the floor above. He assumed the man had gone to dispose of the body.

In the shower, Danny finally broke down. He collapsed to the floor and sobbed uncontrollably, eventually falling asleep under the constant downpour, rinsing away the stains on the outside but never getting close to the ones beneath the surface.

When Danny woke, he found himself reinvigorated in a clean bed, as though he'd slept for hours. He had no idea if it was morning, afternoon, or evening. The man must have returned and discovered him in the shower. At the end of the bed were fresh, long white shirts, snacks, and a drink. Among the snacks was a large bar of chocolate, which he eagerly unwrapped and consumed. With his mouth crammed full, Danny crawled to the end of the bed and looked down at the floor where he'd dismembered the body. Or had he? Could it have been some delusional nightmare? He climbed from the bed and inspected the floorboards. The reddened discolouration of the grain suggested it was not his imagination.

Walking over to the table, Danny reached underneath for the set of keys he'd hung on the loose screw, out of sight. Confirmation of his harrowing ordeal. The car key had a fob with buttons; perhaps the brave policeman could yet be his saviour. Danny went back to the bed, tucked into more snacks, and drank plenty of bottled water. He pulled one of the new long white shirts over his head. It was very baggy and dropped down to the backs of his knees.

Climbing onto the bed, he repeatedly pressed the buttons on the fob, hoping to unlock and lock the car. He knew that with his dad's car, when these buttons were pressed, it made a sound and caused the lights to flicker on and off. If the car was close, maybe someone would see and call the police. *Hope!* Here it was again, dangerous but worth clinging to, even by the slimmest of margins.

He'd been pressing the buttons for around thirty minutes when the door to the room opened. Danny quickly tucked the keys under his pillow. The man came down the steps and paced slowly back and forth along the side of the bed.

'Something has been troubling me about the police officer. You see, I reckon he travelled here by car. He must have, right?' he said, turning to the boy. 'What do you think?'

Danny shrugged his shoulders. 'I dunno.'

'No, I don't suppose you would. Unless, of course, you found the keys to *said* car. Did you?'

'No.'

'Hmm! So if I search the room, I won't find them anywhere?'

Danny didn't reply. He simply shook his head from side to side.

'Okay. If I find the keys in a dark corner of the room, I guess I can accept you had no knowledge of them. However, if I find the keys in a place only you could have placed them, well, you have no idea what I'll do to you.'

Scared by the man's threatening, slow tone, Danny's body shuddered.

The man continued, 'What if I said I could make your punishment ten times worse than anything you have suffered so far? Worse than anything you could ever begin to imagine. Would that change your mind?'

Not wanting to give up his last hope, Danny thought hard about whether to hand over the keys, even though deep down, he knew he had to. The man would find them under his pillow. It would be stupid to think he wouldn't look there. As for a worse punishment, he dared not think how the man could make him suffer more than he already had. Danny reached under the pillow and nervously held out the keys, worried he would be punished regardless. The man moved slowly towards him, his eyes menacing and intense. He took the keys from the boy's hand, nodded in appreciation, and left the boy alone.

18

Lenny

When Lenny woke up in bed with a smile on his face and Olivia Reid beside him, he hadn't bargained on spending the rest of the morning at the police station answering questions about his missing friend, Colin Hargreaves. Since the previous afternoon, nobody had seen or heard from him. His wife had reported him missing overnight, and when he failed to make an appearance at the station, his superiors had set the ball rolling to find him. It was completely out of character for Colin. Calling his phone had drawn a blank, and as yet, they hadn't located his car. They were ready to track his phone by GPS if it were reactivated.

After informing detectives he hadn't heard from him, Lenny considered whether Colin had a theory about the case and had gone off to investigate alone, which really pissed him off because they'd agreed to share any information. As soon as Lenny left the station, he resolved to drive to Harlow, the last place they had been together. He wanted to work out if Colin had observed something he hadn't. A long shot, but it was better than sitting around doing nothing.

*

At Parndon Mill Lane, Lenny parked in the same gravel lay-by as before and headed down the dirt path to where William Harvey's body had been discovered. The thought of that poor boy drowning in the pond and how terrified he must have been made him so angry. And to think there might be another boy being held captive at that very moment. He took a good look around, but nothing obvious stood out. As on the previous occasion, he drove down the road to the mill to check if Colin's car was parked outside; it wasn't. Having always struggled to think on an empty stomach, Lenny spotted a middle-aged couple standing by the water's edge, wandered over, and enquired whether they knew where he could get some decent grub. They recommended The Moorhen pub and grill, which was not too far away, and gave him directions.

When it came to food, Lenny was a traditionalist and ordered golden-battered cod, chips, and mushy peas, with a nice pint of Guinness to wash it down. He opted to have his lunch in the beer garden next to the canal. If it weren't for Colin going AWOL, the clear blue sky and glorious sunshine would have made it a perfect day to sit beside the river eating fish and chips. But truth be told, Lenny was deeply concerned for the welfare of his friend.

Lenny sipped his pint and then licked the foam from his top lip. 'Where are you, Col?' he muttered as he stared out at the River Stort and took in the sight of the colourful narrowboats moored along the bank.

The waitress brought his food out to the table, smiled, and said, 'Enjoy your meal, sir.'

'Cheers, love,' he said, smothering it in salt and vinegar.

While tucking into his cod, he glanced across the car park and observed indicator lights continually flickering on and off. Not just any car – the exact same model as Colin's silver Mercedes.

'Fuck me,' he said aloud, dropping his knife and fork onto the plate.

The family on the nearby bench were horrified by his use of language in front of their children, for which he apologised. Lenny shifted his legs out from under the garden bench and got to his feet.

'It can't be,' he said, doubting himself.

He walked across the car park to double-check. As he approached, the indicator lights continued to flicker, but as soon as he arrived at the car, they stopped. He tried the door; it was locked. Through the window, he recognised Colin's notebook on the passenger seat. No doubt about it, he'd found his friend's car. He couldn't work out why the car was locking and unlocking. Wouldn't someone have to be pressing the fob?

Lenny banged on the boot of the car. 'Are you in there, you silly old sod?' he said, tongue-in-cheek. As expected, there was no response.

Glancing around, he tried to fathom where he could be. A sudden shortness of breath and a strong sense of gloom came over him. He couldn't make light of this any longer and called the detective he'd spoken to that morning to let him know he'd found Colin's car. As the call ended, the car clicked and the doors unlocked. Lenny scanned the immediate area and identified a burly man with short, jet-black hair, wearing a dark red hoodie across the car park, close to the bench where his unfinished meal was growing cold. The man froze on the spot, his hand out in front of him, holding something: keys? Lenny noted the man's thick black eyebrows just as he pulled up his hood to obscure his face. For an eerie moment, the man stared directly at him and proceeded to pat himself down as though he'd forgotten something. He turned slowly and strolled calmly in the opposite direction.

Suspicious of the man's odd behaviour, Lenny followed, picking up his pace as he walked. He tailed the man into the fairly crowded beer garden at the rear of the pub and surveyed the crowd; there was no sign of him. He continued walking until he came upon Moorhen Marina. Increasingly stressed, Lenny searched between the rows of narrowboats. Nothing. He marched back to the beer garden for another look.

'Shit!' He'd lost him.

When the first police officers arrived, Lenny explained everything. Though it wasn't much to go on, he gave them a description of the man. While the officers searched the area, Lenny sat in his car. Plenty of questions churned away in his mind, but only one remained at the forefront: had Colin found the killer? It seemed plausible. Lenny was certain the man in the car park had Colin's car keys, which meant he'd come within a stone's throw of him, and the more he thought about it, the more it angered him. He hoped to God he was wrong, but his expectations of finding Colin alive were fading fast. The way things were looking and his not having been in touch with anyone made him uneasy.

Before the police arrived, Lenny searched Colin's unlocked car and took his notebook. He opened it up and browsed through it. At first, nothing much jumped out as to why he'd gone back to Parndon Mill Lane. However, there were notes about serial killers around the world, such as Ángel Maturino Reséndiz, who was suspected of twenty-three murders and known as The Railroad Killer. Andrei Chikatilo was convicted of fifty-two murders and nicknamed The Butcher of Rostov. The S-Bahn Murderer, Paul Ogorzow, was charged with eight murders. Gary Ridgway, the

Green River Killer, was convicted of forty-nine murders. Colin went on to mention Bryan Miller, the alleged Phoenix Canal Killer, and John Sweeney, another murderer connected with canals.

Colin had certainly done his homework, researching killers linked in some way to railways, canals, and rivers. He had obviously been trying to figure out patterns and similarities in an attempt to understand what type of person they were looking for. Due to Parndon Mill being close to rail tracks and a river, it made sense why Colin had returned to the area. Nazeing, where the remains of the other two boys were found, was also next to a river. Not to mention Tumbling Bay, the location of Charlie Davis. Lenny couldn't dismiss the possibility of a connection.

On the way home, Lenny's mind went into overdrive, asking himself why Colin hadn't stuck to their agreement of sharing information and why he had gone searching for the killer on his own. Then it occurred to him – what if Colin acted on guesswork and stumbled across him accidentally? Lenny changed direction to make an unplanned stop at Tumbling Bay.

The shadow of a large cloud cleared as the evening sun unrolled the way ahead, casting its radiance upon the recently cut grass, seared to a golden brown. He detoured along a trampled path in the undergrowth until he stood next to where Charlie's body had been discovered. He thought back to the strange hallucination he'd had in the café. 'What were you trying to tell me, Charlie?' he said. 'What were you pointing at?'

Lenny walked towards the line of trees until he saw the canal. The railway tracks were less than a mile away. A long narrowboat crawled along the River Lea. The man at the tiller waved in his direction; Lenny felt compelled to return the greeting. On his way back to the car, he received the phone call he'd been dreading.

The police had found what they believed to be the body of DCI Colin Hargreaves. For Lenny, there was no uncertainty about it.

By the time he arrived back in Harlow, the sun was setting. He approached two constables in The Moorhen pub car park and asked to speak to the detective in charge so he could pass on some information, though it was more a case of wanting to introduce himself in the hope of working together.

A tall, suave-looking man in a sharp suit approached. 'Lenny Grey?'

'That's right,' Lenny replied and held out his hand, only to see the detective snub his handshake.

'DCI Harry Baxendale,' he said. 'I understand you wanted to see me.'

'Yes. As you're probably aware, Colin is . . . was a good friend of mine. We were pooling our resources to track down the murderer of Charlie Davis and who knows how many other young boys.'

'I am well aware of who you are, Mr Grey. You're the infamous killer clown hunter.' He smirked. 'We can't confirm the identification of the body yet. As for sharing information, that's not going to happen on my watch. Now, if you'll excuse me, I have a crime scene to investigate before it gets too dark.' The detective walked away.

'The railway!' shouted Lenny.

Baxendale stopped in his tracks and turned. 'What about it?'

'Colin was working on a theory that the killer is using the railway network to find the boys. He holds them captive somewhere, and when he's finished with them, disposes of their bodies in the waterways.'

'It's an interesting theory and one we'll consider, but we have a few other leads we're looking into right now,' said the DCI in a dismissive tone.

'The killer was right here in this car park, just a few short hours ago. He wouldn't have got far. If we act now, we can catch him before he strikes again.'

'Firstly, there is no "we". Secondly, do you realise how many miles of track there are? How many stations? He could have departed from the train anywhere. By the time we even begin to organise a search of that magnitude, he'll be long gone. Now, I really have to get on.'

Although it felt like Baxendale didn't want to know, Lenny accepted the detective's view. Logistically, it was an impossible task and far too late; the killer could be anywhere by now. He turned to walk back to his car.

'Mr Grey!'

Lenny faced the detective.

'For what it's worth, the corpse is that of our colleague and your friend. An officer found him submerged in water in the woods opposite Moorhen Marina. His body . . . let's just say it's not in a good way.'

Lenny had already guessed it was Colin, but hearing the words out loud didn't lessen the blow. Angry, frustrated, and distraught, he was gutted to have lost not only a friend of many years but also the one person who could have helped him catch the killer.

'I'm sorry about your friend – I truly am,' said the DCI, no doubt recognising Lenny's distress.

'He was cut into pieces, wasn't he?'

The detective nodded. 'I've seen some really bad shit this year, and this is right up there. We found him stuffed inside—'

'Hessian mailbags?'

DCI Baxendale seemed surprised at just how much Lenny knew as he nodded once again. 'I should tell you to keep away from this case and leave it to us, but I know I'd be wasting my breath. We will find him, Mr Grey,' said Baxendale, who turned and marched back towards the crime scene.

On his way to the car, Lenny contemplated the detective's sudden change of heart. Perhaps he sympathised with someone losing a friend and despaired over the loss of a colleague, or maybe he wanted this evil bastard stopped just as much as Lenny did.

The drive home was difficult and emotional. Over the years, Lenny had spent many nights alone, but tonight, the thought of going back to his empty apartment and drowning his sorrows in a whisky-filled glass wasn't going to cut it. Before leaving Harlow, he'd called Olivia and told her everything. She insisted he go straight to her flat next to Tobacco Dock in Wapping. He was never going to refuse her offer.

Within the hour, he was on her sofa with a glass of brandy. Alcohol wouldn't make him feel better, but it wouldn't make him feel any worse. They talked for a while, and Lenny regaled her with tales of mischief, trials, and tribulations between him and Colin.

'I remember this one time back in the early '90s. Colin had just become a detective constable and wanted to impress his new boss. He planned to work through the night, researching information for a case so he could hand it in first thing the next day. I offered to help, so he sneaked me into the basement room where the files were kept.

'Now, many police stations back then were old and outdated, with faulty wiring everywhere, and health and safety wasn't a big deal. We were down there for hours but managed to get it all done. Anyway, there were rows and rows of tall shelving units, and the chairs we'd been using had wheels. I came up with the bright idea that it might be fun to sit on our chairs and race from one end of the aisle to the other – best of three, loser gets the beers type of thing. We were using our feet to push ourselves off the wall at one end to give us extra speed.

'The next morning, he set off to work, notes in hand and a big smile on his face. When he arrived, there was a fracas outside the building. Overnight, there had been a serious flood in the basement that blew the fuse box and started a fire that practically destroyed the offices upstairs. One of us had ruptured a pipe on a radiator when we were pushing ourselves off the wall. Handing in his work was obviously a no-no. He could never admit he'd been in the building that night. If he had, he'd probably have lost his job.'

When Olivia stopped laughing, she asked, 'Didn't they have CCTV?'

'No. I don't think there was any. Even if there had been, it would have been on a video recorder, and everything was destroyed.'

'So, which one of you caused the leak?'

'We never found out. We certainly had some good times, though.' Lenny sipped his brandy. 'I shall miss him,' he said, his eyes red and glazed.

'I'm sure you will,' said Olivia, placing her hand on his.

'I have to find the bastard, Olivia. More than anything.' Lenny's body slumped, and tears rolled down his cheeks. The last time he shed a tear was during the Bosnian War when he came across a mass grave of men, women, and children. It broke his heart to see such horror. He had obviously been sad many times since; he'd just found other ways to bury the pain. The distress he felt now had been building for eight years, and after recent events, it had come streaming to the surface. His friend's murder – the last straw.

Olivia put her arms around him, pulling him into her body. She squeezed and held him tight, knowing exactly what he needed right now. Even the toughest shell eventually breaks.

'You'll find him,' she said.

19

Harper

It was the morning after the horrifying events at the Riverside Tower Hotel, and Harper hadn't slept at all – couldn't. Wild fury burned within him as he blamed himself for what had happened to Elaine. For most of the night, he'd paced the room, cursing under his breath and snarling. While Elaine slept, he'd cleaned her bloodied nose and face. In the shower, he had punched the ceramic tiles until his hands were raw and cut to the knuckles. All he wanted was to set off for home as soon as they were able. In less than an hour, the hotel would come alive, and they could blend in with the other guests and leave without attracting attention.

Harper woke Elaine, who was still groggy and could barely walk, let alone drive, which meant he would have to take the risk. Good job he'd managed to get in some recent practice. Supporting Elaine, they sauntered through the lobby and car park with barely a glance in their direction. Once he'd found his way out of the city with the help of the satnav, it was relatively straightforward. Elaine dozed off as soon as he'd buckled her into the passenger seat. She'd slept for hours, which was probably a good thing. He wasn't ready to talk – not yet. Driving helped to calm him, but it wouldn't take much to bring him back to boiling point.

Waking up in a panic, Elaine broke the silence. 'My God! What happened last night?'

'It's done,' he said, keeping his eyes on the road.

'What's done? I can't remember a thing. Why can't I remember?'

'What's the last thing you *do* remember?' Silence ensued, and Harper glanced sideways several times as she trawled through her memory.

'The table,' she said. 'I was sitting at the table drinking with Edward Horner and, oh – I don't know.'

'Had quite a bit to drink, did you?'

'No! At least, I don't think so. I thought I was being careful, but my headache suggests otherwise.'

'Well, you didn't get him outside as we'd planned, but you did get him drunk enough to make my work easier,' he said. Her mind appeared to draw a blank. Harper had hoped this might be the case. He'd already worked out from her odd behaviour that she'd been drugged. He knew all about benzodiazepines, and partial amnesia was a common side effect. If she couldn't recall the awful events at the hotel, he was *not* going to remind her.

'So, everything went okay?' she queried.

Without making eye contact, he said, 'As well as it could go under the circumstances.' Despite doing his utmost to conceal the truth from her, she clearly sensed some form of deception.

'You need to pull into the next services a mile or so up ahead,' she said with a yawn, wiping the sleep from her eyes.

'What for?'

'Diesel. We won't make it home on what's left. Plus, I need to use the bathroom,' she said, yawning once again. Elaine stretched as much as she could in the seat. 'Wow, I feel completely wiped out.'

'That makes two of us,' he replied.

'Thank you for driving. I'll take over once I've freshened up and had a coffee.'

'Sounds good.' The thought of sleep finally appealed to him. It would certainly help bring down his inner rage.

Elaine caressed the unseen bruises on her face and then examined the marks on her wrists. She didn't ask about them, which pleased him; he wasn't prepared for more questions.

At the service station, Harper went to fetch the coffee and croissants, while Elaine went to use the facilities. Sitting at a table, he contemplated how to explain the bruising. Having rushed her out of the hotel, she was bound to use the mirror in the bathroom. As Elaine approached with a determined expression, it was evident she wanted answers.

Elaine threw herself onto the seat and whispered loudly, 'That old bastard hit me last night. I knew you weren't telling me everything.'

'You're starting to remember?'

'It was pretty fucking obvious when I saw the state of my face. Then I had these messed-up flashbacks.'

'Okay, tell me what you know, and I'll fill in the blanks.'

She pulled the lid from her coffee and stirred in the contents of a sugar sachet. She blew to cool it down and took a cautious sip. 'I don't know how it happened,' she said. 'But somehow, I stupidly ended up in his suite. There was another guy there – Peter? Yes, Peter. He was the one who hit me – I think. Actually, I'm sure he did. Perhaps they both did. Everything is so fuzzy.'

'They drugged you, Elaine. That's how you ended up in Edward's suite.'

She frowned and tilted her head. 'How did he know who I was?'

'They didn't know who you were, and they didn't care. You could have been anyone. It wouldn't have made a difference to them. From what I gather, you were not the first person they'd drugged and taken to their room.'

Elaine's face paled, overcome with dread. Harper guessed what she was thinking.

'Was I—'

'No!' he jumped in.

'How do you know?'

'Because I was there. When I entered the room, Edward was roughing you up. I'm not saying they wouldn't have, but I know nothing else went on.' The relief on her face was clear. She relaxed in the seat and released the tension from her body.

'How did you find me?'

'That was the fortunate part,' he said, and explained how he'd interacted with the young man in the lift with the drinks trolley, gained access to the room, and taken care of both Edward Horner and Peter Stafford.

For the remainder of the journey home, Elaine took the wheel. Mindful of meeting Alice at the wedding reception later that evening, Harper was grateful for the rest. Though conflicted that he hadn't told her the whole truth, Elaine appeared to have accepted his account of what had taken place in Edward's suite.

When he came into her life and opened her eyes to what had happened when they were children, he'd forced her to see the past so she could understand who she really was, telling her it was the only way she could move forward. But having been locked away for most of *his* life and having learned so much over the past couple of years, he now had a different perspective. He hadn't admitted it to Elaine in the caravan, but he regretted revealing the harrowing truth about their past. He'd come to accept that *truth* wasn't always the best option. The one saving grace about everything they'd been through together – it was all over – retribution complete and the atrocious beginning of their lives left to stravaig in the winds of time.

In the car with Elaine outside the Forest and Vale Hotel in Pickering, Harper debated whether to attend the wedding reception. To say he was nervous would be an understatement.

'Can't you come in with me?' he asked.

'Don't be silly,' said Elaine. 'Besides, I'm not invited.'

He watched a few guests enter the hotel while others lingered outside, smoking. Seeing all these people only added to his nerves because they weren't just any people; they were Alice's family and friends.

'Go on. This is what you wanted – to be ordinary – to do normal things. Now's your chance,' she said.

'I know. It's just – Alice's parents will be inside. I'm not sure I'm ready to take this kind of step.'

'You'll be fine. It's not like you're asking for her hand in marriage. It's just a party, and you're her guest.'

'True. How bad can it be, right?' he said, straightening his tie.

'That's the spirit.'

After a deep breath, Harper opened the car door and stepped onto the pavement. Having been informed that pastel blue, grey, and cream were the colour schemes for the wedding, Harper was wearing a light grey two-piece suit and black shoes.

'Do I look okay?'

'You look great, Harper – or should I say, Simon?' She laughed.

He smiled, closed the car door, and headed towards the hotel. As he entered the lobby, he immediately saw Alice waiting inside the doorway. His eyes widened, taken aback by how beautiful she looked in her pastel blue dress. Upon seeing Harper's expression, Alice unveiled a bashful smile, turned her head away, and then back again.

'Wow! You look incredible,' he said as he approached.

'You're obliged to say that, but I'd have given you a swift kick in the shin if you hadn't. You've scrubbed up rather well yourself.'

'No, I really mean it. You look stunning.'

She blushed. 'Thank you. Most guys wouldn't be so direct.'

'Oh! Was that a bit much?' he asked, genuinely worried he should have kept the thought to himself.

'Not at all. It's actually quite refreshing,' she replied, her fingers grazing lightly against his. 'I saw you in the car outside with your friend. I wasn't sure if you were going to come in.'

'Just my nerves holding me back. I'm glad I did.'

Alice tenderly took his hand. 'I'm glad too.' She smiled and kissed his cheek. 'Come on. I must warn you, some of my family can be a little overwhelming, but they are eager to meet you.' She escorted him into the main function hall.

Considering how anxious Harper felt beforehand, so far he'd handled everything very well, showing an honest and natural charm that others seemed to love, especially Alice's mother, who instantly fell head over heels for him – just as her daughter had. Not being clued up on reading the signs, Harper remained oblivious to how she felt about him. Anyone other than Elaine showing kindness or affection was new to him, and he embraced it. He welcomed the ordinary things that so many took for granted.

Sitting at a table with a bottle of lager and a white paper plate in front of him, he picked at his selection from the refined buffet.

Alice soon joined him with a plate of her own. 'You've certainly been a big hit with everyone.'

'Really?' he said modestly.

'Absolutely! My mother wishes she were twenty-five years younger, and my teenage niece thinks you're *dope*. That's a good thing,' she added upon seeing his puzzled expression. 'Now the bride wants to ditch her new hubby and elope with you.'

'They're just being kind. You have a lovely family.'

'You're so affable,' she said.

'Not always.'

'I find that hard to believe.' She placed her hand on his. 'What have you done to your hand?' she asked, noticing the cuts from where he'd punched the ceramic tiles at the hotel.

'Oh, it's nothing – I caught my hand while changing the gas bottle at the caravan.'

Alice's father approached the table. 'Simon, I hope you don't mind if I steal my daughter for a dance?'

Harper rose to his feet. 'I don't think a father needs permission to ask his daughter to dance, Mr Shaw,' he said, and watched as Alice was led into the crowd.

A feeling of contentment overcame him as he observed Alice dancing with her father. This was the kind of moment he'd always wanted to experience. To him, it was like a scene from a movie he'd watched while locked away. Except now, here he was with a starring role. He was about to sit down.

'Oh no, you don't,' said Alice's cousin, resplendent in her magnificent wedding dress. 'You have to dance with me – you're not allowed to refuse the bride.'

'I wouldn't dare.' He smiled.

Heads turned to see the bride dancing with an unfamiliar face. They surely must have wondered who he was and where Alice had found him. He just hoped nobody recognised him from an old picture plastered across their television screens three years earlier.

The bride leaned into his ear. 'I don't know how you did it, but well done.'

He pulled back, baffled by her comment.

'For making Alice fall completely in love with you,' she clarified.

'Oh, I don't think that's the case,' he said.

'You don't have a clue, do you?'

Harper looked across the dance floor to see Alice staring at him, her eyes glazed over, her face full of pure joy and adoration. His heart fluttered like the wings of a baby bird preparing for its first magical flight. For the first time in his life, he felt . . . love.

'I do now,' he said, smiling at Alice, who in turn reciprocated.

'The few who have attempted to win her heart have failed miserably. There must be something very special about you.'

'I can assure you there isn't,' he muttered under his breath.

One song ended, and another began. Alice moved directly towards Harper for the next dance, while her father took his turn with the bride. They moved gently in harmony, cheek to cheek, wrapped in loving arms and delicately placed hands. Their heads drifted slowly apart like petals on a lake. Neither could drop their gaze. Eyes acting like magnets, their faces drew closer together until each one's breath blew a soft breeze against the other's lips.

A deliberate pause prolonged their desire to connect. Their eyes closed, and with effortless grace, their lips pressed together. They were lost in a spell of pure melodic motion, enveloped by an energy that flowed freely between them.

The kiss lingered after the song had ended, and the DJ shouted something about livening up the party with some cheesy classics. As soon as Sweet's 'The Ballroom Blitz' blared out, they broke from their kiss and stared at each other. Alice was playfully pulled away to perform some idiotic but fun dance moves. Harper returned to his seat to observe from the sidelines. He found it all highly entertaining.

Alice's mother sat in the chair beside him. 'I thought you'd be up there with the others,' she said.

'I'm not much of a dancer, Mrs Shaw. I tend to leave such things to those with a bit more talent.'

'I can't imagine there are many things you are not good at,' she said.

'Believe it or not, Mrs Shaw, that was the first time I've ever danced.'

'Well, there is certainly something about you, Simon, and it must be something very special because I've never seen Alice like this around a man. And please, call me Laura.'

Harper smiled and turned his eyes towards Alice, who was still dancing. On the table in front of them, he noticed a young woman sobbing, being consoled by one of the other guests. He turned to Laura and couldn't help but enquire what was wrong.

'Oh, that's Andrea. She has really struggled to get over the death of her husband. He was a police officer killed during that terrible incident in Helmsley several years ago. I'm sure you must have heard about it.'

He paused, disconcerted by the reply to a question he wished he hadn't asked. 'Yes,' he said, unable to add anything more. The shock on his face was masked by the natural response of anyone hearing such awful news.

'She was pregnant at the time. The trauma forced her into labour, and she had a very distressing birth, but the baby was fine. Unfortunately, Andrea has found it difficult to cope with both grief and motherhood. She named the baby Sean after his father. A lovely thing to do, don't you think?'

Harper's thoughts had returned to the scene that day and the knife he'd thrust into the stomach of a young police officer who'd knelt over him. He couldn't be sure which officer she was talking about, but for some reason, this was the instance that came to mind. He'd taken the life of a husband and father of an unborn child. The heavy burden he carried and the revulsion of what he'd done flattened him – reminding him of the monster he truly was. His stomach churned. Sweat formed on his brow. With the walls closing in, he needed some air.

'Yes, it was a beautiful thing to do. I'm sorry, Mrs Shaw, you'll have to excuse me for a moment,' he said, desperate to make his escape and get out of the stuffy, overcrowded room.

The air outside wasn't much fresher due to the hot summer evening, but it was enough to subdue the nausea created by his guilt. Leaning forward with his hands on his knees, he deliberated (and not for the first time) whether he could live with his actions. The crimes he'd committed were beyond redemption, so why did he feel there was a chance of a brighter future? Although he didn't believe he was the same person, he did not hesitate to kill Edward and his sleazy friend in the hotel room. But that was different, wasn't it? Edward had it coming, not only for what he had done to him as a child but also for what he had done to Elaine, and no doubt many others.

Then it occurred to him that he'd never change. If someone he loved were attacked and seriously hurt, he wouldn't think twice about taking the life of whoever was responsible. Murder was something that came all too easily to him. In truth, he was struggling, and he knew there would come a day when he would have to make the ultimate choice: if he couldn't move on from all the horrific events in his life, he would have to end it. Why should he wait? Perhaps it *was* time. He would never find enough peace in this lifetime or the next to forgive himself.

It would be best if he called Elaine and got her to come and pick him up as soon as possible. He scrolled to her name on his phone and was about to call her—

'Simon, are you okay?' asked Alice.

'Yeah, I'm fine. I just needed some air,' he said, slipping his phone back into his pocket. 'I'm good now.'

Noticing his agitation, she said, 'We can stay out here for a while if you like. Or, if it's all a little too overwhelming, we can go up to our room.'

He looked at her, puzzled. 'Our room?'

'I thought I'd surprise you.' She smiled.

He fell silent, raised his eyes to the starry night sky, and took a long, deep breath. From the garden, the loud music and out-of-tune singing coming from the main hall convinced him that going back to the party was the last thing he wanted to do. He couldn't face seeing Andrea again. Did that make him a coward? Maybe it did, but he couldn't change anything he'd done, just as he couldn't change what had happened to him all those years ago.

'So, how about it? Would you like to go up to our room?'

'I'd like that very much.'

Alice reached for his hand and led him back inside the hotel and up to the room.

Alice made them coffee while he went to the bathroom. He let the cold tap run for a bit and cupped a handful of water, burying his face in his hands. He repeated the process several times. The colder, the better. Something about the cold water on his face made him feel inwardly cleaner. It had more than just a soothing effect – for a few measly seconds, his sins were washed away. No matter how fleeting the moment, he loved the idea of his life appearing like a blank manuscript – a story yet to be written.

He stared at his reflection in the mirror; where others saw ocean-blue eyes, he saw a sea of molten lava. It always brought him back to the inferno of his eternal damnation. Usually, he'd avoid staring into his eyes; there was far too much truth to be seen, and he hated the horrors behind them.

In the cream armchairs on either side of a small table, they sipped their coffee in silence, well, other than the faint distant droning of music from downstairs, that is. The complete change in his demeanour in such a short space of time would have been obvious to Alice. She put her cup down, leaned forward, and held his hand.

'Why don't you tell me what's wrong? Maybe I can help,' she said.

'I'm fine.' He lied; nobody could help. There was nothing anyone could ever do to make it better. It wasn't as though he could talk about who he was, what had happened to him, or the things he had done. His soul was tortured and could not be saved.

'I can tell you're not fine.'

He removed his hand from hers and stood. 'Perhaps I should leave.'

'No! Please, don't go,' said Alice, hastening to him and placing her hands on his cheeks. 'I want you to stay. We don't have to talk if you don't want to.' She laid her head on his shoulder and wrapped her arms around him.

Harper stayed, and it wasn't long before they were in bed. The distant pounding of music eventually stopped, and for a while, they just lay there, inches apart, with only the silence of the night for company. Alice shifted her arm across and let it rest alongside his. He felt a palliative comfort in the warmth of her skin against his. It didn't remove his bottomless pit of pain, but somehow it alleviated the depth to which it would sink. In her presence, he found serenity.

In time, his hand found hers and their fingers interlocked. Turning his head sideways on the soft white pillow, Alice's eyes glistened in the darkness, gazing back at him. She had a magic about her. He had never dreamed this could happen. Not to him. Good things didn't happen to tainted people. He wanted to kiss her. He longed to feel her lips on his, to taste her on his tongue. He shifted onto his side, placed his hand delicately on her face, and stroked along her eyebrow with his thumb. Their heads drifted closer together, and the tips of their noses touched. The light of the moon through the window shone a spotlight on the lovers.

'We don't have to,' she said.

Harper looked into her eyes. 'I want to.'

Their lips met, and at first, the kisses were soft and light, gradually increasing in intensity as they became overwhelmed with desire.

20

Elaine

When Elaine dropped Harper at the wedding reception, she concealed her own nerves about the situation. Though he was excited to be seeing Alice again, she understood why he was holding himself back; being around so many strangers did not come naturally to him. What made her uneasy was how he would react if something went wrong – a misplaced word or a drunken fracas. Would he be the new, controlled Simon, or the hot-headed Harper?

On the drive home, she concluded it was all part of letting him go and that it was time for him to stand on his own two feet. She wouldn't be there to watch over him once he made his own way in the world. However, it was Harper who had been there to watch over her the previous night. She had completely misjudged the situation at the hotel. She should have known it was impossible to predict the actions of an animal like Horner, and to her horror, she learned the hard way. Elaine remembered much more than she had let on . . .

In the service station bathroom, Elaine stared in horror at the marks on her face. She leaned forward for a closer inspection. But for the glow of her reflection, the room around her went dark. The mirror rippled like water as liquid hands extended towards her. Paralysed by an unseen force, the hands grasped her head and pulled her face through the mirror to the other side.

Elaine saw herself on a small sofa in Edward's suite. The top of her dress had been pulled down, and the man she knew as Peter was at her breast, his hand up her skirt. She lashed out at him, only to see him strike her across the cheek. Everything went black, and she reeled away from the mirror in shock.

She returned to Harper, angry yet composed, ready to confront him – desperate to know the truth. He gave a reasonable account of events, though she had a feeling he was trying to protect her from something. Partly satisfied, she finished her coffee, ate her croissant, and drove them home.

When they arrived at Sablefall Farm, Elaine marched straight upstairs to take a shower. She stripped off and gazed at her naked body in the full-length mirror. There were marks on her shoulders and ribs. She examined the pain around her wrists, where obvious bruises had not yet formed.

Soaping herself in the shower, she paused, her attention drawn to a dull ache along the inside of her thighs. She traced the bruised skin, fingers trembling as she moved lower. A sickening clarity swept over her – this was what Harper was trying to shield her from.

Vomit projected from her mouth and splashed against the ceramic tiles, rinsed away instantly by the constant fall of water. She covered her mouth to suppress the enraged screams threatening to burst out. Tears flowed from her reddened eyes as she sank to the floor. Though Harper had completed their mission, she couldn't help but feel she'd somehow failed, let Harper down, let herself down. She wrapped her arms around her shins and pulled her knees tightly into her chest. Her only comfort, however small, was that all those abhorrent men had paid with their lives.

Lying in bed, her sad and tired eyes felt as heavy as her miserable heart. At least her murderous days were behind her, unless, of course, Lenny came up trumps and found the man who'd killed her son. For now, though, it was time for rest and sleep. She appreciated and loved how Harper had tried to protect her. In turn, she would protect him by not revealing what she really knew had occurred in Sir Edward's suite. They had shared enough pain; she saw no need to add to his.

Unfortunately, her rest was shorter than she would have liked. Tom would be back with the children soon, and he would be curious to know how her face had ended up in such a state. It was not a conversation she was looking forward to. Her marriage had started with enough lies; adding more wasn't something she wanted to do, but what choice did she have? Elaine did her best to conceal the bruises with make-up – there wasn't much she could do about the swelling on her cheek.

Elaine waited on the porch to greet her husband and children. First up was Michael. A reluctant teenage hug and a mumbled 'hello', and it was straight off to his bedroom. Emily was a different story; always ready for a cuddle with her mother. As she embraced her daughter, Elaine took a moment to appreciate the bond between them and felt instantly revived. Aware of Tom studying her face with a quizzical look, she winced with embarrassment and raised her eyes. 'An accident at work. I'll tell you about it later.'

Within the hour, Tom cornered her, wanting to know what she'd done. Having previously told him she was assessing a property out of town that needed major refurbishment, it seemed a plausible explanation to blame her injuries on tumbling down a precarious staircase. Tom bought it; why wouldn't he? He had no reason to doubt anything she told him. That was what hurt the most – he trusted her, and so far, she'd done nothing but lie. Well, that was about to change. With their vengeance complete, she had no reason to tell any more.

Later that day, Elaine left to pick up Harper and take him to the wedding reception. In the car, she realised she'd already broken her no-more-lying-to-Tom pledge by telling him she was popping over to see Lila. It scared her how easy it was to lie. That it hadn't registered was even scarier.

In the car outside her house, Elaine took a few deep breaths. The last couple of days had physically and emotionally drained her. She needed to slow down and spend some quality time with the family, focusing solely on them. Her phone rang in her jacket pocket. When she saw it was Lenny, she sighed in frustration – more out of tiredness than anything. Elaine closed her eyes, deep in thought, caught in two minds about whether to answer. She wanted to switch the phone off, but knowing it was likely an update about Charlie, she answered.

Lenny wanted to talk. He had news and thought it best to share his information face to face. If they needed to discuss matters in person, they had previously agreed to meet in Nottingham, a halfway point between London and Helmsley. Lenny chose a place called 'Kitty's Café' and gave her the postcode. She stepped up onto the porch and noted Tom hovering outside the front door.

'Is everything all right?' he asked, having no doubt observed her prolonged time alone in the car.

'Yeah, it's fine. I just need a big hug,' she replied, moving in close to him. Tom put his arms around her. 'It's been a horrible couple of days, and I'm so tired.'

'Well, you're home now. You can take a few days to relax.'

For now, she thought it best not to mention she'd be off to Nottingham tomorrow. Just thinking about the drive there and back was exhausting. It wasn't a journey she was ready to face, but come morning, *if* she managed to get a good night's sleep, it might be a different story.

'Is Emily in bed?' she asked.

'Yeah, and Michael is in his room.'

'Where else would he be?'

'True. Look, why don't you take a seat on the bench, and I'll make us a nice cup of tea?'

'Sounds like a good idea, but first, I'm going to look in on the children. I'll meet you back here,' she said.

Michael's door was slightly ajar, and she entered without knocking. With the exception of his mother, he hated anyone coming into his room. In front of his monitor, with his gaming headset on, he was blasting aliens to smithereens with his friends online. She walked over and placed a can of lemonade on his desk. He glanced up, acknowledged her with a smile, and went back to shooting slimy monsters. She leaned in, gave him a quick hug, and kissed the top of his head.

The glow of a dim night light on the bedside table showed Emily was asleep, her copy of *Charlotte's Web* open on her chest. Elaine removed the book and placed it beside the lamp. Her foot brushed against Matthew, the teddy bear; he must have fallen out of bed. Elaine carefully placed him under the covers with Emily, tucked them both in, and planted a kiss on her forehead. Emily rolled over and snuggled into Matthew. For a moment, Elaine stood beside the bed, watching over her daughter. A little late for regret, but it now bothered her that she had put vengeance before her children. At no point had she considered the consequences of being arrested for murder or, worse, being murdered herself, which could have been the case had Harper not been there to save her after her lack of foresight.

Tom sipped his tea on the bench. As she walked over, ever the gentleman, he reached down and grabbed her cup from the floor. She nestled beside him with her feet up as he placed his arm around her shoulders and passed her the tea. Graced with a benevolent breeze, the last flickers of the sun had disappeared from view and taken away the lustre, leaving the prerequisite twilight to pave the way for darkness. There was no need for words to spoil the natural quietude. At the end of a long day, birdsong was more than adequate.

Tom was far from stupid, and Elaine often wondered if he had an inkling of what she'd been up to. He'd worked out that Harper was her brother three years ago and had never said a word, not until he brought it up in the hospital. At the same time, he informed her of his knowledge about the case involving the abuse at Sablefall Farm, a case his father had worked on and had been threatened into leaving well alone. To his father's shame, he'd obeyed his superiors; however, he'd always held on to the police report of what supposedly happened on that lamentable night. Tom had given Elaine the files to look through, but they told her nothing she hadn't already learned from Harper.

Tom and Elaine rarely talked about the past, and she certainly wasn't going to tell him about Harper. As far as Tom was concerned, Harper Darmody was dead. Bearing in mind that Harper had almost killed him during the massacre, there was no telling how he'd react if he found out he was alive. Things were much simpler without mixing her two worlds together. Elaine snuggled into Tom and rested her head contentedly on his lap, letting her eyes slowly drift closed. Tom gently removed the cup that was tilting precariously on her thigh.

21

The Boy

In his tiny bed, Danny woke with a forceful flinch, his long hair saturated and bonded to his pale skin by sweat oozing from the pores on his face. Another nightmare about cutting up the police officer's body. Even if he survived his ordeal, it would plague his thoughts forever. He heard the rumbling sound beneath the floor again. Definitely not a sound he was familiar with, and he remained uncertain about what it could be. He'd never heard the noise this late before.

For a while, he lay there thinking about how much time he had left. Countless tears had rolled down his cheeks, and once more, they erupted from his tired, blackened eyes. So many times, his thoughts fluctuated between wanting to live and wanting to die. Right now, his choice was life. He had come so close to being set free; he could almost feel his mother's arms wrapped tightly around him and smell the lavender perfume she always wore. How he longed to see the beautiful and familiar faces of his family again, especially his mum and dad.

Through his soft and fractured voice, he said, 'I'm sorry I wandered off and got lost. I thought the man would help me find you. He said he knew where you'd be. I was so afraid, and I – I believed him. I hope you can forgive me. If somehow I do make it out of here, I promise to be a good son. If I don't, please know that I love you all so very much.' The remnants of his childlike and fantastical innocence hoped his words would be transported in a magical pocket of air and drift back home to his loving family.

A little later, standing over the toilet, his body lurched forward uncontrollably, and his urine missed the pan. The floor beneath him seemed to be moving. He shifted his feet to keep his balance and looked around, worried and confused. The whole room shook as if struck by an earthquake. It had happened before, but not with such ferocity. The rumbling noise below stopped, replaced by the sound of running water, lots of it. Heavy feet stomped above. Unsettled by the ruckus, he climbed back into bed and pretended to be asleep. A few minutes passed – nothing but silence. Danny lay wondering what could have made the room shake so abruptly. Eventually, he drifted off to sleep.

The next day was no different from any other. The man had brought him his breakfast, and everything appeared normal. At first, he wasn't sure he'd woken up during the night at all. Perhaps it was another dream. Then he observed the patch of water on the floor from where he'd missed the pan. He cleaned up and commenced his habitual routine of taking a shower and doing his daily exercises – push-ups and sit-ups, as many as he could. He paced back and forth across the length of the room, but upon hearing movement just outside the door, he quickly sat on the bed. The man entered and stared at him for a few seconds. It was peculiar. Different. The man walked across to the other room, opened the door, and went inside.

Danny listened to the man moving things around. What could he be up to now? The dreaded music wasn't playing, so he knew he was safe from a more sinister motive. After a few minutes, the man stood in the open doorway, glaring in his direction.

'You've proven to be the most resilient and resolute boy I have found. I'm going to share something I've never shown to anyone else before now,' he said, a hint of excitement in his voice.

The man disappeared inside the other room and returned, pushing a narrow wheelchair covered with a large white sheet. There was something concealed beneath the sheet, but Danny couldn't work out what it could be. The man pushed the chair to the middle of the room and turned it to face the bed.

'Are you ready?' the man asked in an eager, almost manic state.

Nervous and afraid, Danny nodded. Like a magician performing a trick, the man ripped the sheet away with excitement. Danny gasped and slid backwards on the bed, away from the hideous sight of decayed skeletal remains seated in the chair: a body adorned in rotting clothes, moulded to the bones. He could not prise his eyes away. Strands of red hair, withered and matted, clung to the skull of the corpse.

'I'd like to introduce you to Ozias. At least, that's what he told me to call him. I never did find out if it was his real name. I suppose it wasn't important. You could say I am who this man used to be, and you – well, you are who I used to be. I hope one day you will become me, but we'll see.'

Puzzled and horrified, Danny remained still, his eyes wide, mouth open, and heart racing. The man calmly sat cross-legged on the floor beside the wheelchair.

'I was a small boy at thirteen, a lot smaller than you. My parents had taken me to some music event or something – I can't remember. Anyway, like you, I'd wandered away from my parents. When I returned to the spot we'd settled at earlier in the day, they were gone. They'd simply packed up the blanket and picnic bags and left me all alone, or at least that's what I was told. You see, a man had been watching us from a distance. Actually, he was watching many families, keeping an eye out for children who looked vulnerable.

'When he saw me standing there, all forlorn and looking around for my family, he approached. He said my father had asked him to take me back to the car, where they were waiting for me. I was a distressed little boy who had no reason to doubt him. Before I knew it, I woke up right where you are now – with that very chain attached to my ankle.'

Danny frowned and tilted his head to the side. 'You were here, in this bed?'

'As I told you, I was who you are now.'

'And that's the man who took you?' asked Danny, pointing.

'Yep. This is the old bastard who brought me here.'

'I don't understand. If this happened to you, why are you doing the same to me? Didn't you want to get away and go home?'

'Oh, I wanted to go home more than anything, but after nine years of captivity and torture, it didn't seem to matter any more. In some twisted way, I'd found where I was supposed to be.'

'Nine years? You were a prisoner for nine years?'

'Yes, but I wasn't chained to the bed for all that time. After a couple of years, he removed the shackle from my ankle and told me I could leave any time I wanted – with one condition – I had to kill him first. If I were to leave without doing so, he said he'd find me and make me watch while he slaughtered my entire family. He would have, too. He was an evil old bastard,' he declared, glancing up at the skeleton.

'At first, I just cleaned up around the place – dirt, blood, whatever. He taught me to cook, and on the odd occasion, he'd even let me drive. As time went on, I helped dismember the bodies of boys and girls he brought home. Eventually, I was tasked with more responsibility and sent out to find, befriend, and bring back children for him. It then dawned on me that I'd become his accomplice. This went on for a few years.' The man got to his feet and turned to face the skeleton.

Danny couldn't understand why the man was telling him all this. 'Why did you do it? Why did you bring back other children for him? Why didn't you go to the police?' Danny asked, anger and frustration increasing in his voice.

'Because I enjoyed it. Ozias had given me his trust. He had put his life in my hands, and in some strange way, it felt amazing. When I brought a child back for him, he would look at me with such pride. It gave him fulfilment. We developed a unique bond.'

'It's sick!' said Danny. 'You took children from their families and led them to their deaths.'

'Actually, we didn't. We only took runaways or children in care homes. The children nobody would miss. Those were the rules – until I broke them. I took a young boy from a fairground. I didn't set out to – it just happened. It was too easy. My friend here wasn't too pleased when he read about the boy's family in the newspapers. Not happy at all, were you, Ozias?'

The man grabbed the bottom of the skeleton's jaw and moved it up and down as he said, 'No, I bloody well wasn't.' He faced the boy, laughing at his own distasteful joke.

'He beat me so badly when he discovered what I'd done. Then he made me kill the boy. It wasn't quite how I'd imagined my first murder. In my mind, I had pictured it very differently. That was the night I knew things had to change.'

'You said he had a rule to only take children who wouldn't be missed – and yet he took you. You had a family. I bet your family missed you.'

'Occasionally, a killer breaks with tradition and pushes their boundaries. My parents kicked up one hell of a storm, and it scared him. He decided to go back to how things were, but after what happened with Charlie, the boy I took, I didn't want to go back.'

Danny's eyes widened at the mention of Charlie, the first name on the list carved under the table. The man slowly circled the wheelchair as he spoke, glaring at Danny with enthusiasm.

'Watching that kid's parents suffer was special. A *huge* rush. That's when I knew I wanted to do things my way, and I wasn't going to let Ozias get away with beating me, not any more. After I strangled the boy and dumped his body, I waited until Ozias was asleep, and then I slit his throat. Now that was pretty spectacular. The blood just kept gushing and gushing as I watched his life slowly fade away, the movement of his chest diminishing with each breath, his eyes straining to an agonising red as death approached. Magnificent.'

The man grabbed the handles and turned the wheelchair. 'Right, enough excitement for you, my old friend,' he said, giving the chair a shove towards the open doorway of the other room. 'Off you go,' he said, waving. 'I'll put you back in your box in a sec. He doesn't like to stay out too long – it's bad for his complexion.' Smiling, he turned his attention back to the boy. 'I bet you're wondering why all the drama, so – let's move on, shall we?'

Danny observed the man walking over to the other room, collecting Ozias on the way. Seconds later, he reappeared carrying a long chain, similar to the one attached to his ankle. He closed the door behind him. The man resembled a child with a new toy on

Christmas morning. Using heavy-duty pliers, the man linked the chain to the same bolt in the floor and laid it out across the room. Danny was terrified. His body shuddered, and his stomach turned. Whatever the man was up to, it wasn't good.

'I've been aching to do this for a while now, and I have to say – I'm very excited. Are you ready? Wait! Don't answer yet. I'm getting ahead of myself. I need to calm down.' The man stood still and took a couple of deep breaths to compose himself.

He hurried up the three creaky steps and left the room, leaving the door ajar. As soon as he returned carrying what appeared to be two small axes, cold shivers clawed their way up Danny's spine. His fears of something bad about to happen were confirmed. The man placed the hatchets on the table.

'I'm about to give you the gift of a lifetime, boy. I know you're not going to like it – at least, I don't think you are. But I, for one, am going to love it.' He smiled, unable to contain himself.

If Danny's face could have turned a shade whiter, it would have. Every time he attempted to swallow, it felt like sharp sand sliding down the back of his throat. The man exited the room and came back with a bulging blanket thrown over his shoulder.

'I bet you're forming an idea of what's to come in your head now, aren't you?' said the man, placing the blanketed pile gently on the floor beside the table opposite Danny. 'Ready?' he said, and removed the blanket to reveal a sleeping and clearly drugged young boy. 'Ta-da!' he sang, spreading his arms wide.

Danny's eyes widened with terror. This wasn't far off from what he had imagined. The boy, dressed in a yellow and white striped T-shirt and blue jeans, looked to be around his age. The man shackled the end of the chain to the boy's ankle and fetched the hatchets from the table. He laid one axe on the floor next to the sleeping boy and placed the other on the floor beside the bed.

Revelling in the moment, the man said, 'Rules, rules, rules. Let's keep it simple – there are none. If you wanted to take that axe to his head right now while he's sleeping, there is nothing to stop you. It wouldn't be sporting, but as you have come to learn, life isn't fair, is it?' he said with a complete lack of empathy.

'Why are you doing this?' asked Danny.

'Because I can.'

The man's cold-blooded and unemotional manner distressed Danny. 'Who, who is he?'

'Does it matter?'

'It matters to me,' he answered, teary-eyed.

'Well, you'd best hope he feels as concerned about you when he wakes up, which, incidentally, shouldn't be too long from now.'

'So, this is my gift of a lifetime? *Some* gift!'

'No, no, no. This is not your gift. I haven't told you that part yet. Your gift, my boy, is freedom.'

'Freedom?'

'Yes. You can leave, go home to your dear old mummy and daddy, or – you can stay here and live chain-free with me.' He smirked. 'I think you know the option I would like you to choose.'

'Why would you let me go?'

'Because you're different. No other boy has shown such tenacity and desire to live. No other has fought back like you.' The man was almost bursting with pride.

'Is that boy getting the same choice?'

'Don't be silly. By your hand or mine, *that* boy is going to die – except, I'll take my time and kill him slowly.' He grinned.

'Kill him and I'm free to leave?'

'Or stay with me.' The man smiled with sickening gusto. 'We could have lots of fun. So many places to see, people to kill.'

'And if I don't kill him?'

'As I said, he dies regardless. Either he'll take your life or I'll take his, and you, you will stay chained to that bed until your time is up.'

'Some choice!'

'Oh, don't be so miserable,' the man scoffed. 'This is a one-time offer, Danny boy. I'll never give you this opportunity again. It's simple – kill or be killed – or die chained to that bed. Whatever happens, only one of you is going to live, and personally, I hope it's you.'

'You said my name.'

'Yes, I did, didn't I? That's never happened before.' He turned to leave the room. 'Make the right decision.'

Danny shouted, 'Wait! You've told me the name of the dead guy, but what about yours? What's your name?'

The man smiled again. 'You're the first to ask. Call me Zeph,' he said, placing his foot on the bottom step.

'Zeph!'

The man stopped but did not turn to face him.

'Is there a time limit?'

'We'll see how it goes,' he said and carried on his way, closing the door behind him.

Danny stared at the boy asleep on the floor. He recalled how terrified and alone he had felt when he first woke up in this room. Then he glanced at the axe on the floor by his bed.

22

Lenny

Considering it was the peak of summer, the mid to late evening seemed dark and soulless. He had been parked outside Mrs Wells' house for almost two and a half hours, waiting for her to return. Nobody could ever accuse him of being an impatient man. The previous night, he'd gone through the notes from their first meeting and recalled something she'd said that now troubled him.

Usually, Lenny wouldn't overlook such key information, and he hoped it was nothing important. He'd already chastised himself for not paying enough attention during his last visit. If he'd heard correctly, the missed information could change everything. He'd thought about calling her but decided against it, preferring instead to catch her at home.

To amuse himself while he waited, he tossed scrunched-up paper in the direction of an empty takeaway coffee cup he'd secured with tape to the dashboard. There were balls of paper scattered across the dashboard, the passenger seat, and the floor. He didn't have to wait much longer before Mrs Wells returned. Lenny gave her a few minutes to settle indoors and then made his way across the road and rang the doorbell.

'Mr Grey! How nice of you to call by unannounced,' she said, sarcasm at the ready.

'Hello again, Mrs Wells. I'm sorry to inconvenience you. I just wondered if you could clarify a few things from when we last spoke. It shouldn't take very long.'

'Well, if I remember correctly, you were rather preoccupied with the biscuit plate.'

Lenny's cheeks reddened.

'I suppose you'd better come in,' she said. 'As it happens, it's not a bad thing you've shown up again, but I'll get to that before you leave.'

Just as before, Mrs Wells led Lenny to the same immaculate room, sat down, made herself comfortable, and gestured for Lenny to sit opposite.

'So, how can I be of service?' she asked.

You could start by fetching some tea and biscuits. Lenny took out his notepad, licked the tip of his thumb, and sifted to the right page.

'If we could go back to when you were searching for your car. You said that you saw the clown with the boy. Is that correct?'

'Yes, that's correct.'

'Only, a while later, you said you saw the balloon floating off and then noticed the boy with the man.' Lenny tapped his pen against his chin.

'Yes. That's exactly what happened.' Mrs Wells didn't seem to understand why he was so confused.

'But you stated it as though it was the first time you'd seen the man when previously you mentioned seeing him with the boy before that particular moment.'

'No, Mr Grey. You have it all wrong. The first time I saw the boy, he was with the clown. The next time I saw the boy, he was with the man.'

Lenny's heart jumped as he realised her statement had been completely misinterpreted. 'A different man and not the clown? We are talking about two different men?'

'That is what I said. It's what I have said all along. Have I done something wrong?' Mrs Wells could see Lenny was not best pleased.

'No, Mrs Wells. It's not your fault. This should have been picked up during the first line of inquiry,' Lenny said, wondering how Colin had not queried her wording and made such a glaring error. 'Do you think the two men were together?'

'I don't believe so. At least, that's not how I perceived it at the time. I assumed the clown was helping the boy find his father. The men barely exchanged words. Actually, I'm certain they were not together.'

Although he hid it well, inside, Lenny was vexed. Hours upon hours were wasted searching for a man dressed as a clown.

'Is that everything?' she asked.

'Yes, Mrs Wells. That's made things very clear. Thank you for your time. I'll be off then,' he said, rising from the armchair.

'Oh, wait. There's something else. I almost forgot,' she said and left the room. Moments later, she was back. 'I asked my son about the mobile phone with the pictures you mentioned. It turns out he hoards all these old gadgets – keeps them in a box. He charged it up – and what do you know? It still works. There are some pictures from the fair and the circus. Here,' she said, passing him her old iPhone. 'If it dies, I'm sure you can find an old charger for it somewhere.'

'This is very helpful. Thank you.'

Mrs Wells looked hesitant. 'One more thing . . . I wasn't sure if I should mention it or not,' she said, taking the phone from his hand. She scanned through the photo gallery to a picture of her son with the big top behind him. 'Now, I don't want to get anyone into trouble because I can't be one hundred per cent certain.' She pointed to a man in the background of the picture with a large camera dangling from a strap around his neck. 'This man here. He was the pushy gentleman who I believe bumped into me on purpose outside the circus tent. I didn't hang around to find out what he wanted, but I assumed he was trying to take and sell his photographs.'

'What about him?'

'Well, as I said, I can't be certain, but when I browsed through these pictures, I remembered the man I saw in the car park with the boy. He was wearing what looked like the same long tan coat.'

Lenny squinted to see the face in the picture. 'I know you can enlarge these pictures, but I'm a bit of a dinosaur when it comes to these things.'

'Tap the screen twice,' she said.

Lenny focused on the man's face. It may have been an old picture, but there was no mistaking the jet-black hair and thick matching eyebrows. His muscles tensed. It was the man he'd seen in The Moorhen car park.

'This is him,' said Lenny. 'The man I've been searching for.'

In the car, Lenny bashed his hands against the steering wheel, angered by his dead friend. He couldn't fathom how someone as experienced as Colin had completely messed up the witness interview.

When Lenny arrived at his apartment, Olivia was whipping up a stir-fry in the kitchen. They had made plans earlier in the day and arranged to have dinner together at his place, and he'd called ahead to let her know he'd be home soon. He hadn't decided what to do about the new evidence. Although he knew he should send the image to DCI Harry Baxendale, deep down, he wished he could share it with Colin. He figured he would email it to the DCI in the morning. *Maybe.*

At the table, he poured wine into the glasses Olivia had already laid out. He wasted no time sinking his own and immediately poured himself another. Lenny's preoccupied disposition hadn't gone unnoticed as she dished up.

'What's wrong?' she asked, approaching the table with two plates.

As she set the plates down and took a seat, Lenny went over to his jacket on the back of the settee to retrieve Mrs Wells' iPhone. He navigated his way to the image and placed it on the table in front of her.

'See that man in the background?' He pointed. 'That's who we're looking for,' he said, returning to his chair.

'You mean this is the killer?'

Lenny nodded as he forked noodles and chicken into his mouth. 'The picture is eight years old, but it's definitely him. That's the night he took Charlie Davis,' he said, waving his fork around. 'It's also the bloke I saw in the car park with Colin's keys.'

'Where did you get this?'

'The witness.' Lenny held up his hand to stop her next question. 'Long story,' he said, not wanting to explain Colin's ineptitude.

Olivia studied the photo. 'I must say, he looks pretty good for a dead man.'

A picture of perplexity, Lenny said, 'Dead man! What are you talking about?'

'Well, I have some more news for you, but it can go no further. My job would be on the line.'

'Liv, I'm not about to put your career in jeopardy.'

She sipped her wine. 'Your friend, Colin – he had a bite mark. My colleague found traces of DNA and ran the obligatory tests. The man's name is Joseph Webster.'

'And you're telling me he's dead?'

'That's the strange part,' she said. 'Joseph Webster went missing seventeen years ago at the age of thirteen. Several witnesses stated that a boy fitting Joseph's description left a music festival with an older, scruffy gentleman, whose only distinguishable features were a limp and a long, dark grey beard. Joseph's father applied to the court for a presumption of death declaration using the seven-year rule. I actually remember reading about the mother and father fighting in court over the ruling.'

'Yeah, that rings a bell. The father was trying to help his wife move on and grieve for her son – something to do with her deteriorating mental health. The judge agreed with the father, and the wife committed suicide three days later.' Lenny emptied his wine glass and stepped away from the table.

'So the young man in the photo is Joseph Webster?'

'It would seem so.'

Lenny paced the room, thinking, trying to understand. 'It makes no sense,' he finally blurted. 'How can *he* be responsible for murdering Charlie Davis, the other children, and for killing Colin? I don't get it. Why would an abducted child take other children and slaughter them in such a brutal fashion?'

'Probably forced into it by his captor,' she said. 'It can happen.'

'So, we could be dealing with two killers?'

'Doubtful! I'd imagine the young pupil killed his master and took over the lair.'

'What makes you say that?'

'Nature! Be it human or animal, he'd want to do things his way – his territory, his rules. You can't have two dominant males ruling the same space. It's only natural they would eventually turn on each other.'

'But if he killed the person who took him, why not leave? Go home?'

'Go home to what? We're talking about a thirty-year-old man here, Lenny. He's not a child any more. Not when he killed Charlie, and not when he most probably killed his abductor. You need to forget he was once like those boys and imagine the awful things he has been through, seen, and done. He is no longer an innocent victim – he is the pupil turned master of his own domain, and sadly, death is all he knows.'

Olivia made sense of the disorder inhabiting Lenny's mind. He sat down at the table, picked up his fork, and deposited more chicken and noodles into his mouth.

'This is cold now,' he said.

Lenny set off just before ten the next morning to meet Elaine. He arrived in Nottingham in the early afternoon after almost three hours on the road. He managed to get to Kitty Café first and found himself surrounded by cats – something he hadn't expected. While he waited, he made a fuss over a tricolour calico that enthusiastically jumped up onto his lap.

'I see you've found yourself a new friend,' said Elaine, appearing out of the blue. 'You look like a supervillain from a James Bond movie.'

To conceal his embarrassment, he removed the cat from his lap and gently placed it on the floor. 'No friend here,' he said. 'I can't stand cats.'

'Hmm! Not how it looked to me when I walked in.'

Lenny blushed. 'I was just, you know, waiting.'

'Oh, believe me, I know.' Elaine wasn't going to let him forget this in a hurry.

'Look, cat fur all over my bloody trousers,' he said, picking the hairs from his trousers. 'I've heard of these places, but I never planned on paying a visit.'

'Then why arrange to meet in one?'

'I didn't do it on purpose,' he said, as another cat jumped onto his lap.

'So the name "Kitty Café" didn't give it away, then?'

'No – I misread the name online and assumed it was named after the owner.' He put the cute black cat on the floor.

'Yeah, I bet.'

'Shall I get the coffee?' Lenny asked, wanting to move on.

'No, it's okay. I'll get them. You carry on making furry friends.'

When she returned with two lattes, Lenny was besieged by more cats. 'They've definitely taken a shine to you, haven't they? I would never have regarded you as a cat magnet.'

'I'm not. They're furry little f—' Lenny refrained from swearing, 'freaks. Anyway, what have you done to your face?'

'Oh, it's nothing, just an accident at work.' She sipped her coffee. 'So, you have some news for me.'

Lenny poured sugar into the mug and stirred. 'Actually, since we spoke, there have been surprising new developments.'

She must have sensed his change of manner, and her instincts kicked in. 'Oh my God, you've found him, haven't you?'

'Not quite.' Lenny pulled out Mrs Wells's old phone, selected the picture, and passed it to Elaine. 'This photo was taken the night your son was abducted. That man there is who we're looking for. His name is Joseph Webster.'

Elaine's memory flashed to a past incident. 'I remember this man,' she said, a bemused expression sweeping across her face. 'He was the photographer outside the circus tent. He took a photo of my boys. It couldn't be him, though. The man I saw leading Charlie away was dressed as a clown.'

'I've gone over everything – you know I have. Every statement Robert and you gave at the time, and everything you've told me since, including Robert being around the back of the house of mirrors with his floozy when your son went missing. I even spoke to the man who was working on the attraction that night and the witness who saw your son in the car park.'

Lenny sipped his coffee before continuing. 'One of the last conversations Robert had with Charlie was about picking up the photograph. I believe Charlie came out of the house of mirrors, saw his dad wasn't there, and decided to go to the circus to collect the photo, but the photographer had left moments before. The clown took Charlie and caught up with the man in the car park. The bloke dressed as the clown thought he was doing a good deed. As for why he didn't wait with Charlie, I have no idea. Perhaps he thought he'd done his bit. Anyway, the witness saw a man put Charlie in the car and drive off. Not the clown – this guy.' He pointed at the man in the picture.

Elaine appeared shell-shocked. 'I don't understand. The witness never mentioned anyone other than the clown.'

'Actually, she did. I picked up on a minor detail in her statement that confused me and went back to get clarification. It was easy to miss,' he said in Colin's defence.

'Fuck, Lenny. No!' Elaine's outburst caused several heads to turn their way. She leaned in closer, lowering her tone. 'It shouldn't have been missed. This was my son,' she argued. 'Wasn't your friend Hargreaves the investigating officer? Colin Hargreaves. I'll bloody kill him.'

'You can't.'

'Oh, I don't mean it, Lenny. I know it wouldn't have changed what happened. I'm not that stupid. I'm just so *fucking* angry.'

'No, I meant you can't kill him because he's already dead.' He placed his mug on the table.

'What? How?'

'He found Charlie's murderer and got himself killed in the process. It hasn't been released to the press yet.'

'How did *he* find this – Joseph Webster?'

'Colin didn't know his name. I only found that out yesterday. I think he stumbled across this guy by accident.'

'How can you be certain the witness is correct? Perhaps she's mistaken. It's been a long time.'

'I know she's correct because when I found Colin's car, I saw the very same man. I tried to follow but lost him in the crowd. The thing is, Elaine, that's why I wanted to see you. The man saw me too, and if, like most serial killers, he's been monitoring his killing career through the media, he will likely know who I am, and there's every chance he could link me to you through our association.'

'You think he might come for me?'

'I'm just saying this is a dangerous man, and you need to be careful.'

'So who is he, this Webster? How did you find out his name?'

'I can't tell you. I've already revealed more than I should have,' he said, keeping his promise to Olivia.

Elaine's comeback was blunt and to the point. 'Don't piss me about, Lenny. Remember who pays you to find out all this information.'

For a moment, Lenny considered her statement. 'Okay, but look – this is all strictly confidential. You can't repeat anything I tell you. This could cost someone very close to me their job, and I can't have that.'

'Oh, come on, don't be ridiculous. Who am I going to tell? This has always been between us, Lenny. You know I want to find this bastard before the police.'

'And what are you going to do when I find him for you? If Colin couldn't take him on, what chance do you think you have?'

'Perhaps you're right. Things do have a way of spiralling out of control – recent events have taught me that, and it's not a road I want to venture down again. On the other hand, you said Colin stumbled upon him accidentally. That won't be the case for me. I'll be prepared.'

'Oh, you'll be prepared, will you?' he mocked. Her blank stare prompted him to continue. 'All right! DNA was extracted from a bite mark on Colin.'

Lenny explained how Joseph Webster had been abducted as a child and, at some point during his captivity, had been declared deceased. He likely became part of an evil double act, playing a role in the abduction and murder of an unknown number of children before going solo and starting a killing spree of his own.

Like Lenny, Elaine found it hard to believe such a young boy could be groomed into committing such appalling crimes. A cat jumped onto her lap and settled down, purring loudly.

'So, what are you going to do now?' she asked, stroking the cat.

'I'll start from Colin's final location and continue searching railway stations.'

Elaine frowned. 'That could take forever! Do you know how many train stations there are in the vicinity of these murders?'

DCI Baxendale had said the same thing. Lenny sat forward. 'Look, Elaine. We know more about this guy than we ever have, and I know what he looks like. We have never been this close.'

'Are the police searching the stations too? Have you shared the picture with them?'

'They're not interested in my theory, and no, I haven't shared the picture with them – yet.'

'You mean you're going to?' She didn't look happy.

'I will if I don't find him soon. He has to be stopped, Elaine. As you know, it's not just your child he's murdered, and I don't want the death of any other kid on my conscience. Do you?'

Her expression betrayed her forthcoming answer. 'No, I don't, and you're right – he does need to be stopped. Regardless of my personal feelings, there's a lot more at stake here. If you don't find him by this time next week, give the police his picture and tell them everything you know.'

Elaine grabbed the cat from her lap and stood up. She walked around the small table and passed the cat to Lenny. 'Here you go, have your little friend back,' she said, putting her handbag over her shoulder.

'Oh, cheers,' he replied, placing the cat on the floor. 'Earlier in the conversation, you mentioned something about recent events – were you talking about the massacre, or has something else happened?'

'No. There's nothing else. I am sorry about your friend, and, well, thank you – for everything.'

'You don't have to thank me. As you said, you're paying me.'

'I shouldn't have said that. I know finding Charlie's killer has always been at the forefront of your mind too. I hope to hear from you soon. Take care out there, Lenny.'

He watched Elaine leave, and his eyes drifted towards the cat he had just placed on the floor. 'Oh, come on then,' he said, tapping his hands on his thighs.

23

Harper

Waking up before Alice, Harper lay there for a while, staring at her, wondering how on earth he'd met someone so special. His thoughts then turned to the woman crying at the wedding reception, Andrea, and all the other lives he'd taken that day. An atrocity committed by a man who still resided somewhere inside his shattered mind, a man he no longer knew but from whom he could not hide. It didn't matter how much he'd changed; he would always be the tortured little boy who became a killer. There was no coming back from what he'd done. No such atonement existed. His mind had become the confined cell from which he'd spent most of his life longing to free himself. Now, he was a permanent resident in the tiny room of his own creation.

Alice deserved so much more than the chaos he would bring to her life. Without disturbing her, he slipped from the bed and got dressed. He reached out to caress her face but stopped short. His hand lingered close to her cheek; her strong, magnetic glow of warmth drew him closer. How he craved to touch her soft skin one last time. His ocean-blue eyes could no longer hold back the wall of water. A heavy tear fell, hitting his hand and bouncing a tiny droplet onto her cheek. She stirred but did not wake. Harper withdrew his hand and quietly walked out of the hotel room.

After taking a taxi back to his caravan in Beadlam, he started to sort through his things. He stuffed what little he had in the way of personal belongings into a holdall. He needed to leave this place, get as far away as he could, but where would he go? Harper viciously grabbed the holdall and threw it against the window, roaring at the top of his voice. An inferno of agony, a deep and relentless pain, flowed through his entire body. He slumped to his knees and punched the floor. If there was a hell, his journey was only half complete. Perhaps it was time to go the rest of the way.

A loud knock woke him. He jumped up from the floor and walked over to the door, pushing it open. Numerous young children, mostly boys in various stages of decomposition, were standing outside the caravan. Their tattered and threadbare clothes dangled from their bodies – some with shoes, some without.

'Help us!' they said in unison.

He stumbled backwards in shock and fell on his backside. The front door swung shut. *What the hell was that?* Another loud knock followed.

'Go away!' he shouted.

'Oh, that's a nice way to greet someone.'

'Elaine!' Unsettled and dubious, he clambered to his feet. 'The door's open.'

Relieved to see her enter the caravan, Harper brushed past her to look outside. There was nothing there. He pulled the door closed but remained troubled by what he'd seen. *Was it real?*

'What's the matter?' Elaine asked.

'It doesn't matter. It's nothing.'

'It's hardly nothing! You look like you've seen a ghost.'

'You could be right about that,' he said.

'Have you been taking your medication?'

'Of course.'

'What happened?'

Harper shook his head. 'Nothing. It was a dream, that's all. I'd just woken when you knocked.'

'You do look tired,' she said.

He walked over to the sink. 'I'm making tea. Do you want a cup?'

'I wouldn't say no,' she said, sitting on the sofa.

He yawned. 'What's the time, anyway?'

'Half six or thereabouts. Heavy night, was it?' Elaine smiled.

His lack of sleep from their trip to London must have caught up with him. That and the stress. 'You could say that.'

'Do I get any details?'

'No.'

Elaine noticed his holdall on the sofa next to her. She peeked inside to see some of his clothes, underwear, his toothbrush, and a flannel. 'What's with the bag? Going somewhere?'

'Maybe. I don't know.'

'Harper, tell me what's wrong?'

He stared out of the window above the sink, his mind a cavern of darkness and despondency.

'Did something happen at the wedding, with you and Alice?'

'Elaine, stop. Please, just stop with all the questions. Everything is fine,' he answered as he poured the tea, brought it over, and sat down beside her. 'So what brings you to my *bedlam*?' he asked, using a pun about the name of the village where he lived to mask the seriousness of his quandary.

'You know that's not how it's pronounced.' She sipped her tea. 'Anyway, I came to see you about something I might need your help with.'

'Sounds intriguing.'

'For the last three years, I've been paying someone to find the man who took and killed Charlie. Well – he's getting close. It turns out this man has killed more children. I've given my guy one more week to find him. If he doesn't, he'll tell the police everything he knows and let them handle it.'

Harper placed his cup on the small table in front of them. 'Why not hand over what you've discovered to the police now?'

He took her prolonged silence as an answer to his question. 'Oh! I get it. You want to kill him yourself. I don't mean to sound insincere, Elaine, because I know how much you want this man, but are you out of your fucking mind? Have you already forgotten what happened at the hotel?'

'No, of course not. That's why I need your help.'

'You had my help then, but it still went wrong, didn't it?' He rose from the chair, went over to the sink, and gazed once again out of the window.

'Please, Harper. It may come to nothing. I'm asking for this one last favour before you go wherever it is you're going. One week. Just wait one more week. Your passport and other documents will be here by then. You'll be a new person with a new life and a new beginning.'

After a brief pause, he muttered, 'Only when the embers have been extinguished should you walk away from the fire.'

'What is that, some kind of saying?'

'I don't know. It's what a patient at Rampton Hospital used to repeat on a daily basis. He probably read it in some fire safety guide. But he compared embers to traumatic memories – that you need to deal with them, not walk away and leave them to smoulder and spread. Only now do I understand what he meant.'

In the field outside the window, the young dead children stared back at him. Somehow, he knew the boys were connected to Charlie. 'What are the chances of your guy finding the killer?'

'I'd have to say high. He's pretty resourceful, not to mention relentless.'

'Okay. If he finds him, I'll help you.' Harper turned to Elaine as she jumped up from the sofa and threw her arms around him.

'Thank you,' she said, laying her head on his shoulder. 'You know, it doesn't matter who you think you are – you'll always be my little brother.'

She pulled back with a smile, fetched her cup from the table, and finished her tea. 'Right, I'd better get a move on,' she said.

'You off home?' he asked, glancing out of the window to where the children had been standing. They were gone.

'Fat chance. I promised I'd call in to see Lila. I've barely seen her since the day of the wedding. I can't keep putting her off.'

Not in the mood to sit around all day, Harper went for a walk, took in the country air, and contemplated his next move. He received a text message from Alice.

> I missed you this morning. Hope you're okay. I
> just wanted to thank you for being my plus one last
> night. You were a big hit with my family. Talk soon.
> xx

Even in his current state of mind, her simple text message brought a smile to his face. By leaving or doing something worse, he would never have to face up to disappointing her. Now he'd be here for at least another week. He could never come close to imagining how she would feel if she discovered the truth about him or how *he* would feel for possibly destroying her life if it ever came out. She'd be known as the woman who'd slept with one of the UK's most notorious killers. The thought of not seeing her again tore him apart, but for her sake, he needed to keep away. Without replying, he turned off his phone and put it back in his pocket. It was for the best.

At the end of the road, he saw a pub and made straight for it. He entered, ordered a pint of beer, and sat at a table in the corner. A quiet drink in a country pub. He'd walked past the premises a few times and, until now, had never ventured inside. Until Alice came along, he'd kept his promise to Elaine and stayed away from public places. Not far from where he sat was a well-used pool table that nobody seemed interested in. When he'd finished his pint, he went to the bar, ordered a second, and returned to his seat. On a nearby table, a young couple in their early twenties quietly argued. The more heated the argument became, the louder their voices grew, attracting stares from several customers standing at the bar.

'What are you staring at?' the young man shouted.

As the couple stood to leave, the man locked eyes with Harper. 'You got a problem, you tosser?'

Harper didn't respond and turned away. Clearly rattled, the man shook off his girlfriend's attempt to stop him from going towards Harper. He placed his hands on the table and leaned over until his face was barely an inch from Harper's, who remained calm and continued to stare straight ahead, avoiding eye contact.

'Did you want to say something to me?' the man snarled.

'I think you should leave,' said Harper, without turning to face the young man.

'Are you gonna make me?'

'I think you should leave now, boy.'

'Boy! Did you just call me a fucking boy, you old cunt?' Further provoked, he straightened up and removed his hands from the table. 'How about I break your fucking neck?'

Harper remained completely still and didn't say another word. *Rage* – it had ignited. The man's aggression only added fuel to the fire that burned within. He lifted his glass to his lips and gulped down some beer in a futile attempt to cool down his inner furnace. He calmly placed the glass back on the table. The people at the bar, including the landlord, pretended to go about their business as if nothing was going on, each one taking a subtle glance over before quickly turning away, not wanting to get involved.

'That's what I thought,' said the young man, further aggravated by Harper's lack of movement or response. He reached out a hand and, with his index finger, tipped Harper's pint glass over and backed away from the table.

Beer splashed onto Harper's lap, and yet he kept his cool. The pub had been fairly quiet when he walked in, but now you could hear a pin drop. The reaction of the patrons made Harper wonder if it wasn't the first time they'd witnessed this kind of behaviour from this yob. Harper rose from his seat, his blue jeans soaked through around the crotch area.

The thug laughed. 'Oh, look at the poor old man. It looks as though he's pissed himself.' He stepped towards Harper.

'You stupid little prick,' said Harper, stepping out from behind the table to confront him.

The thug punched Harper in the face and knocked him off balance. Harper was quick to recover and advance. His outstretched hand grasped the young man's neck and tightened around his throat, lifting him from his feet and carrying him until his back smacked against the oak-panelled wall. His face turned bright red as Harper hoisted him higher.

Out of the corner of his eye, Harper saw the glimmer of a silver blade in the man's hand, coming down at him. The blade tore through the cloth of his sweatshirt and penetrated his left shoulder. Agony forced Harper to release his grip. The youngster dropped to the floor, coughing and struggling for breath. Not allowing him time to recover, Harper kicked him in the face. The man's nose exploded, and blood splattered the wall and carpet; his nose was bent out of shape.

Harper reached down, grabbed his shirt, and dragged him away from the wall. Sitting astride the man's chest, he punched him several times in the face. A woman shouted for him to stop, breaking his concentrated anger. He looked up and saw the anxious faces of patrons and the thug's young girlfriend a few feet away, staring at him.

Undeterred and back on his feet, Harper dragged the man along the floor towards the pool table, lifted him up, and laid him across the table. He fetched a pool cue from the rack and whacked the thick end of the cue against the man's ribs.

'Please!' shouted his girlfriend.

Interrupted again, Harper moved to the end of the table, turned the cue horizontally, and pressed it hard against the man's throat.

Groping for the cue, he rasped and hacked for words and finally said, 'I'm sorry.'

Harper eased the pressure on his neck. 'What was that?'

'I'm sorry.'

Removing the cue, Harper stepped back from the pool table, trembling with fury, his eyes fixed on the man. 'Not good enough,' he said, lunging forward and bringing the cue down on the young man's face. About to do so again—

'Please, stop!' cried his girlfriend.

Harper observed a terrified young girl with tears streaming down her cheeks. He couldn't understand her sympathy for such an animal. Was the strength of real love unconditional? Surely not for someone who was cruel and violent.

He glanced at every face in the room. Their eyes were solely focused on him, with varying expressions of disapproval. Although he hadn't started the brawl, there appeared to be a general air of condemnation for *his* actions, and *not* for the brutish behaviour of the young man who had callously stuck a knife in his shoulder. A figure of perplexity, Harper placed the cue on the table next to the battered young man.

Stepping out from behind the bar, the landlord said, 'You should go before the police get here.'

With a faint nod of his head, Harper eyed the knife handle protruding from his shoulder. He walked back to where he had been sitting and reached under the table for the empty pint glass, which, bizarrely, he handed to the landlord.

The landlord grabbed a beer towel from the bar and proceeded to wipe the glass. 'You were never here,' he said, setting the glass on the bar. He then walked to the pool table, picked up the cue, and wiped it down before placing it back on the rack among the others.

Heading towards the exit, Harper paused next to the tearful girlfriend and said, 'You could do better,' then continued on his way out of the door.

When he arrived at the caravan, he found Alice waiting for him on the steps outside. She grew concerned when she noticed the blood on his shirt, followed by the knife in his shoulder, and hurried towards him.

'What the hell has happened to you?' She helped him up the steps and into the caravan. Not that he needed help; he didn't seem fazed at all, which bothered her somewhat.

'Some idiot in the pub pulled a knife on me.'

'He didn't just pull a knife,' she said. 'He stuck it in you.' Alice made him sit at the table. 'I think we should go to the hospital and call the police.'

'No, I don't want to make a fuss. Anyway, it's not a big knife. I'll just pull it out.' He reached up for it, only to see his hand batted away by Alice.

'The size of it is not the point. I'm sure you're not supposed to just *yank* out a knife by yourself.'

There was absolutely no way Harper could involve the police, which automatically ruled out a visit to the hospital. He pointed to a kitchen drawer a few feet away. 'There are some clean tea towels in that drawer. Could you get them for me, please?'

'I really think you should let me drive you to the hospital.'

His reply came in the form of a blank stare.

Knowing he wasn't going to do as she suggested, Alice placed her hands on her hips, huffed, and went to fetch the towels.

'Right, for this next bit, I probably will need your help,' he said.

'No, Simon, I can't do that,' she answered, guessing what he wanted her to do.

'Please, Alice,' he asked as she put the towels on the table in front of him.

She frowned and shook her head. 'I can't believe I'm agreeing to this.' She stood behind him. 'Okay, how should I do it? Do I pull it out quickly or slowly?'

'Keep it straight and just ease it out nice and slowly. Then quickly help me get this shirt off.'

Alice remained apprehensive as she wrapped her hand around the knife handle. Forming a grimace on his face, Harper yelled through gritted teeth as she started to ease the blade free. She tossed the knife onto the table and immediately grabbed his sweatshirt, pulling the material over his head and freeing his arms. Blood flowed from the wound. She reached for a towel, folded it, and pressed it hard against his shoulder. Harper placed his hand on top of hers, where it stayed for a minute or so.

'You can take your hand away now,' he said.

She carefully removed her hand from under his. Harper got to his feet and ambled over to the sink. He turned on the cold tap and leaned over, soaking his shoulder to clean the injury. He did this for a couple of minutes, giving Alice plenty of time to search his phone for Elaine's number, which she entered into her phone.

'Can you pass me another towel?' he asked, turning off the tap. Before he had the chance to turn, Alice was already there, pressing a clean towel against his shoulder.

'Let's get you settled in the bedroom, and I'll go out and buy some bandages,' she said.

He sat on the bed with his legs up and his back pressed against the headboard to keep pressure on the wound.

She pulled her keys from her pocket and marched towards the door. 'Right, I won't be long.'

'Alice,' he said, stopping her in her stride. 'Thank you.'

24

Elaine

Lila lived with her children in the lovely end-of-terrace house she had inherited from her mother. They made polite small talk on their way through the house to the kitchen, where Lila stopped to make coffee and Elaine continued out into the garden. Following the horrendous events at Sablefall Farm, the relationship between the pair had been strained; however, things had improved significantly over the past year. The basis of the tension was the body of Lila's missing husband turning up on Elaine's property. At one point, they could barely raise their eyes to each other, let alone exchange a word. A conversation was needed, but both were at a loss about how to begin one. The situation was hard to read and difficult to navigate, and Elaine left Lila alone to grieve with her children, considering whether she even wanted to learn the truth.

Although Lila knew her husband had been killed by Harper Darmody, it remained unclear to her why he had gone to Elaine's house in the first place. He had no reason to be there, and it left her feeling ambivalent. She certainly didn't want to believe they were having an affair, and it made her physically sick to think of her husband and best friend together. She had tried so hard to bury the notion of such betrayal, but it was no good – the thought always found its way back into her mind. It had to be dealt with.

When the time finally came, Elaine wasn't surprised when she opened the front door to see a stern-faced Lila. Elaine had prepared for the moment but had not planned on telling her the truth, thinking it would be unpleasant for Lila to hear about her husband's constant lewd behaviour towards her. However, when she came face to face with her friend, it wasn't lies that spilled from her mouth but the truth; from her confrontation with Ashton in the upstairs bathroom on the day of Lila's barbecue to his assault against her on the doorstep of her home on the night he was killed.

Lila believed every single word; she knew her husband and what he was capable of. She went on to tell Elaine about all the crazy thoughts that had gone through her mind, and with everything out in the open, things were soon back to normal and their friendship was stronger than ever. Lila also admitted that once she was over the shock of Ashton's death, she had become serene and happier – so much so that she was riddled with guilt. Elaine reassured her that she had nothing to feel guilty about.

Lila brought two cups of coffee out to the garden, where Elaine was relaxing in the evening sun. 'You were saying?' she said.

Puzzled, Elaine couldn't recall the conversation she'd started upon entering the house.

Lila reminded her. 'Something about cats.'

'Oh yes. I had a meeting in Nottingham and popped into one of those cafés with cats strolling about the place.'

'You lucky thing. I've always wanted to go to one of those.'

'I'm not sure what to make of them. Some of the cats seem happy and sit on your lap, while others appear fairly anxious.'

'You'd think cats in a café would be against some kind of food hygiene law, wouldn't you?' said Lila.

'Yes. But then again, I bet they keep the mice away.'

Lila soon steered the conversation in a different direction. 'Are you going to tell me then?'

'About?' Elaine acted clueless.

Lila glared at Elaine. 'You know what!'

'Oh, the bruises. I fell down some stairs in an unsafe property I was viewing. I should have been more careful.'

'Yes, you should. Why do you keep taking risks in those old buildings? One day, you're going to break a leg or worse.'

'It's my job!'

'Can't you get someone else to view the properties?'

'The newer ones, yes, but I love to view the older buildings. They have history and many tales to tell. It's sad that I have to decide whether the purchase of the property is worth the cost of renovating.'

After a further discussion about their children and how Lila's son was playing the role of Bill Sikes in a school production of *Oliver*, Elaine said, 'Oh, I have something I want to show you.' She reached into her pocket and placed a tarnished silver-plated St Christopher necklace on the table.

Lila glanced at the item. 'Other than a tatty piece of jewellery, what am I looking at?'

Elaine smiled. 'You don't remember it, do you?'

Lila thought for a moment before it came to her. 'It's not?'

'It is.'

'No way.' Lila picked up the necklace. 'I gave you this when we were children. I can't believe you've kept it all this time.'

'I found it in my old keepsake box the other day. I'd forgotten I'd held onto it. I was reminded of when I was taken away after my mother's death. Night after night, I'd kiss the St Christopher and pray your mother would bring you to see me. The children's home was such an unforgiving place, and I missed you so much. As time went on, I realised you weren't coming. I took it off and put it away in a small shoebox, along with some other bits and pieces of my past life.'

Clearly overwhelmed, Lila had tears in her eyes. She jumped out of her chair and threw her arms around Elaine. As Lila pulled away, Elaine attempted to conceal her own tears. How she wished to confide in her friend about what had happened at the hotel, but opening up about one thing would inevitably lead to so many other questions she'd be unable to answer.

'Are you okay?' asked Lila, seeing Elaine wipe a tear from the corner of her eye, perhaps sensing something deeper.

'Yeah, I'm fine. I do, however, need to ask a favour.'

'Elaine, you know I'd do anything for you, anything.'

'If something were to happen to me, I'd appreciate it if you could check on my children now and then – make sure they are okay, that sort of thing?'

'Oh my God, something *is* wrong. Are you unwell?'

'No, nothing like that. Everything is fine. I just think I should have plans in place if, well, you know. It's not as if my life has been without tragedy, and there is no one I trust more to watch over my children.'

Lenny's unspoken suggestion about Joseph Webster coming to find her had struck a nerve. Having already asked Harper to help meant she was taking his warning seriously, especially after recently discovering how things don't always go according to plan.

'I'd be honoured to keep a watchful eye over Michael and Emily, but to be honest, I reckon your tragic days are behind you. You don't deserve any more pain.'

'Sadly, we don't always get what we deserve.'

*

Tom had dozed off in the armchair while Michael and Emily were sitting at either end of the sofa watching one of the many *Pirates of the Caribbean* movies on the television. Elaine observed them from the doorway, out of sight. Michael's attention drifted between his phone and the film, while Emily appeared completely engrossed in the on-screen action.

Elaine walked along the hall to the kitchen, grabbed a large round bowl from the cupboard, and filled it with a giant bag of sweet and salty popcorn. Her phone vibrated, and she retrieved it from her pocket. An unknown caller, but she answered anyway.

'Hello.'

'Hi, is that Elaine?' asked a softly spoken voice.

'That's me.'

'It's Alice, *Simon's friend*. I'm really sorry to bother you, but—'

'Has something happened?' Elaine was quick to assume the worst.

'No, he seems fine, but he was involved in some kind of altercation in a pub earlier and received a knife wound to the shoulder.'

'Oh my God! Is he hurt badly? Did he go to the hospital?' Elaine asked, hoping he hadn't.

'That's actually why I'm calling. I've given him some strong painkillers, cleaned the wound, and bandaged it for him, but I think he should get it looked at properly and have some stitches. He's sleeping now and doesn't know I'm calling you. I'm worried about him and thought it best to let you know. I don't understand why he won't go to the hospital.'

'Hates them,' Elaine replied quickly. 'Has done ever since he was a child. Are you with him now?'

'Yes. I thought it best to stay over, but I do have to leave early in the morning.'

'You're very kind to stay the night. Leave when you have to, and I'll pop by and check on him. You did the right thing by calling me.'

Alice breathed a sigh of relief over the phone. 'You don't know how pleased I am to hear you say that.'

'Thank you for letting me know, Alice.'

'No problem. Erm, one more thing – other than his shoulder, is Simon okay?'

'I think so. Why do you ask?' Elaine worried that Harper had said something he shouldn't have or that Alice had found out something about him.

'It's just that last night at the wedding reception, he was fine and appeared to be having a great time – then out of nowhere, his mood quickly went downhill. And this morning, he left the hotel before I woke. He didn't reply to my texts or calls, which is unlike him – and now this.'

Relieved it wasn't about something more serious, Elaine couldn't think why Harper would be acting so strangely. She thought back to their conversation earlier in the day – about the bag he'd packed and how he didn't want to talk about what was wrong. With recent events and the changes going on in his mind and life, it was difficult to pinpoint any one thing in particular.

'I can't think of anything off the top of my head. I'll have a word with him in the morning and see if I can get him to open up.'

'Thank you, Elaine.'

'No problem. I'll talk to you soon.'

'Okay. Bye.'

Elaine put her phone on the worktop and carried the bowl of popcorn through to the living room. Michael and Emily looked pleased to see her as she plonked herself down on the sofa between them. The children reached out to help themselves to popcorn.

'Oi! This is mine. Go and get your own,' Elaine teased.

Emily snuggled into her mum, and Elaine placed her arm protectively around her daughter.

25

The Boy

They had stared at one another for what seemed like hours, neither boy prepared to drop his gaze. So far, no words had been exchanged. Danny hadn't slept at all, patiently waiting for his new roommate to come around. He didn't have to wait too long, and when the boy finally opened his eyes, he was clearly terrified. Danny knew the feeling all too well.

When the boy saw Danny on the bed, he scrambled backwards until he hit the wall. His eyes scanned the room to take in his new surroundings and soon fell upon the axe on the floor next to Danny's bed. Seconds later, he caught sight of the one close to him by the table. He scurried across the floor, grabbed it, and quickly retreated to his spot.

While the boy slept, Danny refrained from touching the axe by his bed. That's not to say it hadn't crossed his mind more than once to do what the man had suggested and kill the boy in his sleep. Freedom and the thought of going home were a tempting proposition, but he soon talked himself out of such wickedly evil thoughts. Once the boy had picked up the axe, though reluctant, Danny had little choice but to do the same.

The door to the room opened, and the man entered with two identical trays containing an apple, a sandwich wrapped in cling film, and a bottle of water. He glanced in turn at the boys and, seeing the hatchets in their hands, smiled. 'I suspected it might take a while for the gravity of the situation to sink in.'

The man placed one tray on the table and walked towards the trembling boy in the corner, who clung to his blanket as tightly as he held the axe. He knelt down, placed the second tray close to the new boy's feet, and studied him in silence for a moment.

'There is no doubt in my mind that Danny boy over there *will* eventually come at you. It just takes him a while to accept what he has to do to survive. He certainly has more to gain than you. So, if *you* want to live, don't trust or turn your back on him.'

'He's lying!' said Danny. 'He has no intention of letting you live.'

The man smirked and said, 'Watch your back.'

He collected the tray from the table and walked over to Danny. 'Remember you asked if there was a time limit? Well, now there is. I'm going to be gone for a while, and when I return, I expect to see only one of you alive.' He placed the tray on the bed. 'Make your food last, boys,' he said on his way up the steps, closing the door to the room behind him.

Danny listened until he heard the distinctive slam of what he assumed to be the main door. The man had gone.

Hours passed, and so far, the boys had only moved to bring their trays closer, eat a piece of fruit, and drink some water. Danny was desperate to use the toilet, and after holding it in for at least half an hour, he could wait no longer. He thought about taking the axe with him, but not wanting the boy to be afraid of him or to believe what the man had said, he left it on the bed. By constantly holding the axe, how could he gain his new companion's trust?

The new boy watched his every move as he ambled over to the toilet. If the boy attacked him now, it would mean certain death – a risk he was willing to take. With his back to him, he wondered if the boy was considering his advantage. In any case, it was too late now. The clinking of the boy's chain indicated movement.

Thwack!

Danny's heart thumped. He dropped to the floor with a twist to instinctively protect himself and see what was happening. The boy swung his axe.

Thwack!

'What are you doing?' asked Danny.

'What does it look like? I'm trying to break the chain.' He swung the axe again. The clanking sound of metal on metal echoed around the room. The boy examined where he'd struck the chain – a link had become wedged in the floorboard.

Danny got to his feet. 'Did it work?'

The boy yanked the chain to free the link from the floor. 'No,' he said. 'It hasn't even made a dent.' He sat down and sipped his water.

His heart still racing, Danny flushed the toilet, washed his hands in the sink, and sat on the edge of the bed. He was relieved the boy didn't seem to be a threat.

'Is it true?' asked the boy. 'Is the man going to kill me?'

Danny nodded mournfully, a sinking feeling in his stomach as tears formed in the other boy's eyes. 'He wants *me* to kill you, and if I don't, *he* will.'

'Why does he want you to kill me?'

'He told me if I kill you, I could go home.'

'Do you think he means it?'

'I don't know. I doubt it.'

'Why don't you do it?' asked the boy.

'And give him what he wants? I don't want to be like him.'

'Why is he doing this to us?'

'Because he can. He's a monster,' said Danny.

The boy couldn't suppress his feelings any longer and started to cry. 'I don't want to die!'

Danny had no response to his roommate's heartbreaking statement. Anything he said would be of little comfort. Unless they were saved, the boy would die.

Leaving the axe on the bed, Danny walked over and sat beside him. 'What's your name?' he asked, putting his arm around the boy.

'Connor.'

'There is still time for us to be saved, Connor.'

'How?' Connor looked up expectantly with tear-stained eyes, his chest rising and falling with every heavy sob.

'A policeman was here, but the man killed him. He'll surely be missed, and there is a good chance they'll track him to this very place.'

'But we could be somewhere else by now,' said Connor.

Bemused by his comment, Danny asked, 'What do you mean, somewhere else?'

Connor pulled back from Danny and turned to face him. 'You don't know, do you?'

'Know what?'

'When he was carrying me, I glimpsed through a hole in the blanket . . . we are on a boat.'

Danny fell silent, thinking – the noise of water below – the rumbling sound of an engine. *Drive*! The man said something about Ozias letting him drive. It all made sense. How had he not worked it out before now?

Danny got to his feet and paced the room. 'Are we on the sea?'

'No. It looked more like a small river. I saw another boat going by. One of those long ones.'

'Like the ones you see on a canal?'

'Yes! Exactly like one of those.'

Danny was bursting with a renewed sense of hope; adrenaline surged through his veins. Boats like these were made of wood. They could use the axes to cut a hole in the side of the boat and signal for help. Danny hastened over to the bed, grabbed the axe, and stood on the mattress. He plunged the axe into the padded material.

Connor soon guessed what he was doing and joined him. The boys repeatedly swung their axes against the padded wall, tearing away the material until the axes made a clanging sound. Danny tore away the material with his hands and uncovered a sheet of metal underneath. Despite their frustration, the boys kept pounding their axes against the metal, making dents but failing to break through. Tired and getting nowhere, they stopped and sat on the bed with their backs to the wall.

Desperate to cling to his newfound hope, Danny turned to Connor and said, 'Somehow, the policeman knew to search for a boat on a canal. He must have told someone. We could be saved at any moment.'

'What if he didn't? What if no one is coming?'

Danny hated to admit defeat, but reluctantly, he had to accept that Connor could be right. If the policeman had told someone, then surely more police would have come by now. He buried his head in his hands, then sat upright and said, 'What if we kill him?'

His comment took Connor by surprise. 'But how?'

Danny held the axe in front of him. 'We have weapons. We just need to work out a plan before he gets back.'

26

Lenny

The nearest train station to The Moorhen pub was Harlow Town. Lenny deemed it the best place to begin his search. Olivia had scanned the image of Joseph Webster onto photographic paper for him to show to staff and random passengers, and after a couple of hours, nobody had recognised the man in the picture. He left his car and boarded a train to Harlow Mill, then on to Sawbridgeworth, continuing right up to Bishop's Stortford. It seemed pointless to go any further north, as there was nothing to suggest the killer had ventured that far, so he headed back down the line towards Harlow.

Not far into his journey, uncertainty set in, and he considered whether it was a waste of time searching the stations. What were the chances of bumping into Webster again, let alone finding someone who might recognise a man from an eight-year-old photo? The air of confidence he had set out with had burst, and he accepted this was far too big a job to do by himself.

Resting his head against the window, the lush green countryside drifted past. Every now and then, he would catch a glimpse of the River Stort as it twisted and turned its way through the grassland, its path inextricably linked with the railway tracks. At one point, the river passed underneath the train as it crossed a bridge. Lenny watched as the narrowboats gracefully nosed their way through the water.

Lenny sprang upright and observed the river fade into the distance and then curl back towards the train. There was another way for the killer to travel between Harlow and London, and he hadn't considered the waterways as a possibility – until now. Colin had touched on it in his notes, but what kind of criminal would choose such a leisurely mode of transport? A quick getaway would be impossible. On the other hand, that could be how the killer had managed to go unnoticed for so long. As the train pulled into Harlow Town station and the narrowboats came into view by The Moorhen car park, he remained on board.

The train passed the Gallery at Parndon Mill, close to where the last body was discovered. After Roydon Station came Roydon Marina, home to plenty of moored boats. Next was Broxbourne, the closest station to the two children Colin had first called him about.

Lenny rode the train down to Enfield Lock, where he departed and took a taxi just over a mile to Smeaton Road, back to the place where it had all started for him – Tumbling Bay. He gave the driver some money and told him to wait.

Sitting where Charlie's body was found, he stared at the river less than forty feet away and recalled his hallucination in the café when Charlie had turned into water. The boy had pointed to the River Lea, telling him where to look. It would have been easy to dispose of bodies under the cover of darkness and with minimal attention. The police either hadn't considered the killer using a boat or, like him, had supposed it very unlikely. Except for Colin, that is, who set about leaving no stone unturned and trekked the paths along the local river, searching the narrowboats.

*

Lenny burst through his front door, rushed straight into the bedroom, and turned on his ancient desktop computer that hadn't been used for some time. While the old girl fired up, he went to the kitchen, poured himself a much-needed whisky, and downed it. He sighed, poured another, and took it with him back to the bedroom, where he slumped into his tatty black leather office chair. Lenny searched for UK canal maps and clicked on a site, examining the map in great detail. Any doubts were now gone; he felt it in his gut, or was that the burning sensation of whisky?

Finding the killer wasn't going to be easy, but it was going to be more straightforward now he knew where to look. He had to work out which direction Webster had gone from Moorhen Marina and how far away he could have got. Next to the keyboard, his phone rang. He sipped his whisky and answered.

Lenny's first hello was a croaky whisper, so he cleared his throat and tried again. 'Hello.'

'Lenny Grey?' a voice queried.

'Yeah, that's me.'

'It's DCI Harry Baxendale.'

'What can I do for you?'

'How's your search going?'

Lenny smiled. 'Since you're calling to ask me, I assume you're not having much luck yourself.'

'Your assumption is correct. Look, nobody knows this case better than you, and DCI Hargreaves clearly knew enough to locate this sick psychopath. I'm guessing you're a lot closer to finding him than we are. I admit I may have been too hasty to dismiss your help. If you have any ideas or suggestions, I'd appreciate your input.'

As much as it usually pleased him to hear a detective squirm, this wasn't one of those times. Children's lives were at stake, and even Elaine had conceded that catching this maniac was more important than her own selfish vengeance.

'I'll tell you what, there is something I'm currently looking into, and if it pans out, I'll be sure to let you know,' said Lenny, knowing he might not be able to keep that promise. It would depend on whether Elaine still wanted to deal with the killer herself, which he was almost certain she would.

'Can't you tell me what it is now?'

'I think it's best I check it out first. I wouldn't want to waste your time.'

'Fair enough, but you should know – another boy is missing.'

Lenny fell silent. The abduction of yet another boy hit him hard. He took a swig of whisky to help quell the blow and asked, 'When and where was he taken?'

'The night before last from a campsite in Hoddesdon. The parents were in one tent, their two sons in another. Their youngest got scared and chose to sleep with his parents, leaving the older boy on his own. The father went to wake him in the morning, but he'd vanished. So he could have been taken at any time within a seven-hour window.'

'What's the name of the campsite?'

'Lee Valley Recreational Park, Dobbs Weir.'

'Okay, if I find out anything, I'll get back to you.'

'Lenny, be careful – and don't do anything foolish.'

Lenny hung up and immediately searched on Google Maps. He found the park mentioned by the DCI and saw that it ran directly alongside the canal. He picked up his phone and called the detective back.

'That was quick,' said Harry.

Lenny asked, 'Have you thoroughly searched the canal and the undergrowth around the recreational park?'

'Why would I do that, and what would I be searching for?'

'The body of Daniel Logan.'

'The other missing boy. What makes you think he's dead?'

'If the killer has taken another boy, it's unlikely the Logan kid is still alive.'

'I do hope that's not the case, Lenny. Unlike you, I can't afford to make assumptions. So, until we have some firm evidence to suggest otherwise, I won't be searching for a body. Anyway, I don't have the resources. As well as taking over from DCI Hargreaves, I'm also heading a team investigating the murders of five men over the past two and a half years, and the only lead I have is a dodgy CCTV image of a woman and a witness photofit resembling the man who almost killed you three years ago.'

'Harper Darmody? No chance. That's surely a coincidence.'

'That's what I thought, but regardless of how unbelievable it might sound, I don't have the luxury of not following up leads when presented with witness evidence. Besides, after the last two murders, I can't entirely rule it out.'

'What do you mean?'

'I can't talk about all this over the phone,' said Harry.

Lenny took the bait. 'Fancy a pint?'

In less than an hour, the pair met up at a pub in Stratford called The Cow. While Harry got the drinks, Lenny browsed through the menu and made a mental note to bring Olivia here at some point. It was perhaps a little too *gastropub* for his liking, but he knew she would love it.

At first, the detective attempted to get Lenny to disclose what he was looking into regarding Joseph Webster, but Lenny had a way of manipulating the conversation to suit his own needs. He took a sip of his lager and got straight to the point.

'So come on, Harry. Talk to me. What's got you thinking that Darmody is still knocking about?'

'This can go no further, Len. If we're going to get along and occasionally share information that's beneficial to both of us, then we need to trust each other.'

'I completely agree,' said Lenny with a wry smile.

'I'm serious, mate.'

'Oh, I'm only messing. I know how this works. Colin and I worked together for years.'

Harry took a sip of Guinness and wiped the froth from his top lip. 'First up was Denley Parker.'

'Yeah, I remember reading about his murder in the papers,' said Lenny. 'Pretty gruesome.'

'Then came Alan Whitehall.'

'Let me guess the third – Malcolm Hayes?'

'How did you know?' asked Harry.

'Three well-to-do blokes all killed in such a brutal and calculated way. I can see why you'd think it was the work of the same killer, but how does that bring you to Harper Darmody? He was an animal, a psychopath – more your spur-of-the-moment kind of guy. Not exactly a man with a plan,' said Lenny, taking another swig of lager.

'I agree, and he wouldn't have even been on the radar if not for the murder of Sir Edward Horner and Peter Stafford.'

'The Home Secretary? What a load of old cobblers! You've been watching too many conspiracy movies.'

'Former Home Secretary,' Harry corrected him. 'Now, do you want to hear me out or not?'

Lenny smiled. 'Yeah, go on. I'm game.' He rested his elbows on the table.

'Their murders were violent and aggressive. It was a frenzied attack – the kind committed by someone whose mind had snapped.'

'There are plenty of nutcases out there, Harry. I get you're under pressure from above, but you can't just pin all these murders on a ghost because you have no evidence.'

'If you let me finish, I'll get to the bloody point.'

Lenny sat back in his chair and folded his arms.

'Edward's father was Judge Lawrence Horner, and guess who that judge was known to be close friends with? Denley Parker.'

Harry Baxendale finally had Lenny's attention. Not even *he* could dismiss such a strong link as pure coincidence, but he was eagerly waiting to find out where Harper Darmody fitted into all this.

'I examined a lot of CCTV footage from the hotel after being told Sir Edward was seen in the bar talking to a woman called Dr Rowan Heder, which, incidentally, happens to be an anagram of Edward Horner.'

Lenny reached inside his pocket for his pen and notepad and wrote down the name. 'So it is.' He smiled. 'How clever.'

Harry pulled out a scanned picture. 'Witnesses identified this woman.' He placed it on the table.

Not the best image, but Lenny instantly knew it was Elaine. Though taken by surprise, he played it down. 'Who am I looking at?'

'Are you honestly trying to tell me you don't recognise her?'

Lenny picked up the picture and examined it closely, shaking his head. 'It's quite blurry, and she does have her head slightly turned away from the camera, but no, I can't say I do,' he said in a nonchalant manner, placing the picture back on the table.

A smile crossed the detective's face. 'So you don't see Elaine Burgess in that picture?'

'That's not Elaine.' Lenny laughed and picked it up again, pretending to look closer. He then tossed it back on the table. 'No! Definitely not her. What are you up to, Harry? This is ridiculous. Are you seriously trying to suggest Elaine Davis – sorry, Burgess – killed these two men?'

'Not necessarily on her own,' said Harry. 'Take a look at this.' He passed him the reconstructed picture of a man who looked similar to Harper Darmody.

As soon as Lenny saw the face, his blood boiled. Not because of his own run-in with Harper, but because Elaine had lied to him all this time. He did his utmost to conceal his anger from the detective, which wasn't an easy thing to do.

Lenny handed back the picture. 'Nope! Again, I can't see the resemblance. This could be anyone.'

'Okay. If you say so,' said Harry.

'This is all complete nonsense. You can't possibly think Elaine and Harper are going around bumping people off.' Lenny didn't want to believe what he was hearing, mostly because it wasn't something he'd considered until now.

'I read your book. The names other than Elaine and her brother might be fictional, but the accounts are based on their abuse at the hands of their father, who went on to invite others from his grotesque circle to join him. One such person being—'

'Denley Parker!' said Lenny.

Harry didn't bother to acknowledge that he was correct and continued. 'I believe all of these men were there on the night you described in the book when Elaine put a hayfork through her father's neck. Except for Peter Stafford – he was collateral damage, but from the stories I've heard, he got what he deserved. They all did. One person I haven't mentioned yet is Elaine's former psychiatrist, Dr Graham Walker. It's no coincidence he took a leap down a flight of stairs in Symi at the exact same time Elaine was there on her honeymoon.'

'You know, it's funny,' said Lenny as he took a long swig of his pint. 'Earlier, you spoke of trust and shared information, yet when I called you back, you tricked me into meeting you tonight so you could get me to identify your suspects. You knew I'd ask to meet up when you dangled the carrot at the other end of the phone.'

'Do you maintain that it isn't Elaine in the CCTV image?'

'It's definitely not her.'

Harry sipped his Guinness and said, 'Okay.'

The small space across the table between them seemed like miles. Both men knew the truth, but out of sheer loyalty, only one of them had reason to refute the other's claims.

'What are you going to do?' Lenny asked, breaking the short silence.

'As I said, those men had it coming – either by taking part in the abuse or helping to suppress the truth from coming out. I know something bad happened back then. That much is obvious. There is no hard evidence to suggest that any of what I've said is correct. It's pretty much all circumstantial. Even though I believe the book is an accurate account, I'm sure if it came to it, you'd say most of your novel is fictional – but murder is murder, Lenny, and as a detective, it's my job to investigate. I will be heading up to Helmsley with a colleague to ask Mrs Burgess a few questions tomorrow afternoon. It wouldn't hurt if she were given a heads-up that a certain DCI is going to pay her a visit.'

Harry downed the rest of his pint and stood to leave. Before doing so, he leaned down, placing his lips close to Lenny's ear. 'Trust and shared information, Lenny. I'm not interested in Elaine . . . but I can't say the same about her brother. He murdered innocent people, and that is something I am concerned about.' Harry straightened up. 'Talk to you soon,' he said, and casually walked towards the exit.

Lenny processed the conversation with DCI Baxendale. Was Harry someone who could be trusted or not? Difficult to tell. He may have pulled a fast one, trying to get him to identify the siblings, but he also gave him the opportunity to warn Elaine. The lesson he'd learned from their meeting was not to get on the wrong side of the DCI. Harry was clearly an efficient and intelligent detective.

27

Harper

Harper's eyes adjusted to the darkness of the bedroom. Muffled voices from the television at the other end of the caravan suggested Alice was still around. The unbearable ache in his shoulder caused him grief as he moved to get out of bed. He perched on the edge to let the agony subside before ambling towards the sound.

The mellow lighting revealed Alice asleep on the beige sofa, her head resting peacefully on a pillow from the bed. Harper stared and smiled, unsurprised that she had stayed with him. It was her nature to do so. He grimaced in pain as he reached up to a cupboard above the sofa, pulled out a blanket, and carefully covered Alice. Crouching down, he gently swept the hair from her face and let the back of his fingers rest on her soft, warm skin. He walked to the fridge and fetched two small bottles of water; one he opened and drank straight away, while the other he left beside Alice for when she woke. Harper turned off the television and switched off the light on his way back to bed.

Morning came, and Alice had already left. There was a note on the table letting him know Elaine would be coming over at some point. She hoped he wouldn't be upset that she'd called her. He wished she hadn't, but how could he possibly be upset with her? It was nice to have someone other than Elaine caring about him. His air of comfort morphed into sorrow. Whatever his relationship with Alice was, it wasn't going to last much longer. She would be going her way, and he would be going his.

Sitting outside on the steps with a cup of tea in his hand, Harper appeared relaxed and peaceful. The sky gleamed; the veiled sun was on the verge of breaking through the light grey clouds, though it never delivered on its promise. Harper didn't register Elaine's car pulling up nearby. She stood in front of him, but he stared right past her, focusing on the dead children who had gathered outside his caravan, as though waiting for him to do something for them. Their unsettled manifestations skipped, jumped, and ran around playing tag and other games.

'Hey!' Elaine called out.

The children froze on the spot and turned their heads towards the pair. Harper snapped out of his intense gaze. 'Hi! Sorry, I was miles away.'

'You're telling me.' Elaine looked behind her, trying to work out what he was so taken with.

He motioned his cup towards her. 'I suppose you want a cup of tea?'

'Sure! Then you can tell me all about yesterday,' she answered, following closely as they went inside.

'Yeah, Alice let me know she'd told you.'

'And I'm glad she did.'

Harper made the tea and joined her at the table, knowing he was about to get an earful.

Elaine coiled her hands around her cup. 'So, come on, tell me what happened.'

'It was nothing really. Just an argument.'

'You put a young man in hospital,' she argued.

'I didn't start it.'

'Maybe not, but you certainly finished it.'

'How do you know he was taken to hospital?'

'The local shop. Beadlam is a small place, and people gossip.'

'I only wanted a quiet drink. I never went there in search of trouble.'

'That may well be the case, Harper, but trouble always finds you. You need to learn how to avoid it. Every confrontation doesn't have to end with someone seriously hurt or dead.'

'Confrontation isn't easy to avoid when trouble sticks a knife in your shoulder. Anyway, I could have killed him – I didn't. I'd say that's an improvement on my part, wouldn't you?'

'Don't be a smartarse! One minute you say you want to be free of violence, and the next you're having bar brawls down the local. Hardly lying low and changing your life.'

'Just yesterday, you asked me not to leave, and why? Because you want me to help you kill someone. So don't you think you're being a tad hypocritical?'

Her stumped reaction said it all.

'Let me take a look at that shoulder,' she said, briskly changing the subject. As she approached, her phone pinged in her back pocket. She helped pull the shirt over his head and unwrapped the bandage. 'Alice has done a good job. I'm impressed.'

'She was quite intent on making sure it was clean,' he said.

'I meant I'm impressed with her. She's a good woman.'

'Yeah, she is. Far too good for me.'

'At least you're aware of that fact.'

Harper turned to see Elaine smiling. He returned the smile and let her put a new dressing on his shoulder.

'Doesn't mean it couldn't work,' she said.

'It wouldn't be fair. I refuse to weigh her down with my baggage.'

'Then don't. You're starting anew, so leave the baggage behind.'

'You know it's not as easy as that.'

'I do know, but you've been punished enough in this life. Harper Darmody has almost served his purpose, and when the time comes, you need to let him go. Within your grasp is an opportunity most people can only dream of – a chance to hit reset.'

Elaine's words sent his mind into overdrive and his heart rate spiralling. Could it be possible? Was Alice's car breaking down the catalyst for change? With her, he was different. She had a unique ability to lift the heavy burden of guilt from his shoulders.

Elaine applied tape to secure the bandage and said, 'I was wrong and selfish to ask for your help to kill Charlie's murderer. I understand if you've had enough. I don't blame you. I do think you should wait for your new identity, though. As for Alice – if she wants something more, you'd be a fool to let her go. It's not difficult to see the positive effect she's had on you. Anyway, I'd better get back home.' Elaine moved towards the open door and out into the glare of the bright morning sun.

'Elaine?'

She delayed taking the first step down from the caravan but didn't turn to face him.

'You're right about Alice – she is a good woman. Is there a future with her? I don't know. I'll have to wait and see. But I am still going to help you.'

Without saying a word, Elaine continued on her way. Harper watched her projected shadow on the caravan floor slowly withdraw from view.

*

For the rest of the day, Harper hung around the caravan, thinking about what Elaine had said. She'd opened his eyes to the distinct possibility of a new life and encouraged him to seize the opportunity with both hands. Whether Alice would play a major role by his side was out of his control. He could only hope. All these thoughts were new to him: unplanned and unexpected. Could an unanticipated life truly lie ahead? If it did, he vowed to make every moment count.

Harper and Alice had exchanged the odd text throughout the day while she spent some quality time with her parents. By late afternoon, they'd petered out altogether. Her last message had informed him she was about to curl up with a book and have an early night. His phone pinged again just after ten, waking him on the sofa. It was a message from Alice; she was on her way over. Though pleased, he couldn't help but wonder about her sudden change of mind.

Before she arrived, he made a hasty effort to tidy up. Not that it was messy – just a plate on the side and a couple of dented cushions. The headlights of a car beamed through the curtains. Excitedly nervous, he didn't know what to make of all these feelings and emotions he was experiencing for the first time.

Harper opened the door ready for Alice, put the kettle on and prepared two cups. He stood with his back against the work surface and waited. When she appeared in the doorway, his stomach fluttered.

'I wasn't expecting to see you tonight. The kettle's on,' he said. In her hand, he noticed something wrapped inside a carrier bag. A present?

Without a word and just a casual sideways glance, she walked straight over to the table and sat down. She placed the bagged item on the table in front of her and avoided looking in his direction.

Something was different about her. A strange coldness. The tense atmosphere in the room brewed along with the tea. It had never been this way between them.

Strained.

Awkward.

Uncomfortable.

Perhaps she'd chosen this moment to bring an end to whatever this was. Fun, a fling, a relationship? He had no idea. They'd never really discussed feelings and whatnot. Deep down, he always knew she would return to her life. Her career. Why wouldn't she? This was *never* going to be permanent.

His heart thumped. He fought with difficulty to maintain his composure. Uncertainty boiled in his stomach. Worry. Stress. This was similar to how he had felt right before he found Elaine in the hotel room. Standing firm and keeping it together, he carried the tea over to the table and sat opposite her. Her powerful stare invaded his, attempting to burrow into the secret world behind his eyes, searching, reading, examining.

'Is everything okay?' he asked.

Alice opened the bag and placed a book in front of him: a copy of Lenny Grey's novel, *The Dancing Bear*. Harper knew what the book was about but hadn't read it; he couldn't bring himself to. Elaine had warned him away from the story that told of their lives as abused and traumatised children, the ensuing cover-up, and the harrowing aftermath. He couldn't speak, unsure of what to say or what she knew.

'Is this for me?' He picked it up, pretending to have no knowledge of the book. He glanced at the front cover and turned it over to view the back. 'What's it about?'

'Why don't you tell me?' she asked calmly, failing to hide the frailty behind her croaky voice. She sipped her tea in a feeble attempt to appease the dryness in her throat. Her eyes welled quickly, and a tear fell, slowly making its way down her flushed cheek.

Concealed behind his bewildered guise, Harper disliked where this was heading. He thought about trying to maintain the pretence but couldn't lie to Alice. She watched the veil lift from his sunken face. Reality dawned for both of them. Harper got to his feet and walked over to the sofa. He was done. He stood with his back to Alice.

'What do you want to know?' he asked reluctantly.

He waited in silence for the question he expected. The seconds passed like minutes. Perhaps it was a question even Alice didn't want the answer to.

'It's you, isn't it, the character in the book – the brother? Those three scars you have – they are bullet holes. And the woman is Elaine – your sister.' A sad discomfort in her voice betrayed the truth she knew would follow.

'Yes.' He bowed his head in shame and waited for her next words, words he imagined would be accompanied by a tone of disgust and revulsion.

Alice's hand unexpectedly touched his shoulder, and he turned hesitantly to face her. They gazed into each other's watery eyes, where an uncontrollable flow of broken pieces waited to fall. She placed her hands on either side of his face.

'I'm so sor—'

'Shhh,' Alice whispered, putting her finger to his lips.

There were no words powerful enough to describe the living agony and torture of Harper Darmody's mind, body, and soul.

'Everything that happened to you is not your fault,' she said softly. 'Everything you have done is not your fault.' Alice paused to swallow the lump of sadness in the back of her throat. 'The boy in the book never had a chance. The person who committed those crimes three years ago *was* that little boy. But standing before me now is the man that boy never had the chance to become.'

With his face in her hands, Alice drew closer to him and placed her lips on his. She eased away. Heartbroken breaths caressed each other's faces. 'Until it was too late,' she said in a tearful undertone.

Alice removed her hands from his face and backed slowly away. Harper detected no shame, disgust, or revulsion in her expression – only love. He watched helplessly as she turned and walked to the door. She paused and gazed at him with loving, sorrowful eyes. Then she was gone.

Harper fell to his knees, lost in his emptiness – a dire consequence of a ruined and unlived life. With his head in his hands, he pulled at his hair, almost ripping it from the roots. He yelled at the top of his lungs. He thumped his fists continuously against the sides of his head and then lunged his body forward, intentionally smacking his head against the corner of the small wooden coffee table. He lay there, blood seeping from a cut on his forehead, staring at the door. His distorted vision glimpsed a figure in the doorway before his eyes closed, and he slipped into unconsciousness.

In the early hours of the morning, darkness enveloped the lonesome caravan pitched away from the few others on the site. Harper opened his eyes on the sofa in the dimly lit living area. He reached up to comfort the throbbing wound on his head and found a damp flannel draped across it. Dried blood adorned the side of his face.

'Ah. You're awake at last.'

Harper snatched the flannel from his head and shot upright to see who was there, perhaps a little too quickly for his pounding headache. He drew in a sharp breath, rubbed his eyes, and identified a familiar face sitting at the table with a pistol in front of him. Probably the same pistol that had fired three bullets into him.

'It's all right, don't look so shocked. I'm not here to finish the job. If I wanted to kill you, I'd have done it already,' said Lenny, motioning towards the gun. 'This is more for my safety.'

It seemed Lenny was more concerned with how *he* might react to seeing the man who had so nearly ended his life. Harper lay down and covered his eyes with the flannel, unperturbed that there was an armed man just a few feet away.

'More surprised than shocked,' said Harper. 'Right now, I couldn't care less if you put a bullet in my head.'

'As I said, I'm not here to kill you.'

'If you're not going to use it, at least put it away. I might be tempted to use it on myself.'

'Aww, has someone had a bad day?'

'Not great. Look, what are you doing here, Lenny? I'm sure you haven't just popped round for a nice friendly chat.'

'I need you to come with me.'

'Do you, now? And why would I go anywhere with you?'

'Because your sister asked me to come and get you.'

Harper pulled the flannel from his eyes and sat up on the edge of the sofa. 'Is this about Charlie's killer?'

'I'm not sure – maybe. I went to see her earlier today, and on my way home, she called and asked me to turn the car around and come back. She wouldn't say why and texted me your address – told me to come and pick you up. That's all I know.'

'I suppose we'd better get a move on then,' said Harper, rising to his feet.

'You should probably go and clean yourself up a bit first. I'll wait for you in the car.' Lenny grabbed the pistol and climbed out from behind the table with a loud groan. 'Don't be long.'

There were hardly any cars on the dark country roads, and why would there be at stupid o'clock? Anyone with good sense would be snuggled under the nice warm covers of a comfortable bed. Harper caressed the prominent bump on the side of his forehead. Although the bleeding had stopped a while ago, the soft moonlit night would now and then highlight the weeping cut in the centre. He didn't know which hurt more: his head, his shoulder, or his heart. He noted how tired Lenny looked, his eyes glazed over and straining.

'So what happened to your head?' asked Lenny. 'You were out cold on the floor when I found you.'

'It's not your concern.'

'Fair enough. You haven't got the hump with me then – for shooting you, I mean?'

'Not really. I'm certainly not saying I've forgiven you. I am pissed off about your book, though.'

'Not to your liking?'

'I haven't read it, nor will I. But let's just say it hasn't done me any favours.'

'You'd best take it up with your sister – it was her idea, her story. All I did was put it into words.'

They drove in silence for the remainder of the short journey. As the car ventured up the drive to Elaine's house, Harper appeared unsettled. 'Stop the car,' he said.

'Why, what's wrong?'

'Just stop the car.'

Halfway along the drive, Lenny brought the car to a halt. Harper opened the car door and stepped out to scan the grounds. Quiet and still, barely a breeze brushed his skin. There were no lights on at the front of the house, which seemed strange if she was expecting them. The porch light was usually on at night. He climbed back inside the car.

'Something is wrong,' said Harper.

'Like what?'

'I'm not sure.'

'Well, let's go and find out, shall we?' Lenny turned off the headlights and continued up the driveway to the house.

Harper exited the car while Lenny fetched his pistol from the side door pocket before joining him on the drive. He tucked the pistol into his trousers, and they advanced towards the porch steps. Harper drew Lenny's attention to the glass on the floor by the front door – the light above had been smashed. Lenny reached for the pistol and held it in front of him as they stealthily approached the door, which was slightly ajar. Harper pushed the door wide open, and they peered into the dark hallway. Side by side, they crept through the darkness of Elaine's long hallway. Lenny pushed the living room door open and peeked inside. He turned to Harper and shook his head to indicate that the room was clear. A noise came from the kitchen, and as they neared, the kitchen door swung open.

'You took your time,' said Elaine, much to their relief.

28

Elaine

Before driving away, Elaine stared at the caravan. Very soon, she would be saying farewell to her brother, perhaps for the last time, and it wasn't easy to come to terms with. They might not have been in each other's lives in the traditional sense of siblings, but no matter how far apart they were, the dreadful things they had witnessed would bind them together forever.

She checked the message she'd received while talking to Harper. Lenny was an hour or so away. He'd sent an earlier text to say he would be coming to see her today, and for him to want to talk in person, it *must* be important. Perhaps he'd discovered Webster's location and didn't want to discuss it over the phone. With Tom working away from home for the next three days, she was able to invite Lenny to her place. Michael and Emily were on their school holidays, and so far, because of one thing or another, she'd been unable to spend much time with them. Good job they both had plenty of friends. She had dropped them at Lila's before going to see Harper, and now it was a case of heading home to wait for Lenny.

The last couple of days had been particularly hot. Not quite the heatwave of three years earlier, but almost as humid and uncomfortable. Lenny's car came up the driveway, and Elaine was out front on the swing bench, drinking a glass of lemonade. On the bench beside her was a large, unopened brown envelope. Staring at a particular area of the floor, her thoughts drifted back to that godawful day. It had a habit of creeping up on her, and why wouldn't it? Bodies everywhere, with two right here on the porch, one of them her ex-husband. Elaine had never told Harper that she'd been the one to end Robert's life. Would it have made any difference revealing that little snippet of information? Probably not.

Lenny climbed out of his car; he didn't look happy. He stomped up the steps and stood in front of her, watching her peacefully sway back and forth on the bench.

'Everything okay, Lenny? You look, dare I say it – annoyed.'

'Oh really! I'd go further and say I'm bloody furious. For the past three years, you've had me writing your book and running around like a blue-arsed fly trying to find your son's killer, and all this time, you've been on a killing spree of your own.'

Elaine held her feet firm, bringing the bench to a stop. Her skin grew cold. This was not good to hear. The question that popped into her head was how he could have possibly found out.

'You and your "dead brother," who, might I add, is not quite as dead as you'd have people believe, have been scheming and murdering those perverted old bastards who abused you.'

Gobsmacked, Elaine thought it horrendous enough that he knew about the murders, but Harper! She needed to think fast – tell him whatever he'd found out wasn't true—

'Don't you dare!' he cut in.

'What?' she asked, as though butter wouldn't melt.

'I can see the wheels turning, Elaine. Don't you dare make a bigger fool of me than you already have. I don't want to hear another one of your half-arsed concocted stories.'

It was pointless attempting to lie to him, and, truth be told, she didn't want to. They may have had an indifferent relationship over the years, but she'd grown fond of Lenny. He turned his back to her and placed his hands on the porch rail. He stared out across the grass, awaiting her response.

'It's true,' she said.

'Which part?'

'All of it.'

Lenny's head dropped at her confirmation. She couldn't help but wonder if he hadn't wanted it to be true, even though he undoubtedly knew it was.

'What possessed you to believe you could go around murdering people and get away with it? Well, congratulations, Elaine – the police know.'

'I gathered that's how you'd found out,' she said, her whole world beginning to crumble. 'When are they coming for me?'

'In a manner of speaking, they're not.'

'I don't understand,' she said, perplexed.

He turned to face her. 'DCI Harry Baxendale is on his way. He could be here any time now.'

'That doesn't explain what's going on.'

'He's not interested in you, Elaine. He's not bothered about the men you have killed. As far as he's concerned, they got what they deserved. I got the impression he would have done the same thing.'

'How does he know? And why is he coming here if he's not going to arrest me?'

Lenny ambled over to the bench and sat next to her. 'The book. He's read the bloody book and put the pieces together. He has no evidence as such. As you know, there isn't any from the past. Everything he has is circumstantial, and any reputable lawyer would get it thrown out of court. He may not even ask, but as long as you stick to parts of the book being fictional and insist you haven't seen Harper since the day he walked out of here three years ago, there is nothing he can do. He wouldn't be doing his job if he didn't question you. He has a dodgy photofit of Harper and a grainy CCTV image of you as Dr Rowan Heder at the Riverside Tower Hotel. Clever anagram, by the way. I'm assuming that's where you received the injury to your face?'

Elaine gave a subtle nod and asked, 'So who tipped you off?'

'He did. As I said, he doesn't want you – but he does want Harper. Baxendale's an intelligent bloke, Elaine. Sharp. So give him nothing he can sink his teeth into.'

'How did he work out Harper was alive?'

'Because he's smart. He knows those murders were committed by more than one person. Like I said, he'd read the book and believed your account. Why wouldn't he? We marketed it as the true story behind the massacre. Then all these high-profile old-timers started getting knocked off in the most horrific and vengeful way. If I'd been in his shoes, I'd have probably worked it out myself.'

The pair sat in silence until Lenny turned to face her.

'Why didn't you tell me, Elaine?'

'Come on, Lenny! How do you imagine that conversation going? "Oh, by the way, Harper's alive, and together we're going to kill a few people!"'

He nodded slowly, clearly understanding her reasoning. 'So, where is your brother hiding out? You know what, don't tell me. I don't care. There is one thing I *would* like to know, though – did you "bump" into Graham Walker while on your honeymoon?'

'Not literally. I would have let him walk away, but he chose not to and took a fall.'

Lenny got to his feet. 'Is your son's killer the last?'

'Yes.'

'Then, after I've had something to eat in town, I'd better go and find him, hadn't I?' He walked down the steps.

'Lenny!' He looked up as she leaned on the handrail. 'Thank you.'

'Yeah, yeah,' he said with a casual wave of his hand.

As he drove away, Elaine picked up the brown envelope and opened it, knowing what was inside. Harper's passport and various other documents to support his new identity had arrived. A doleful expression formed on her face as reality hit home. The thought that he'd soon be gone almost brought her to tears. Now this detective knew about him; the sooner, the better.

Awaiting the arrival of DCI Baxendale wasn't an option, so she called Lila to let her know she was on her way. They had already arranged to take the children to Helmsley Open Air Swimming Pool, where they intended to spend most of the afternoon.

Elaine had taken the children to this particular swimming pool a few times, but this was their first visit since some improvements had been made. The new outer fencing and walkway around the heated pool made a huge difference. After a paddle with the children, Elaine and Lila returned to their chairs and watched from afar.

While telling Elaine about her son Ryan's rehearsal for the school play, she noted a woman staring in their direction and said, 'Don't make it obvious, but do you know the lady in the bright red vest and shorts over there?' She nodded furtively towards the woman. 'She keeps looking this way as though she knows one of us, and I certainly don't recognise her.'

Elaine waited a moment and then turned, pretending to see what the children were up to. Emily waved from the opposite side of the pool, where she was standing with her toes over the edge. Elaine waved back and shot a swift glance at the woman, who seemed amused by something as she stared out at the pool. Perhaps there was a familiarity about the woman, but nothing noteworthy. She'd probably seen her around town. A child's scream filled the air.

'Emily!' Lila shouted, jumping to her feet.

Elaine reacted as soon as she saw Emily underwater and ran towards the pool, diving in to get her. When they came to the surface, Emily coughed and spluttered as her mother carried her to the side. She lifted Emily from the water, and Lila pulled her out. Elaine was soon out of the pool and by her daughter's side. Almost every pair of eyes was on them as Elaine patted Emily's back to help clear her airways of the water she had swallowed.

Meanwhile, Lila made her way around the pool, heading in the direction of an older girl with a churlish smirk on her face. 'Why the hell did you do that?' asked Lila, furious with the teenager.

'Do what? I didn't do anything,' the girl replied.

'Yes, you did. I saw you.'

The woman in the red vest and shorts appeared on the scene. 'Don't you dare shout at my daughter!'

'Your daughter! Did you tell her to do it?'

Elaine observed the argument as she comforted an upset Emily.

'Of course I didn't,' the woman replied.

Given the girl's reaction to her mother's denial, it was obvious she was lying, and Lila didn't hold back. 'You bloody liar.'

Elaine left Emily with Michael and marched around to join Lila as a small crowd gathered. 'What happened?' she asked.

The woman turned to Elaine. 'This silly bitch accused my daughter of pushing your little girl into the pool.'

Lila jumped in. 'Who are you calling a bitch? Besides, it was more like a violent shove in the back.'

'It's just kids having a bit of fun.' The woman smiled.

Elaine said, 'So you admit your daughter pushed mine?'

The woman hesitated. 'Yes, but she was only playing.'

'What she did is extremely dangerous, and I hope you'll have a serious talk with her about her behaviour.'

'Yeah, sure. Of course, I will,' the woman replied flippantly.

Lila was fuming and didn't want to drop the matter, but Elaine calmly ushered her away, and they returned to where their things were.

Elaine put a towel around Emily, and they gathered their belongings before going to the changing rooms. All the while, Lila disputed letting the woman get off so lightly – a woman who, for some unknown reason, seemed to have it in for them. As they exited the changing rooms, Elaine spotted the woman in the red vest and her daughter packing up their things.

On their way to the car, Elaine stopped to check the sports bag. 'Damn, I left Emily's costume behind. I'll just pop back for it and meet you at the car.' She handed the keys to Lila and the bag to Michael.

The receptionist recognised Elaine and let her through. She marched into the changing room and found the woman's daughter alone, changed, and putting her wet things in a bag. When the girl turned, she was startled to see Elaine in front of her. Elaine grabbed the young girl by the throat and forced her against the wall.

Wide-eyed and shaking with terror, the girl mumbled nervously, 'I'm sorry. I shouldn't have pushed your daughter.'

'No, you shouldn't,' said Elaine, releasing her grip on the child's neck. 'But you did.' She punched the girl in the stomach. The teenager doubled over. 'You touch my daughter again, and I'll break your fucking legs. Do you hear me?'

'Yes, I hear you,' she cried. 'But it was my mum who told me to do it.'

'Why would she tell you to do such a thing?'

'Because you live at the murder house. She said it's your fault all those people died.'

Elaine sat the girl on the bench. 'Where is your mother?'

'In the toilet.'

'Stay there and don't move.'

Only one cubicle was occupied. Elaine stood back and waited. The chain flushed, and as soon as the door unlocked, she rammed the bottom of her foot hard against it, forcing the door to slam into the person on the other side. She pushed the door open and saw the woman in the red vest seated on the pan, her hands hovering close to her smashed and bloodied nose.

The stunned woman stared up at her. 'You fucking bitch! I'm calling the police.'

Elaine huffed and raised her eyebrows. 'Now, why did you have to go and say something so stupid?' With a cold, menacing look in her eyes, she strolled into the cubicle and closed the door behind her.

Several minutes later, there was a gentle tap on the cubicle door. A frightened voice called out, 'Mum, are you in there?'

The door eased open. Elaine looked up to see the woman's distressed young daughter as she held her mother's head in the toilet bowl.

Elaine smiled. 'It's okay, we're all done now.' Clutching a handful of the woman's hair, she pulled her head from the pan, her face awash with blood and water. 'We've had a nice chat and agreed to forget all about our little misunderstanding, haven't we?'

The woman nodded. 'Yes, it's fine. I'm okay, Shannon, sweetheart,' she said, offering reassurance to her daughter.

Elaine stepped calmly from the cubicle and past the girl. 'Help your mother, and don't forget what I said.' Elaine washed her hands at the sink and left.

She knew there were people in town who had deep-seated anger about what had happened, but she never expected her children to become the target of such spiteful behaviour.

'You took your time,' said Lila as Elaine got comfortable in the driver's seat.

'Yeah, I couldn't find her costume anywhere,' she said, putting on her seatbelt.

'That's because it was in the bag, Mum,' said Michael.

Elaine looked around and pulled a face. 'Silly me.' She caught Lila staring at a small bloodstain on the thigh of her jeans. 'I'm so hungry,' she said, trying to deflect Lila's attention. 'Who's up for McDonald's?'

The children cheered with delight, and Lila replied, 'Sure, why not?'

Although Lila didn't question her, Elaine could tell her friend had an inkling she'd gone back for the woman in the red vest. The subject wasn't brought up during their meal, perhaps due to the presence of the children, though she suspected a conversation would be forthcoming at some point in the near future.

After dinner, Elaine dropped Lila and Ryan off and returned home. Up ahead, she saw a black four-door saloon parked outside the house. Seeing her arrival, two men stepped out of the car; she guessed one of them was DCI Baxendale.

'Kids, I want you to go straight up to the house,' she said before exiting the car.

'Who are those men, Mum?' asked Michael.

'Important clients from work.'

Michael and Emily did as they were told. Elaine stared at the DCI and his colleague. She took a deep breath and walked over, her hair still damp from swimming.

'Mrs Burgess?'

Elaine nodded and shook his hand.

'I'm Detective Chief Inspector Harry Baxendale, and this is Detective Constable Krishen Burman. Would you mind answering a few questions for me?'

'Not at all, but could we do this away from the house?'

'Of course. Wait here, Krishen,' he ordered.

They strolled across the grass towards the play area by the huge old oak tree.

'You seem to have blood on your jeans,' he said.

'Do I?' Elaine examined her jeans, pretending not to know it was there. 'Oh, yes. So I do.' Lenny was right about this guy being on the ball. 'My daughter had a nosebleed while we were at the pool.'

The detective appeared to accept her explanation, took a deep breath, and smiled. 'I love the fresh smell of recently cut grass,' he said. 'Did you know the smell is a distress signal from the grass, crying for help?'

Elaine said, 'Why don't we cut the chit-chat and get straight to the point? Lenny told me you were coming.'

'Yes, I hoped he would save us from going through the rigmarole of pointless questions you didn't want to hear, and I didn't want to ask.'

DCI Baxendale was different from what she'd expected. In a good way. It pleased her that he too seemed keen to get this over with.

'I haven't seen Harper,' she said. 'That's why you're here, isn't it?'

The DCI smiled. 'Yes. That is indeed why I'm here, but I thought we weren't going to do this frivolous back-and-forth. We both know that's not true.'

He observed the pretty floral wreath under the oak tree. 'I assume the wreath is for your mother?'

'Yes, it is.' For him to know this was the tree from which her mother hung herself, he'd certainly done his homework.

'Do you think she deserves it – to be remembered?'

'We can't always know the reasons why people make bad decisions or do dreadful things. But if, in the end, they accept responsibility for their actions, do they not deserve some form of forgiveness?'

'Do you believe Harper Darmody deserves forgiveness?'

'Unfortunately, that's not for me to decide. However, Liam Bennett does.'

They stopped under the shade of the tree. 'What about you?' he asked. 'Do you think you deserve to be forgiven?'

'I'm not asking.'

'Perhaps you should.'

'My conscience is clear, Detective.'

'Is it?'

Elaine held her tongue. He was aware of her murderous activities, which made her consider whether he was referring to Dr Neville Brown's death at the hospital, his being the only murder she looked back on with deep regret. It sometimes crossed her mind whether she could have approached him, asked him to forget he'd ever seen her file, but if he'd said no, what then? Her one chance to keep her children would have been gone. But how could the detective know? There was no autopsy, and it was reported that Dr Brown's death was due to a brain haemorrhage related to his severe head trauma.

'I know I'd be wasting my breath asking you the whereabouts of Harper – but I will find him, Mrs Burgess.'

'I can only wish you the best of luck on that front.' The detective was trying to read her, to find some kind of clue. She gave him nothing, exactly as Lenny had told her.

'Okay, we'll leave it there for the moment,' he said. 'Now, I apologise in advance, but I need you to look at these because my colleague is probably watching from the car.' He showed Elaine the CCTV image of her and the photofit of Harper. 'I'm guessing you have an alibi for your whereabouts on the night Sir Edward Horner and Peter Stafford were murdered. If you don't, get one, just in case. Given his important status, I might not be the only one looking into this. Lucky for you, nobody but me knows about this image of – let's say, someone who looks remarkably similar to you. That's not to say someone else won't pick up on it. I just thought you should see it in case it comes back to haunt you. All I'm here about is Harper Darmody.'

Elaine remained quiet and stared at the grainy image of herself in the lobby. It brought back unpleasant memories. He was right about her having an alibi. She had paid for a room at a different hotel in Newcastle on the same night. She'd also hired an escort who could pass for her to stay there. It was difficult to understand why he was being so helpful.

'Why did you apologise?' she asked.

'Because it didn't go to plan. I think something went horribly wrong that night.'

Christ, Lenny's assessment was spot on – Baxendale *is* smart. She just hoped he wasn't clever enough to find Harper before he vanished forever.

'Right, I've taken up enough of your time and it's a long drive back to London,' he said.

'May I ask a question, DCI Baxendale?'

'Of course.'

'How come you're not taking me in for questioning?'

'Because you've been through enough over the years. This visit was just a formality to cover my back. Only four of us know the truth – best it remains that way.'

He walked away and then turned to face her. 'Oh, just one more thing – if you are considering going after Joseph Webster, I'd advise against it – he's unlike anything you've come up against before. Take care, Mrs Burgess.'

Elaine had settled on the sofa with the children to watch a movie. It was Emily's turn to choose, and she picked something Michael might pretend not to enjoy: Disney's *Christopher Robin*. Elaine's guilt at not being around much of late had played a part in providing the parade of snacks on the table in front of them. How she wished Tom were here too. He'd recently expressed how much he hated working away from home and sleeping in hotels, preferring to spend his evenings relaxing at home with his wife and the children. She got the impression he missed his old job.

With the movie over and their stomachs full of all the wrong things, Michael disappeared to his room, where he would likely insert his earbuds and listen to music while messaging friends for the remainder of the evening. Emily, on the other hand, had just about managed to keep her eyes open until the end of the movie and was ready for bed.

After tucking Emily in, she gazed at her. If she'd lost her little girl today at the pool, it would have destroyed her completely. There was no coming back from the loss of another young child. Throughout the evening, she reflected on whether she'd overreacted earlier, but having already lost a child, she couldn't see how any rules applied. Keeping them safe was everything.

At nine-thirty, Elaine made herself a cup of cocoa and selected a book to read in bed. Before heading upstairs, she checked the back door in the kitchen; she'd forgotten to lock it earlier, which was often the case. Tom had repeatedly warned her about locking windows and doors. On her way up, it occurred to her that she hadn't switched on the porch light. She went back down, flicked the switch, and, through the frosted glass above the door, saw that the light had failed to come on. Elaine put her cup of cocoa on the console table, opened the door, and stepped out onto the porch to check.

It was near dark, but light enough to see that the bulb and glass casing had shattered. Tiny shards lay scattered about the floor below. Could the bulb have exploded? Maybe one of the children broke the light and failed to tell her. Emily had been out on the porch playing with her ball earlier. She hated getting into trouble and was prone to telling the odd fib, so there wasn't much hope of getting a confession. Oh well, it wasn't a big deal. She'd clean up and sort it out in the morning.

Elaine walked to the edge of the porch and scanned the area in front of the house, but only as far as the fast-fading light would allow. Her skin turned cold, and she folded her arms, overcome with a sense of unease. Perhaps Lenny had planted the seed in her head when he'd suggested that Charlie's killer could come for her. She wouldn't be difficult to find – she lived in the so-called murder house, for Christ's sake. A quick internet search of her name, Lenny's, or Charlie's would pretty much pinpoint her exact location. Was she being paranoid? She shrugged off the idea, took one last look around, and went back inside the house.

The light flickered on the bedside table next to the cup containing the dark remnants of unconsumed cocoa. Elaine had fallen asleep with the book she'd been reading wide open on her chest. Registering her name being called, she stirred and bolted upright. Wiping the sleep from her eyes, she saw a tall, sturdy man with shiny black hair and thick eyebrows standing at the end of her bed. In front of him, Michael and Emily were bound to wooden chairs – their pale, ghostly faces and dying eyes staring at her as blood oozed from the gaping lacerations across their necks. She couldn't move, couldn't scream – shocked into paralysis.

Her focus returned to the man standing over them – the man from Lenny's picture, Joseph Webster. With his unusually large eyes and a grotesque smile, his arms loomed from behind his back, a small axe in each hand, rising slowly upwards. With a savage, euphoric expression on his face, Webster closed his eyes and thrust the axes towards the heads of her children.

In a cold sweat and trembling under the covers, a long, sharp scream woke Elaine. 'Emily!'

Elaine leapt from the bed, the book flying from her chest as she raced to Emily's bedroom. She burst through the door to find the bedside lamp switched on and Emily sitting up in bed, crying, tears flooding her cherubic cheeks. She hurried to comfort her on the bed.

'Oh, baby. What's wrong? Did you have a bad dream?'

'No,' she cried. 'There was a man standing by my bed, staring at me.'

'It was just a dream, sweetheart.' Elaine wrapped her arms around her daughter and rocked her gently.

'No, Mummy. It was real. He is a bad man, and he said horrible things.'

'Aww, what did he say to my baby?'

'He said bad things would happen to me and Michael, and that he would kill you.'

'Sweetie, no one is going to hurt us, okay? No one!' Elaine gazed into her daughter's eyes to reassure her that she was safe. 'I have dreams about monsters too, but they are just dreams. They're not real.'

'Are you sure it wasn't real?' Emily asked.

'I'm sure, sweetheart. It's just pretend – our imagination trying to scare us.'

'Mummy – am I still dreaming?'

'No, sweetheart. We are both wide awake.' Elaine smiled.

'Then why is the bad man standing with Michael by the door?'

Elaine's smile vanished. She turned and saw Joseph Webster standing in the doorway, his hand tightly pressed over her terrified son's mouth. Gripped in his other hand was the silver shimmer of a long, sharp knife. Elaine jumped to her feet and pulled Emily from the bed, hiding her little girl behind her.

'Please don't hurt my son.' Her heart thumped, and beads of sweat turned into drops. She was face to face with Charlie's killer.

'You shouldn't have tried to find me,' he said.

'I – I don't know what you mean. I don't know who you are or what you want.' In her panicked state, it was all she could think to say, hoping he would believe her and leave.

'If you're going to play games with me, I'll slit your son's throat right now.' Webster wasn't buying her pretence and pressed the cold steel against the tender skin of Michael's neck.

'Stop!' The palm of her outstretched hand emphasised her cry. Her other hand shielded Emily behind her back, out of sight. 'Okay, I'm sorry. No more games. Please, just let my son go. This is between *you* and me. Don't take the lives of any more of my children.' There was no holding back her tears.

'You should have let things be.' He removed the knife from Michael's throat and brought his arm down by his side.

'Let things be? You killed my son!' Elaine struggled to control eight years of pent-up anger as the blood boiled in her veins. Being so close to the man she loathed ripped the scabs from her unhealed wounds and laid them bare.

'And if you're not careful, I'll kill another one,' he said, calm and callous.

She couldn't win like this, not while he held the power. 'You sick, fucking coward. Why don't you let my son go and take me on?' she said, trying to goad him. 'I'll shove that knife so far up your arse the coroner will have to crack open your chest to prise it out.'

Webster rammed Michael's head into the doorframe. He dropped to the floor, unconscious, blood trickling from a deep cut. Screaming with rage, Elaine ran towards her son. As Webster was about to advance and attack her, he was tackled by Tom, who appeared from nowhere, taking him to the floor on the landing. Elaine fell to her knees and held Michael in her arms, relieved as his eyes opened. Over by the bed, a petrified Emily sobbed. Elaine was unable to see what was happening outside the room as Tom fought the man.

Tom shouted, 'Shut the door and lock it!'

Elaine got to her feet and dragged Michael further into the room, away from the opening. She raced back to the door and peered out into the landing. Webster was on top of Tom as they grappled, with Tom trying to prevent him from reaching the knife a couple of feet away. Webster punched him repeatedly while Elaine debated whether to help Tom or protect her children. Her brief delay was all it took for Webster to stretch across Tom's body and brush his fingers over the handle. She saw the frantic expression on Tom's face as he watched the man wrap his hand around it. Webster thumped the butt of the knife into Tom's forehead.

In an act of desperation, Tom crashed his head into the man's face, knocking him sideways and forcing him to drop the knife. Tom grabbed it firmly and lunged towards the man – the blade missed by a fraction and sank deep into the wooden floorboards. The man scrambled to his feet and ran. Tom pulled the knife free and gave chase. Webster sped past the bedroom, heading for the stairs, glaring at Elaine as she slammed the door shut. She heard Tom's footsteps close behind.

29

The Boy

The boys had their plan but grew restless and tired as they waited for the man to return. Every monotonous minute dragged into the next. Danny may have been there longer and grown used to the endless days of misery, but even he had succumbed to impatience, eager to bring an end to his harrowing captivity. He yearned to return to his family, his messy bedroom, and the comfort of his own bed. Thoughts of home crossed his mind repeatedly during his time there, only to be cast out as he accepted his fate – a tormenting cycle of hope and loss.

On the tatty bed, he lay staring up at the dark, padded ceiling. A young boy, desperate to sense the love of his mother and father – a love he would never again take for granted. Quiet tears fell, the pain of loss deep in his heart. His eyes were drawn to a small black object next to the fluorescent light. It wasn't there before; he would have noticed. The man must have placed it there recently while he was sleeping.

He stood on the bed for a closer look and guessed it was a camera. Zeph must be recording them. He had set the boys up to do battle, so why wouldn't the sicko want to watch? Soon, with Connor's help, he would take on the sadistic killer of so many young boys. Failure wasn't an option. Desperately tired, Danny's eyes gradually closed.

He woke sharply to find Connor by the side of his bed, axe in hand, his bright, beady eyes glaring down at him.

'I think I heard something outside,' he said.

Danny sat up and listened but couldn't hear a thing. He climbed out of bed and moved as close to the door as he could. Still nothing. 'What did you hear?'

'I'm not sure. It was like a knocking sound. I suppose it could have been another boat passing by.'

'Yeah, maybe,' said Danny.

Connor returned to his side of the narrow room, and Danny ambled to the sink to splash cold water on his face. Still tired, he no longer wanted to sleep. It wasn't safe. Not only could the man come back at any time, but he also wasn't sure if he could trust his roommate. There was something about the look in Connor's eye when he woke to find him standing over his bed, distant and contemplative. Did Connor have a different plan from his – the one they had spent hours discussing and forming? Then again, Connor could have attacked him several times, yet he hadn't. Maybe they were both suffering from paranoia and thinking the same thing. The man had emphasised to Connor not to trust him, so why would he? He was bound to have doubts.

Danny dried his face on the dirty towel and sat on the bed. He stared across the room and couldn't tell if Connor's eyes were closed or if he was squinting, secretly watching his every move.

'You awake?' No reply.

'Connor!' he called, louder this time. Not a flinch.

As Danny moved towards him, Connor shot upright and tightened his grip around the handle of the axe.

Danny stopped abruptly. 'Are you okay with everything?'

'Sure. Sorry – I fell asleep.'

'I mean, are you okay with our plan?' Connor's silence was his answer, and not the one he wanted. 'We can do this,' he said confidently, in an attempt to put Connor at ease.

'I'm – I'm just – scared.'

Connor wasn't lying; the fear in his eyes was obvious. It was exactly the same for Danny. Every muscle in his body ached, and he didn't know why. Perhaps the emotional strain and constant tension were taking their toll. He walked over to Connor and knelt in front of him. Unsure he could trust him, Danny was taking a huge risk.

'You're not alone,' said Danny. 'I'm just as scared and want to get out of here alive. All we have to do is stick to the plan. One way or another, this *will* end for us.'

'How will it end, though?'

'It doesn't matter how – as long as it ends.' Danny patted him on the shoulder and walked back to the bed. 'How long was I asleep earlier?'

'A few hours.'

Danny had to gain Connor's trust, and fast. He knew they would soon come face to face with the monster, and in a bid to prove that Connor had no reason to fear him, Danny refrained from touching his axe and frequently turned his back. It was brave, even stupid, but for his plan to work, he needed Connor to believe in him. Occasionally, he felt Connor's eyes burning into the back of his head – or was he being paranoid? It didn't matter. It had to be done. The risk was worth the end result.

30

Lenny

Any words to explain the awkward, angry silence in the room would be a gross understatement. They were all sitting at the kitchen table, Elaine and Tom on one side, Harper and Lenny on the other. Irate stares were fired back and forth, all unsure how to begin the conversation. The huge lump on Tom's forehead could not be ignored. It was worse than Harper's. And let's not forget Elaine's swollen cheek from the incident at the hotel.

Lenny raised his hand in the air. 'I'll go first, shall I?' he said. 'Two questions. Why did you call me to come all the way back? And what in God's name is wrong with Tom's head?'

Tom piped up, pointing at Harper. 'Why is that psychopath in our house?'

Harper replied calmly, 'I'm not a psychopath. I have a mental illness.'

'I'll give you a bloody mental illness,' said Tom as he shot to his feet.

The lack of words exchanged seconds ago no longer seemed to be an issue.

'Tom!' Elaine shouted. 'Sit down.'

'He shot me,' said Tom. 'Damn near killed me. He killed my colleagues, including two of my friends,' he said, referring to Andrew James and Liz Morgan.

'Tom! Please, just sit down.'

Tom stared at his wife, eventually taking his seat.

Lenny said, 'If we're laying it all out there, he shot me too.'

'He shot the front door, not you,' said Elaine. 'All you got was a splinter.'

'Splinter?' said Lenny. 'It was more like a stake.'

Lenny continued to bicker with both Tom and Elaine while Harper sat quietly, watching the three of them shout and holler, mostly about him.

'Enough!' yelled Harper, banging a hand on the table.

The three of them fell silent and stared at Harper. He said, 'I could apologise for what happened, but would it honestly make a difference? Would it make you happy? Make everything all right? I don't think so. Any apology I give doesn't help those who died or their families, does it? What's done is done. We all know the circumstances behind that day. I would like nothing more in this world than to take it all back. Make it right. But that's not possible. I have to own what I did. Now, give me your pistol, Lenny.'

'You ain't serious? He's not, is he?' Lenny queried of Elaine.

'Give it to him,' she insisted.

Lenny reached for his pistol and reluctantly placed it on the table in front of Harper, who immediately picked it up, checked to make sure it was loaded, and unexpectedly placed it in front of Tom.

'Other than those children upstairs whose father I murdered, you have more reason than anyone else here to kill me. So, if you want to take my life, Tom, do it. Nobody will stop you.'

Lenny observed Elaine sheepishly turn her head away at the mention of the children's father. He then looked at Tom and sensed the temptation in his eyes to reach for the pistol. Would Harper really allow Tom to shoot him? A question soon answered as Tom rose to his feet, picked up the pistol, and pointed it at Harper.

Elaine shouted, 'Tom, no!'

'Let him be,' said Harper. Tom's hand visibly trembled. 'You're a good man, Tom. Shooting me won't take that away, and nobody would hold it against you. You'd probably be branded a hero.'

Lenny had no feelings about the outcome. Granted, it wouldn't be pleasant to observe, but he'd seen worse. Turning to stare at Harper, he perceived something within his eyes that hadn't been there on the day he stood over him and Elaine, brandishing a shotgun. On that day, his eyes were unemotional and dead; now, they were the eyes of a tired and pained man – a man who desired his life to be over. There was something else – regret. A whole lot of regret.

'Put the pistol down, Tom,' said Lenny.

'Why? He deserves to die.'

'Maybe Harper Darmody deserves to die – but you'd be killing Liam Bennett.'

'What the hell are you talking about?' asked Tom, completely bewildered.

'Those are not the cold, dead eyes that we both looked into on that day, Tom.'

'What does it matter? He's in that bloody head somewhere.'

Lenny rose to his feet. 'Give it here,' he said, taking the pistol from Tom's hand.

He pressed the pistol against Harper's temple. 'Tell me where Harper is, and I'll shoot him for you. Is he here?' Lenny moved the pistol a few inches to the back of Harper's head. 'How about here?' He moved it once more, placing it against Harper's forehead. 'What about here?'

Tom flopped dejectedly into his seat. Elaine reached out to caress his fingers on the table, but Tom pulled his hand away.

Lenny put the pistol in his pocket and sat down. 'Right—'

'Hold on, Lenny,' said Elaine. 'I have something I need to say.'

They stared at her, anticipating the next revelation. She looked at Tom with a sorrowful glint in her eyes, and his expression suggested he couldn't take much more. Elaine extended the silence as they waited with bated breath.

'Harper didn't kill the children's father – I did.' She bowed her head, not wanting to see her husband's reaction.

Lenny wasn't at all surprised by her admission. Having recently found out what she was capable of, there was nothing more Elaine or Harper could do that would shock him.

'Well,' said Tom, shifting back in his chair in disbelief. 'This just keeps getting better and better, doesn't it?' He stood up again and, this time, paced around the kitchen.

'I thought I killed Robert?' said Harper.

'He may well have died anyway. I was just—'

'Helping him along,' said Lenny.

'Yes. No. I mean, sort of. Oh, shut up, Lenny!'

'Will all of you just be quiet!' said Tom, upset, angry, and still pacing. 'So let me see if I've got this right. Harper here is a mass murderer, who my wife,' he stared at Elaine, 'has been hiding from the authorities for the last three years. On top of that, the two of you have been gallivanting about the country on some murderous vendetta. And you,' he said, pointing at Lenny, who in turn innocently pointed a finger at himself, 'you've been secretly working for Elaine, searching for Charlie's killer, *and* got your detective friend killed in the process.' Tom let out a long, exasperated sigh. 'All of this has been going on right under my nose, and furthermore, I wouldn't have had a clue about any of it if the killer hadn't broken into our house tonight, scared the life out of the children, and hurt Michael.'

It now dawned on Lenny and Harper why they were sitting in Elaine's kitchen.

'Is Michael okay?' asked Harper, before Lenny had the chance.

'Yes, he's fine,' said Elaine. 'Just a nasty cut on his head. They were both shaken up, but they're sleeping now. They'll be okay.'

'I did warn you he might come looking for you,' said Lenny.

'I know you did. I just didn't think—'

'Just a minute!' Tom interrupted, further enraged. 'You knew a psychotic killer might come here, and you failed to tell me?'

'Tom, I honestly didn't think he would come to the house.'

'That's your problem, Elaine. You don't think. What about the children? What about their safety? You send this joker' – he pointed at Lenny, who was visibly offended – 'off on some harebrained pursuit, and he practically invites him into our home. I'm flabbergasted. I don't know what to say. If my plans hadn't been cancelled at the last minute, I wouldn't have been here to stop him. I dread to think what would have happened. This is all an unbelievable nightmare.'

Tom leaned against the kitchen counter, refusing to return to the table. He understandably didn't want to be near any of them and couldn't even look at Elaine. Lenny couldn't blame him. To be honest, he was surprised Tom was still in the room, let alone the house. Tom had been deceived by his wife, and he was hurt. Deeply hurt. The bottom line: Tom was right – about most of it anyway. Lenny could have argued about being in any way responsible for Colin's death, but what was the point? For the next few minutes, silence ruled the room. None of them knew what to say or what the next move should be until, unexpectedly . . .

'We have to catch this guy,' said Tom. 'I don't mean next week, next month, or next year. We have to catch him now. While he's out there, Elaine and the kids are in danger. There's no reason why he wouldn't try again, no reason at all. Lenny, what do we know about him?'

Lenny was surprised by Tom's sudden turnaround; then again, Tom was a police officer with around thirty years' experience. Bringing calm and a sense of control to a situation was what he did best.

'We know his name is Joseph Webster, and he cruises the canals on a boat, most likely a narrowboat,' said Lenny, keeping it short.

'The canals!' blasted Tom. 'Do you realise how many miles of canals there are in the UK?'

'Just over two thousand,' said Lenny, having done his homework.

'It would be like looking for grey hair on a white sheep,' said Tom.

'Not quite,' said Lenny. 'I can show you exactly where he was five days ago. By estimating the average speed of four miles per hour, it shouldn't be difficult to pinpoint how far he could have gone in that time in either direction. Do you have a map?'

Elaine shot out of her seat and rushed towards the kitchen units. 'There's a map in the messy drawer. Michael needed it for some school project a while back.' She opened a drawer and sorted through an array of takeaway menus, user guides for household items, and various other bits and pieces. Upon finding the map, she unfolded it and spread it out across the table.

Lenny and Tom hunched over and examined the waterways.

'Now, I can't be exact without calculating the mileage on a computer, but five days ago, he was here.' Lenny pointed to the area of the canal in Harlow, where he'd seen him at The Moorhen car park. 'He wouldn't have had time to get this far north by boat. So, to get to this house, he probably came by car—'

'He did,' said Tom. 'I chased him from the house. He got into a car that he'd parked out on the road. By the time I reached the end of the drive, he'd driven too far away to see anything helpful. Elaine told me this Webster is pretty much a ghost and that checking the vehicle database would be useless.'

'She's right,' said Lenny, continuing to point his finger at the possible route on the map. 'Let's assume he took his boat north from Harlow. Bishop's Stortford is as far as he could have got. It's the end of the line for boats going in that direction. If his car was parked between there and Harlow, it's likely he would have driven straight up the M11 motorway, joined the A14, and then taken the A1 before cutting across to Helmsley.

'We should start at Bishop's Stortford and work our way down to where the River Stort joins the River Lee Navigation in Rye. We then follow the river down as far as Cheshunt. The other area we need to search is across this way from Rye to Hertford. He most likely keeps his car somewhere around this area. Any other place would involve parking restrictions. From here, he could easily pick up the M25 and follow either the A1 or the M1.'

'That's still a wide area to cover, Lenny,' said Tom.

'It is, but with four of us searching, we'll get it done faster,' said Lenny.

'Four of us?' Tom questioned, staring at Harper. 'Oh no, you're not seriously considering letting him loose in the English countryside, are you?'

'The more of us involved in the search, the quicker we'll find him,' said Lenny.

'What makes you think he'll go back to the boat?' asked Harper.

'It's where he lives,' said Lenny. 'It's all he knows. Plus, there is a strong possibility he has a boy captive on the boat, perhaps two.' Lenny was clinging to the hope that Danny Logan was still alive. 'There's a reason Webster and the bastard before him got away with this for so long, so it's likely the boat will be moored on its own, away from prying eyes.'

31

Harper

The unlikely quartet launched their hunt for Joseph Webster. After a quick search on Elaine's laptop, Lenny's estimations were deemed accurate enough to stick to his suggested search area. Harper and Lenny set off in the early hours, with Tom warning Harper not to draw any unwanted attention to himself. They certainly didn't need to add to the trouble they had already found themselves in. Tom had taken charge and been very specific with his instructions. He'd said they should split up and search multiple locations at once, eventually coming together somewhere along the route. If either of them found Webster, they were to alert the others.

Lenny had dropped Harper in Hertford, from where Harper would work his way along the River Lee Navigation up to The Boathouse Café Bar in Roydon. Tom, who was beginning the search from Cheshunt, would eventually meet him at the café by the River Stort. Still angry with Elaine, it was evident Tom didn't want to pair up with her himself. He especially didn't want her and Harper left to their own devices. Elaine had stayed behind to make arrangements regarding the children. Once Michael and Emily were in Lila's care, she was to drive to Bishop's Stortford and meet up with Lenny, where together they would search downriver until they met up with the others.

After walking three miles along the canal with the sun beating down, Harper stopped for a rest. The pain in his shoulder and the bump on his head probably contributed to his fatigue. With many of the narrowboats covered over and seemingly moored for some time, he had only found it necessary to closely inspect a couple. When he examined the map with the others the previous night, it had been difficult to take into account how long and daunting the walk would be. Wherever the others were in their search, he wondered whether they were having similar thoughts about how difficult it would be to find this man. He reflected on his conversation with Lenny during the journey from Helmsley.

The bickering started as soon as they walked out of Elaine's front door, and after admitting he could do with an hour or two's kip, Lenny reluctantly agreed to let Harper drive first. When he eventually woke up, Harper had a question waiting. 'How are we supposed to find this elusive narrowboat?'

'Use your imagination. Knock, peek through windows, or force entry. Look for anything out of place or suspicious.'

'Force entry? Isn't that illegal?'

'Are you having a bubble? After everything you've done, you're worried about breaking into a bloody boat?'

'Point taken.'

'There's a service station coming up,' said Lenny. 'Pull in there, and we'll swap. After a question like that, you could probably do with getting some shut-eye yourself.'

*

Lenny had told him about the remains of the young boys and how Webster had killed an unknown number of children. Imagining his nephew, Charlie, being among the victims was distressing. He regarded the dead children staring at him from across the canal. For some strange reason, they had appeared at intervals along his walk. Charlie was not among them – perhaps his spirit had moved on. But why hadn't these children done the same? Were they waiting for the killer to be caught? Their remains to be discovered? He had no idea.

It occurred to him what a hypocrite he was. The people he'd killed were all someone's son or daughter. What right did he have to stop this man, and why were the manifestations of dead children following him? So many questions, but maybe it wasn't about him at all. Why would it be?

Harper examined his phone. No calls or messages. It seemed nobody had spotted Joseph Webster yet, though that wasn't the only reason he had checked his phone. He had hoped to hear from Alice, but so far, nothing. Maybe she'd deleted his number, ending all contact forever. He wouldn't and couldn't blame her. She had made things very clear, and it hurt. It hurt deeply.

Harper sighed and continued walking. It wasn't long before he came across a narrowboat on its own, covered with a blue tarpaulin. He lifted the tarpaulin slightly and knocked loudly on the side. It looked as though it had been moored in the same place for a while. On the deck, he noted an oddly shaped object underneath the cover and climbed aboard to investigate. It was a rusting blue bicycle, and thankfully, it wasn't chained up. Harper smiled at his good fortune and hauled it over the side. He climbed on, and off he pedalled. He was a little unsteady at first as he hadn't ridden a bike since he was a child, but he soon got the hang of it. It appeared the old saying, "It's like riding a bike," was true.

*

Thanks to the bicycle, Harper made it to The Boathouse Café in good time, needing to examine only four narrowboats on his route, two of which he had to break into for a closer look. There was nothing suspicious about the boats making their way along the river; they appeared to be occupied by families or older couples. Getting to the café before Tom allowed him to get something to eat and a much-needed cup of tea. Harper sat outside on the decking overlooking the marina. Out of boredom, he counted up to two hundred moored boats. He didn't fancy inspecting all of those on his own.

The longer he waited and contemplated how many boats roamed the waterways, the chances of finding the killer seemed increasingly unlikely. His phone pinged. He assumed it would be Tom or one of the others checking up on him, but it was a text from Alice. She wanted to meet the following day for a chat. Harper smiled and replied instantly, agreeing to meet her and ending his message with two large Xs. Now he had something to look forward to; he hoped the day would end quickly and they could all head home without any drama. Elaine had promised Tom that if they hadn't found Joseph Webster by late evening, Lenny was to turn over his information to DCI Baxendale.

Three cups of tea, a cheese toastie, and a slice of cake later, Tom arrived. He also needed food and refreshment. Understandably, things remained tense between the two. Tom was disgruntled, and rightly so.

Tom took a bite of his sausage sandwich and sipped his tea, all the while peering across the table at Harper.

'Did you know I wouldn't shoot you?' asked Tom with his mouth full.

'I don't know you well enough to second-guess whether you would or wouldn't.'

'Did you care? If I'd pulled the trigger, I mean?'

'No.'

'Is that how fine the line between life and death is for you?'

'There is no line, Tom. The words are too closely related.'

'How so?'

'They're only separated by three letters.'

Tom tried to conceal his smile, but he couldn't prevent his lips curling at the sides as he bit into his sandwich. It appeared Tom found him as difficult to comprehend as Elaine and Lenny. All three doubted his sanity, and at times, Harper doubted himself.

Sweat amassed on Tom's forehead as the hot sun bore down on them. Two suited men walked past their table. Harper observed Tom give one of the men a long, hard stare. A look of recognition? Tom looked around at the table where the two men had made themselves comfortable in the shade.

'Couldn't you have picked a table in the shade?' said Tom, picking up a napkin and wiping the moisture from his forehead.

Tom seemed frazzled – in more ways than one. 'I like the sun,' said Harper.

'You take after your sister,' said Tom, more flustered by the second. 'Do you see her as your sister?'

'When I came back three years ago, I didn't.'

'And now?'

'Yes, I think I do.'

'So who are you? Do you even know?'

'Your wife thinks I'm neither Liam nor Harper. She reckons I should make a fresh start.'

'But what about you? What do you believe?'

'I love Elaine, and I'd do anything to protect her.'

'Sounds like a brother to me,' said Tom, stuffing the last of his sandwich into his mouth and sipping his tea. He glanced over

Harper's shoulder and once again turned to check out the table behind. Tom faced Harper, leaned in close, and whispered, 'You need to go. Now!' He glared over Harper's shoulder and faintly nodded towards the car park.

Harper leaned back, stretched his arms, and took an imperceptible glance over at the car park, immediately spotting armed police officers heading stealthily towards the café. Either Tom recognised the man at the table behind as a detective, or he'd set about turning him in and changed his mind. There was no time to think or ask questions. Harper shot up from his seat.

'He's clocked us!' shouted a man at the table behind Tom.

'All units, move in!' the other yelled into a handheld radio.

Harper lifted the chair and hurled it towards the detectives. He climbed over the railings and jumped the short distance onto the path below. He raced along the marina jetty, voices behind – shouting for him to stop. Approaching the end of the jetty, there was a loud bang, followed quickly by another. Harper dived into the water and swam beneath the surface, holding his breath for as long as he could. Eventually, he sprang from the water, gasping, and scrambled onto the shore in the corner of the marina.

'There!' a voice shouted.

Harper looked back; standing at the edge of the jetty, eyes fixed on him, was the same tall detective he'd thrown the chair at. Armed officers ran in the opposite direction, no doubt making their way around the side of the marina to give chase. There was no time to catch his breath. Harper scrambled to his feet, took one last look at the detective, turned, and ran through the low trees and small bushes. He had to get out of the area fast; a helicopter was probably minutes, if not seconds away.

Harper sprinted along the grass on the outskirts of Roydon Marina Village and then onto a paved road, with holiday lodges on either side of him. Sirens from police cars grew louder as they closed in. He charged through a row of thick bushes and came to a stop at the edge of another body of water. Close by, he spotted a footbridge. After crossing the bridge, he stopped to catch his breath. In front of him was a long, wide grassy clearing. To his left were rail tracks. To his right was the River Stort, where he saw narrowboats moored in the distance. Loud voices were getting closer, followed by what he feared most: a helicopter. He raced out into the open clearing towards the canal. Glancing back, he saw officers – lots of them – chasing on foot.

Harper made it to the trees and continued, out of sight, through the bushes along the edge of the canal. He jumped into the river and swam across to the other side, between two moored narrowboats. Climbing out of the water onto the path, he got to his feet. Gasping for air, Harper leaned forward, placing his hands on his knees. Water dripped from his body onto the ground, along with drops of blood.

Across the river, police officers shouted as they searched the bushes. Above the trees, the helicopter approached the grassy clearing. Harper darted along the private path and out onto the main road. There was a level crossing on the other side of a small bridge, close to the railway station. Red lights flashed, and a piercing bell rang out. The barriers were down, and cars queued. He raced the short distance over the bridge and saw the train, already at the station. He climbed over the barrier, crossed the tracks, and hauled himself up onto the platform.

'Oi! You can't do that!' a man shouted from the signal box.

Ignoring the man, Harper raced towards the train. A loud beeping signalled that the doors were about to close. He boarded the carriage just in time.

Breathless and perspiring, he slumped into a seat by the window as the train pulled out of the station. He watched the helicopter circling above the trees and scanning the undergrowth near the clearing. It didn't look as though the police had seen him board the train. Observing police officers standing behind the barrier, Harper slid from his seat and hid below the window as the train passed through the level crossing.

Sitting upright in his seat a few seconds later, he let out a huge sigh of relief and winced, bringing a hand to his left side, just above the hip. Lifting his shirt, he saw where the bullet had grazed his flesh. Thankfully, it wasn't too bad, but it hurt like hell. He pulled out his phone, but as he'd already assumed, it was dead due to his dip in the water. Slouching in his seat, he wondered who could have tipped off the police. His best guess would be Tom or Lenny, but there was one other person, and he hated himself for even considering the thought – Alice.

32

Elaine

Lila had expressed concern when Elaine showed up at her house so early and asked her to look after the children. Elaine had said it was an emergency and that she'd explain everything when she returned to pick them up the following day. Lila didn't hesitate or feel the need to quiz her on the matter – always the good friend.

Elaine arrived at The Port Jackson pub in Bishop's Stortford, looking every bit the part for a long, painstaking search on a hot summer's day: a lightweight jacket over a white T-shirt, a pair of blue jeans, and her old Converse trainers. From a distance, she saw Lenny sitting outside overlooking the canal, typically tucking into a feast. She went to the bar to get herself a coffee.

She had arrived later than expected due to making a last-minute detour. Before Harper left with Lenny, he'd told her about what had happened with Alice and how she'd worked out who they were. Upon seeing Elaine's troubled expression, he added that Alice would never say a word to anyone. Elaine wasn't so sure. While Harper was upstairs taking a shower, she took the opportunity to call Alice, having already entered her number when she had called about Harper's shoulder. They arranged to meet at a café in Pickering after Elaine had dropped off the children.

*

Alice had chosen Caffé Stop, the only place in the area she knew would be open before 9.00 a.m. Elaine was able to park right outside and found Alice sitting on a black leather sofa by a large window, away from the earshot of others. The café itself was clean and nicely decorated. The exposed brickwork on a couple of walls and around the edges of the windows added to the warm, cosy, country feel. Elaine joined her on the sofa rather than sitting on the one opposite. The waitress came over, and Elaine ordered two cups of coffee.

Alice dived straight in. 'I'm guessing you've spoken to Simon – or is it Liam? Perhaps Harper?'

'Yes,' said Elaine.

'You don't have to worry about me opening my mouth if that's what you're worried about.'

'He already told me you wouldn't say anything, but I won't lie – it's more comforting to hear it for myself.'

'Did he send you?'

'God, no! He wouldn't do that.'

'So, what is it you wanted to see me about?'

'To be honest, Alice, I don't know what I'm doing here. I imagined I might be able to persuade you to rethink and give him another chance – but I get the feeling I'm wasting my time.'

'He lied to me, to my family.'

'Only about his name.' Alice glared at her. It was about a lot more than a name, and Elaine knew it. 'Okay, I get it, but what did you want him to tell you – the truth? How would that have worked out for him?'

'I expected . . .'

Alice paused mid-sentence as the waitress approached with the coffee and placed the cups on the table. As soon as she walked away, Alice said, 'I expected not to fall for the pretence of a personality that doesn't exist.'

The two women emptied one sachet of sugar into their respective coffees and stirred. Elaine sipped hers immediately and sighed with relief. 'Oh, wow. You have no idea how much I need this,' she said, taking another sip. 'It's pretty good coffee.' Elaine placed her cup on the table. 'Do you really believe he pretended to be someone he wasn't when he was with you?'

'I don't know, maybe. It felt real.'

'What makes you think the man you fell for doesn't exist?'

'Can you honestly tell me that you believe he does?'

'Since his reappearance after what happened on that dreadful day, there have been changes in his personality. I should have noticed, but I was selfish. I was so intent on keeping him to myself and protecting him that I didn't want to acknowledge them.'

'Protecting him or protecting others?'

'Both, I guess. Alice, I can't explain the complexities of the mind, and I can't tell you what you should or shouldn't do. What I can tell you is that he's not the man who came back into my life three years ago, but I think you already know that.'

Elaine picked up her cup and drank the rest of her coffee. She rose to her feet, stepped away from the sofa, and looked to ensure that nobody was listening. 'So the answer to your question is yes – the man you fell for does exist. You read a book, and all you know is of a harrowing past belonging to someone else and the monster that man became. Simon is neither. You love him. I can see it in your eyes. Everybody has doubts and uncertainties, but don't let the truth be concealed by self-denial.' Elaine walked away, leaving Alice to contemplate in silence.

With one more stop to make, Elaine parked next to Harper's caravan and used a spare key to let herself in. Her attention was immediately drawn to the small patch of blood on the carpet where he had intentionally hit his head. On the floor next to the shelving unit was the holdall he'd prepared in readiness to leave. She reluctantly placed the brown envelope containing his new identity papers on the table. An end in sight, with a new beginning now closer than ever. On the one hand, she was content. On the other, it meant losing him forever, and it pained her.

All Elaine could do was hope Alice would reconsider walking away from Harper, but she understood the difficulty of her decision. It all came down to whether she could look beyond the horror story and see him for the man she'd fallen in love with.

Lenny looked up as Elaine pulled a chair out from under the table. 'You're late,' he said.

'Traffic.' She glanced across at his plate with a bemused expression, trying to see what possible delights were hidden beneath the layers of red and brown sauce. 'What *are* you eating?'

'Full English,' he answered, bursting the egg yolk with a forkful of black pudding.

She said nothing and quietly sipped her coffee, even holding her tongue when she noticed the yolk running down his chin.

When Lenny devoured the remainder of his breakfast and guzzled down the last drops of tea, his satisfied expression suggested he'd just consumed the finest meal of his entire life. Something she'd come to like about Lenny was his simplicity. He wasn't about possessions and fine dining or jetting off around the world to exotic destinations; he was a grounded man who fought with strength and passion for what he believed in.

Elaine had long since forgiven him for his misguided accusations regarding Charlie; however, he had been spot on when he'd implied there was an inner darkness about her. She'd known he was right all along, and now, so did he. In the past, it might have been a bad thing to have him know so many secrets about her, but now – now it was different. Lenny was different. They had become entwined in a common goal to find Charlie's heartless murderer.

Many strange events had occurred since her son's death, and she had often speculated whether life was predestined, leading to this point. The paths of five people coming together to hunt an evil monster couldn't come down to mere happenstance. If not for her, Lenny, and the deceased Colin Hargreaves, no one would have known about Joseph Webster or the killer who had come before him. How many young children had the pair killed between them? A question that would probably go unanswered. The more she reflected, the more confident she became about finding him. There were no coincidences. All things happen for a reason. She had never been more certain.

'Elaine!'

'What?'

'Blimey, at last,' said Lenny. 'You were away with the fairies. I've already called you three times. Shall we get a move on?'

'Yes, I think we should. We can't afford to waste any more time.'

Lenny said, 'Regardless of how positive I sounded trying to convince Tom that locating this bloke was possible, the chances are slim. You know that, right?'

'I thought the same at first, but *we* will find him,' she said.

'I've always loved your optimism.'

Lenny took out his phone to check the time and saw he'd recently received a voicemail from Olivia, sent the night before. *Bloody phone networks!* He grinned like a Cheshire cat as he listened.

'I never thought I'd see the day,' said Elaine.

Unusually bashful, Lenny quickly put his phone away. 'Right, come on then, let's find this bastard.'

Lenny dropped Elaine off at the top of the road, where she crossed over to the path on the other side of the river. She was to continue on foot, and Lenny would drive the car to Tanners Wharf, where they would swap over. If either of them found anything suspicious, they were to call the other. There were only three houseboats on her part of the journey, none of which were worthy of further investigation.

At Tanners Wharf, they made the scheduled change. Lenny had barely walked a mile before he was on the phone to her, complaining about his aching feet. Nevertheless, he carried on, taking a short rest here and there. They swapped places again at South Mill Lock and Twyford Lock. Despite his earlier fuss, Lenny persevered, and they continued their arduous search down to Spellbrook, Tednambury, and stopped for a longer rest at Sawbridgeworth Lock.

Sitting in the car with the engine running, the air conditioning blasted a cool breeze into their hot faces as they each consumed a bottle of water. With the sweat pouring off Lenny, Elaine could tell he was feeling the strain and insisted on making the nearly five-mile trek to Burnt Mill Lock on her own, where they would meet at The Moorhen pub and grill. At that point, they would have covered around nine miles of the river between them.

Twenty-five minutes into her walk along a quiet stretch of the river, Elaine was sure the killer must have gone in the opposite direction from The Moorhen and hoped Harper or Tom would have more luck. She checked the time: almost two in the afternoon. As she put her phone away, it rang. Tom called to explain what had happened in Roydon and how Harper could be wounded.

She snarled furiously down the phone, 'How did the police know he'd be there, Tom?'

After a short pause, Tom said, 'I called them.'

Stunned into silence, Elaine didn't know how to respond. Further along the river, she observed a red and green narrowboat moored to the side, shaded by a long line of trees. It appeared to be an old boat, about seventy feet in length, with one end modified to a higher level than the rest. She continued walking, the faint sound of its engine growing louder as she neared. A man stepped onto the raised deck by the tiller. Her heart raced, fiercely knocking against her chest. She quickened her pace and raised the phone to her ear.

'I've found him, Tom,' she said, her voice brimming with determined satisfaction.

'Who, Harper?'

'Webster!'

Elaine ran as fast as she could as the narrowboat steadily pulled away from the riverbank. She drew level with the back of the boat and glared intently, locking eyes with Webster, who was clearly startled to see her.

The gap widened as she closed in. She had to make her move before it was too late and leapt into the air to make the four-foot jump onto the boat. Her feet landed on the gunwale, and she slapped her hands on the roof to pull her body tight against the side. The phone slipped from her grasp, and she watched it slide across the top and over the edge.

Elaine climbed onto the roof. Joseph Webster was marching towards her. She scrambled to her feet and lunged headfirst into his midriff, forcing him to fall hard onto his back. Elaine landed on top of him and wrapped her hands around the front of his neck, a profound look in her eyes.

He lashed out with a fierce punch to the side of her face, causing instant numbness and a constant ringing in her ears. Her grip remained firm. The second punch knocked her off him. Webster got to his knees, reached an arm around her neck, and placed her in a headlock. He squeezed tightly; Elaine couldn't breathe. She tried to pull his arm away, but he was too strong. Desperation kicked in, and she thrashed her legs around, growing weaker by the second. Suffocating. Darkness loomed as black fog billowed inside her head. Elaine's eyes closed.

33

The Boy

Heavy footsteps above signalled that the man had returned with no idea what he would find waiting for him. A few minutes passed before the door to the pitch-dark room opened. A dull streak of daylight exposed fresh blood on the floor.

Spatters and drips.

An eerie silence.

A continuous click as the man attempted but failed to switch on the light. He lingered in the doorway above the three steps, his shadow cast across the floor. Perhaps he was apprehensive about entering, knowing one of the boys might be dead, but the other was armed.

Zeph called into the room, 'I see you boys have been busy, but which one of you is victorious, I wonder?' His attempt to gain a response was unsuccessful.

'Danny!' he called.

Not a sound crept from within the room.

'You boys had better not be messing with me.'

Reluctant to enter, Zeph listened for the faintest sound. Nothing. He stepped cautiously down and edged closer to the centre of the room. Fear was indiscriminate and could burrow into the blackest of hearts. Something crunched beneath his feet. He knelt down and saw the shattered remains of the long tubular bulb and the camera.

'I see you found the hidden camera. Clever boy!' he said, staring into the blackness. Increasingly frustrated by the silence, he scanned the shadows. 'You'd both better be unconscious or dead.'

Standing near the metal plate, Zeph reached down for one of the chains and fed it slowly through his hands, drawing it towards him until it became taut. He took one step forward and stopped, unwilling to stray into the unknown. With more effort, he pulled on the chain, dragging something heavy along the floor. He glimpsed a shackled leg and continued to draw the body closer. Danny's bloodied white shirt came into view. He paused, sighed with disappointment, and dropped the chain.

Reaching down for the other chain, Zeph once more fed the slack through his fingers until it became tight. He heaved the dead weight and saw Danny's body move; the other boy was snagged behind him. Visibly anxious, Zeph inched towards the prostrate body, Danny's face concealed by the shadows, his torso missing an arm. Nervous, Zeph knelt down, grabbed Danny's ankle, and pulled his body closer until he saw the side of his face. Stunned, he dropped the leg and looked up . . .

Danny emerged like a ghost from the darkness, running, screaming, wielding the axe high above his head, his face drenched in blood, his eyes full of hate and rage. He scowled at the man and swung the axe towards his chest. Zeph stepped sideways and reached out to grab the handle. He yelled in agony as the axe cut into his shoulder, but he managed to minimise the blade's impact. Danny attempted to pull the axe back, but the man was far too strong.

Zeph stared into his tired, psychotic, and bloodshot eyes, recognising a face as unfeeling as his own. 'Damn, boy. It's like looking in a mirror.'

With his other hand, he shoved Danny in the chest with enough force to send him onto his backside. Zeph glanced at his bloodied shoulder and tossed the axe across the room. Danny jumped up, once more on the attack, pummelling his fists into the man's body. Zeph wrapped his arms around the boy and restrained him. Danny wriggled and struggled to break free, frustrated that he had failed in his plan to kill the man. Holding the boy tightly, Zeph dropped to his knees. It took a while, but eventually, Danny stopped thrashing around and fell asleep.

The Plan

To keep turning his back on Connor was dangerous, but with time running out, Danny had no choice. The monster could only be taken down if his companion played his part. Danny had discussed in detail with Connor how they were going to trick the man, and once everything was in place, they would strike and catch him unawares. For it to work, he needed to gain Connor's confidence, and at last, it looked as though he'd won him over. Yes, Danny had a plan, all right.

Connor walked past him towards the toilet and placed his axe on the floor. Danny turned away to give him some privacy. When he'd finished, Danny informed him about the camera on the ceiling and the need to disable it. He persuaded Connor to climb onto his back and strike it with the axe.

Danny's nerves were on edge. His hands trembled, and his legs were restless. Zeph would be here soon – he could feel him getting closer. It was more than instinct – he'd become connected to the man in some sick and twisted way. He breathed deeply, needing to calm down and compose himself. 'You can do this,' he said quietly, and then turned to Connor. 'He's close.'

'How do you know?'

'I just do. We need to get ready.' Danny grabbed the axe from the bed and stood.

Connor approached, gripping *his* axe. 'Which one of us is lying down to play dead?'

'I don't mind. But we need to hurry up and decide,' said Danny, urgency in his tone.

Both boys waited for the other to volunteer. Danny took control and said, 'Okay, I'll get on the floor, but it means as soon as his attention is on me, you need to hit him with the axe. You need to strike fast, and you need to strike hard. Aim for his head if you can.'

'His head? I don't know if I can do that,' said Connor.

'You can do it. You have to. It's our only way out of here.' Just as Danny had expected, Connor was clearly troubled by the task he had set for him.

'I'll play dead,' said Connor.

'Are you sure?'

'I don't know. Yes! You kill him.'

'Okay then,' said Danny, and walked to the gap between the toilet and the bed. 'You need to lie on the floor here.'

'Why there?'

'Connor, we discussed this. We need to confuse him. He'll assume I'm on this side of the room, and when he approaches you lying here, he won't be expecting me to attack from the shadows. If *you* want to attack him, then we need to go to your side of the room.'

'No, it's fine. I get it.' Connor slowly dropped to his knees, his eyes locked on Danny.

Paranoid tension remained. Danny could sense Connor wondering whether he was right to trust him.

Connor lay on his back, his hand not letting go of the axe.

'It's better if you lie on your front,' said Danny.

'Why? What difference does it make?'

'Because he might see you breathing. We don't want to alert him in any way. Once you're in position, I'm going to smash the light, as we talked about. When he finds your body, I will attack. Then you quickly get to your feet and join in.' There was reluctance and uncertainty on the young boy's face. 'It's going to be all right, Connor. We can do this. If we're going to get out of here alive, we have to do this.'

Finally, a hint of faith appeared in Connor's eyes. Danny placed his axe on the bed – a final show of trust and togetherness. Connor rolled onto his front, and Danny knelt to help situate his body into a more realistic pose: one leg bent, the other straight. He told Connor to spread his arms wide and stood to see if it looked believable.

'It's still not quite right. Something is missing.' Danny bent down again and wrapped his fingers around Connor's axe, attempting to pry it from his grasp. 'This needs to be on its own a few inches from your fingers.' Connor was reluctant to let go. 'It will look more natural,' said Danny. Connor sighed and released his grip on the axe. Danny moved it a short distance from Connor's hand. 'Yes, that's perfect. Right, I'd better get into position.'

Danny walked a few steps, stopped, turned, and ambled back towards the bed. 'It would help if I took the axe with me, don't you think?'

Connor looked up and smiled nervously. 'Well, you're not going to do much damage without it.'

Danny grabbed the axe from the bed and gripped it tightly. 'No,' he said calmly. 'You're right about that!' He swung the axe into Connor's back.

Connor's horrendous scream expressed a thousand words of betrayal as Danny struggled to pull the axe free. Connor reached for the axe on the floor, an inch from his straining fingertips. Danny managed to prise the axe from Connor's back and swung it with force, chopping through the flesh and bone of Connor's skinny arm. Another ghastly scream erupted from the poor boy. Danny tugged the axe free from the floor and glared at the severed forearm, the fingers twitching against the wooden handle. Ready to strike again, Connor cried out. He fixed his sad, terrified eyes on Danny and pleaded with him to stop, but it was far too late to stop now. Danny had to finish this.

'Blood! That's what was missing. Zeph would never have bought my plan without plenty of blood,' said Danny, repeatedly burying the axe in Connor's back.

After a mere few seconds of merciless violence, he glanced down at what he had done with no hint of shame or regret. His face was awash with deep red blood, dripping from the end of his nose and chin. Using the bloody axe, he cut through the jeans on Connor's chained leg and removed his trousers. He took off the boy's shirt and dressed him in one of *his* oversized white ones. Danny backed away towards the fluorescent light and, using the axe, jumped up to smash the tube. Complete darkness swallowed the room.

A little over ten minutes later, footsteps thumped above. Zeph was back. Danny moved into position, his chain scraping quietly along the floor as he prepared for his final battle. A disturbed expression formed on Danny's face. An unnerving grin. Unhinged. The scared little boy within was gone.

His face clean of Connor's blood, Danny was woken in bed by the clanging of the bucket hitting the floor. Adjusting his eyes to the restored lighting, Zeph dropped some towels and a couple of hessian bags next to the bucket. Despondent, Danny chose not to look over the side of the bed at the spot where he'd hacked Connor to death. He didn't want to believe he had committed such an atrocious act, but he had, and he didn't need to see the body to know it was true.

Danny knew what he had done and why he had taken the life of the other boy. Connor's death was supposed to set him free, but not in the way the man had promised. He didn't trust Zeph and had used Connor's body as a decoy to kill him as well, removing any doubts about securing his freedom. Danny struggled to get his head around having gone through with it and failing. A shudder of guilt, shame, and disgust rippled through his body. He sank into his pillow. He had taken poor Connor's life for nothing.

'You did well, Danny boy. Though I knew you had it in you, I wasn't sure you would go through with it.'

'Do I get to go home now?'

'I don't know about that.'

'But I did what you wanted.'

'Attacking me was not part of the deal. Besides, after the horrible things you've done since you've been here, do you really believe there is a place for you out there in the real world?'

'You were never going to let me go, were you?'

Zeph smiled, suggesting he had answered his own question.

'You caught me good,' said Zeph, caressing his shoulder.

'I wish I'd killed you!'

'I know you do, Danny boy. I know you do. Right, the bucket is over there with the cleaning stuff. You have some work to do.' Zeph turned to leave.

'Clean it yourself!'

The man stopped in his tracks with his back to the boy. For a moment, Zeph remained still; then he stormed across the room in a rage and wrapped his large hand tightly around Danny's throat, forcing his head deep into the mangy pillow. 'Do not test me, boy. You've seen what I can do, but you have no idea what I'm capable of or how miserable I can make your worthless existence.'

Danny's pale face strained but failed to redden, a sign of his weakening state of body and mind. The man released his grip and backed away. Gasping, Danny crawled from the bed, grabbed the bucket, and walked over to the shower to fill it.

'There are bags next to the body. Chop him into pieces, and I'll dispose of the remains. When you're done, leave the axe on the top step in front of the door. No more silly games.'

With the man gone, Danny got to work. Unlike before, he found his despicable task surprisingly easy. Two hours later, a blood-spattered Danny heard a muffled commotion above. There were loud thumps and – was that someone yelling? On his knees, Danny's gaze turned to Connor, his body cut into pieces in front of him. He stared into the open eyes of Connor's severed head and felt nothing. The door to the room burst open, and Zeph appeared, dragging the body of a woman by her ankles down the steps and into the middle of the room.

'We have a special guest,' said Zeph, marching across to the other room and reappearing with a small tool in his hand. 'Pass me the axe.'

Danny didn't wait to be asked twice and took it over to him. Zeph grabbed the axe and chopped through the dead boy's lower leg to release the chain. The man seemed to be in a hurry and used the tool to undo the shackle, which he then placed around the woman's ankle. Back on his feet, he tossed the tool on the floor in the other room and closed the door. Zeph picked up the axe and raced across the room towards the steps. The room shook violently with a loud bang, and the man lurched forward, almost losing his footing. A crunching sound reverberated around the room, quickly followed by an ominous scraping sound. Zeph righted himself and dashed up the steps and through the door, slamming it shut behind him.

The boat had obviously hit something, and judging by the noise, there could be serious damage. With Zeph stomping around above, Danny walked over to the unconscious woman. She had some swelling and a nasty cut on her cheekbone. It looked painful. Danny nudged her to see if she would wake. When she didn't, he hurried to the sink and soaked a clean piece of cloth. After he'd gently cleaned the blood from her face, he continued to put the remaining parts of Connor's body into the bags. As soon as he finished, Danny sat beside the woman on the floor and waited.

34

Lenny

Thoughts of being younger, fitter, and healthier plagued Lenny's mind. Although he would have struggled to walk any further, he hated leaving Elaine to continue and complete the long trek on her own. On his way to The Moorhen, he received a call from Tom, asking him to divert to The Boathouse Café in Roydon. Tom didn't give a reason, but his voice expressed urgency.

Passing two police cars at the entrance, Lenny pulled into the car park, fully aware that some kind of commotion had taken place. There were more police vehicles parked up ahead. Could it be something to do with Joseph Webster? Had he been captured or perhaps killed? Quite a few people were milling about outside the café – probably customers and staff, excited by the police presence and wanting to see what was happening.

Lenny exited his car and approached a man who had just buckled his young child into a car seat. 'What's going on?'

'I don't know much, really. There were loads of armed police chasing some guy. I think they've still got a helicopter in the area.'

'Yeah, I noticed the helicopter from the road. Did they catch him?'

'I don't think so. Rumours are going around that the police shot him. I don't know whether that's true or not. You know how quickly people like to exaggerate and gossip.'

'Did you hear any shots fired?'

'We were inside, where it was quite noisy, but I'm pretty sure I did.'

Lenny spotted Tom in the distance on the grassy bank by the river, talking on his phone. 'Okay! Cheers, mate.' Lenny walked over, hoping Tom could elaborate on what had happened.

As Lenny neared, Tom finished his conversation and appeared agitated, pacing up and down, fumbling with his phone and returning it to his ear. Lenny's phone rang. He reached into his pocket and saw it was Tom.

'Tom!' he shouted.

Tom turned and disconnected the call. 'I was just calling you.'

Lenny held up his phone. 'I can see that. What the bloody hell is going on?'

'Elaine has found Webster.'

'What? She never called me!'

'No, on the phone, just then. She found him while I was talking to her about Harper. I heard her running, and then the phone went dead. I tried again, but nothing.' Tom was clearly panicked.

'Well, where was she?'

'I don't know,' Tom snapped, frustrated and angry. 'That's why I was calling you.'

Lenny called her mobile. Nothing. He then checked his watch. 'Right, come on. She can't be too far from where I dropped her off. The quicker we get back there, the quicker we'll find her.'

Lenny recognised DCI Baxendale over by the café, who in turn saw him from the decking. He motioned to Lenny, suggesting he wanted to talk. There was no time to stop and chat with the detective; he and Tom needed to get to Elaine. They hurried over to Lenny's car, and as they pulled away, Lenny glanced at Baxendale in the rear-view mirror, standing in the road.

'What were you talking to her about Harper for? What's going on, Tom?'

'The police came for Harper at the café. I think he's been shot.' The echoes of Tom's betrayal hung in the air.

'Oh, Tom, please tell me you didn't?'

Tom sighed and glanced sideways. 'I did. I thought it was the right thing to do at the time.'

'And then?'

'And then I didn't. I told him to run.'

'I doubt Elaine will forgive you.'

'I know.' Tom bowed his head in regret. 'Let's just find her before something bad happens.'

As they continued towards Sawbridgeworth Lock, their voices fell silent; both were worried, contemplating different outcomes. Neither wanted to believe the worst, but Lenny accepted that the worst was a distinct possibility. The two men had been dragged into the aftermath of what had occurred thirty-odd years previously and the consequential lives of the siblings.

'What made you change your mind and tell Harper to run?' Lenny was desperate to distract his mind from worst-case scenarios.

Tom took a long, deep breath, pausing before giving his answer. 'I wanted the man who killed those people to pay for what he did. Before he pulled the trigger and shot me, I stared deep into his eyes. They were dark and soulless. Pure evil. You don't forget a moment like that. Not ever. But sitting across from him today,

I don't know. Call me crazy, but it wasn't the same man. I looked into those eyes, and suddenly, it all felt wrong. Like I was wrong.'

Lenny shifted in his seat. 'If it helps in any way, Tom, I don't believe you're crazy or wrong. Don't forget, I stared into those wicked eyes as well. You're not the only one who sees a change in him. I'm not saying he couldn't lose it again, but I think a few scores have been settled, and they are both ready to move on with their lives.'

'I just hope I did the right thing, Lenny.'

'Do you know exactly what happened to him in the past?'

'Are you trying to sell me a copy of your book?'

Lenny glared at Tom.

'Yeah – I know the whole story. My father was one of the arresting officers that night. I bet that wasn't in your book! Like many others, he was forced to keep quiet. He wasn't content with doing nothing at all, though, and stole the files containing the original crime and arrest reports.'

'What? You mean you have the original reports? Does Elaine know?'

'Of course she knows. She told me to burn them.'

'Burn them! Why would she ask you to do that? They could have helped prove everything in the book was true.'

'I wasn't sure at the time, but in light of recent revelations, we both know why,' said Tom. 'If she had released the real names, they wouldn't have been able to make them pay for what they did.'

'So, you knew the names of all the men involved?'

'Yes.'

'And you didn't put two and two together when they started getting bumped off?'

'I haven't looked at that file in years. I recognised Edward Horner's name, but come on, Lenny, why would I think Elaine was responsible?'

'I suppose,' said Lenny. 'Did you burn the file?'

'No. My father must have believed that one day the truth *would* come out, and he'd be able to supply invaluable evidence for the investigation. I held on to the files in case Elaine changed her mind, but after yesterday's revelations . . .'

'Yeah, it's probably best if you burn the files at the first chance you get.'

'I will.'

The car pulled onto Mill Lane, and Lenny parked in the same place as before, just over the bridge by Sawbridgeworth Lock. He and Tom stepped out of the car and looked around. Lenny walked a few steps along the path Elaine had taken and stopped. There were no boats in sight.

Standing behind Lenny, Tom said, 'Well, what should we do now?'

Lenny pointed. 'I think *you* should start heading in that direction, and I'll drive down a little further than she could have walked and make my way back towards you.'

Tom nodded. 'Sounds like a good idea,' he said, immediately setting off along the riverside path.

Lenny drove to Sheering Lower Road and stopped to consult his tatty, ancient paper map. He continued a little further down the road until he came to a padlocked double gate. Fortunately, Lenny gained access via the wide gap to the side of the gate. Driving through a large muddy puddle and across the field by way of a beaten-down path made by a tractor, he came to a stop at the railway tracks. Checking both ways, he continued along the tractor route until he arrived at Feakes Lock.

Certain she couldn't have reached this point, he locked the car and stood on the bridge. A little way down the river was a red and green narrowboat that must have recently passed through the lock. He hoped to God it wasn't the boat they were searching for and walked in the opposite direction along the path towards Tom.

35

Harper

The train pulled into Harlow Mill Station. Harper was happy to have had a rest after his gruelling escape from the police. The wound above his hip was distressing, but it wasn't going to deter his search for Joseph Webster. Now without a phone, he hoped to bump into Elaine en route.

As the train doors opened, he spotted a mauve sweater draped over the back of a seat. He swooped in and snatched it without anyone noticing, then stepped onto the platform. On his way out of the station, he pulled on the sweater to hide his bloodied shirt. A middle-aged couple climbed out of a taxi. Harper jumped into the back seat and asked the driver to drop him by the river.

On the short journey, the police helicopter hovered over the fields in the distance. He smiled at the irony of it all; he was desperate to find Webster, and the police were desperate to find him. Harper imagined he would become old news when the crimes of Joseph Webster came to light. Not forgotten, but old news nonetheless.

As the taxi pulled into a near-empty car park belonging to a riverside brasserie, the driver called out the fare and twisted around in his seat. Harper reached into his damp jeans and pulled out a few soggy banknotes. He handed a twenty-pound note to the driver and told him to keep the change. The man took the wet cash, completely oblivious to Harper's dishevelled appearance.

In the far corner of the car park next to the restaurant, he opened a wooden gate that led to the riverbank path. With one hand nursing his side, he looked at the path ahead: scenic but arduous. A narrowboat was moored close to the brasserie, with a bright pink girl's bicycle lying on the deck, the garish colour *screaming*, "Here I am!" Did he dare steal another bike? A child's bike, at that.

Harper cycled along the thin, bumpy dirt path like a man without a care in the world, enjoying a charming bicycle ride in the countryside, taking in the delightful sights along the river. Of course, this was not the case at all. For one, he was a grown man riding a pink child's bike, and secondly, he'd been shot. Yes, it may well be just a flesh wound, but it still smarted like a son of a . . .

Inside, he was the same as ever, confused about his identity and hurting from all that had gone before. Alice was the only person who had made him forget who he really was, but he couldn't expect *her* to save him from his dreadful past. Life wasn't that simple. He didn't even know whether she wanted him or if *she* was the one who'd turned him in. Had the text he'd replied to alerted the authorities to his location? He no longer suspected Lenny, and if it wasn't Alice, the only other person was Tom. Why did he need to know when it didn't even matter? It wasn't as though he could blame any of them for turning him in.

He hadn't been cycling for long, but he was now far enough away from the town to be in the middle of nowhere. Trees and bushes lined the river on both sides, beyond which were fields stretching out as far as the eye could see. Up ahead, a narrowboat appeared to be coming to a stop beside the path. Slowing the bike as he approached, the damage to the front of the boat at water level on the far side was hard to miss. It had clearly been involved in a collision of some kind. A man came into view and leaned over the side to inspect the damage.

Harper stopped alongside and shouted, 'Looks pretty bad!'

The man looked over. 'Yeah, I think it's worse than I suspected.' He wandered across the deck. 'It happened a little way back. Another boat hit me. Some people just shouldn't be on the river.'

The men were locked in a deep, prolonged stare, attempting to assess each other. The man's account sounded reasonable, and his behaviour appeared normal, but what was Harper's normal? His instincts were on high alert. Was it possible for one killer to detect another?

'Nice bike,' the man teased, injecting humour into the tense silence.

Harper smiled. 'It's my daughter's.'

'Anyway, I should probably try to repair my boat before it sinks.'

'I reckon that's a good idea,' said Harper. He scrutinised the boat. Black curtains covered the windows, two of which were boarded up from the outside and painted red to match the main colour.

Before leaving, Harper said, 'This other boat, the one that hit you, how far away is it?'

'About a mile or so by now, I should think.'

The other boat could be the one he was looking for. Harper cycled past the name *ZEPHYR*, painted in large white capital letters on the side of the boat. A strange sensation of being watched came over him, as though the man's eyes burned along with the sun into the back of his neck. Harper glanced over his shoulder, but the man was nowhere to be seen. He cycled on for about four minutes and stopped. Something didn't feel right. A nagging voice was telling him to go back. Harper turned the bike around and cycled to a bend in the river, where he observed the red and green narrowboat in the distance. He contemplated whether he should go back and investigate further. Could he afford to ignore his gut feeling? Across the river, the dead children glared at him. Whether they were there or not, he listened to his inner voice and cycled back towards the boat.

As he neared, there was no sign of the man. He deduced that he was below deck assessing the damage from inside. Harper stopped and stared at the weathered white lettering – *ZEPHYR*. He dismounted, laid the bike on the ground, and moved in for a closer look. A lighter shade of green covered the previous name, with the white letters added over the top.

On closer inspection, the outline of the old letters underneath spelled out the name *OZIAS*, which meant nothing to him. He looked again at the name *ZEPHYR*. 'Zeph,' he said. 'Joseph.' Looking up, the ghosts of the dead children were standing all over the roof and deck. This *was* the boat, and he'd found Joseph Webster.

Vigilant, Harper climbed quietly aboard the front of the narrowboat, wincing in pain as he stretched. He nursed his side, the mauve sweater dampening from a slow bleed. A helicopter whirred in the distance. Not wanting to alert Joseph Webster, he crept along the deck and under the canvas canopy to the door. It was locked. There was no way of breaking in without being heard, so he would have to try the entrance at the other end.

Harper turned his back, and the door squeaked open behind him. He paused, sighed, and quickly spun around. A small metal toolbox smacked against the side of his head, knocking him to the deck with a loud thump. Disoriented, he scrambled to his hands and knees. His eyes flickered as sporadic drips of blood fell from a cut above his temple and soon became a constant trickle. Needing to act fast, Harper rolled onto his front. The toolbox crashed down beside him, tools littering the deck. Webster dove on top of him and punched his face.

With his head forced to the side, Harper spotted a long, thick screwdriver and a Stanley knife within his reach. Webster grabbed his head, raised it, and smashed it onto the floor. Dazed and weakening, Harper stretched to reach one of the tools, blindly scouring the deck. He located the screwdriver and plunged it into Joseph Webster's side, sending him rolling away in agony.

Webster's hand covered the wound but couldn't prevent the blood from surging between his fingers as he crawled towards the edge of the boat. Harper sat up, weak, half-dazed, but desperate to make good his advantage. He launched himself at Webster and thrust the screwdriver into his back. Less than a foot from the edge, Joseph's body dropped down, prostrate on the deck.

Harper collapsed onto his back in agony, wiping the blood from his left eye. He needed a moment to catch his breath, and he took it. Clambering to his feet, he examined Webster, the screwdriver sticking out of his back. The boat shuddered and tilted at the front, almost throwing Harper off balance. Webster wasn't joking when he'd said it could sink.

Lenny had implied that a young boy *could* be imprisoned on the boat. Harper knelt down and heaved the lifeless body of Joseph Webster over the edge into the water. His body vanished beneath the surface of the murky water. Harper staggered across the deck, through the open door, and down the steps.

36

Elaine

Elaine moved her head first and then slowly opened her eyes. She bolted upright and, not for the first time, felt intense pain in her jaw and cheekbone. A mixture of musty and putrid odours attacked her senses as she took in her surroundings and fixed her eyes on a gaunt young boy covered in blood beside her. Pleased to see he was alive, Elaine wrapped her arms around him and discerned he'd longed for someone to make him feel safe – a temporary comfort, but it was better than nothing.

With gentle hands, she eased him back to look into his tired and withdrawn eyes. He stared back at her, tears rolling down his cheeks, which she wiped away with her thumb.

'Are you hurt?' she asked.

'No, it's not my blood,' he said, his voice as subdued as his demeanour.

With the boy clearly traumatised, she didn't want to ask whose blood it was. 'What's your name?'

'Daniel, but everybody calls me Danny.'

'Daniel Logan?'

'Yes,' he said, a spark of light in his eyes because she knew his name. 'Are you a police officer?'

'No. I'm not with the police, but I know who you are. Some friends and I have been searching for the man who has been keeping you captive. I'm going to get you out of here.'

'But how?' he asked, rattling the chain attached to his ankle.

Elaine observed the shackles around both their ankles. Hiding her concern, she got to her feet, exuding positivity. 'It's okay, I'll find a way.' She walked over and examined the metal plate and the iron ring that held the chains in place. Reaching down, she pulled on the chain to test its strength and then headed towards the door.

'They don't reach either of the doors,' said Danny, which she soon discovered.

Studying the room, it was difficult to conceal her reaction to a mass of blood on the floor. Danny had moved and was now sitting on the edge of the bed, watching her every move. His demoralised countenance told her he was less than optimistic about getting out of there.

'We will get out of here,' she said, sitting next to him.

Her mind raced, determined to find a way out of this dreadful situation. On the far side of the room, against the wall, were two large hessian mailbags that she'd previously glimpsed. Realisation struck, and her stomach turned. 'Danny, whose blood is all over you and on the floor?'

He hesitated, then pointed to the bags. Elaine laboured over to peek inside, knowing it wasn't going to be pleasant. An animal, perhaps a dog or something. She opened the top of one bag and recoiled at the dismembered limbs of a child. Overcome with nausea, Elaine retched. She thought she'd seen everything, but this was something else, and it chilled her to the bone.

'I'm sorry,' said Danny.

Troubled by his reaction, she asked, 'Why are you sorry?'

'The man – he made me do it.' Danny covered his face with his hands and sobbed.

Elaine rushed over to comfort him once again, sickened by what he'd been forced to do.

'I just wanted to go home,' he said.

'And you will. I promise.' She pulled him close and stroked the back of his head. 'I'll get you home,' she said, uncertain it was a promise she would be able to keep.

'You said you'd been searching for Zeph. Why?' asked Danny.

She deliberated for a moment and said, 'A few years ago, he took *my* boy.' Her eyes welled up. She had come so close to making the bastard pay, and now, having not waited for the others, her thoughts were rife with self-condemnation.

'What was your son's name?'

'Charlie!'

Danny pulled back, rose from the bed, and held out his hand. She took hold and let him lead her across the room. Reaching the table, he let go and turned it on its side. Danny knelt down, showed her the list of boys, and pointed to the first name etched into the wood. 'This Charlie?'

Hand to mouth, Elaine fell to her knees. She hadn't even considered that her son had been imprisoned in this very room, possibly killed here. Elaine ran her finger over Charlie's name, reliving the hurt she had experienced many times over. Fresh. Constant. As ingrained in the wood as it was in her heart. Her fingers caressed the names of the other boys. So much had been taken away. So much agony.

They returned to the bed, and after a while, Danny fell asleep in the comforting warmth of her embrace. The poor lad must have been physically and mentally exhausted. The best therapy in the world wouldn't be able to heal this damaged little boy. She scoured the room, frantically searching for a means of escape, which didn't look at all possible. All her hopes were on Tom, Lenny, and Harper.

Harper! She hadn't had time to process that he'd been wounded or Tom's attempt to turn him in. Why had Tom done such a thing and betrayed her? All things considered, perhaps he was right to. She should never have expected so much from him. It pained her to think how selfish and unfair she'd been to her husband.

Cold water crept over Elaine's feet, rising up through the floorboards and jolting her thoughts to the present. There must be a burst pipe or something. Danny clung to her as she tried to ease away and lay him down. Even in sleep, he sought solace and safety. Staring intently at his face, she recognised him from her vision of the boy in her bathtub, but how—

The door opened, and Joseph Webster stomped down the steps into the room. Elaine glared at him, full of scorn – tempted to attack but scared for the boy's safety. Webster returned a cold, blank stare as he stormed across the room towards the other door.

'I'll deal with you later,' he said, clearly concerned about the water beneath his feet.

He entered the other room and closed the door. After a minute or so, there was a knocking sound. Repairing the leak, perhaps? A loud crashing noise vibrated throughout the boat, followed by an eerie rumbling. Then, except for the modest waves of water lapping against her feet, silence. Her white trainers were stained with a pink wash from the blood on the floorboards and underneath. Elaine removed her feet from the water, bringing them up onto the bed. Panic set in.

'Danny, wake up,' she said, stroking his face.

His eyes opened, filled with hope and excitement, but reality dawned and his buoyant demeanour faded.

Elaine pointed to the floor. 'Has this happened before?'

Danny sat up, looked down from the bed, and shook his head, worried. 'Are we sinking?'

'I don't know, Danny. I don't know what's going on.'

'The boat hit something soon after the man brought you in. It shook quite badly.'

Elaine leapt from the bed and hurried over to the table. She flipped it on its side, snapped off one of the legs, and stood the table upright, resting it against the wall.

On her way back to Danny, the boat jerked. She lost her balance and slipped, getting soaked in the process. Scrambling to her feet, she perceived a tilt to the room, and the water was deeper in one corner. She jumped on the bed and hid the table leg under the covers. A loud thumping noise in the other room forced her to grip the table leg. The door opened, and there he was.

'Harper!' she said, surprised and relieved.

'Elaine!'

Aware of the boy close behind her, he rushed over to the bed, observing the shackles around their ankles. He grasped the iron ring that was bolted to the floor and pulled in vain.

'There's a tool!' Danny shouted. 'The man tossed it on the floor of the room over there.'

Harper raced off to find it as Elaine and Danny climbed from the bed to peer through the open door. As the boat jolted with a deep, prolonged groan, the chained pair stumbled to the floor. The table fell, and the two mailbags containing the Connors' remains tipped over, spilling their contents into the water. Harper was on his hands and knees, frantically scouring the floor under the water, the level of which was rapidly rising. His hand surfaced, holding a small object.

'That's it!' said Danny. 'That's the key thing.'

Elaine and Danny got back on the bed, pulling their feet from the water.

Harper splashed across the room with the Allen key, dropped to his knees in front of the boy, and removed the shackle from his bruised and reddened ankle.

'Right, kid, get up on the deck and wait for us,' ordered Harper, moving across to free Elaine.

Danny waded across to the other room, the water level rising with each step. He reached the stairs and headed up towards daylight. Elaine turned her attention back to her brother as he unfastened the shackle.

'Is Webster dead?' she asked.

'Yeah.'

She caressed the cut on his head and observed blood seeping through his sweater. 'Is it bad?'

'It's just a scratch,' he said. She got the impression he wasn't being truthful.

With the shackle removed, the pair made for the stairs to catch up with Danny. Elaine regarded the skeletal figure in the wheelchair and turned to Harper, who seemed unperturbed by the sight and was more concerned with getting off the boat.

As Elaine placed her foot on the first tread, a dark shadow loomed in the doorway above, blocking out the light. Danny glared down at them, and standing tall behind him was Joseph Webster, with a Stanley knife pressed firmly against the boy's throat.

'Move back,' said Webster as he and the boy descended.

Retreating slowly into the bedroom, Elaine focused on Danny, who was trembling with fear, his neck bleeding due to the pressure being applied by the blade.

Before following them into the room, Webster paused to collect something from a small drawer of a shabby old chest. He ordered Elaine and Harper to stop when they reached the bed, unconcerned that the blood-red water was now at knee height. As another grating creak bellowed from the sinking narrowboat, getting the boy off the boat was Elaine's main priority.

Webster kept his distance from the pair and handed whatever he had collected from the drawer to Danny. 'Hold it out to the lady, Danny boy.'

Elaine stepped forward, saw another Allen key in the palm of Danny's hand and knew instantly what Webster wanted her to do. As she took the key, she observed a constant stream of blood running down the side of Webster's hip and leg. His wound must be very bad, possibly fatal.

'Place the shackle around his ankle,' said Webster, gesturing towards Harper.

Elaine hesitated; there had to be something she could do.

'Come on, get on with it, or I'll slit the boy's throat.'

He meant it and wouldn't think twice. She glanced at Harper, hoping somehow he'd have a plan, but he nodded for her to get on with it. Elaine crouched down and reached into the water, combing the floor for the shackle. Her heart raced as she remembered the other key – it had to be nearby. After locating the shackle, she kept searching, and then her fingers brushed over it. Relieved, Elaine glanced at Harper and signalled with her eyes as she slipped the spare key into the side of his shoe, hoping he'd feel it and understand. She wrapped the shackle around her brother's ankle under the water.

'Where I can see!' said Webster. 'Don't take me for a fool.'

Harper lifted his foot onto the bed, and Elaine fastened the shackle in place with the key.

'Now, find the other shackle and come over here,' said Webster.

Once more, she bent down and blindly scoured the floor. Retrieving the shackle, she approached Webster.

'Reach down and put it on, and don't try anything stupid,' he said.

Elaine bent over and placed the shackle around her ankle.

'Not yours!' he said.

Elaine scowled at him in defiance. 'No. I'm not putting it on Danny.'

'I'm not asking you to put it on the boy. I want you to put it on me.'

At first baffled, Elaine grasped his awareness that, regardless of the outcome, he was going to die. Joseph Webster had chosen to go down with the only place he had ever really known as home, and he was taking Harper with him, possibly because Harper had struck the fatal blow. She happily fastened the shackle to Webster's ankle. Elaine stood upright when she was done and glared into the callous eyes of the man who had taken the life of her son.

Another violent quake vibrated through the boat. Everyone struggled to keep their balance as it listed at an alarming rate. The fluorescent light flickered out, and, other than a sliver of daylight creeping through the open doorway, the room fell dark. Webster ordered Elaine to turn on the switch by the door, allowing the red light to cast its devilish glow upon them.

'Give me the key and the boy is yours,' said Webster.

Elaine didn't delay. She put the key in his hand, and in turn, he pushed the boy towards her. Danny flung his arms around her waist.

Webster smiled. 'You get your freedom after all, Danny boy. You've earned it.'

Elaine gazed at Harper, tearful yet hopeful.

'Take the boy and get out of here, Elaine,' said Harper, ready to accept his fate.

She remained still, torn between getting the boy to safety and helping her brother, but deep down, there was only one option – save Danny.

Harper gave a faint smile and flicked his head to the side. 'Go.'

Mindful that the water had risen above Danny's waist, Elaine eased him forward in front of her. Guiding him through the door towards the steps and daylight, she glanced over her shoulder. Harper's eyes were focused on Joseph Webster. She hoped he would find the key, free himself, and escape, though it crossed her mind that she might never see her brother again.

She paused on the steps when the two men roared, followed by the sound of them charging through the water. Worried about the Stanley knife in Webster's hand, she wanted to turn back, but there was no time. The water climbed the steps behind her. *Get the boy out.* She hurried Danny through the door and onto the sloping deck, shocked to see water surging over the gunwale. At this rate, it wouldn't take long to sink.

With one side of the narrowboat beneath the water, the side they needed to jump from was higher than the riverbank. They eased their way steadily up to the gunwale. The gap between the boat and the bank had also increased in distance.

'Can you make that jump, Danny?'

Danny gazed nervously at the four-foot gap and the three-foot drop. With her hand on his shoulder to steady his balance, he shivered with fear. 'Listen, I'll jump first, then I want you to jump over to me. I'll catch you, okay?'

Danny nodded apprehensively, and as Elaine prepared to jump, her name was called. Tom and Lenny were running along the footpath. Tom arrived first, with a weary Lenny straggling further behind.

'Come on, kid,' said Tom. 'Jump across to me.'

Elaine helped Danny balance on the edge of the gunwale.

With urgency in his voice, Tom shouted, 'You can do it. Come on!'

Danny peered anxiously at the water below and then jumped into the safety of Tom's waiting arms. As he settled the boy on the path, a dishevelled Lenny finally arrived.

Tom returned to the edge of the path. 'Come on, Elaine. Jump!'

Balancing on the gunwale, Elaine stared first at Tom, then at Lenny, contemplating whether to go back and help Harper. A whirring helicopter circled above. The police had arrived, and distant sirens grew louder as they neared.

'Come on, Elaine!' said Lenny.

'I have to go back!' she said.

'Elaine, no. Just get off the bloody boat!' shouted Tom.

As she turned, the boat shuddered and listed further. Her foot slipped, and she fell backwards, sliding down across the deck, headfirst into the submerged gunwale.

37

The Boy

Danny stood on the path, concerned as the woman who had saved him fell from view. The man who'd caught him jumped into the river and swam around to the other side of the narrowboat. The other man moved closer, pulled him away from the edge, and put a hand on his shoulder to offer comfort; it had the opposite effect.

Loud voices and clumping footsteps on the path drew his attention to armed police officers rushing towards them. Coming from the other direction, more officers approached at speed, among them two suited men, ties flailing over their shoulders as they ran.

The boat creaked and groaned. It wouldn't be long before the bulk of it disappeared beneath the murky surface. Someone yelled as the man swam into view with Elaine, keeping her head above water as he brought her towards the bank. Police officers moved to the edge, ready to help pull her from the river.

A tall, suited man who had arrived with the police stepped closer to observe the sinking narrowboat. He then watched Elaine being pulled from the water before approaching Danny and the man beside him.

'You should have called me, Lenny,' he said, clearly upset. 'I thought we had a deal?'

'You're the one who broke it, Harry. Besides, you seemed more interested in catching Harper Darmody.'

It made Danny uneasy as Harry examined his pale face, the lash marks on his limbs, and his long, bloodied white shirt.

Harry turned to Lenny. 'The boy from the boat?'

Lenny nodded.

Harry stooped down. 'Hi there, buddy. I'm Harry Baxendale, a detective. Can you tell me your name?'

Danny hesitated, anxious about the woman being resuscitated on the path, and then answered, 'Danny Logan.'

The detective appeared relieved and happy. Danny supposed they hadn't expected to find him alive, his parents included. He looked past the detective to check on Elaine, who still wasn't moving, her face a pale blue. A police officer repeatedly pressed down on her chest. The man who had jumped in to save her was now on his feet, standing close, watching with an anxious look on his face. Paramedics in their familiar green uniforms raced along the path with their bags.

Water and vomit surged from Elaine's mouth as she coughed and spluttered. Danny smiled, thrilled she was alive.

A loud rumbling noise had everyone turning to watch the narrowboat as it succumbed to its fate and thumped against the riverbed, with only a fraction of the roof protruding from the water.

'Call the diving unit and tell them to hurry,' Harry said to his colleague.

The colour slowly returned to Elaine's face as a paramedic tended to her. A blanket was thrown over Danny's shoulders, and Harry asked another paramedic to take him to the ambulance. Danny ran straight to Elaine and into her arms.

Elaine hugged him. 'It's all over, Danny – you're safe now. Go with the nice lady. She will look after you, I promise. They are going to take you to the hospital and make sure you're okay. I'm sure your parents will be there to see you very soon.'

'Will you come and see me?'

Elaine smiled. 'Of course I will.'

She eased him towards the paramedic who led him away. He glanced over his shoulder at the woman who had saved him from the monster. At that moment, he trusted only her and hoped she would keep her word and visit him in the hospital.

After being checked over in the back of the ambulance, Danny was left alone for a few minutes. His muscles relaxed, and warmth flowed through his body with an overwhelming euphoria of freedom, something he'd lost hope of having many times, especially after his failed attempt to kill the man. Very soon, he would be reunited with his parents and sister, and it troubled him. He wasn't sure he wanted to see them yet and didn't understand why. Would things simply return to how they had been before, or would his life never be the same again?

Lingering within his emotions was a form of unexpected anguish. Not for cutting up the police officer or taking the life of Connor in such an unnecessary and calculated way. No, what he sensed was an immense loss. Not the kind you feel for a loved one – but different. Though he hated Zeph for what he'd done and for what he had made him do, in some bizarre way, Zeph had liked and respected him. Reflecting on their encounters, the pride he had witnessed in Zeph's eyes had given him a sense of belonging. Danny burst into tears. It was an odd feeling to be both happy and sad at the same time.

'Hey, Danny.' Harry Baxendale stepped into the ambulance and sat opposite him.

Danny wiped his eyes, attempting to conceal that he'd been crying. The detective reached out to place his hand on Danny's arm to offer reassurance, but Danny flinched. Harry pulled back, not wanting to cause further distress.

'Are you okay to talk?' asked Harry.

'I guess.'

'I've called your parents to let them know you are safe. They're understandably over the moon and can't wait to see you. I wouldn't be surprised if they get to the hospital before you do.'

'Do I have to see them right away?'

The detective seemed surprised. 'No, of course not. You will probably be in the hospital for a few days, so you can rest and take all the time you need.'

'Will they be angry with me for not wanting to see them straight away?'

'Not a chance, Danny. You've been away for a long time and have been through a terrible ordeal. You can see them when you are good and ready. You are safe, and that's all that matters to them. They will understand. I'll come and visit you at the hospital very soon, okay?'

Danny was exhausted, which must have been obvious to the detective and probably one of the reasons why he didn't push him too hard. He no doubt wanted to make his acquaintance and earn his trust. Danny wasn't silly; he knew how this worked. The next time he saw him, there would be questions galore. The detective would want to know every single detail about his captivity.

As Harry climbed out of the ambulance, Danny had another question. 'Why did the other man give his life for mine?'

Harry appeared mystified. 'Which man?'

'She called him – Harper.'

Confused and with a hint of displeasure, the detective said, 'I'm afraid I can't answer that, Danny. People are unpredictable. They do the strangest things.'

Danny watched him walk away and reached under his long shirt into the side of his underpants to retrieve a neatly folded tissue. He slowly unfurled it to reveal the piece of nose belonging to Colin Hargreaves and a young boy's little finger – Connor's finger. Danny examined the items with a hint of satisfaction.

As the paramedic appeared, he carefully folded the tissue and tucked it back inside his underpants. The paramedic closed one of the back doors, and for a brief moment, Danny's face was divided by light and darkness: the bright side – an innocent young boy who had been through a traumatic experience, and the dark side – a boy who smiled with menacing pride. The other door closed.

38

Lenny

And then there were three. Lenny, Elaine, and Tom stood on the edge of the riverbank, staring down at the roof of the sunken narrowboat, ignoring the hustle and bustle around them. Their thoughts and emotions a mixture of many – Lenny gazed at Elaine. He felt for her. She had finally received retribution for Charlie's murder and, along the way, had saved the life of another young boy – but it had come at the cost of losing her brother all over again. It was bound to hurt, but in time she'd feel good about reuniting parents with their missing son. In some way, they had all contributed to bringing an end to the evil and despicable Joseph Webster.

Other than being relieved this was all over, Lenny had no idea what was going through Tom's mind. His marriage to Elaine would no doubt involve a long, drawn-out conversation, but how Tom felt about Harper was another story. He rightly harboured a grudge and even attempted to turn him in, only to change his mind at the last second. Now Harper had sacrificed his life to save the Logan kid; Tom surely had no regrets about telling him to run.

'I'm going to need statements from all three of you,' said Harry, wandering up behind them. 'It seems you've all failed to mention that Harper Darmody was on the boat.'

Elaine wasn't ready to talk and walked away.

'Elaine!' called the detective.

'Not right now, DCI Baxendale,' said Tom, following after her.

'You'll get your statements,' said Lenny, continuing to stare at the river. He understood why Harry was cheesed off, but now wasn't the time.

Harry stood beside him. 'What was Darmody doing on the boat?'

'Saving the life of a young boy.'

'I don't get it.'

'None of us do, Harry. Sometimes, there are no explanations.' Lenny patted him on the shoulder and walked off.

'Where are you going?'

'Home, Harry. I'm tired, and I'm going home,' he said without looking back.

Before setting off, he'd called Olivia twice, but she never answered. Needing to hear her voice, he listened to her last message again. She'd replied to his missed call from the previous night when he'd informed her that he wouldn't be home. Olivia had spent that night at his place and left him some dinner in the fridge. He hoped she'd be at his place when he arrived home later; if not, maybe the dinner from a day earlier was still waiting for him.

They hadn't been together long, but it was long enough to open his eyes to what he'd been missing all those years. He'd always put work first. Having someone to love had never been on the agenda. *Love! Was that what this was? The sneaky bastard*! He had never thought it would happen.

On the journey home, he contemplated the years since the death of Charlie Davis; it had been his desire as much as Elaine's to find the killer. He could never have predicted that Harper Darmody would be the one to stop him. Nevertheless, that was how it had turned out, and now it was all over; he felt a sense of relief. But what would he do now? How about writing another book? Perhaps Harper deserved a better ending, to be remembered as more than just a mass murderer. Once upon a time, he was Liam Bennett, the boy who never had the chance to grow up – a little boy who had paid a high price for protecting his sister. It could be fitting to say he'd gone full circle, sacrificing his life to rescue Elaine once again, along with Daniel Logan. He had come into the world as Liam Bennett, and satisfyingly, that was the person he'd left it as. He truly was *The Boy Who Died Twice*. Great title, Lenny thought.

He pulled into a petrol station close to home, not only to fill up the car but also to pick up some flowers for Olivia. They were the last bunch in the bucket and looked withered. After complaining and asking for a discount, Lenny paid full price.

After reversing his car into the assigned space in the underground car park at his apartment complex, he walked towards the lift. A quick glance at the visitor parking section revealed Olivia's car. A surge of comforting warmth rushed over him. The last couple of weeks had been difficult, and today had seemed like the longest day ever. A snuggle on the sofa would feel heavenly. In the lift, he did his best to fluff the dried, wilting flowers into shape, certain she would be pleased with his efforts. After all, he was new to all this.

Once through the front door, he kicked off his shoes and hung his jacket on the rack in the entrance hall. He ambled along the hallway into the large open-plan living area, placing the flowers on the worktop. The huge window displayed the early evening sun over the city skyline. He received a text from Tom, informing him that Elaine had briefly fallen unconscious after the incident and had been admitted to hospital as a precaution. Tom told him not to worry and that he would keep him updated. Lenny wasn't surprised and attributed it to years of mental exhaustion. There was only so much the mind and body could take after such an emotional ordeal involving personal tragedy and profound vengeance.

Olivia wasn't around, so he strolled along the hallway to the bedroom. Lenny quietly opened the door and peeked through the crack: the blinds were closed and the room was fairly dark. He discerned the shape of her body under the covers. She must have had a hard day and taken a nap. As tempted as he was, he didn't wake her and closed the door. Back in the kitchen, he fetched a glass and poured himself a whisky.

On his way to the window, he noted the television remote on the laminated floor beneath the sofa. He picked it up and placed it on the glass table. Over by the window, he stared at the tall buildings that cast shadows over the streets of London, plunging them into premature darkness. Lenny sipped whisky from the glass, closed his eyes, and tilted his head back. He breathed deeply. The immense relief of a weight lifted made him emotional. A tear slipped from his eye and drifted down his cheek. The golden sunset penetrated the window and fell across his face. He opened his eyes and raised his glass.

'Here's to you, Colin,' he said, taking another sip. 'We got him, Charlie . . . we got him.'

Lenny sank the remainder of the whisky and placed the glass on the worktop. He glanced at the fridge and considered yesterday's dinner. Nah, not hungry. Joining Olivia for a nap, on the other hand, was very tempting. He entered the bedroom, stripped down to his underwear, and gently slipped into bed so as not to disturb Olivia, who, for once, had the duvet pulled over her shoulders.

Flat on his back, his head pressed into the pillow, he could have sworn he'd never experienced a more comforting sensation. Torn between not wanting to move and not wanting to wake Olivia, he couldn't resist turning onto his side and snuggling into her back.

Her skin was cold, so he put his arm around her. Closing his eyes, Lenny was ready to drift off to sleep.

Something wasn't right – the bedsheet and cover were damp. Maybe there was a reason she'd gone to bed early. Perhaps a fever. No! It wasn't damp. It was wet. His recent contentment deserted him, and now he was consumed with fear. He hesitantly lifted the duvet and glanced beneath.

'No,' he said softly, ignoring the metallic smell that filled his lungs. 'No, no, no!' He ripped away the cover.

Blood! A puddle of wet on top of dry. She was covered in it, and so was he. Lenny pulled her over and knew immediately – Olivia was dead. He ran his hands and eyes over her body, uncertain of what he was searching for, but then he found it – an entrance wound on her right side below her ribs, no doubt piercing her liver. Lenny drew her head to his chest and sat there crying, with Olivia in his arms.

For almost two hours, the forensic technicians busied themselves in Lenny's apartment while he sat on the sofa in a complete daze. Every person was attired in white overalls, gloves, and foot covers; even Lenny. His clothes had been placed in evidence bags and taken away for examination. Beside him on the sofa was DCI Harry Baxendale.

If Lenny had fetched his dinner from the fridge, he would have seen the sharp, bloodied steak knife used on Olivia. It lay casually on top of the mashed potatoes and sausages she had lovingly prepared for him the night before. Harry had sent the knife to the mortuary and asked forensic pathologist Arthur Potts to pull the clear fingerprints from the handle and run a match as soon as possible.

It wouldn't take long to confirm if Lenny's suspicions were correct. The killer had left the prints on purpose, wanting Lenny to know who had carried out such an atrocious act – wanting the world to know. Lenny already knew. Webster. He had never been more certain of anything, and it left him completely devastated. Before returning to the boat after his failed attempt to get Elaine, Webster must have sought him out and instead found Olivia. Consumed with guilt and unbearable anguish, Lenny couldn't move – inconsolable. Olivia was gone, and he blamed himself.

'Len, I don't know what to say.'

'Then don't say anything, Harry.' Lenny's reply was low and gruff, his voice replicating the desolation within.

'Divers have recovered three bodies from the boat. They're being taken to the morgue right now. One of them is bound to be Joseph Webster. I find it difficult to believe he would have come here to kill—'

'Webster did this!' said an enraged Lenny. 'He came here for me and killed Olivia instead.'

Harry fell silent, clearly aware this was an argument he'd never win. All they could do was await the results from Arthur Potts.

'You can't stay here tonight, Lenny. Do you have somewhere else you can stay?'

'I'll probably book into a hotel.'

Both men stared straight ahead at nothing in particular, blocking out the activity going on around them.

A fuss in the corridor outside the apartment caused Harry to get off the sofa and head out to see what was happening. Lenny sat forward and raised his eyes to the heavens. He covered his face with his hands. Olivia's death had filled him with grievous anger. He released a tormented roar of pain, clenched his fists into balls, and brought them crashing down onto the glass coffee table in front of him, shattering it into pieces.

39

Elaine

Having been told she would be fine, Tom had gone to collect his car. Elaine was glad for some time alone, but lying in bed, her mind raced. She couldn't switch off – stressing about Harper and all that had happened. She had regained consciousness in the back of the ambulance, and despite not wanting to go to the hospital, the paramedics weren't taking any chances. Tiredness, shock, or almost drowning were all possible causes, not to mention everything else she had been through of late. The doctor wanted to run some tests and keep her in overnight.

Tom soon returned and sat in the chair beside her bed. Neither said a word. The tension between them hovered like thick fog. He received a phone call and informed her that three bodies had been recovered. Distraught, Elaine turned onto her side, away from him, pretending to be asleep. As tired as she was, sleep seemed impossible; she constantly thought about how agonising the final moments of Harper's life must have been.

She pictured him standing on the bed, his face pressed against the ceiling, making every last breath count until he became submerged. His body writhed in panic as he began to strain. The intense need to breathe forced his first intake of water, resulting in a futile attempt to cough it out. He swallowed, his airway narrowing as water filled his stomach. The lack of oxygen to his brain rendered him unconscious, followed by the final beat of his heart. Tears fell from her eyes. *Shouldn't have left him. Shouldn't have left him.* Four words that played on repeat in her head. A brimful of guilt she would always carry.

Elaine turned her head on the pillow and glanced at Tom, a blank expression on his face. Having deceived him many times over, he had every right to be angry with her. She also understood why he'd come so close to handing her brother over to the police. She had put him in an impossible and distressing position that went against everything he'd ever believed in. Tom was a good man, and she had asked him to sacrifice all the qualities she admired and adored. Not only had he protected her and the children the night Webster came to the house, but today he'd jumped into the river to save her life. Could he ever forgive her? She could only hope.

'I love you, Tom,' she said, her voice tired and weak.

Caught off guard, Tom looked up and rose from the chair. He leaned over and kissed her lips. 'I love you,' he whispered.

'I know. I've come to a decision.'

'Oh! What's that?' he asked, uncertain of what her next words would be.

'We should move, find somewhere else to live.'

'What about the house?'

'There's bad energy surrounding that property. Too many terrible events have taken place. I'll get the house boarded up for now and maybe, in time, have it demolished.'

Tom understood and agreed. He leaned in to kiss her again when her phone vibrated on the bedside cabinet. 'It's Lenny.' Tom passed her the phone.

'Hello, Lenny. This isn't a good time.'

'Olivia's dead.'

She turned to Tom, horrified. 'What? How?'

'Webster.'

The conversation was brief, and Elaine couldn't get out of bed fast enough. She explained things to Tom, got dressed, and discharged herself from the hospital. They were soon on their way to Lenny's apartment. Tom had already cancelled his plans to stay at a hotel near the hospital, and while he drove, Elaine browsed her phone for another hotel and booked two rooms. She called Lila to check on Michael and Emily. Considering what they had been through, they were doing okay.

Tom dropped Elaine off at Lenny's place and carried on to the hotel. She was to meet him there later. In the lift, she contemplated a question that had plagued her for the whole journey. Was Olivia's death her fault? If she hadn't hired Lenny to find Charlie's killer, he would never have met Olivia, and she would still be alive. But would Lenny have continued to search for the killer regardless? Knowing his feelings about her son's death, it was possible. The ifs and buts were endless, perhaps pointless. Poor Lenny. She'd seen the look of adoration on his face earlier in the day when he'd listened to her message on his phone. Never before had she seen him with such a natural and exuberant expression. He'd be heartbroken.

Elaine stormed along the corridor and caused a scene with two uniformed officers who were preventing her from entering Lenny's apartment.

Seconds later, Harry showed his face. 'What are you doing here, Mrs Burgess?'

'Lenny called me.'

Harry sighed. 'Of course he did.'

An anguished roar echoed from inside, followed by the thunderous smashing of glass. Harry raced back into the apartment. Elaine brushed past the police officers.

Standing beside Harry, she stared at a dazed Lenny and the shattered remains of the coffee table beneath his feet.

'Lenny!' she called.

He turned to her, a lost and confused look on his face. The agony behind his eyes was intense; however, he did seem relieved that she was there.

'Elaine,' he said, stepping towards her.

She threw her arms around him, and Lenny wept on her shoulder.

Harry raised the palm of his hand to stop the two officers from interfering.

Elaine said, 'Change into some clothes and gather your personal belongings. I'm getting you out of here. I've booked us into a hotel.'

Lenny pulled back but remained still, not knowing what to do or what he was allowed to do. Elaine glared at Harry.

'Okay,' Harry conceded. 'I'll help him pack some things, but please, Elaine, can you make your way out into the corridor without touching anything?' He looked at the officers. 'The same goes for both of you,' he commanded. 'Come on, Len.'

Along with the officers, Elaine left the apartment.

Ten minutes later, Lenny appeared. Harry had allowed him to wash and change into fresh clothes. Elaine thanked the detective with a weak smile and a faint nod of her head.

They had barely made it twenty feet along the corridor when Harry called Lenny's name.

'I just spoke to Arthur. You were right . . . Webster's prints *are* on the knife. I'm sorry.'

Elaine waited impatiently in the taxi while Lenny fetched something from his car. She was on edge, worried he might not return. Should she have let him wander off alone? She climbed out of the car, but her fears were allayed when he appeared out front. Not a word was exchanged on the way to The Stratford Olympic Hotel. Elaine was all too aware that words were never a comfort in times like these. People expressing the best they had to offer would fall on deaf ears for the person on the receiving end, who would rather have quiet and solitude. Grieving was personal.

Having booked the two best rooms available, Elaine collected the keycards from the front desk and escorted Lenny to his suite. Lenny laboured into the luxurious room and perched on the end of the bed. Elaine had never seen him this way – crushed. Since she had known him, she had witnessed many facets of Lenny Grey, not all of them pretty, but this – this was a side of him he had never shown: wretched and pitiful.

'Is there anything I can get for you?' she asked.

He looked up, his eyes doleful and pleading, begging for this not to be real. 'It should have been me.'

Elaine's eyes welled. She dropped to her knees in front of him and placed her head in his lap, devastated by his loss, her loss – the whole damned mess. His hand rested on the back of her head. The minutes passed by unnoticed as they consoled each other in silence. Eventually, she felt his hand fall away as he slumped back onto the bed. He had fallen asleep, something she could only wish for. She removed Lenny's shoes and left him on the bed.

Elaine walked along the plush, carpeted corridor and entered her and Tom's room. Tom had left a note saying he'd booked a table for dinner and would meet her in the main restaurant and bar. Thankfully, he'd unpacked the suitcase. She changed into an elegant black dress (the colour of which seemed appropriate) and freshened up in the immaculate natural stone bathroom. Elaine hadn't thought about food and wasn't at all hungry. A drink, however, would not go amiss after such a long and eventful day.

She strolled down to the sumptuous bar and found Tom sitting at a table out on the gorgeous sky terrace with an open bottle of white wine nestled in a bucket of ice. He topped up his glass and poured Elaine a large one. With the sun fading fast over the horizon, she gazed in amazement at the clear night view overlooking Queen Elizabeth Olympic Park and the city beyond. For a few seconds, she was taken away, mesmerised by the twinkling bright lights of the vibrant city below, as though the day had never happened. The gentle breeze caressed her skin.

'It's beautiful, isn't it?' said Tom.

He brought her crashing back to reality. Good things never seemed to last. 'Yes,' she replied with a half-hearted smile. 'It's magnificent.'

Tom rose from his seat and carried the wine to her. The glass touched her lips, and the wine disappeared immediately. The bottle was soon emptied and replaced by another, and then another. With neither of them hungry, food was put on the back burner. They barely spoke. Words were irrelevant and unnecessary.

Their tolerable silence was interrupted by loud fireworks bursting across the skyline like an invasion. Guests swarmed onto the terrace to watch the spectacular show from an event taking place in the Olympic Park below. Soon after the fireworks ended, she sent Tom back to the room with her discarded Louboutins while she went to check on Lenny before going to bed.

Elaine knocked and waited in vain. He was probably sleeping. She chose not to disturb him and sauntered along the corridor towards her room. She stopped; an unknown force prevented her from going any further. A voice inside her head told her to turn back. She listened.

She entered Lenny's room with the spare keycard. There was no sign of him. A tingling cold sensation fluttered across her shoulders, and a desperate concern took hold. She hurried towards the bathroom and slowed when she saw the floor saturated with what appeared to be diluted blood.

40

Lenny

It came as no surprise when Harry uttered Webster's name in the corridor outside his apartment. Joseph Webster wanted someone to pay a fatal price for hunting him down and would have been incensed after failing to get Elaine. Lenny was a suitable alternative. Unfortunately, it was Olivia who became his next victim, and Lenny was crippled with self-reproach. He wished it had been him lying lifeless on a mortuary slab.

A desperate desire to turn back the clock consumed him, but Lenny was well aware of the reality of life, and the horror of what had happened was not going away. It would remain with him, along with all the other hellish nightmares he had witnessed. There was only one question churning away at him now – did he want to continue living in such an atrocious world?

In the lift, Elaine must have sensed his mind ticking over as her hand reached for his. Her warmth and affection were evident through her touch. The last eight years had been tough, and what had started with pure hatred for each other had blossomed into a friendship neither could have foreseen. She had changed him, made him see life through different eyes. He had learned how childhood trauma could have a detrimental impact on the future outcome of someone's life, and the ripples that followed resulted in consequences for so many who lay in its path. Chaos theory in its full sadistic splendour.

They stepped out of the lift into the lobby of his building. 'I need to get a couple of things from my car. I won't be long,' he said.

'I'll come with you.'

'No, you go on ahead. I'll meet you out front.'

She had a dubious expression on her face. 'Elaine, it's okay. I'll only be a few minutes.'

Her eyes might as well have been glued to his back as he walked towards the door leading to the underground car park. Her anchored stare lingered even after he had disappeared from her view. Lenny opened the boot of his car and removed the tyre. Underneath was his pistol, which he slipped into his trousers behind his back, out of sight.

As well as the pistol, he took some notebooks to deceive Elaine into thinking they were what he wanted to collect from the car. He walked through the front door of his building and saw Elaine step out of the taxi, ready to come and find him. Lenny appreciated her concern.

The journey to the hotel seemed to take forever. He was glad Elaine didn't put him through needless chit-chat. Then again, it might have kept him from constantly seeing the horror of Olivia in his bed. No – silence *was* better. Lenny took nothing in as the streetlights and passing cars highlighted the bleak outlook on his face. Occasionally, he sensed Elaine turning to look at him. Words attempted to escape her mouth, but she managed to catch them before they crossed the threshold.

*

By the time they reached the hotel, Lenny was on autopilot, oblivious to everything around him. On the edge of the bed in the hotel room, he stared straight ahead, not really knowing how he had got there. Becoming aware of Elaine's muffled voice, he looked at her, with no idea what she was saying. Lenny searched for words . . .

'It should have been me,' he said.

Before he knew it, Elaine was in tears, her head nestled in his lap. Grief-stricken and unsure how to react, he rested his hand on the back of her head. After a few minutes, awkwardness set in. He wanted her to leave. *Why wouldn't she leave?* Would it be selfish and uncaring to ask her to go? Probably – but he wanted to be alone.

Lenny closed his eyes and fell backwards onto the bed. It was a polite last resort to make someone leave you in peace. She moved – and then took off his shoes. Why had she done that? He couldn't imagine himself removing anyone's shoes. *Was it a woman thing?*

Elaine finally left the room, and Lenny sat upright. The first thing he noticed was his shoes positioned neatly under the coffee table. Another curious thing she had done. He got to his feet, removed his leather jacket, and tossed it onto the bed. *Minibar, minibar!* Seconds later, it was open, and he dove in. Time wasn't wasted on selection; he didn't care what it was as long as it contained alcohol.

The next two hours passed quickly, and there were empty bottles of this and that scattered about the room. He'd even called room service to bring him a bottle of whisky. Wearing only his baggy white underpants, Lenny was sprawled out on the sofa with the bottle gripped in *one* hand and his pistol in the other.

Booming fireworks outside caused him to stir, and the sound of water slapping against the tiled floor in the bathroom spurred him into action. Lenny slammed the bottle down on the table and struggled to push himself up from the sofa. After two unsteady steps forward, he stopped and turned back for the whisky.

'Can't leave you behind,' he mumbled, reaching down for it.

Holding both the pistol and the bottle, he staggered to the bathroom.

'I'm coming, Olivia,' he said.

The water flowed over the rim of the stylish freestanding bathtub. Lenny splashed through the water and, with his hands full, wrestled to turn off the taps.

'I ain't hanging around down here no more. It's all bollocks,' he slurred.

Lenny attempted to push down his underpants while stupidly clinging to the whisky bottle. Raising his leg, he strove to free his foot from the cotton, lost his balance, and plummeted into the bathtub, accidentally firing the pistol. Waves of water surged over the edge. The bottle fell from his grasp and smashed onto the tiled floor. He splashed around and finally steadied himself by gripping the sides of the tub with his hands.

Lenny sputtered and gasped; the water was turning red. 'What the—?'

Confused and sensing an intense throbbing pain, he eased his right foot above the water – something was missing. He had inadvertently shot off his big toe.

With a deep scream and a few obscenities, Lenny clambered out of the bath. As soon as his foot hit the broken glass on the floor, more coarse words were blasted into the atmosphere. He hobbled over to the window and sat on the tiles, his back against the white net curtains. Fireworks lit up the night sky behind him. He reached for a fresh white towel from the unit that supported the hand basin.

Pressing the towel firmly against his wound, he grimaced. 'For fuck's sake!'

After a few seconds of applying pressure, he noticed blood seeping from the sole of his other foot. A closer examination revealed a shard of glass embedded in the skin. Lenny tightened his fingers around the shard and eased it free. He rested his head against the window and closed his eyes.

Lenny was woken by someone knocking on the main door. It couldn't have been important as they didn't knock a second time. They probably had the wrong room. A chill brushed over his naked form. He reached for another towel and draped it over his shoulders. The sight of his sorry feet, surrounded by a pool of blood, was a stark reminder of his earlier fiasco.

'What the fuck, Lenny?'

Elaine was standing in the doorway, her face a picture of astonishment at the scene in front of her. He ripped the towel from his shoulders and covered his privates.

'Yeah, that's made a difference,' she said sarcastically. 'What the hell have you done?' She knelt down and examined the cut on his foot.

'I messed up.'

She removed the towel from his other foot and gazed in shock. 'Oh my God, Lenny. Where's your toe?'

There was no hiding his pain nor his embarrassment. 'I shot it off.'

'What were you aiming for, your brain?'

His sheepish expression betrayed him. It was clear to her what he'd hoped to achieve. Elaine glanced around for the pistol.

'It's in the bath,' he said.

She turned to him, her expression a mix of anger and heartbreak. 'Oh, Lenny.' She sighed and fetched him a robe.

Elaine grabbed the remaining two towels, wrapped them tenderly around his feet, and helped him up. With his arm over her shoulder, she supported his weight and guided him back to the bed. He lay down and let her take a closer look.

'I think we need to get you to a hospital,' she said.

'Not gonna happen! I ain't going to no hospital.'

'It could get infected.'

'Just get me the gun – I'll finish the bloody job.'

Elaine scowled and said, 'By shooting off more toes?'

A short silence ensued before she broke into a soft smile. Even in his state of emotional and physical pain, he couldn't help but smile with her. Olivia would think he'd been a complete idiot. Their subtle moment of frivolity was brought to an abrupt end by a knock at the door. They glared at each other.

'Shit!' he whispered aloud. 'What if someone heard the shot?'

Elaine concealed his feet with the throw at the end of the bed and marched to the door. The person knocked again.

'Who is it?'

'It's Tom.'

Elaine opened the door and pulled him inside. She poked her head through the doorway and glanced down both sides of the long hall before closing and locking the door.

Tom was immediately aware that something was wrong. 'What's going on?'

Elaine removed the throw and towels from Lenny's feet. 'Someone's had an accident.'

'No shit,' said Tom, completely unsurprised by what confronted him.

Lenny watched Elaine lead Tom to the bathroom doorway and listened to their conversation.

'You know what?' said Tom, upon seeing the state of the room, 'I'm not even going to ask.'

Elaine said, 'I need you to fish the gun out of the bath and take it back to our room. Did you bring your painkillers with you?' She was referring to the medication he took for the injuries inflicted on him by Harper.

'You know I don't go anywhere without them,' he replied.

'Good! Bring those back with you.'

'Am I right to assume we're taking him home with us?'

'Yes. I have everything we need at home from when I took care of Harper.'

'What about the mess?'

'We'll clean it. It will look like we were never here.'

Although still inebriated, the adrenaline pumping through Lenny's body enhanced his alertness. The pain in his feet intensified, and the throbbing where his toe used to be was profound. Elaine returned to take another look at his feet.

'I'm sorry for all this,' he said. 'I just wanted to feel – nothing.'

'I know all too well how you feel right now, Lenny. I'm not going to lie and tell you it gets any better because it doesn't – but it doesn't get any worse either. It slowly becomes manageable.' She continued to tend to his injuries. 'The bleeding has almost stopped. I need to apply a little more pressure to stop it completely before I can clean it,' she said, wrapping it back up. Lenny closed his eyes and winced as she pressed down on the wound.

Tom came out of the bathroom. 'I've got the pistol. I also found your toe. Sadly, there's not much left of it,' he said, holding it aloft.

Elaine was trying hard not to laugh, but then Lenny roared with laughter himself. They all did. As bad as things had been over the past twenty-four hours, they couldn't help but find humour in the extremes of darkness.

41

Elaine

They arrived back at Sablefall Farm early the following morning, having departed the hotel at around 4.00 a.m. Lenny's room had been left virtually spotless, with Elaine raiding an unattended chambermaid's trolley in the corridor for fresh towels and some cleaning products. Their only concern had been a small bullet hole near the bottom of the tiled bathroom wall. Tom improvised and filled the hole with tissue and hair wax after he had dug out the shell. The colour wasn't an exact match, but it did somewhat fit in with the pattern on the tile. Only a closer inspection or a keen eye would notice.

Having seen for herself exactly how devastated Lenny was, she insisted that he stay at her and Tom's place for a while, at least until he'd recovered from the injuries to his feet. Elaine reasoned that the support of his friends could help him deal with the loss of Olivia.

The pair had locked horns on more than one occasion in the past, but over the last three years, he had been more than helpful to her. She certainly wouldn't have found her son's killer without him. Lenny had his moments, but Elaine appreciated him. Maybe it was time to tell him how she felt and how dear he had become to her. On the other hand, he probably knew.

With Lenny settled in the guest bedroom after a painstaking trek up the stairs, Tom finally went to bed. Elaine had managed to get some sleep on the journey home, and now it was time to take care of Lenny's wounds. Using the torch on her phone, she descended into the secret room under the kitchen to collect the medical supplies. She had kept them down there from when she'd nursed Harper back to health. Elaine turned on the main light and bagged the supplies.

Her finger on the light switch, ready to leave, she regarded the small red wooden box. All this time, she still hadn't opened it. It wasn't that she'd forgotten; it was more a case of avoidance. She recalled Harper's words when she found him down here: "You won't like what you find." On that occasion, she had ignored his warning and ventured to open the box, but Harper cried out in pain. She closed the lid and never returned to it, sensing that whatever was contained inside might be better left unknown. Elaine put the bag down and walked over to the table.

Elaine carried the box over to the dusty futon and sat down, resting it on her lap. Just as it had the first time, the hinge of the box squeaked as she slowly raised the lid. At the top were two old photographs: one of a young baby, possibly a boy, and the other (judging by the pink sleepsuit) of an older baby girl. She retrieved them and spotted something more curious underneath – an aged yellow document, the heading of which set her heart racing. The papers were stapled together and letter-folded, the envelope long since discarded. With increasing trepidation, Elaine unfolded the paper and began to read, rapidly being dragged down by an undertow of outrage.

Dear Mr K. Bennett,

This is to certify your purchase of Lot 14, a 7-month-old baby boy whom you have chosen to name Liam Bennett (see the attached new birth certificate and various documentation). The boy was taken from a wealthy family in the United States of America that has an extremely good medical history.

The World Child Placement Society wishes you many joyful years with your acquisition. Should you wish to repudiate or extirpate, please refer to the attached information.

Kind regards,

C. McGinley HBP (Head of Bid and Purchase).

Stress caused a muscle in her neck to spasm violently. Sweat formed on her brow. Stunned, Elaine turned the page to see Liam's birth certificate. There were a few staple holes in the top-left corner, revealing it had been removed and stapled back inside a few times. The next page was about calling a provided number to relinquish responsibility for the product (referring to the child). Whatever this organisation did was horrific. The last page was a receipt, but it didn't reveal the price paid by her father.

So many questions bounced around in her head. Words she didn't understand. She thought about Harper and what must have gone through his mind when he'd read this. It surely added fuel to his burning rage. A final note at the bottom of the last page stated the need to dispose of all evidence pertaining to the product, apart from the new identification. For whatever reason, her father had not carried out the instructions.

The true nature of the document sank in – Liam wasn't her brother. He had been abducted from a family and sold to the highest bidder. This was highly organised child trafficking. Could this organisation still be in business after all these years? Unlikely, but it proved beyond doubt that her father was part of it or at least knew of its existence. Her mother, too. This was proof that what had happened to her and Liam *was* real. She needed to hand these documents over to the police. Maybe something would be done to bring all those behind this abhorrent society to justice.

She put the papers aside and saw another document inside the box. Her heart thumped frantically.

'Oh God, no! Please, no!' She lifted the document and unfurled the pages.

Dear Mr K. Bennett,

This is to certify your purchase of Lot 4, an 18-month-old baby girl whom you have chosen to name Elaine Bennett (see the attached new birth certificate and various documentation). The girl was taken from a children's home in the United Kingdom. We have no further details available.

Elaine couldn't read any further. She looked again at the photographs, no doubt pictures of her and Liam after they had been stolen. With an unsettled stomach and an intense burning sensation in her chest, Elaine jumped up from the futon. She paced over to the wall, pounded her palms against the smoky black brickwork, then stopped to be sick. They had been stolen and auctioned like property. How many other children could there be? Hundreds? Thousands? The thought horrified her. Dr Walker had told her it was bigger than she could possibly imagine.

*

Sitting upright in bed, Lenny browsed through the documents. 'Repudiate is certainly not a word you hear often. It means to refuse to accept, and in this case, it means to reject and return the child. This is bad, Elaine. Really bad. It's worse than just child trafficking.'

'Tell me what extirpate means?'

Lenny hesitated – he clearly didn't want to say.

'It means to kill the child, doesn't it?' Elaine drew her own conclusion. 'But why?'

'Oh, come on, Elaine, you're not stupid. Use your imagination. What do children do?'

'Grow up,' she said.

'They get older and start to question things. A few may confide in someone they trust. In most cases of abuse, a child will usually turn to the one person they truly believe will protect them no matter what.'

'Their mother,' she said.

'Precisely. It's even possible the woman you thought was your mother came through the same system,' said Lenny.

'It would explain why she never said a word at first and then suddenly decided to put a stop to it.'

'She was probably scared. Her whole life would have been lived in fear. I've heard rumours of highly organised child trafficking and what goes on, but I've never seen any evidence. It doesn't mean it isn't happening, though. There were probably many women like your mother who were placed in these positions, some perhaps being mothers themselves. Did you ever witness your parents showing affection for one another?'

'Come to think of it, no. Never. I just considered them to be very private. Most of the time, they slept in separate bedrooms. My God, how could I have missed the signs?'

'You were far too young to look for signs. You were only a kid when all this was going on,' he said. 'The mothers of these children were likely the safety net for this organisation. They would probably be the first point of contact for a child wanting to question what was happening to them. The mothers would then tell the fathers, and for confiding in their mothers . . . the children's lives would soon be at an end.'

Incredibly angry and upset, Elaine said, 'But why? Why would those mothers have allowed it to happen? Why didn't they tell someone?'

'And who would they have told? Look at the kind of people who were involved in your own case and the ensuing cover-up: a High Court judge, a renowned psychiatrist – the Home Secretary, for Christ's sake. The list of high-profile figures involved in this doesn't bear thinking about. These women would have been terrified. You have to pass this information to the police, Elaine – you know that, right?' Lenny waved the documents at her.

'Yes, of course I will,' she replied firmly.

'Okay, good. Just checking. We can't have you rampaging across the globe on another vengeful killing spree,' said Lenny, one eyebrow raised.

Oblivious to Lenny's last comment, Elaine's mind was all over the place, thinking about her real parents and where she came from. Were they still out there, seeking closure?

'Everything is a mess. Is my whole life a complete lie?' she asked.

'Not at all. These papers don't change a thing. Only a few years of your life were a lie. The rest is real. You made independent decisions. You got married. You built a thriving business from scratch. You had three beautiful children. You even got married again. Your life *is* a reality. You may well have had some tragedies along the way, Elaine, but who hasn't? I guarantee you've had more moments of happiness than sadness. And also, however you look at it, Liam is – or was – still your brother.'

Lenny's words conveyed several truths, and as Elaine thought about her children, there were many aspects of her life she wouldn't change. 'You're right. It's no longer about me. Michael and Emily come first now. I need to put all this behind me and move on with my life. I've spent far too long running from ghosts and chasing demons.'

Birds sang while the light breeze woke the leaves and spurred them into a dance. The early morning sunshine pierced through broken clouds to cast scattered shadows upon the ground. From the porch, Elaine observed the shaded contours gliding across the grass: assorted patches of emerald and viridian, nature's mirror ball.

Standing on the porch with a cup of coffee in her hand, Elaine mused over the previous day's events, devastated by the outcome. She had taken her revenge, but not without personal cost – and it hurt. Had it all been worth it? A question she would repeatedly ask herself for a long time to come, but she already knew the answer.

'Mummy, why is Lenny in the spare room?' Emily asked, appearing behind her at the open front door.

'*Mr Grey*,' said Elaine, 'is going to be staying with us for a little while.'

'He said I could call him Lenny.'

'Oh, did he now? Well, that's okay then. I think Uncle Lenny sounds better.'

'He's not really an uncle, though,' said Emily.

'No, he isn't. But I think he's earned the title.'

Emily pointed towards the drive. A car was approaching the house. Elaine ushered Emily inside, telling her to go and wake Tom. She had an inkling of who it might be and sat on the swing bench to wait.

'Good morning, Detective Chief Inspector Baxendale,' she said as he walked up the steps.

'Mrs Burgess,' he replied, giving a subtle nod. 'I'm sorry to trouble you, but I've come for the statements.'

'Aren't we supposed to come to you?'

'A common misconception. It can be either, but under the circumstances, I thought this might be easier. Is Tom around?'

'He is. Do you want me to fetch him?'

'No, it's okay for now. We can start with yours.'

'Did you want to go inside the house?'

'No. Here's just fine.'

An uncomfortable edge lingered. It could be to do with what he knew about her, which was pretty much everything. She ignored the awkwardness and gave her statement, informing him about Lenny's tireless search for Joseph Webster, the killer's visit to her house, Tom's involvement, and finally the showdown on the narrowboat. Though the tension eased as the conversation went on, Elaine remained unsure whether the detective could be trusted. She kept details about Harper to a minimum, sticking to Lenny's original advice about not giving him anything to go on.

Tom stepped out front to greet the detective and realised they were still talking. 'Oh, I'm sorry. I didn't mean to interrupt.' He was about to head back inside.

'No, it's fine, Tom. We're about finished,' said Harry.

Tom folded his arms and leaned against the architrave.

'So, one last thing.' Harry hesitated and then smiled.

'What's funny?' asked Elaine.

'I'm just wondering if it's worth asking where Harper lived.'

'Well, let's consider your question asked. The answer is no. I have no idea where he could possibly have been staying.'

'That's what I figured you'd say.'

'Does it even matter now?' she asked.

'Considering we haven't recovered his body, yes – it does.'

'What do you mean?' said Tom. 'I was told you recovered three bodies.'

'And we did,' said Harry. 'But not Harper's. Not yet, anyway.'

Elaine shot to her feet. Did this mean he'd managed to free himself and escape? She knew it was possible, but with how quickly the boat went down and that he was about to take on Webster, she had major doubts. When Tom divulged to her at the hospital that three bodies had been pulled from the water, any lingering hopes were shattered.

'So whose bodies did you recover?' asked Tom.

As soon as Tom posed the question, Elaine pictured the rotting corpse in the wheelchair. 'The skeleton! Webster, the boy in the mailbags, and the bloody skeleton.'

The detective confirmed with a nod of his head. Elaine saw the puzzled look on Tom's face. He had no idea what she was talking about. Harry explained that the skeletal remains were likely to be those of Ozias Blackwood, the former owner of the narrowboat, and most likely the man who had taken Joseph Webster all those years ago.

Elaine let him know about the table with the boys' names etched underneath. The DCI and his team had a traumatic and gruelling investigation ahead. There were more young bodies yet to be discovered in the canals and rivers around the country, where first Ozias and then his young protégé had disposed of their victims.

When the detective finished collecting Tom's statement in the living room, he stepped back out onto the porch.

'I'm all done. By the way, how was Lenny last night?'

'As devastated as you'd expect. He's upstairs if you need to talk to him.'

'Lenny is staying here? That's very kind of you to look out for him, Mrs Burgess.'

'It's the least I could do. You can go on up if you'd like.'

'That won't be necessary, not right now. I have plenty to go on, and I have a feeling he'd rather be left alone. I'd better get going, then.'

As Harry Baxendale stepped down from the porch, Elaine toyed with the idea of providing him with the documents about her past.

'Detective! Wait a moment,' she said and disappeared inside the house. She returned holding a large brown envelope and moved close enough to look Harry in the eye. 'Can I trust you?'

He stared first at the envelope in her hand and then at her. 'I've seen what you do to those who cross you.' He smiled.

'I'd be grateful if you'd take a look at these.' Elaine handed over the envelope and watched him scan through the papers with a look of horror and dismay. 'I understand if you don't want to follow this up personally or if it's not your department, but you may have a trusted colleague within the force who wouldn't hesitate to thoroughly investigate whatever this is. Someone who wouldn't be afraid of where it leads.'

'Someone immediately comes to mind, and if I can assist with this, I will do whatever I can.'

*

Encouraged by the possibility that Harper could be alive, Elaine drove to his caravan soon after the detective left. Her excitement waned when she opened the door and discovered the envelope containing his new identity, untouched on the table. Even if he were alive, returning to this place would be a huge risk.

She couldn't deny the probability of his body turning up somewhere along the river. It was hard to imagine he'd managed to deal with Webster, free himself from the shackle around his ankle, and escape from the sinking boat without detection. But this was Harper, and she couldn't rule it out. On several occasions, he'd shown how resourceful he could be.

Elaine sat at the table and gazed around the room at his things, most of which were worthless objects she'd provided to make the place appear more homely. She examined the contents of the envelope; along with his identity papers, there was a considerable amount of cash. She removed the passport and opened it. Not the best photograph, but then again, they rarely were. Elaine regarded the name she'd chosen for him: Simon Smith. If you were going to hide in plain sight, she thought it best to go with the most common surname in the English-speaking world.

The caravan rocked as someone stepped onto the bottom tread outside. A shadowy figure appeared at the frosted door panel. Elaine shoved the passport inside the envelope and placed it out of sight on the bench beside her. The door eased open. She felt a rush of excitement, hoping her brother had returned. Her intense build-up of anticipation faded as DCI Baxendale stepped through the open doorway.

'He isn't here,' she said.

Though he appeared to believe her, Baxendale half-heartedly checked the shower and bedroom. As he re-entered the living area, he made himself comfortable on the sofa, stretching his arms across the back cushions. 'So, this is where he was hiding all along.'

She deemed it unnecessary to add to his comment.

He said, 'Let's assume Darmody is alive. Would he come back?'

Delving deep to find an honest answer to his question, Elaine's sad eyes glistened in the natural sunlight shining through the net curtains and the wide-open front door. 'Regardless of the risk, if he were alive, he would have come back.'

'I agree,' said Baxendale, getting to his feet. He walked over to the entrance and stood in the doorway, staring into the bright sun. His hands dangled casually by his sides. 'As far as I'm concerned, Harper Darmody is dead. I hope never to acquire knowledge to the contrary.'

Harry's silhouette faded away like a ghostly shadow. She placed the envelope on the table and waited for over an hour, clinging to a sliver of hope. When Tom called to ask what time she would be home, Elaine locked up and left, only to return in vain later that night. Every single day for the next two weeks, she found herself sitting at the table, staring in disappointment at the envelope.

42

Harper

Joseph Webster ordered Elaine to place the shackle on Harper. After taking the key from Danny, she waded through the water towards him, a forlorn and helpless look in her eyes. For obvious reasons, Elaine wanted to hurt Webster. As for Harper, he wanted to tear the bastard apart and save the boy, but with the boy's life in Webster's hands, it was an impossible situation. Any attempt to take him on at this point would be doomed to fail.

Elaine dropped to her knees and combed the floor beneath the discoloured water for the chain. Her demeanour altered unexpectedly; there was a determined, concentrated manner about her. Harper watched closely as she searched, noting her strange calmness and relieved expression. Grabbing his ankle, she glared up at him with an intense, crazed look in her eyes. Something sharp pressed against his instep.

'Where I can see!' Webster shouted.

From the moment she restrained his ankle, he was on his own. Soon after Elaine had fastened the other shackle around Webster's ankle, a powerful tremor shook the boat. Harper grabbed the bedpost for support as the boat tilted further to one side. The fluorescent light sputtered into darkness. Webster ordered Elaine to turn on the red light by the door, after which he traded the key for the boy. Harper saw the look of desperation in her eyes when she turned to face him, wanting to help, but all he desired was for her to get herself and the boy to safety. He told her to go, and reluctantly, she led the boy away.

Harper turned his attention to Webster, who inserted a false set of white, serrated teeth. No longer was it about survival, as both men had accepted they would probably die. Two men turned into killers by an evil twist of fate, about to clash like caged lions. Tearing hands and sharp teeth. Harper wanted to finish him off, and dying in the process was something he was ready to accept.

They scowled at each other and roared as they kicked up water and came together, eager to strike the first blow. Harper threw a punch and then wrapped his hands around Webster's throat. Harper bellowed in agony as Webster pierced the top of his bicep with the Stanley knife, dragging the blade deep along his arm with such force that it snapped off in the wound. Despite the immense pain, Harper did not lose focus and continued to strangle his adversary.

Beneath the water, Webster thrust a knee into Harper's groin, weakening his grip. He dropped the broken knife, lunged forward, and sank his sharp teeth into Harper's previously injured shoulder. Harper yelled, and as he shoved him backwards, Webster tore a small piece of flesh from his shoulder and gave a menacing grin before spitting it into the water with contempt.

Despite the blood running down his arm, Harper's chest swelled with the promise of violence as he regarded Webster with a cold, measured calm. 'You want to fight like an animal – so be it.'

He launched himself at Webster and forced him against the side of the boat, pressing his forearm tightly against his neck. Harper's other hand searched for the wound he had inflicted earlier with the thick screwdriver. He found it and burrowed his fingers into the hole, stretching the wound.

Webster grimaced and bawled in anguish; no matter how hard he tried, he couldn't fend off his attacker. He was tiring, growing weaker by the second. Harper gripped the flesh of his stomach and pulled, tearing the skin apart. Webster's scream was drowned out by a loud, continuous creaking as the boat shuddered and started to lean even more.

Both men lost their footing and vanished under the rising water. Webster didn't appear to be conscious. Harper kicked out with his foot and pushed Webster's body away, watching it slowly drift into a dark corner of the room, a blood-like mist trailing from the savage wound.

Harper turned, and a young boy's severed head floated past his face. Unable to hold his breath much longer, he used the chain to pull himself towards the bed. The boat shifted again and appeared to be levelling out. Harper swam onto the bed and climbed to his feet. He raised his head above the surface, coughing and spluttering as he gasped for air.

Water surged through the outer door, down the steps, and into the room. Time was running out. The boat was going under, and the police were either on their way or already standing on the riverbank. Harper reached down and pulled the Allen key from the instep of his shoe. He held his breath and dipped his head under to unlock the shackle. Free from the restraint, he resurfaced. With the water almost up to his shoulders, he would need to hold his breath one last time to swim underwater through either door and out of the boat.

Harper took several short breaths in preparation. Behind him, Webster's head rose above the waterline, his malicious gaze intent on taking Harper with him. Ready to dive, Harper took a long, deep breath. Webster's hands emerged from the water, and he wrapped the chain around Harper's neck, pulling tight to choke him. Harper grabbed the chain but could do nothing. Webster didn't bother to take a breath as he calmly dragged Harper down under the water with him.

Panicked groans and bubbles spewed from Harper's mouth as he struggled aimlessly. As both men hovered above the mattress in the faint glow of the red light, Harper's flailing left hand brushed against something on the bed. He tore away the covers, grasped the table leg, and rammed it into the gaping hole in Webster's side. As Webster let out a horrifying, garbled yell, Harper spun around, looked into Webster's dark eyes, and forced the piece of wood deeper into his torso. Webster floated away from the bed, the weight of the chain pulling him to the floor.

Harper removed the chain from his neck and attempted to surface. His head hit the ceiling. There was no air. Water now occupied every square inch of the boat. He swam as fast as he could towards the door, water filling his lungs. He reached the steps and saw daylight above, but he slowed down, his eyes widening, life leaving his body. He thought about Elaine being safe and then focused on Alice . . .

43

Lenny

Mourners ambled along the path away from the beautiful stone chapel. Sombre expressions graced most faces, but several people were smiling, perhaps talking about a fond memory of the deceased or even gossiping about somebody's dreadful hat. A smile didn't necessarily mean people were happy, just as a tear didn't mean they were sad. Some mourners grouped together while others chose to stand alone. Lenny preferred his own company, more so at times like this. It was his way. He'd been called a misanthrope in the past, but that wasn't exactly how he saw himself. He didn't dislike humans – just the bad ones, and he'd encountered plenty.

Lenny hated funerals and avoided them when he could. Now, in the same week, two funerals had come along at once: first Colin's and now Olivia's. Over the past fifteen years, he'd avoided all but his father's funeral. He hadn't conversed with his father for years before he died, not because he didn't want to; he just couldn't. Alzheimer's had put a stop to that. After numerous visits to the care home, it occurred to him that it was no longer his father sitting in the chair, staring into oblivion – so he stopped, concluding his father was gone and only an impostor remained. It was the most difficult decision of his life, but he couldn't cope with bearing witness to such a merciless disease. The shadow beast hunting him was a growing concern.

Olivia, how he bloody missed her. So little time together, and he was angry and resentful. He'd had other relationships, though not quite as short. Okay, that's a lie, but the big difference was the overwhelming feelings that were unrecognisable compared to anything he had experienced until she came along. It wasn't just love for him; it was first love. A friend's wife once told him that when you find that special someone, you just know. At the time he'd fobbed it off as total bollocks, but now he knew what she meant.

While everyone watched the coffin vanish behind the curtain, he could only visualise finding her in his bed. Of all the atrocious things he had witnessed, this stood out above all, perhaps because it was so personal. What a wicked and cruel memory. Elaine had told him to focus on standout moments between them, and eventually, the good would outshine the bad. He had taken her advice, even to the extent of meditating.

For his first attempt, Lenny got comfortable in the armchair, and after several minutes of focusing on his breathing, he reminisced about the time he and Olivia had gone for dessert at an ice cream parlour. He put a splodge of ice cream on the end of her nose, and when she went to do the same, she accidentally knocked his Knickerbocker Glory into his lap. "Bit of an overreaction," he'd said. They laughed, and it might not have been the funniest story, but it was their story – one of those in-jokes between couples. Elaine's suggestion hadn't worked so far. He would stick with it, though.

Leaning on his walking stick, Lenny stared at the clear blue sky and the sun streaming across the cemetery. *Wasn't there supposed to be rain and black umbrellas on days like this*? At least that's how it appeared in the movies. The air was fresh with a modest chill, and the early morning dew lingered, with tiny droplets of water weighing down the strands of dark green grass. Lenny regarded his shiny black wet shoes – the price of walking across the grass. He had taken painkillers before squeezing what was left of his swollen toe into a shoe – the price of having shot himself in the foot.

Lenny had offered his condolences to Olivia's family and was surprised that her mother and father knew of him. To know she had spoken of him to her parents felt very special, more than anyone could know. He looked up from the ground and saw Harry Baxendale walking towards him. *Oh, what did he want?* It was kind of him to attend, but general chit-chat – *nah*, he wasn't in the mood.

'Lenny.'

'Harry.'

'There isn't much I can say that hasn't been said.'

Harry was right; there wasn't. Conversations were always repetitive and awkward at funerals.

'What's with the stick?' Harry asked.

'Oh, it's nothing – I twisted my ankle.'

'I see. So, what are you going to do next?'

'I had a couple of ideas before . . .' Lenny didn't finish the sentence and lowered his head. 'Now, I just don't know.'

'I'm sure you'll think of something. I've checked out your background – you've proven to be a very resourceful man over the years. Who knows, maybe I'll need your assistance now and then.'

'I don't think that's gonna happen,' said Lenny.

'I wouldn't rule anything out – not yet. Just keep an open mind.'

Lenny didn't respond. It wasn't the best time to make decisions regarding his future.

'Well, take care of yourself, Lenny. Perhaps we'll talk soon.' Harry walked away as Elaine approached.

'Elaine.' Harry acknowledged her with a dip of his head.

Elaine smiled but didn't reply.

'Hey, Lenny. You okay?'

'Not really. But I will be.'

She glanced down at his foot and said mockingly, 'How's the toe?'

'Get stuffed,' he said, breaking into a smile. 'Better.'

'You will get through this,' she said reassuringly.

Lenny sucked in the fresh morning air. 'I know. I know.'

44

Elaine

Much to Emily's disappointment, Lenny had returned to his apartment in London. As the weeks rolled by, Elaine's visits to the caravan grew less frequent as her hopes dwindled. There was still no sign of Harper's body, and experts suggested the current could have carried him anywhere along the river or out to sea. The weeks turned into months. Every time Elaine opened the door to the caravan and saw the untouched envelope on the table, her heart sank. Without stepping over the threshold, she pulled the door closed and left. Her deep-seated pain hadn't gone unnoticed, and Elaine recognised how Tom agonised over her despair. The couple had lost the ability to conceal their anguish from one another.

Almost a year to the day since the narrowboat went down, they had moved into their new home closer to Helmsley town centre. Sablefall Farm had been boarded up, and plans were in place to tear the house down. Elaine had applied for planning permission to build three large new houses on the property. Though it was for the best, Elaine struggled to sever her connection to the old house.

For the past few weeks, Tom had tried to convince Elaine to sell the caravan, repeating that it was time to let Harper go. On the night of their first anniversary, she reluctantly agreed. It didn't take long to find a buyer, and although Tom offered to go and remove the last of Harper's belongings, he suggested it might give her some closure if she did so herself.

When she pulled up outside, she discovered all the curtains were closed. Tom was the last person to come here, so it was most likely his doing. Elaine traipsed over to the caravan, inserted the key into the door, and paused. She had been here many times throughout the year, but on this occasion, a strange sensation prickled the back of her neck. Something was different, and it wasn't just the curtains. With a euphoric rush, she pulled the door open. Her determined gaze promptly focused on the table. The envelope was gone.

Elaine scurried inside and drew a blank in her search for Harper. She glared at the empty table where the envelope had sat for months. Had Tom removed it and packed it away somewhere? Surely he'd have mentioned it. She scanned the floor next to the shelving unit; the holdall was no longer there. Was it possible? Could Harper have survived and returned for his new identity and personal belongings?

Elaine was excited yet reluctant to believe it was true. Maybe Tom had done this. It would be just like him to let her live with hope in her heart. When she returned home, she would confront him at once. No! Why ruin the dream that Harper could be somewhere out there? She recalled the strange sensation that had overcome her outside the caravan.

What if?

45

Alice

London's South Bank bustled with activity. People flocked to the area come rain or shine. So far today, it had been a mixture of both. Wet paving slabs dried quickly in patches as the hot sun soaked up the rain. On a bench overlooking the River Thames, Alice could have been admiring the splendid view of the Palace of Westminster, but she wasn't. Instead, she watched a small puddle shrink from the outer edges until it faded from existence, and with so few memories and no pictures, she feared Simon would do the same.

Today marked the anniversary of his drowning on the *ZEPHYR*. There were times she cursed the man she'd fallen desperately in love with over such a short period, but mostly she felt blessed to have met him. His baby cried in the pram beside her – another reason to be thankful that Simon had come into her life. Then again, wasn't it she who'd entered his? After all, it was his door she'd knocked on when her car broke down, and she'd been the one to make all the first moves, something she'd never done in her life up to that moment.

Alice took Milena out of the pram and fed her milk from the bottle. Milena had inherited her father's ocean-blue eyes, while her hair had subtle hints of dark auburn. As she sat feeding the baby, Alice finally took in the sights around her and observed people going about their day.

She had moved to London as planned to start her new job at the literary agency. When she discovered she was pregnant, she didn't know what to think or how to feel, but soon after, she was overjoyed. How she wished Simon could have met their beautiful daughter.

After the conversation with Elaine in Pickering, it didn't take her long to send him a message about meeting up; sadly, it wasn't to be. At that point, she had no idea she was pregnant, yet still wanted to discuss the possibility of a future together. Everything had developed so quickly between them, but sometimes that's how it happened: love didn't have rules. Would he have moved to London with her? She liked to believe he would have jumped at the chance. She missed him so much.

When informed of her pregnancy, Elaine was over the moon, and a few days after the birth, she paid them a visit and handed over a substantial cheque. "A gift," she said. Elaine also wanted to pay an impressive monthly sum into Alice's bank account to help with expenses. Alice was reluctant to accept either offer, but Elaine was insistent. She went on to say that while uncertainty remained around Harper's demise, she would stay out of her niece's life. Elaine feared that knowing he was alive and where he was could jeopardise his new identity and safety.

Alice wasn't as optimistic and had convinced herself that Harper was dead. She didn't want to put her life on pause and live for the moment he walked back into their lives. How would that be fair to her or to their daughter? Quite simply – it wouldn't.

During the pregnancy, she struggled with the notion of whether to tell Milena about her father, thinking it would be unfair for her to inherit the kind of legacy Harper had left behind. He *certainly* wouldn't have wanted his child to carry such a burden, but when she gazed lovingly into those baby blues, she knew she'd have to tell her something about him, and deep down, she wanted to. Alice would avoid the tragic truth and let her know of a man who had shown her *love, warmth,* and *grace* – the meaning behind Milena's name.

With the bottle almost empty and the baby fast asleep, she sat for a while, cradling her daughter in her arms. After an unpredictable start to the weather, it was turning into a lovely afternoon. The river shimmered with flecks of glorious sunshine on every ripple. She looked at her watch: time to go home. She had rented an apartment around the corner and was expecting the delivery of a manuscript she needed to read for work. Not wanting to wake the baby, Alice carefully returned her to the pram and covered her with a blanket.

A light breeze brushed over her shoulders, and with it came a sense of rapture. Alice detected a presence. Goosebumps formed on her arms, and the fluttering in her stomach was accompanied by a warm rush inching its way up her spine. She glanced around with excited anticipation, but there was nothing. He wasn't there and never would be. Sadness washed over her as she pushed the pram and headed for home. A few steps on, a shadow was cast over the ground ahead. Alice stopped, her heart racing. She slowly raised her head – a familiar face stood in front of her. As he stepped forward, she ran the final few feet into his arms.

AVAILABLE NOW
A Whisper Away From Evil

Turn the page for a preview of the third installment in the Godless Creature series and continue the story . . .

On a bleak December night on a Kent motorway, Detective Inspector Harry Baxendale is called to a fatal car crash that's anything but routine. A man is dead, and a teenage girl seen by witnesses at the scene has vanished. The next morning, a traumatised young woman is found lying on a centuries-old grave near the crash site – claiming to have narrowly escaped abduction.

As Harry and Police Constable Lucy Fenton search for answers, their investigation leads them through a tangle of mysteries, secrets and lies, while the body count begins to rise.

Still reeling from the loss of his partner, former journalist Lenny Grey is reluctantly drawn into the case. His discoveries take him from an eerie Kent graveyard to the icy streets of Toronto, uncovering a chilling link between present-day murders and the tragic fate of twin sisters wronged in the eighteenth century. As Christmas and New Year's approach, a final confrontation looms – and Harry is forced into a choice that will haunt him forever.

1

December 18

9.10 p.m.

Propelled by fierce winds, rain pelted down on the Kent motorway. Numerous emergency vehicles with flashing blue lights lined both sides of the incident, illuminating the gloom. Twinkling like stars, thousands of tiny glass fragments littered the road. In the midst of it all lay the wreckage of an old white Ford Transit van and a dark blue Mazda MX-5. The southbound section of the M2 between junctions four and five had been closed, much to the annoyance of tired motorists eager to get home and out of the dismal December weather. Strewn across the saturated road were unrecognisable parts of both vehicles. On its side, the van took up both lanes, while what was left of the overturned Mazda was a good four metres or so further ahead on the grass verge. A black four-door saloon pulled up beside a police car. A man dressed in a dark suit and tie stepped out.

A uniformed officer wearing a high-visibility jacket approached him and said with a broad Welsh accent, 'I'm Owen Carrick, Roads Policing Lead Investigator. And you are?'

'Detective Inspector Harry Baxendale. I've been assigned to assist in the investigation. Please tell me why I'm out here in the pissing rain?'

'Possible homicide. Just over an hour ago, a van rammed into the back of a car that was parked on the hard shoulder.'

'It happens far too frequently, but surely it's an accident. No one in their right mind would plough into a stationary vehicle on purpose,' said Harry, who considered it a waste of his time being called to a road collision.

'A witness says the Ford Transit accelerated along the hard shoulder towards the Mazda instead of braking to lessen the impact. A passenger in the same vehicle concurs.'

'Maybe the van driver was distracted or dozed off.'

'I start every road death investigation with the mindset of unlawful killing, and usually, I'd agree. However, I've been doing this for a long time – something is definitely off with this one.'

'Fair enough. I'll bow to your experience,' said DI Baxendale as he approached the van. He pulled a pair of latex gloves from his side pocket and slipped them on.

'In the van, we have a twenty-nine-year-old deceased male. The Forensic Collision Investigation Unit is on the scene and has discovered the gentleman's wallet.' Owen checked his notes. 'Vincent Perry from Chatham. The deceased has significant injuries, so I hope you have a strong stomach, Detective.'

Harry cast his eyes over the severe damage to the front of the vehicle and peered through what little remained of the shattered windscreen. A short burst of camera flashes gave him a brief glimpse of the driver's broken body. The camera flashed a couple more times before the FCI emerged from the back of the van holding sealed evidence bags containing the wallet, an iPhone, and various scraps of paper. Harry turned his attention from the bags and asked her if it was okay to take a closer look.

'Be my guest,' she answered, and turned to Owen Carrick. 'You can have the coroner remove the body now.'

'Thank you, Sally.'

Rain rattled against the side of the van above as Harry crouched down and poked his head inside the cab. He spied the word 'DAD' tattooed across the middle fingers of the dead man's left hand. Owen Carrick wasn't kidding about the man being messed up. Harry observed the severe damage to the side of his face and skull and the cloying, metallic odour of blood in the air. He noted Perry hadn't been wearing his seat belt. If you were going to intentionally crash into someone, wouldn't you want to protect yourself as much as possible?

As though listening in on his musings, Owen said, 'You've noticed the seat belt, haven't you?'

'Yeah.'

'Doesn't make sense, does it?'

Getting to his feet, Harry answered, 'No, it doesn't. Unless he didn't intend to survive.' He looked towards the second vehicle and approached. 'Who do we have over here?'

'Now, this is where it gets strange,' said Owen.

'I'm all ears.'

'Despite the vast amount of blood on the steering wheel and dashboard, there's no victim. We're still checking the vicinity, but so far, we've failed to locate a body.'

Harry's puzzled expression fell away as he closed in on the overturned car, taking in the extensive damage. Although a two-seater, the back of the car had been crushed forward, almost into the front seats.

'Jesus,' he said, crouching down to examine the interior. He stood, glanced along the hard shoulder, and pointed to Sally, who was taking measurements with a member of her team. 'Is that where the van struck the car?'

'Yes. There is still a lot of work to do, but Sally is confident the driver made no attempt to brake. The position of the van suggests he may have changed his mind at the last second and tried to swerve around the Mazda.'

'So the van collided with enough force to push a stationary vehicle nearly fifteen feet?'

'Yes. Sally estimates the van was travelling at more than seventy miles per hour, and the handbrake not being applied in the car didn't help. That's usually the first thing you would do if you'd pulled up on the hard shoulder.'

'Unless you're preoccupied. Though it does seem strange,' said Harry. 'I can't imagine anyone would have got out of this car alive, let alone walked away from it.'

'You'd be amazed at what I've seen people walk away from.'

'I'm sure,' said Harry. 'Could there be another explanation for the blood?'

'Well, this is where it gets even more bizarre. We have several witnesses who claim to have seen a young woman in the driver's seat a second or two before the crash. They pulled their vehicles over further along and trekked down the hard shoulder, half-expecting to see the poor woman's remains. But she'd vanished.'

Harry raised an eyebrow. 'Vanished? That's absurd.'

'Hey, I can only relay what the witnesses have stated, Detective Inspector.'

The rain continued to fall as Harry scanned the carnage, trying to assess the situation. He wiped the rain from his forehead and said, 'Okay. It's a strange one, I'll give you that. But it's not murder until we find a body. I'm assuming you've already expanded the search of the surrounding area?'

'Of course. I've called for more officers, and I'm hoping a police helicopter will be here shortly. Meanwhile, I have officers checking recent admissions at local hospitals. With any luck, we'll find the driver within the next couple of hours.'

Harry said, 'The witnesses would have been driving past at *some* speed, so we can't rule out the possibility they are mistaken.'

'I'm not ruling anything out, but the witnesses were pretty adamant.'

'And yet none of them saw her crawl out of the wreckage and leave,' Harry argued. 'Are there any traffic cameras along here?'

'Yes. Across the motorway, up ahead, and further back down this side. I've already got the ball rolling on getting them examined.'

'Great,' said Harry. 'I'll follow up on the witness statements tomorrow. Let me know when you've confirmed the identity of the deceased driver, and I'll find out all I can about him.' Walking away, Harry stopped in the tracks of his wet footprints and turned. 'Oh, and if you find the woman, give me a call.'

Harry hastened to his car to escape the heavy rain. Before heading home, he called Detective Chief Superintendent Malcolm Falconer and left a message updating him about the new case. Through the water cascading down the windscreen, he observed the scene once again. Despite his initial reservations about the collision, he sensed something dark.

About the Author

Gabriel enjoys writing psychological thrillers with plots that twist and turn. Born in London, he now lives on the Kent coast of England with his wife and two cats.
He left school early to work in the building trade as a painter/labourer and went on to become a carpet fitter, postman, and multi-tradesman, though not all at the same time.
Inspirational books include 'Salem's Lot by Stephen King, Flowers in the Attic by V. C. Andrews, and The Rats by James Herbert.

You can find out lots more about me, my books, and
other exciting info on my website:
www.gabrielblake.com

To be the first to receive updates about future releases,
exciting news, and special offers, please subscribe to my
occasional newsletter:
https://tinyurl.com/Subscribe-to-Gabriel-Blake

It would be fantastic if you joined me on Twitter:
https://twitter.com/GabrielBlake_

Follow me on Instagram:
https://www.instagram.com/gabrielblakewriter/

Thank you for reading. If you enjoy my stories, please
know that it means the absolute world to me. You can
show your support for my writing by recommending my
books to others or leaving a rating or review wherever
you can. Subscribing to or following me on social media
is also a massive help.

Godless Creatures